TESSA HARRIS read History at Oxford University and has been a journalist, writing for several national newspapers and magazines, for more than thirty years. She is the author of 11 published historical novels. Her debut, *The Anatomist's Apprentice*, won the Romantic Times First Best Mystery Award 2012 in the USA. She lectures in creative writing and is married with two children. She lives in the Cotswolds.

Facebook: Tessa Harris Author
Twitter: @harris_tessa

T0030622

Also by Tessa Harris

Beneath a Starless Sky
The Light We Left Behind

The Paris Notebook

TESSA HARRIS

ONE PLACE. MANY STORIES

HQ
An imprint of HarperCollins*Publishers* Ltd
1 London Bridge Street
London SE1 9GF

www.harpercollins.co.uk

HarperCollins*Publishers*
Macken House, 39/40 Mayor Street Upper,
Dublin 1 D01 C9W8
Ireland

This paperback edition 2023

First published in Great Britain by
HQ, an imprint of HarperCollins*Publishers* Ltd 2023

ISBN: 9780008564445

This book is produced from independently certified FSC™ paper
to ensure responsible forest management.

For more information visit: www.harpercollins.co.uk/green

Printed and bound in the UK using 100% renewable electricity
at CPI Group (UK) Ltd

For Gill

I have spread my dreams under your feet;
Tread softly because you tread on my dreams.

He Wishes for the Cloths of Heaven, WB Yeats

Prologue

Hamburg

August 1939

With every step Katja's dread grew. Forcing herself up to the first floor, each stairwell echo tolled a warning bell until she reached the landing. It was as she feared. The door of her apartment was open a crack. Someone had been – or still was – inside. Her temples began to pulse as she stiffened and stepped across the threshold. As her heart thumped against her ribs, she started padding down the corridor, careful not to make a sound. But she didn't have to go far to see that while she was at work, there'd been an intruder.

Moving silently past the kitchen, she stopped dead to confront the chaos in the salon. Cushions tossed to the floor, drawers emptied and hurled, ornaments broken; there'd been an intruder all right, but this was no random burglary. The place had been ransacked and Katja knew just who'd done it and what they were looking for.

The framed photograph of her father, that her mother used to kiss every night, lay cracked on the rug. Alongside it were the African beaded bowls, which had been flung from the cabinet. The Swiss clock, whose cuckoo had lost its call years ago, had been wrenched off the far wall, and her mother's plaster statue of the Virgin Mary was smashed to smithereens. Dozens of books had been torn from their shelves too; pages ripped out of some. All the objects in that cramped little apartment had been uprooted, like trees in a forest after a hurricane. And every object held a memory. But memories, Katja told herself, could be kept in the heart. It was the notebook that mattered.

Throwing away all caution – the intruders were long gone – she raced to her room to dive down by her bedside and tug at the square of carpet. They'd torn off her bedding and pillows, but they hadn't ripped up the floorboards. Still on her knees, Katja reached for the pliers hidden in her bolster and, with her heart pumping so loudly it blocked out all other noise, she prised up the wooden plank. Lying there, untouched, was the notebook. She'd already risked her life for these pages, and she would again. There was no time to waste. They'd be back in little over an hour. She knew it. She had to leave. It was now or never.

Her open suitcase lay discarded on the floor by the shutters. Hurriedly, she grabbed the clothes left scattered across the room – blouses, skirts, underwear – and threw them inside. She paid much more attention to the notebook, slipping it under tissue paper in her leather hatbox. Luckily, she'd had the foresight to take the passports and train tickets with her to work. They were safe.

She'd been tempted to hail a taxi, but she knew she had to watch the cash Dr Viktor had given her. It would be riskier too. The driver might easily identify her, so she trudged down to the end of her street, lugging her suitcase and the hatbox, and caught a tram at the junction. It was half past six and workers poured out of offices and factories like ants. There were no free seats on the tram, so she was obliged to wedge her body in the aisle, against a very large woman, who occupied two spaces.

Ten bone-shaking minutes later, the central *bahnhof*, with its impressive clock tower and huge swastika banner, loomed in front of her. The tram pulled up outside. Men and women were streaming through the massive doors. There were families too, some leading dogs or carrying cats; the fortunate few with money enough to flee while they still could. Before war was declared. She would join them, trying to lose herself in the faceless crowd. The sooner the better. Hefting her luggage along the aisle of the tram to the exit, she'd just tagged on to the end of the queue when two black saloon cars raced onto the station forecourt. They screeched to a halt by the entrance.

'Gestapo,' muttered the large woman to her neighbour.

The passengers paused for a moment to watch eight policemen rush into the station, the tide of commuters parting to let them pass. Katja didn't know who they were looking for, but she feared it could be her. Stepping off the tram, she proceeded into the station.

Inside the cavernous building, capped by a huge glass roof, the constant noise was magnified. Announcements of arrivals and departures, not to mention the incessant drone of voices and footsteps, made it hard for Katja to think. She looked up at the large clock. The train at Platform 5 would be boarding in ten minutes. She dived away from the throng to stop by a newspaper stand. A businessman in front of her offered a few coins in return for the evening edition.

'What's going on?' he asked, as the policemen rushed past them.

The vendor, a war veteran Katja guessed from the patch over his eye, shook his head. 'Some secretary shot her boss this morning. Maybe it's to do with that.'

His words chilled her. They confirmed she could be the one they were hunting. The Gestapo wanted to frame her for murder. Fumbling in her purse, Katja slipped on her mother's old glasses that she'd brought in case she needed a disguise and

3

quickly covered her blonde hair with a headscarf tied under her chin. Catching sight of her reflection in a shop window on the concourse, she prayed her new look would be enough to throw the Gestapo off her scent, just until the train left the station.

Bobbing and diving through the crowd, still lugging her suitcase and hatbox, she made it to Platform 5 as the guard was about to close the gates. Two young women just ahead of her were being bundled off to an office by an official. She wondered what crime they were suspected of.

'Ticket, *bitte*,' Katja heard a guard snarl.

In anticipation, she'd taken out her documents and had them in her hand so she could present them coolly and calmly. Looking around as she waited, she could see a commotion further along the concourse. Black-capped heads bobbed like gulls through the sea of commuters.

'*Danke, fräulein*,' said the guard, seemingly satisfied.

Handing her ticket back, he let her pass, but then . . .

'*Reichpass, bitte!*'

A customs official was glaring at her. Her stomach flipped as she handed over her French passport with a disarming smile. She bit her lip as the official studied the document carefully. Could he tell it was fake? Could he see where the photograph has been pasted, or the stamp forged? She held her breath.

The official looked up. '*Französisch?*' he asked with an arched brow.

'*Oui*,' she lied.

'Off!' He pointed to her headscarf. A tug revealed her blonde hair, and its revelation made her feel vulnerable. Naked even, as the guard inspected her.

An agonising moment later, the passport was returned and Katja breathed again. With her acting skills rewarded, she marched through the gates, her head held high, and onto the platform. Her seat was in a carriage towards the middle of the train. Both her arms ached with the weight of the baggage, but she made it.

4

Checking her ticket, she boarded and moved along the crowded, smoke-filled corridor to find her compartment. There was one seat left. The others were occupied by a family. A mother and father, two children and an older woman – a grandmother, she presumed. Together they sat in silence – the atmosphere surrounding them so fearful it almost hung from the luggage racks – and when the grandmother shifted in her seat to adjust her hat, Katja could see why. She caught a glimpse of her dark eyes, sunk deep into shadowy sockets. Her haunted expression gave her away. Equally terrified, but for different reasons, she joined them.

From her seat Katja could see another station clock on the platform. Two minutes until the scheduled departure time. Time stood still. She needed to count down the seconds to make them pass quicker. *One hundred and twenty*, she mouthed to herself, just as, from somewhere nearby, there was a shout. The father turned his head towards the window. A second later, a Gestapo appeared outside, to be joined swiftly by another. One barked an order.

One hundred, whispered Katja as she took out her book of poetry from her handbag.

The mother and father swapped uneasy glances. Footsteps now along the corridor. One of the children, a little girl, began to whimper.

Seventy.

A shadow appeared across the carriage floor. A passing Gestapo glanced inside. Katja buried her head inside the book but was horrified to hear the door slide open. For a heartbeat she froze.

'You!' yelled the Gestapo.

Her head shot up to see the policeman lunge at the father and heave him up by the lapels. 'Out. You Jewish swine!'

Sixty.

The little girl's whimper became a full-blown cry. Her slightly older brother joined in as their father pleaded.

'But we have papers,' he cried, fumbling in his coat pocket.

5

'Out,' shouted the Gestapo, as his colleague began tugging at the grandmother.

Forty.

'Out! Now! You old Jew!' he screamed, suddenly pointing a gun at her.

Thirty.

'Please. No,' cried the mother, drawing her little girl close.

One Gestapo drew a cosh and hit the father's trembling hands, sending his papers flying. 'Out, I say!'

Twenty.

The frail old woman was plucked easily from her seat and flung into the corridor. She was followed quickly by the little boy, but he bit the Gestapo on the hand and was rewarded with a slap to the face that sent him hurtling backwards. Distraught at the sight, his mother dived screaming into the corridor, while her husband was finally bundled out of the carriage by the other Gestapo. One by one they were manhandled onto the platform.

Inside Katja was screaming too, but she held her tongue. Only a few more seconds. She had to hold it together.

Ten.

A jolt from below. The locomotive sprang into life. A pillow of white steam rose from the platform, swallowing the distraught Jewish family wailing below. The terror Katja had seen in the mother's eyes swelled the outrage that boiled in her veins, but knowing she was powerless, she forced her gaze towards the clock. She could barely see its face anymore through the steam, but she didn't need to.

Three.

The screech of the whistle cut through the mayhem and the carriage juddered and sprang forward.

One.

She was on her way to Paris. To freedom. To the bookshop. And to Daniel.

Chapter 1

Hamburg

Seven months earlier

Adolf Hitler stared down on the city, master of all he surveyed. One arm held out stiffly in the familiar salute, the other placed firmly on his Aryan heart. But it was his look that made passers-by stop in wonderment, as he glowered thirty metres above the traffic-choked road. His enormous blue eyes were piercing and hypnotic, enough to strike admiration – or terror – into anyone caught in his unblinking gaze. Anyone like Katja Heinz.

That morning Katja was travelling away from Hamburg city centre to a leafier district – leafier in summer that is – to the university. In warmer weather she might have walked to the interview from her apartment block. But today was not a day to linger. An icy wind blew from the Elbe and leaden clouds threatened snow. The thermometer hadn't risen above -10° Celsius for the last seven days. Another week and they'd open the Outer Alster lake to skaters.

It used to be her daily journey, sometimes with her father, but mostly with fellow students. Although parts of the route were still familiar after six years, the memory seemed an age away; of a much happier time when people could read what books they wanted and say what they truly felt. They were poor, yes, but at least they'd been free to express themselves.

This time Katja found herself next to the tram window, misted by the breath of so many passengers. A small man in a shabby coat, reeking of cigarette smoke, pressed against her apologetically. With her gloved hand she rubbed a small circle on the glass, to look out as they bounced and jolted through a canyon of grey buildings.

As they came to a halt at the first stop, more commuters boarded. The smoker sitting next to her, an office worker she supposed, rose to make way for another passenger. She'd assumed he was giving up his seat to a woman, but when she was suddenly elbowed in the ribs, and a swastika armband flashed before her, her scalp tingled with fright. One of Hitler's thuggish brownshirts had planted himself in the seat next to her, crossing his arms to take up maximum space. She turned away to avoid eye contact. Even now, she lived in fear of being discovered and decided to alight at the following stop, albeit half a kilometre away from the main university building. She would be too early for her interview, but at least now she had time to pay a visit to a favourite haunt. Pinching her coat collar against the biting cold, she headed toward Herr Wortzman's bookshop.

The only colour that burst out of the ubiquitous grey on a morning like this was the blood red of the Nazi banners and flags that hung from every office block and municipal building. A boy was selling newspapers on the street corner. Waving a copy of the *Hamburg Echo* in front of her, he called out '*Führer to visit city*.' That was why, she told herself, the giant billboard had appeared, heralding the arrival of Germany's saviour. The nerves that she'd managed to control on the tram suddenly re-emerged.

She'd hoped looking at the latest books in Wortzman's window might take her mind off what she knew would be a challenging interview at the clinic. She was aware that she wasn't really qualified for the job, but when she was summoned, she was thankful for the chance.

A sudden gust sent the familiar rusty sign creaking on its hinges and told her she had arrived at her destination. A few moments browsing, she hoped, would settle her nerves. It had been a while since her last visit to the shop, but instead of the excitement she used to feel when she first caught sight of the books in the window, this time she was underwhelmed. Behind the smeary glass, the displays looked as tired as Herr Wortzman whom she could see behind the counter. Before the Burnings, he'd reminded her of a walrus, with his bushy moustache bracketing his mouth and his big belly matching his laugh. Now even his whiskers seemed to have lost their zest for life and drooped.

The Burnings, the *Säuberung*, or cleansing by fire, had scarred her and her family for life. Back in May 1933, Nazi students had built great public bonfires with any books they said were anti-German. Thousands of volumes were destroyed, not just in Hamburg, but across Germany. Before that, Herr Wortzman's window had been crammed with titles from all over, from France and Italy, from Britain and America, as well as Germany. Some had glamorous covers that dared you to open them, like the beautiful people on the front of *This Side of Paradise*. Some had intriguing titles, like *The Invisible Man*, or *The Time Machine* that beckoned you in. Others, like ones by the French author Jules Verne, invited you to explore different worlds.

Now, in place of all those enticing hardbacks and exotic titles of the Weimar years, the plain red cover of the Führer's *Mein Kampf* took pride of place in all bookshops; the volumes stacked high, dwarfing all others. When Herr Hitler first came to power and many thousands of copies were sold, her father told her people read his writings because they were curious, not because they agreed with what he wrote. Today, however, after everything that had happened and was still happening, she couldn't be so sure. Rather than soothing her nerves, it seemed browsing Herr Wortzman's window had produced the opposite effect. Thrusting her hands into her pockets, Katja strode on through the quiet suburb, and less than ten minutes later arrived at her destination feeling even more agitated and uneasy.

The plaque on the red brick building told her she was at the right place. The Clinic for Neurological Disorders was attached to the University of Hamburg Hospital but housed in a separate wing at the side. It had its own entrance overlooking a quiet square bordered by linden trees. Pausing before mounting the shallow steps, Katja took a deep breath to compose herself. She needed this job. The Jewish firm of solicitors where she'd worked as a secretary had been forced to close down four years before. After that she'd found low-paid secretarial work in a soap factory, slaving away for a foul-mouthed boss. There were bills to pay. Her mother's medication cost a small fortune, let alone the rent. A prayer fluttered across her lips: 'Please God, give me strength.'

An elderly receptionist, whose skin was as wrinkled as the ruching of her blouse, directed her down a long, ill-lit corridor.

'You will wait outside to be called,' she croaked.

A distinct smell of disinfectant hung in the air, even though this was not a surgical but a psychiatric clinic. Everything appeared clean and efficient, and the corridor walls were hung with paintings of alpine scenes: lakes and mountain vistas. As she walked past them, Katja supposed they were meant to help patients relax, but they only succeeded in making her feel as if she was back at school; about to enter the headmistress's study.

As her eyes adjusted to the gloom, Katja could see another figure at the end of the corridor, also waiting to be called for interview she assumed. The person, a woman, looked up when Katja approached and gave her an unfriendly scowl. She was big-boned and wore no make-up, and when she shifted in her seat a

10

shaft of light bounced off her lapel badge. She was a member of the Party. The Nazi Party. *Who did she remind her of?* Katja often compared real people to characters in novels. She hated herself for it, but it was a habit that had stayed with her since she was a child. This woman reminded her of the horrible workhouse matron in *Oliver Twist*.

Katja, flustered, turned away to slip off her coat. She'd just taken a seat, when the door opposite opened and a tall uniformed nurse with a clipboard, who reeked of carbolic soap, called a name. The candidate rose confidently, tugged at her jacket and followed the nurse. Just before she disappeared from sight, she glanced backwards with a smug look on her face.

Silence descended once more on the corridor and the minutes began to pass slowly. Katja sat stiffly, gripping her handbag like a buoyancy aid in choppy waters, as doubts crowded in on her. The anxiety pressed so heavily on her chest that she was starting to think about walking out. The humiliation would be too much to bear. She should never have applied for such a job. She had no medical experience, and she could tell the other candidate was in a different league; confident and self-assured. Convincing herself that she had absolutely no chance of success, she was about to gather up her coat, when the call came. The other candidate flashed her a triumphant smile as she left, and Katja was summoned inside.

The tall nurse with a waspish expression led her into a sort of anteroom, and through double doors into a large office. Two men sat at a table in front of a window. Katja assumed they were doctors and had expected them to be in white coats, but they both wore normal business suits and that put her more at ease. One, the older man, stood to offer his hand. His face was friendly, framed by silver wings of hair. If the other candidate was the horrible matron, this man reminded her of Oliver Twist's kindly benefactor Mr Brownlow.

'Fräulein Heinz, I am Dr Viktor. And this is my colleague,'

he said, gesturing to the younger, sullen-faced man with thick spectacles, who remained seated. 'Dr Ulbricht.'

Katja felt the younger doctor's eyes bore into her through his magnifying lenses. His hair was greased back and crested a high forehead, reminding her of Bram Stoker's *Dracula*. But it was the Party badge, displayed proudly on his lapel, that made Katja want to turn tail. Pitted against the other candidate with the same political allegiance, she had no chance.

'I see you have not come far,' said Dr Viktor lightly, looking at her résumé on the desk through pince-nez. Katja's face relaxed a little. 'That is good. We need our staff to come into work even when the snow is knee-deep,' he told her, with a laugh in his voice.

Dr Ulbricht appeared unamused as he looked down at her résumé in front of him. 'So,' he began. 'I see you have no experience whatsoever of working in a medical setting, Fräulein Heinz.'

Even in her worst nightmare, Katja hadn't expected such brutality straight away. It set her off balance. 'No, sir, but . . . well I have good typing and shorthand speeds and . . .'

'It's not necessarily a drawback,' Viktor intervened, slipping his colleague a disapproving sideways look. 'Do you think you could adapt?' he added, his voice softening.

She'd been thrown a lifeline. 'Oh, yes, sir,' she replied. 'I am very versatile and my filing . . .'

Ulbricht cut her short. 'I see you once worked for a firm of attorneys. Jewish attorneys.' He spat out the word Jewish and leaned forward to skewer her with a suspicious look. 'Are you a Jew?'

Katja's eyes slid over to Dr Viktor, as if to appeal to him to rescue her, but he remained impassive. Switching back to Ulbricht, she replied: 'No, sir. I am not. I am a Christian.'

He gave a satisfied nod, then leaned back, twirling a pencil through his fingers. 'So why did you cut short your literature studies at the university?'

It was a question she'd been dreading and no matter how many times she'd tried, she still couldn't come up with a convincing answer. The Nazi racial laws had forced many of her fellow students who were Jewish to abandon their studies, but she had to leave for a different reason. Because of her father, her Vati.

'I ... I, well,' she began. Once more she found herself appealing to Dr Viktor for help. 'The course was not to my liking,' she replied, and instantly knew it made her sound arrogant. She started to squirm like a worm on a hook and Ulbricht only added to her pain.

'Were our great German writers not good enough for you?'

Did she really have to tell them about the Burnings and how her father died as a direct result of them? The doctors would surely recall the story instantly if she told them her real name and that Vati had been a professor at the university. They might even have known him personally. Even though it happened almost six years ago, the horror was still so raw and painful.

'Well?'

The pleasure in Dr Ulbricht's eyes at seeing her struggle finally gave way to impatience. He threw the pencil down on the desk. 'I do not believe in niceties, Fräulein Heinz. I saw little point in interviewing you, but Dr Viktor seemed to think we should. So, tell me why we should employ you as the department receptionist?'

Katja's mouth suddenly went dry. 'I am very punctual and organised, and my filing . . .' she repeated.

This time, Dr Viktor interrupted her. 'Many young women are good at filing, Fräulein Heinz, but what special qualities could you bring to this job?'

In that moment Katja knew all was lost unless she took a gamble and told the truth. She steadied her gaze and stuck out her chin.

'I can bring understanding to your patients,' she replied.

'Understanding?' repeated Ulbricht, his voice tinged with disdain. He retrieved the pencil and twirled it once more. '*You* would not be—'

Dr Viktor lifted his hand to silence his colleague. 'What do you mean by understanding, Fräulein Heinz?' he asked, tilting his head.

Katja suddenly pictured her mother at home. Widowhood had turned her into a shell of a woman, drained of energy and any interest in life except for the pigeons she fed daily from her balcony. 'I know what anxiety and depression look like,' she replied thoughtfully.

'In what way?' pressed Viktor.

Katja shifted in her seat, aware of Ulbricht's glare upon her. 'I know a huge wave hits you, barrelling you round and dragging you down. You cannot think straight or eat. The effort of simply moving your limbs or lifting your head is too much because the force is pulling you down, down. Someone might offer a hand to pull you out, but you can still fall back and drown. And for the person who reaches out, but loses their grip, the pain can be just as bad. They can be dragged down too. They know they need to be strong, but it's hard for them to keep their own heads above water at times. They can need help as well, to escape the wave; the great crushing depression that threatens to engulf them.'

Katja stopped then, bringing herself back into the moment. She shifted her focus to see both doctors staring at her. She had said too much. It was Dr Viktor who broke the silence. He cleared his throat.

'You have obviously been touched by issues of mental health, Fräulein Heinz,' he remarked. 'Someone close, I presume.'

Katja blinked and a stray tear broke lose. There was no use pretending anymore. She had made a fool of herself. She may as well leave immediately. Her eyes slid from one man to the other. 'I'm sorry. I should go.' She made to move, but Dr Viktor said: 'Please, Fräulein Heinz. I asked a question. I would like an answer.'

Katja sat back down again, even though she wanted to leave so badly. 'My mother,' she replied. 'She has not been well. Not since my father passed.'

Dr Viktor nodded. 'I am sorry to hear that,' he said. 'So how do you escape?'

'Sorry, sir?' Katja did not follow.

'How do you escape the great wave?' Viktor explained. He seemed genuinely interested.

Katja's gaze locked on to his. 'I read novels, sir,' she replied. 'They take me to different places. Help me forget.'

Dr Viktor's lips lifted in a smile. It meant he could appreciate what she was saying, and Katja no longer felt so alone. But Dr Ulbricht would have none of it.

Flinging the pencil down on the table once again, he narrowed his eyes. 'Your personal misfortune is no concern of ours. I see no point continuing with this interview. We will write to you with our decision, Fräulein Heinz.'

Katja was being dismissed. 'I'm sorry, I . . .' She looked to Dr Viktor for a stay of execution, but he simply dropped his gaze and she saw his shoulders heave in resignation.

'Good day, Fräulein Heinz,' insisted Ulbricht. 'We've heard all we need to,' he added, glancing towards the door. 'Nurse Wilhelm will show you out.'

A smell of carbolic soap wafted into the room and the tall nurse suddenly appeared, giving Katja no choice but to leave.

'Good day, gentlemen,' she mumbled above her own wretchedness. 'I am sorry I wasted your time.' She had been made to feel worthless. Perhaps she was. Perhaps she was drowning too. There had been a moment when she believed Dr Viktor might offer her his hand and lift her from the water. He did not and she walked out of the clinic feeling as if she, too, was being sucked down into the murky depths.

Chapter 2

Paris

The Citroën driver swerved to avoid the pedestrian, while at the same time blasting his horn. Leaning out of his open window, he pointed to his own head and shouted an aggressive '*Fou!*' at the man he'd narrowly avoided hitting, before driving off at high speed.

The fortunate man wasn't truly 'mad', just very distracted and seemed almost unaware of his lucky escape. He simply raised his gaze as he turned into rue de l'Odéon – he had previously been ambling along with his head in a book – and gave a little shrug. He'd made it to the penultimate page of Hemingway's *A Farewell to Arms* and was determined to finish it before he returned it to the lending library a little further down the street.

Everyone who was anyone in Paris knew about Shakespeare and Company – the bookshop and subscription library. The portrait of William Shakespeare hanging on a bar above the shop door gave the Bard thick brows and a wry Gallic smile. It made him look distinctly French, but everyone also knew the shop sold mainly books written in English.

Daniel Keenan wasn't a Parisian, despite his frequent use of the shrug to signify indifference. In fact, it was also obvious Daniel Keenan wasn't French even before he opened his mouth. In his late thirties, he dressed in tweed, wore a cravat and brown brogues and sported a floppy trilby-cum-fedora on his head. Most people took him for an Englishman, and a rather eccentric one at that, although this only angered him as much as being mistaken for a German. If there was one thing he hated more than comments about his particular dress, it was being mistaken for a '*Rosbif*' – the French slang for an Englishman. He was as Irish as a shamrock, or the Shannon River, or James Joyce – whom he knew quite well – and had grown up regarding the English as oppressors. And now, after what the soldiers did to his family, killers too.

Daniel read the novel's last page standing on the street, between the florist and the *brocante* shop. When he finished, he closed the book reverently, so as not to disturb the finality of the story, as if the very act of closure might ruffle the words before the next reader could begin them. As a journalist himself, he admired Hemingway's precise prose; no lurid descriptions, no flowery sentiments, just an innate skill for phrasing sentences in such a way that allowed the reader to see beyond the words, to reach an unspoken understanding.

The bell over the bookstore door tinkled when Daniel opened it, alerting the bird-like woman behind the counter to his arrival. Although he'd read the last page outside on the street, he suddenly wished he'd saved it for the sanctuary offered by the shop. It was a place where novels were treated like the relics of saints by Catholics, and where, instead of religious scenes or stations of the cross adorning the walls, portraits of writers like Whitman, Poe and Wilde were revered.

'Oh Daniel!' chirped the petite woman, looking up from a stack of volumes. '*Bonjour.*' Her hair was cut in an efficient, masculine bob, and she gave off the air of an excited schoolboy.

Daniel removed his hat and crumpled it into his jacket pocket.

'*Bonjour, Mademoiselle Sylvia*,' he replied, the solemn look on his face remaining unchanged. He advanced towards the counter and handed over both novels – the other one being DH Lawrence's *The Rainbow*.

'You enjoyed them?' asked the bookseller, opening the covers one by one to return the cards to their frontispiece pockets. Despite the fact almost everyone addressed her as '*mademoiselle*', Sylvia Beach was, in fact, American, although she had spent most of her life in Paris.

Daniel nodded. 'The Hemingway in particular.'

Her lips twitched coquettishly. 'Ernest is wonderful, isn't he?' she replied, placing the stamped books on a trolley to her right. She'd come to know her fellow American well over the years, and out of all the writers whom she knew personally, 'Papa', as he was known, was one of her favourites. His swarthy good looks and his swagger made him a hit with most women, even though everyone knew Sylvia had no interest in the opposite sex. 'I shall introduce you to him.' Her voice suddenly trailed off. 'If he ever visits again.'

'He's in Spain right now, isn't he?' asked Daniel.

'Correct.' She suddenly perked up. 'He's reporting on the civil war, but knowing Ernest, he'll be taking on the fascists single-handedly too.'

Daniel found himself vaguely amused at the picture Sylvia had just conjured, but it still couldn't coax a smile. He rarely smiled these days, unless he was drunk, but the civil war in Spain he found particularly worrying. His editor on *The Parisian* – a light-weight, second-rate magazine – was an American, who slugged back bourbon with his morning coffee and liked the easy life. Chuck Patterson had insisted 'the Spanish business' would all blow over soon enough. He was of the opinion expatriates in Paris were much more interested in the latest scandals and new restaurant openings than in General Franco. Daniel knew he was probably right, although quietly he worried the war would spread, and that France would be dragged into it. Today, however, he kept his thoughts to himself.

There was a pause as he stared into space, as he often did these days. But knowing that Daniel's pauses were so often filled with grief, Sylvia leaned over towards him, a look of concern on her face.

'We're having a soiree at Gertrude's apartment tomorrow evening,' she told him kindly. 'Why don't you come?'

Gertrude Stein was the darling of the avant-garde, and her salons were legendary. Daniel had been introduced, but didn't much care for her, finding her too loud and showy. There was a time when he'd been attracted to such people, but not anymore. Not since his loss.

Seeing the hurt still lingering in his eyes, Sylvia paused then cupped her hand over his on the counter. He looked down at it, as if puzzled by her touch. 'It will pass,' she told him softly. 'The pain will lessen, but the memories will remain.' She squeezed his hand. 'The good ones.'

Daniel looked up and stared at her blankly for a moment. She meant well, he knew, but she had no idea what he was going through when every flame-haired beauty in the street was his Grace, and every green-eyed cherub his Bridie. How could she understand? She had never been married. Never had a child. Never suffered the unbearable sense of loss that he had felt over the past fifteen months and twenty-two days. He missed his loved ones' conversation and companionship desperately, but it was justice he craved just as much.

'Thank you,' he told her, not out of gratitude, but politeness.

Sylvia backed away from the counter. 'I'll leave you to browse then,' she said, cocking her head in the direction of the lending library.

It was true, the novels helped him forget. When he was lost in their pages, he lived in the author's world, not his own. They allowed him to walk in other people's shoes: offered him respite.

Yes, novels helped him forget, but Daniel Keenan had done enough forgetting for one day. He had recently come to the realisation that he couldn't hide in books forever. 'Another time,' he told her softly, and with that he strode out of the bookshop to return to his office, biting back the tears that Sylvia's kindness had stirred.

Chapter 3

Hamburg

Three days after her interview at the clinic, Katja arrived home from work, and checked her post, as she always did, in the pigeonhole in the communal hall. She leafed through the correspondence. Among the usual bills was a plain white envelope. Flipping it over, she saw the address of the clinic printed on the back. This was the letter she'd been waiting for, even though she was certain what it would say. She was right.

> *Dear Fräulein Heinz,*
>   *Following your recent interview for the post of receptionist at the Clinic for Neurological Disorders, we regret to inform you . . .*

The rejection came as no surprise. She'd already accepted she wasn't the right candidate for the job. Besides, since the interview she'd had a nightmare. In it she'd dreamed Dr Ulbricht was a vampire, sucking the lifeblood from her. She could never have worked for him in any case. Screwing up the letter, she stuffed it in her pocket and hurried up the stairs to her mother.

'Mutti, I'm home,' she called opening the door to the apartment. This she did every time she returned from work because since the Burnings, as well as depression, her mother suffered from terrible anxiety. As she was climbing the stairs, Katja had also resolved not to mention the letter of rejection from the clinic. That would only make matters worse.

The apartment was always chilly. Whatever the weather, her mother would insist on keeping the French doors open so she could see the pigeons on the balcony. Katja hung her coat over a hook in the narrow hallway and shivered as the cold air touched her skin. 'Mutti. It's me,' she called again.

The main room remained unchanged since her father's death six years before. Mutti had insisted it become a sort of shrine to him, cramming it with various souvenirs from his visits to Africa.

Professor Reinhart Lemmerz had been an anthropologist. He'd made it his life's work to study different cultures, and the German colony of Kamerun was where much of his research had been conducted before the Great War. The ivory carvings, beaded bowls and necklaces made of conch shells he'd collected on his travels, all made impressive *objets d'art*. Among the framed photographs of him posing with various tribal chiefs in startling headdresses, there was a larger one that pictured the professor proudly holding a copy of his very own book *An Interpretation of Central African Cultures*. It was the fruit of many years of labour. He'd even won a prestigious prize for it, although that was rescinded when Adolf Hitler came to power.

Advancing towards the sofa, Katja found her mother crumpled in a heap under blankets. Walking over to the *kachelofen* in the corner, she palmed its painted tiles to find only the faintest residue of warmth. On a small table nearby, lay a hunk of untouched salami and crumbs where there'd been a slice of rye bread.

'Oh Mutti,' Katja said, half scolding. 'You didn't give it to the birds again, did you?'

Mutti lifted her grey head from the arm of the sofa. 'You're home,' she whispered, holding out a hand.

Katja took it. It was as cold as the glazed porcelain of the plate. 'Yes, I'm home,' she said with a gentle smile, her gaze lingering over her mother's pallid complexion. Her eyes were sunken. She'd lost more weight.

'How about some chicken soup?' Katja asked, taking the plate and turning for the kitchen.

Mutti shook her head. 'What would I do without you, my Kati?'

It was a question her mother asked at least twice a day and every time Katja answered in her head. She knew she would fade away. Or worse. There'd been a terrible time when she'd swallowed a bottle of pills while Katja was at work, and another when she'd taken a knife to her wrists. Hopefully, those days had been left behind them, but Mutti's reliance on Katja remained. She simply could not exist without her help.

A well-rehearsed smile lifted Katja's lips in reply. 'You'd manage, somehow,' she said brusquely, as she always did. She couldn't allow herself to sound mawkish. 'Now, let me heat up that soup.'

Katja had just resumed her journey to the kitchen when there was a knock on the apartment door. She frowned. Frau Cohen, their widowed neighbour, would always call out to announce her presence. Hardly anyone ever knocked, apart from Dr Spier, when her mother took a turn for the worse, or Father Fischer, who occasionally came to recite the rosary with her.

Carefully, Katja drew the chain across the door and opened it a crack. A thick-set man stood with his back to her on the landing. He was wearing a smart grey overcoat and held a homburg in his hand. The minute he turned she recognised him.

'Dr Viktor,' she said, unable to hide the surprise in her voice.

'Fräulein Heinz, forgive the intrusion.'

For a moment she could only stare at her unexpected visitor.

'Is this an inconvenient time?' he asked, his breath rising like smoke in the cold air of the landing.

Katja bit her lip and shivered as she quietly stepped over the threshold and shut the door behind her. 'I'm sorry, I can't invite you in, Doctor. It's my mother,' she began. 'I'm afraid she . . .'

Dr Viktor nodded, as if he needed no further explanation, but he didn't appear to be fazed. He lowered his voice. 'You received a letter from the clinic?'

Feeling slightly awkward, Katja dipped her gaze and shook her head. 'I didn't expect to get the job.'

'You were a good candidate, but Dr Ulbricht—'

'Please. You don't have to explain.' She cut him off with a smile.

'But I wanted you to know . . .' he began, then stopped himself as soon as he heard footsteps below. A second later, a young man in a flat cap and shabby jacket was striding up the stairs, two at a time. He glanced at the doctor and at Katja but didn't acknowledge either of them. He simply carried on to Frau Cohen's door on the opposite side of the landing, where the widow lived with her son Aaron. The stranger tapped three times in a rhythm. Katja had heard several visitors to the apartment knock like that before and had already guessed it was some sort of a secret code devised by Aaron. Like all Jews in the city, he and his mother lived in fear ever since the racial laws came into force.

A moment later, the young man was admitted wordlessly to the apartment, and Dr Viktor resumed his conversation. Keeping his voice low, he told her: 'I was impressed by your manner, Fräulein Heinz, and your attitude.'

Despite the cold creeping into her bones, Katja felt her face flush. The interview had certainly not gone as planned. Compared with the other older, more confident candidate, she must have appeared naive and incompetent.

'It's hard for my mother . . .' she began again. But the doctor flattened his mouth and shook his head.

'You were very brave to speak as you did, from the heart, but please, there is no need to explain,' he told her gently. 'I understand, and that is why I am here.' She eyed him curiously. 'You see, I know who you are.'

Katja turned to stone as her eyes clamped on to the doctor's face. Did he know her secret? If so, was he a friend or foe? But he soon answered her question.

'I knew your father,' he told her.

'You knew my . . .' Katja felt the blood leach from her face. This man, this almost complete stranger who stood before her, knew something about her that she had managed to keep hidden for almost six years.

Viktor's expression remained neutral, leaving Katja not daring to breathe until, after a moment, he said, 'I respected him.'

Slowly, the tension drained from her chest in a long breath, although she still couldn't be totally certain where the doctor's sympathies lay. She was picking her way through a minefield, treading warily. One false move and he could have her arrested.

'We were acquainted through our work.' His remark unsettled her, but then the clinic was part of the university where her father lectured. Both men were senior members of their relative departments, and she supposed the circumstances of his agonising death were, for a time, on everyone's lips. Seeing her frown, he added: 'He was a man of great integrity.'

Katja nodded and let her gaze drop. 'Yes, he was,' she agreed, even though she knew it was his integrity that led to his downfall.

The doctor explained: 'I saw the address on your résumé and remembered Professor Lemmerz had given me his card, so I checked.' The doctor's eyes creased at the corners as he glanced at the front door. 'He invited us to dine here once, but my wife, she . . .' His shoulders drooped at the mention of his spouse, as if the very thought of her weighed him down. He continued to look solemn when he said: 'His loss was a great tragedy, but I'm hoping his daughter has inherited his principles.'

Katja narrowed her eyes. 'I'm sorry, I don't follow.'

He sighed and touched his brow. 'I know you and your mother have been through a lot.'

While she appreciated the doctor was trying to be sympathetic, to say they had been though 'a lot' was an understatement. The manner of her father's death had been horrific enough. Then came more recriminations and threats. Of course, he'd been under pressure for months before his death. All the lecturers were confronted with an ultimatum: swear a vow of allegiance to the Führer or lose your position at the university. And not just the University of Hamburg. Her father was told he'd never work again if he didn't take the oath to Hitler. But before he had given his final answer, there were the Burnings. After those – and her father's death – Katja and her mother had even been forced to leave their apartment for a few weeks, until the whole terrible affair quietened down. They'd needed to hide the pain and the ignominy they'd endured by association and had even changed their family name. Katja had been forced to leave university before graduation and take whatever job she could to pay the bills. It was true, they'd been living in the shadows since the Burnings and now this doctor was shining a light on them. But for what purpose?

Katja blinked and, still afraid to own up to the whole truth, her voice came out weakly. 'Why? Why have you come here?'

Dr Viktor's smile disappeared to be replaced by a serious, solemn expression once more. 'To offer you a job.'

'A job,' repeated Katja, confused. She thought of the crumpled letter in her pocket.

'I have a vacancy for another role, which may be better suited to your talents,' he explained, his eyes twinkling in the light from the solitary overhead bulb on the landing. 'And I wondered if you might be interested in discussing it, if, of course, you haven't already been offered another position.'

He was flattering her and for a second time Katja blushed. 'No,' she said quickly. Then realising her answer might be misconstrued, she added: 'Yes. I mean I don't have another offer and I'm interested to hear about your job, *Herr Doktor.*'

The doctor's mouth twitched. 'I'm glad we understand each other, fräulein. So, if this evening is not convenient, perhaps we could meet another time?'

'Katja!' Mutti's voice sounded muffled behind the door.

Suddenly flustered, Katja rolled her eyes. Without turning, she raised a hand and pointed behind her towards the apartment. 'My mother. I . . .'

'Tomorrow morning at the Café Blau? Say seven thirty?' suggested the doctor.

Katja nodded apologetically, her hand on the door handle. 'I'll be there,' she said firmly, as her mother's reedy voice called again.

'Where are you?'

The doctor dipped his head before replacing his hat, and Katja watched him start to descend the stairs before she returned inside. Closing the door behind her, she leaned back against it and took a long, deep breath.

'Kati, is that you?'

'Coming, Mutti,' she called, as she hurried along the corridor. For the first time in a long while there was a spring in her step.

Chapter 4

It was still dark, but Katja was already familiar with the café where she was to meet the doctor. It sat opposite Herr Wortzman's bookshop, and Vati would sometimes treat her to *kirschtorte* there after a book-buying excursion.

There'd been heavy snow overnight, but the countless footsteps of dock workers and clerks and street girls had already turned it to slush on the pavement. Katja stamped her feet outside before venturing into the café, if only to return some circulation to them. Despite the early hour, the place was busy. Some men drank beer to help them unwind after a hard night's work. Some drank coffee to perk them up before starting their day.

As soon as Katja walked into the café she hit a wall of smoke from cigarettes and pipes, and her eyes immediately started to sting. She hated the very thought of smoking, because every time she saw a flare of a match and the puff of smoke from a cigarette, it reminded her of that night; the night her father was so cruelly taken.

There was no sign of Dr Viktor at the tables, so she headed towards the booths at the back and found him reading a news-paper while puffing on a pipe with a curved stem. His homburg was on the banquette beside him. He rose as soon as he saw her and caught a passing waitress's eye.

'*Ein espresso, bitte,*' he told the girl, before pointing to Katja.

'The same, please,' she said, taking her seat.

'You know this place?' asked Dr Viktor, dampening down his pipe.

Katja's eyes were raised towards the familiar vaulted ceiling painted with gold stars. Even now they were still magical to her.

'Yes,' she replied, tugging at the fingers of her gloves. 'My father and I used to come here a lot.'

'Ah yes, your father. You were close?'

'Yes, very.'

'And politically?'

The words, shot without warning from his mouth, were charged with danger. No one talked politics openly these days and certainly not in a coffee shop when Hitler's spies could be listening at the next table. Katja's gaze darted around her, but her shock only seemed to amuse the doctor. He smiled, deepening the creases round his eyes. 'I should make myself clear, shouldn't I?' he said, just as the waitress arrived with two steaming cups of coffee.

Katja tried to think straight. What did her father have to do with a job offer from the clinic? Her bewilderment showed itself in a frown, and Dr Viktor sensed her impatience.

'I shall get to the point,' he told her, stirring sugar into his coffee. 'I have a notebook.' He shrugged. 'It contains detailed patient notes, and records, that sort of thing, and I need someone to type them out for me. Someone trustworthy.'

Katja was familiar with the importance of patient confidentiality, but there was something in the doctor's manner that led her to believe these notes were rather special.

'Someone trustworthy,' she repeated. She thought of the older woman with the Nazi lapel badge.

'But you hired the new . . .'

The doctor raised his coffee spoon to break her off before she could finish her sentence. 'The new receptionist will have enough on her hands. My project requires . . .' He paused to search for the word. '. . . discretion. No one must know what you are typing.'

29

'I see,' said Katja, a wary edge to her voice.

The doctor continued: 'Transcription will be your primary function, but to anyone who asks, you are also in charge of my diary, including my lecture schedule, and you will take dictation, type my letters and generally ensure the smooth running of my office.'

Katja nodded. 'Yes, sir. I can do that.'

Viktor laid down the spoon thoughtfully and didn't meet her gaze when he said: 'But I feel I must warn you the job carries with it responsibility.'

'Of course,' replied Katja.

But the doctor narrowed his eyes and looked straight at her. 'I mean special responsibility.' His look left hers again and Katja suddenly had the impression he was thinking out loud, even though he was casting around as he spoke. While the booth offered a good degree of privacy, he suddenly appeared more on edge. Clearing his throat, he passed his palm over his grey head, as if tackling how to phrase his explanation. 'This patient whose notes I need transcribing,' he began. 'He is a well-known figure and if word gets out that I am dealing with him, it could be somewhat' – he hesitated – 'embarrassing.'

'Embarrassing?' repeated Katja.

Dr Viktor stiffened. 'Please, fräulein.' He glanced about him once more. 'Discretion must be your watchword, if you are to take this job.'

She nodded. 'I understand, sir.'

Viktor matched her nod, then upped it with a conciliatory tilt of the head and a gentle smile. 'You would work in my office and answer solely to me,' he told her, as if his presence offered her some form of protection.

'What about Dr Ulbricht?' she asked, recalling her humiliating interview.

Viktor snorted. 'There's no need to worry on that score. You'll have nothing to do with him. It'll be just you and me.'

'So, I would be your personal assistant?'

Her acceptance of this job just took on a new dimension. Unthinkingly, she pushed away her coffee cup, but Viktor forced out a chuckle, trying to ease the tension that he sensed she was feeling. He picked up his pipe and tapped out the tobacco into the ashtray. He was allowing Katja to weigh up her choices as she toyed with the handle of her cup in silence.

As Katja weighed up her options, Dr Viktor came to her aid. 'If it's of any help, I believe taking this job would make your father very proud of you. He spoke truth to power and refused to compromise his belief in free speech.' Her head jerked up. 'Knowing what he was like, what he stood for, and how he reviled this fascist regime, I think he would encourage you.'

Katja leaned back on the banquette to study the doctor's expression. She hardly knew this man and yet there was something solid and almost fatherly about him. A feeling that she could trust him was starting to build inside her. She would follow her instinct. After a moment she nodded in agreement. 'If you say so, Dr Viktor.'

A smile spread across his face. 'So, you'll take the position?'

'I will, *Herr Doktor*,' she told him, returning his smile.

He held out his right hand over the table and she took it in hers. His grip was firm, but not too firm, and he cupped his left hand over hers in a gesture of trust.

'Thank you, Fräulein Heinz,' he said.

Both of them were so wrapped up in the moment that they did not notice the man at the counter, scanning the café for a free table. Dr Ulbricht's roving eyes just happened to witness his colleague – his married colleague – smiling, drinking coffee and holding the hand of a young woman who was turned down for the role of receptionist at the clinic. Were they to find out – and they just might – the university board of governors would surely take a very dim view of such an encounter, especially given Viktor's track record.

Chapter 5

Katja handed in her notice at the end of her shift at the soap factory the following day. Her boss, a rough, uncouth man, swore at her. Instead of serving a week's notice, he told her to leave straight away, minus a reference. She walked out of the door for the last time without a second glance. Thanks to Dr Viktor she knew where her future lay.

When she arrived back at the apartment that evening, she found the front door slightly ajar, even though she'd always told her mother to keep it locked.

'Mutti!' she called, hurrying down the hallway.

Her mother was sitting in her usual chair, although she was not alone. Frau Cohen was holding a glass of brandy to her lips.

'What happened?' asked Katja, dropping to her knees by Mutti's side.

'Your mother had a fall. I heard her calling, but she hasn't broken anything.'

Frau Cohen had been a nurse at the Somme in the Great War. It was there that she'd met her husband. They married the following year, but Hans was killed shortly after, leaving her with a baby, Aaron – the son who recently seemed to have acquired lots of suspicious friends.

Despite having visitors at all hours, Katja knew she was lucky to have such a competent neighbour to rely on.

Hilde Heinz smiled weakly at her daughter. 'I'm sorry to frighten you,' she said, reaching out for Katja.

'As long as you're all right.'

Frau Cohen took the empty glass and rose from the sofa. She looked at Katja then slid her eyes towards the kitchen. 'I'll just put this down,' she said.

Katja followed her and shut the door behind her.

'What is it?'

'Your mother is weak. Malnourished. She needs better food.'

Katja nodded. 'I know.'

'Your cupboards are practically bare,' scolded Frau Cohen, opening the nearest one to demonstrate her point. A solitary jar of pickles and two cans of peas were all that remained.

'Yes, but there's no need to worry,' Katja assured her. She had relented and told her mother about the rejection but hadn't had the chance to give her the good news about Dr Viktor's position.

Suspicion sharpened the widow's look. 'Hilde said you were turned down at the university.'

'Yes, that's right,' replied Katja.

'Did they find out?'

She shook her head. 'No, they didn't, but it's all right.'

Frau Cohen leaned back and folded her arms. 'From where I'm standing it doesn't look all right to me. You can't carry on like this. You need food, rent money, medicine for her.' She pointed towards the door.

'I have a new job,' Katja told her calmly. She wanted to shout it from the rooftops. The role would pay her much more than her old one, and she hadn't felt so positive in a very long time.

The widow seemed unconvinced. 'Where?'

'I am to be the personal assistant of a doctor who works at the university.'

'The university? But . . .' Frau Cohen raised a sceptical brow.

'It's all right' said Katja. 'I'll be working for a man who knew my father.'

The elderly woman's eyes momentarily widened then narrowed again. 'Did he indeed?' She leaned in and spoke through her teeth. 'Then I hope you both know what you are doing, because if you get found out . . .'

Katja shook her head. 'No one will find out. I trust him.'

Frau Cohen snorted. 'The Nazis have long memories and . . .'

A sudden loud knock burst into what Katja feared would be a long lecture. It came from across the landing, on the Cohen's door. It was not the usual *rat-tat, rat-tat* so familiar to Katja, but louder and more forceful. Then came the order.

'Gestapo. Open up!'

Frau Cohen clutched at her chest; her eyes wide in alarm, silently imploring Katja to help.

'Open up, or we'll break down the door!'

Quickly Katja ushered her neighbour inside the broom cupboard in the hall. 'Is Aaron out?' she asked the widow, now sandwiched between a bucket and a carpet beater.

'Yes.'

'Then leave this to me,' she said, hurrying to the front door. An officer and two men stood across the landing, one of whom was about to break Frau Cohen's lock with his rifle butt. 'Is there a problem, sir?' she called calmly.

The officer turned, and his eyes swept over her before he said, 'You live here, fräulein?'

She nodded. 'Yes. I saw the old woman go out,' she added.

The officer lifted a hand to his men, signalling them to pause, then turned on his heel.

'An old woman, you say?' He took off his cap and wedged it under his arm. He was quite young with bright blue eyes.

'That's right.'

'And does she live here alone?'

'Oh yes. She is widowed and her only son died last year.'

The officer smirked and returned his hat to his head. 'Is that so?' He pulled it down firmly. 'In that case, she won't mind if we take a look around.'

Before Katja could protest, the officer re-issued his order to break the lock and the door flew back on its hinges, slamming against the wall with a mighty crack. All Katja could do was watch in horrified silence as she heard cupboard doors being opened and drawers being emptied on the tiled floor. She felt so powerless as the sound of crockery and glass smashing punctuated the air like machine-gun fire. She daren't even check on Frau Cohen, whom she knew would be listening to the mayhem. Hopefully, if the Gestapo came across any of Aaron's possessions, they would think the widow was keeping them for sentimental reasons.

Moments later, the officer and his men returned empty-handed to the landing to find Katja still standing at her doorway.

He dipped a shallow bow. 'Please offer my apologies to your neighbour for any disruption we have caused, but it could not be helped,' he said. Politely he touched the peak of his cap, as if he was on an afternoon stroll in the park, before he and his men stomped down the stairs.

'Kati! Kati! What's that noise?'

Katja could hear her mother calling from the salon, but she was more concerned about Frau Cohen. Racing back to the kitchen, she lunged for the cupboard door to let her out. The widow emerged breathless and troubled.

'I told him not to. I begged him,' she panted, stepping out of the gloom.

'I think you had better tell me what's going on, Frau Cohen,' Katja replied. 'For all our sakes.'

She sat the widow down on a nearby chair in the hall and poured a glass of water. 'Deep breaths,' she said, crouching on the floor beside her.

'Kati!' called Hilde again.

'I'm here, Mutti!' Katja craned her neck to call through to the salon, then hooked her gaze under Frau Cohen's bowed head. Her face was pale and, more worryingly, her lips had turned blue.

'I told him not to do it,' the widow kept muttering, shaking her head and gasping for breath. 'I told him it was dangerous.'

'What has Aaron been doing, Frau Cohen?' asked Katja, thinking of the succession of visitors who gave the suspicious knock. 'Tell me, please. I need to know.'

Chapter 6

Paris

Apart from a few staff, Daniel Keenan was the only drinker in the *Poisson Jeune*. It was still early in the evening and not even Cyril, the black pianist, who seemed to play all hours, was at his post. The Irishman cut a solitary figure in his sports jacket and cravat, perched on a bar stool, and staring into the bottom of an almost empty glass of whiskey.

He'd just downed his first double when he heard the patter of heels approach on the wooden floor.

'*Bonsoir monsieur*. You buy a girl a drink?' said the tiny voice behind him. He could smell cheap perfume even before he'd turned round. When he did, he guessed the voice belonged to a girl no older than sixteen. With her rouged cheeks and ringlets, she wore a skirt with a hemline that barely covered her backside. She reminded him of one of Bridie's dolls.

'*Non. Va-t'en!*' he dismissed her, but then, seeing her dejected look, he softly added, '*Chérie.*' Reaching into his pocket, he gave her a note. After all, he told himself, she was somebody's daughter. Just not his.

It'd been a bad day and his hand went up to order another drink. Fifteen months on and he had them every so often. He'd be drifting along, just about keeping his head above water, then something would happen to drag him down to the depths again. Today it had been Gloria Patterson's fault. She was his editor's blonde, bold and brassy wife, who clearly ruled the roost in their household. The nanny was sick, and Gloria had a fitting at Chanel, so she'd marched into the magazine's office unannounced, little Jeanie in tow, and told her husband he had to mind the child for a couple of hours. Even though he knew of her existence, Daniel had never seen the girl before. He guessed she was roughly the same age as Bridie would have been, and he simply couldn't handle her being there. Maybe it was the tousled curls, or the fact that she wore the same white ankle socks threaded with pink ribbon. Or perhaps because she had dimples on her knees. Whatever it was, the child's presence was too much for him. Shortly afterwards, he'd been caught red-eyed over his typewriter.

'Shoot, Dan.' His editor, Chuck Patterson, tended to prefix any declaration with the word shoot. 'I can't have you handing in soggy copy!' He'd been very understanding, and told him he could call it a day just as soon as he'd finished the article he was working on. Those last few paragraphs were hard to write but he made the deadline – it was a matter of pride for him. He handed in the copy and headed straight for the bar.

As Claude, the bartender, filled up his glass once more, another voice, this time one Daniel recognised, leaned into his ear.

'*Monsieur Keenan, comment allez-vous?*'

Daniel would know Madame Geneviève's smoky purr anywhere. Even in his depression, with her black flapper dress that bulged slightly at the waist and diamante cigarette holder that made her look like a sad silent-movie star, she always managed to prise a smile from him.

'I am better for seeing you, Madame Geneviève,' he replied, gesturing gallantly to the bar stool.

'You are early,' she said, perching herself stiffly next to him. Her arthritic knees were clearly giving her trouble and the tops of her bare arms quivered slightly with the effort of mounting the stool.

'I couldn't stay away from you,' he told her. She always brought out the lighter side in him, the one that had largely remained dormant over the past few months.

'You are such a charmer,' she told him, touching him playfully on his arm. There was already a cigarette in her holder, and she leaned in for a light. Daniel obliged. It had become a ritual he was happy to perform every time he saw her.

'Claude,' he called, holding aloft a rolled note. 'Champagne for Madame Geneviève.'

Almost simultaneously, the pianist, Cyril, appeared in a tuxedo and started tinkling the ivories with a blues tune that seemed to suit the mood perfectly. At the sound of the music, Geneviève blew out a great cloud of smoke, then clapped her gloved hands. It wasn't until the smoke cleared that she noticed Daniel's drawn face and frowned. She lowered her voice. 'But you don't look like you're in the mood for fun.'

He shook his head. 'You know it'll be a long time before I'm ready for that.'

She patted his knee sympathetically. 'I've already told you, you can have any of my girls for a special price.'

Keeping his gaze on the bottles lined up behind the bar, he nodded. 'You're most generous, *madame*, but I'm no company for any woman at the moment,' he said with a wry smile.

'*Oh, mon pauvre.*' Madame Geneviève's lower lip jutted out. Since learning of his misfortune, she'd seemed genuinely concerned for him. 'Some of my girls can be good listeners. Marie-Noelle used to work in a hair salon and . . .'

'Thank you, Madame Geneviève, but I really don't need the company of a young woman right now.' He was gentle but firm, and she understood any further attempts to console him would be futile.

Claude placed a bottle of Champagne in an ice bucket before them on the bar just then, but Madame Geneviève waved it away.

'Another time, Monsieur Keenan.' She touched his arm lightly once more. 'I won't take advantage of a man still in mourning,' she told him, before heaving herself down from the stool.

By now the club had started to come to life. Businessmen were being shown to tables by the maitre d', Gilbert, and one of the cigarette girls was already doing the rounds with her tray. Cyril had upped the pace on the piano with a ragtime tune, and behind the rustling curtain on the small stage, the little troupe of dancers was preparing to perform.

Daniel was just thinking about moving on to a quieter venue, or even going back to his own apartment with a bottle, when someone called his name in a familiar American accent.

'Daniel! Is that you?'

'Sylvia.'

She stood beside him looking very dashing in a man's tuxedo. He thought it suited her.

'I'm here with Gertrude and James,' she told him, looking over her shoulder. He followed her gaze and saw them being shown to a table by Gilbert. 'You will join us, won't you?'

Not only did he dislike Gertrude Stein with her showy manner and flashy wallet, Daniel also had a fairly low opinion of his fellow countryman. The famous, or should that be infamous, writer James Joyce was a two-faced scrounger. He'd not hesitated when Sylvia offered to fund the publication of his *Ulysses*, after no other publisher would touch it, then dropped her like a hot coal when a big company in the States made him a better offer. Sylvia had suffered terribly from the fallout and was devastated by his desertion, but somehow the two of them had resolved their differences and judging by this evening's show managed to be friends again.

Daniel shook his head. He dreaded the thought of talking art and philosophy all evening, preferring instead to curl up alone with a bottle of Bushmills and a book. 'You know I'm not good in company right now, Sylvia.'

But she wasn't going to take no for an answer. 'Just one drink,' she pleaded, taking him by the hand. Under cover of a beaming smile, as she led him over to the table where the others were seated, she told him: 'And yes, I do know that, at the moment, my dear, you hate everyone.'

Regrettably, as he summoned what little good humour he could find, Daniel Keenan knew what she said was true.

Chapter 7

Hamburg

Katja wore a sensible grey wool suit, and her blonde hair was styled in an efficient chignon at the nape of her neck for her first day at the clinic. Just a touch of rouge highlighted her cheekbones. After six years of dragging herself into work, today she felt almost excited, until, that is, she encountered the new receptionist. Seated as if on a throne behind her desk, a telephone clamped to her ear, was her formidable former rival.

As soon as she put down the receiver, she eyed Katja and, suddenly recognising her as the defeated candidate, twisted her mouth in contempt and flung out an arm in a salute.

'*Heil Hitler!*' she cried.

Katja, taken slightly aback, muttered a weak '*Heil*' in return. 'I am to report to Dr Viktor's office,' she said, trying to sound as confident as she could.

'Really?' came the reply, as if the receptionist thought there must be some mistake.

'Yes,' replied Katja, confused. 'Dr Viktor is expecting me.'

The receptionist picked up her pen with an exaggerated gesture and used it to scan a large ledger in front of her.

'Why, yes. You are here,' she replied, after a moment's search, tapping the entry with her pen. 'His office is down the corridor, third door on the right.'

Katja thanked her but did not smile. She already feared that after her initial rejection at interview, working for Dr Viktor would not be plain sailing, and she had already made her first enemy. Some of the staff would know her application had been turned down, and yet she hadn't expected to run into choppy waters so soon. Retracing her steps along the familiar corridor hung with paintings of alpine scenes, Katja knocked on the door that bore Dr Viktor's name. Hearing his voice on the other side came as a great relief.

'Come.'

She entered to find herself in a replica of the space where she had been interviewed: a small office with double doors leading onto a larger one. Her eyes swept quickly around the room, once inside, and revealed more alpine prints, a leather couch, filing cabinets and a large desk behind which sat Dr Viktor. He rose to his feet when he saw her and extended his hand once more.

'I'm so glad you're here, Fräulein Heinz,' he told her, gesturing to a seat. 'You'll have seen who we hired to take the receptionist's job,' he said, lowering himself back into his own chair. 'Fräulein Schauble won't take any nonsense,' he told her, before adding with a conspiratorial smile, 'She is from Swabia.'

At the mention of the receptionist, Katja had to return the smile, as if they both understood each other. Swabians had a reputation for being overly tidy and uptight. 'I'm sure she will be most efficient, sir,' she agreed.

'You, on the other hand, Fräulein Heinz, will be required to work behind the scenes. As I said, I need some patient's notes transcribing before I edit them. Is that clear?'

'Perfectly, sir.'

'Good, then let us begin,' he said, rising and stalking across the floor to a large canvass – the Matterhorn, Katja thought. Much to her surprise, when he pulled it gently, the picture opened like a book. Behind it was a safe. Viktor glanced at her to gauge her reaction. She seemed suitably impressed.

'Our little secret,' he said with a wink, before proceeding to grab the dial and move it first one way, then another, followed by two more twists. The doctor gave a satisfied nod as he opened the safe door. Reaching inside he retrieved what looked like a thick, well-thumbed notebook. It was bound in tan leather, while its spine was a darker brown and, from the mottled appearance of the cover, Katja guessed it was quite old. She noticed some of the edges of the pages were dog-eared and stained too. Nevertheless, it seemed of great importance to the doctor. He was hugging it to his chest as he walked back to his desk.

'Here we are,' Viktor said in a hushed tone, setting down the notebook respectfully.

Katja watched in silence as he settled himself once more and drew the book towards him. He laid his hands flat on the cover and stroked it as he studied it, almost reverently, for a moment.

'So, the notes.'

'The patient's notes.'

'Quite.'

Carefully, he opened the cover to reveal lined sheets of paper. 'There are more than two hundred pages here: my detailed observations. And here' – He pointed to a pocket on the inside front cover, bulging with slips and chits of various sizes – 'we have official forms, etcetera. Everything needs to be typed up. Then I shall edit them into chapters, to make sense of them.'

Katja tilted her head slightly and focused on them. She could see they were mainly handwritten in black ink that crawled across the page in a sort of haphazard order that obviously made sense to the doctor as their author, but not immediately to her.

Viktor turned the open notebook round and pushed it over

to her. 'It needs to be kept secure at all times.' He patted one of the pages, and almost as an afterthought said: 'I hope you can read my writing.'

She studied a few words on the first page for a moment, deciphering snatches here and there, but not really following them. Yet there was one thing that did stand out. Every now and again, as she thumbed through the pages, there was a deletion. A thick line had been drawn across some of the letters, rendering them illegible. She looked up with a frown and once more, as if he could read her mind, Dr Viktor explained. 'Those were the patient's initials, but I decided it would be better for all concerned if they were erased.'

Katja was aware that his gaze remained upon her, as if to impress the importance of this patient's identity. For someone to be able to guess a person from their initials alone, she assumed there must be some personal connection. Either that, or they were very well known indeed. She simply nodded.

'You will have seen your typewriter in the outer office,' said Viktor. 'There is paper in the desk. Neither the notebook nor the typing must ever be left on your desk unattended. Never. And you are to make no copies. Understood?' The doctor's words were delivered like rounds from an ack-ack gun. He paused for breath, then asked: 'Do you have any questions, Fräulein Heinz?'

Katja was used to taking orders. She was also used to being left to get on with things at the attorneys' office and the soap factory. She supposed it would be no different here – officious men telling efficient women what to do, then leaving them to fend for themselves and deal with any subsequent problems that arose. Sometimes she wondered what it might have been like if the Burnings hadn't happened; if her father hadn't refused to take the oath of allegiance to the Führer. If he hadn't tried to persuade his colleagues to make a stand against a regime that forced lecturers to teach Nazi ideology. What would have happened, she thought, if she'd been allowed to finish her degree in English Literature.

She wondered what she could have achieved had the situation been different. But a job was a job, and Dr Viktor paid her wages.

'Everything is clear, *Herr Doktor*,' she replied with a nod.

'Good,' he said, slapping the arms of his chair simultaneously as she rose. 'Oh, and Fräulein Heinz,' he called her back just as she reached the door. 'The kitchen is the next door on the left. You know how I take my coffee.'

Just as Katja was filling the kettle from the tap, the tall nurse who smelt of carbolic soap, the one she'd seen at interview, appeared in the kitchen with a water jug. She stopped in her tracks.

'You must be Dr Viktor's new assistant,' she said sharply, looking at Katja disapprovingly. It was almost as if any woman who worked for the doctor was somehow tainted.

Katja smiled politely as she turned off the tap. 'Yes, I am.'

The nurse, with humourless eyes and a mean mouth, fixed Katja with a stare and said: 'I am sure you are aware that Dr Viktor is a married man.'

The remark took Katja by surprise. 'I'm sorry,' was all she could muster at first.

'His previous assistant needed reminding,' added the nurse, setting down the empty jug by the sink before walking out again. Katja was so stunned by this remark that she didn't notice the kettle overflowing. It was only when water started to splash her hand that she finally turned off the tap. Had she really just been warned about the behaviour of her new boss?

*

When Katja did eventually sit down in front of her typewriter, having delivered a cup of espresso, she scanned the first few pages of the notebook quickly. What could they possibly contain to make them so very important, she wondered?

As well as the doctor's handwritten notes, the other official forms, folded in the inside pocket, were filled in by a clinic of some sort, in a place she'd never heard of. She squinted at the name. *Pasvel* or *Basvel*? The ink on the first letter was smudged, and the rest of the word was hard to read. These forms also required transcription, according to Dr Viktor. But their dates puzzled her. They started in mid-October 1918. *Just before the end of the war*, Katja thought. Why should they have any significance now, more than twenty years later? Then she noticed something else. Pinned to one of the inside pages was a medical chit. By the looks of it, it had been signed by a doctor on the front line and dated October 15. She peered at the faded ink. The name of the patient had, of course, been redacted, but the details were clear. According to the form, the soldier – a lance corporal – was exposed to poisonous gas during a British assault on German lines in northern France. It had left him completely blind; unable to see anything at all.

Dr Viktor's own notes were made, Katja assumed, after his initial examination of the mystery patient. His writing was not easy to decipher, but it was just about legible. On one page, an ink splatter bloomed in the corner. There was a slight tear in another. A few were faded, as if they'd been read and re-read many times. She noted down any puzzling words on a pad in pencil, but once her eyes adjusted to the handwriting and she'd begun to read, she found herself hooked.

Dr Regler confirmed the initial diagnosis and asked me to take on the case. I, too, believe that the patient's blindness is not due to the physical effects of mustard gas but to a form of hysteria – a psychological condition whereby intense anxiety is converted into the loss of a physical function.

A door slammed nearby, making Katja jump. She looked up, but realised the noise was outside. She returned to the notes. '*It is*,' Dr Viktor wrote, '*a case of hysterical blindness.*'

Hysterical blindness, mouthed Katja, making a note of the unfamiliar term on her pad. In other words, it seemed this patient's affliction was all in his mind. It was something she'd never heard of before, but she suddenly found the notion fascinating;

that a patient could *think* themselves blind, even when there was no physical reason, came as quite a revelation to her. She thought of her mother then, and how she used to complain of terrible stomach ache. But after Dr Spier had examined her, he'd pronounced there was nothing wrong. 'It's all up here,' he'd told Katja pointing to his temples. 'Anxiety can have that effect.'

She returned to the notes. Such a person must have an extremely complex mind, she thought. No wonder Dr Viktor was making a special study of it. Her curiosity was suddenly piqued in a way it hadn't been before, and she knew it wasn't going to be easy to quell her natural inquisitiveness.

Once she'd familiarised herself with the first few pages, Katja searched the drawers in her desk for paper. First the top, then the bottom. They were empty, as far as she could see, although one of the drawers was stuck. It wasn't easy to open at first, but when she gave it a hefty tug, it had relented. Several sheets of typing paper lay in the drawer, along with something else.

Wedged at the back, and the reason the drawer had been hard to open, was what seemed to be a narrow length of fabric. When she released it, and saw the hearts and flowers embroidered onto it, Katja understood she was holding a bookmark, and at the bottom, in green silk, had been stitched a name. She squinted to read it. *Leisel Levi*. Katja thought for a moment. The name was certainly Jewish, but it meant nothing to her, so she shoved the bookmark back into the drawer once more and took out several sheets of typing paper. Carefully, she fed a sheet into the roller of the large Continental Silenta before propping up the notebook on the desk to her left. Then, taking a deep breath, she lifted her fingers over the keys. To her dismay, she suddenly realised her hands were shaking. She also realised the reason.

After reading only the first few lines of the notes, she understood why Dr Viktor was so anxious to keep them confidential. While she hardly knew anything about medical practice, she'd heard of the Hippocratic Oath – the bond between patient and doctor that mustn't be broken. If this patient were to be exposed as suffering from a mental disorder, he might lose his family, or his reputation, or his profession. And if he were a famous person and the story found its way into the newspapers, he could be undone. By simply handling these secret notes and learning their contents, she could be putting herself in a difficult position.

Banishing all such thoughts, she steadied her hands on the keys once more and typed solidly for the rest of the day. Her progress was slow, but she managed to transcribe what was asked of her and return the original notebook to Dr Viktor at the end of the day.

Nervously, she waited as he read through her work as the clock ticked past the hour when she was due to leave. With every passing second after five o'clock her mother would be growing more anxious.

After what seemed like an age, he nodded. 'These seem satisfactory,' he told her with a smile.

Katja smiled too, relieved that her typing had passed muster. 'Thank you, sir. Will that be all?' she asked, aware that Mutti would be distraught if she wasn't home within the hour.

'You may go,' he replied, rising to return the notebook to the safe.

Seeing her employer so protective of his notes, and after the nurse's cryptic remarks in the kitchen, Katja's first day in her new role had left her a little puzzled. As she caught the tram home from the clinic, she was left wondering what on earth she'd let herself in for.

*

As soon as Katja arrived at her apartment half an hour later, she felt a draft ruffle her hair and heard the flapping of wings. Hurrying along the corridor, she found the balcony doors wide open and her mother outside, surrounded by pigeons. They were perched on the balcony railings and cooing at her feet.

'Mutti!' she shouted, and her cry sent the birds fluttering and squawking into the night air. 'Come inside. It's too cold to be out there!'

Hilde, wearing only a shawl over her shoulders, turned and looked forlornly at her daughter, like a child whose play had been interrupted. 'But they are hungry,' she protested, a hunk of bread still in her hand.

'So are we!' said Katja, trying not to sound angry. Taking her mother by the hand, she led her back into the salon and shut the doors behind her.

Hilde eased herself into her favourite chair, keeping her baleful eyes on the glass doors.

'They will come back tomorrow,' said Katja, rubbing her mother's cold hands.

'They will?' she asked.

Katja nodded and patted her knee as she stood up.

'They will,' she told her, even though she knew Herr Becker in the apartment above, hated the birds. He called them 'vermin' and would poison them all if he had his way. He was a great supporter of the Nazis, and she'd heard him shout 'Jewish filth!' after Frau Cohen and Aaron more than once. *He'd like to exterminate them too*, she thought.

Chapter 8

Paris

With the latest edition of *The Parisian* hot off the press, Daniel Keenan was summoned into Chuck Patterson's office as soon as he arrived at work. Patterson was from Florida and couldn't abide wearing sweaters, so the central heating had to be turned up high when the weather was only a few degrees above freezing, as it was that February morning. He had on a striped shirt with sleeve garters and his feet were up on his desk when Daniel knocked.

'Come,' he drawled.

'You wanted to see me?'

'Sure do, Danny Boy.' He flung down the latest edition onto the clear desk and it skated across the polished surface to land in front of Daniel. 'That piece you wrote on Hitler's speech at the Reichstag.'

'What about it?' Daniel was scanning the headline on the article he'd written about Hitler's most recent threats. *'A warning to France.'*

'Doesn't exactly flatter the Führer, does it?' Patterson pulled his feet off the desk and tucked them under it.

Daniel picked up the offending copy and pointed at the headline in disbelief. 'The man's dangerous,' he replied, a note of exasperation in his voice. 'He's a menace, and France, and America, need to be warned about him.'

Patterson raised an eyebrow and clasped his hands behind his head to reveal sweat stains under his arms. 'Shoot, Danny, we've had a complaint.'

'A complaint?' Daniel let out a gentle chuckle. He liked complaints. It meant someone was reading what he wrote. 'From whom? Pétain or some other fascist?'

'Actually, from one of your friends.' Patterson unclasped his hands, stood up and walked over to the drinks cabinet.

'One of my . . .' At that moment, Daniel couldn't think of anyone.

'Miss Gertrude Stein,' the American replied, pouring himself a bourbon.

Daniel lifted his head to look at the ceiling and barked out a laugh. 'Gertrude Stein is no friend of mine. I've only met her a couple of times, and I couldn't possibly be friends with a woman who thinks Hitler is a peace-loving man.' His smile disappeared. 'She is merely a professional acquaintance.'

Without offering Daniel a drink, Patterson took a slug from his glass and retreated to his desk once more. 'Shoot, Danny. I don't care if she's your long-lost mother, she's influential in this town. In the States too. You don't mess with her.'

Daniel raked a hand through his hair and cupped the back of his neck. 'I get it,' he replied. 'So, what do you want me to do about it? Because I stand by everything I wrote in that piece.'

Patterson sighed heavily. 'You know what you are, Danny Boy?' Daniel hated it when people called him that. 'Pig-headed.' Raising his glass to him, Patterson took another swig of bourbon.

Daniel nodded. 'I'll give you that, all right.'

Patterson slammed his glass down on the desk in frustration. 'Shoot, you're a bloody good writer too. The best I've got.'

Another nod from Daniel. It was nice to be appreciated, even if his editor's tongue had to be loosened by liquor to admit it.

'But you're also too bloody liberal and that's why I'm telling you to go on leave. Catch up on some reading. I've heard you practically live at that place. What's it called?'

Daniel thought of Sylvia's shop. 'Shakespeare and Company.'

'Shoot. Great name for a bookstore. Wish I'd thought of that.'

Even though Patterson was trying to make light of the situation, Daniel wouldn't buy into it. 'I can't believe what I'm hearing,' he replied, his voice raised. 'Hitler has just announced that he's going to annihilate the whole Jewish race in Europe, and you want me to bury my head in a novel.'

'Only for a week, then when you come back nice and refreshed you can cover this for me.' The American pushed a press release in front of him. Daniel glanced at it to read: '*Matters of the Mind.*'

'What the hell is this?' He was in no mood for games.

'A conference of those psycho-type doctors at the Sorbonne.' Patterson pointed to his temple and circled it, whistling at the same time. 'Get something light for us. What makes a woman attractive to a man? What makes a man attractive to a woman? Our readers love that kind of stuff. And a couple of case studies about finding love. Yeah.' He snapped his fingers as he raced through ideas in his head. 'I thought I was ugly but then . . .' He pointed at Daniel. 'And dreams. People love reading about what dreams mean. Oh, and there's some quack giving a lecture about the sex lives of the Nazis.' His striped shoulders heaved in a laugh. 'That should be right up your street, Danny Boy.'

Daniel couldn't believe what his editor was saying. Or rather he could, but he chose to challenge it. 'Chuck. Chuck, you're not serious?' He only ever called him Chuck in private – and in exasperation.

Patterson leaned over the desk and his expression switched to earnest. 'I'm very serious, Dan,' he replied. 'Gertrude Stein is one of the most influential women in France right now. We don't want to upset the apple cart, do we? Play nice and we can all live happily ever after.'

Daniel needed a cigarette but had left his packet on his desk. 'I'll cover the conference, but just this once. You can't sideline me, Chuck, or I'll . . .'

Patterson shook his head. 'Or you'll what? Get another job?' His boss was looking at him with what Daniel took for pity. 'That won't be so easy, Danny Boy. You need to be more than a good writer to be a good journalist. And you need to toe the line to get on.' He picked up a pen and pointed it at him accusingly. 'Remember when you came to me last year? You were broken. I picked you up and gave you a second chance. Don't waste it.'

Daniel caught his glare and returned a look of simmering rage. 'I may have been broken, Chuck,' he retorted, 'but at least I didn't sell out.'

And with that, he stormed from the office, headed straight for a bar – any bar – just as long as the drink helped him forget.

Chapter 9

Hamburg

'Good,' said Dr Viktor, securing the typed page of the transcript into a folder. It was Katja's second week at the clinic, and while she was managing the typing, she found she was constantly being distracted by telephone calls and meetings. That morning was no exception.

'Yes, very good. Now,' the doctor said, glancing up at the clock on the wall, 'I have a consultation in ten minutes. You will show the gentleman through to me as soon as he arrives. Understand? And while I am occupied, you can get on with this.' He slid the notebook across the desk.

'Yes, sir.'

Dr Viktor's patient – a man in his middle age with greasy hair and hooded lids – arrived a little early for his appointment. Katja rang through to check if the doctor was ready to receive him. 'Herr Levi is here, Dr Viktor.'

The man seemed quite nervous, constantly fingering the brim of his hat and tapping his foot as he waited.

'I'll see him now,' came the reply.

A moment later, the doctor was at the door, but instead of his usual welcoming smile, there was a scowl on Viktor's face.

Herr Levi shot up and almost barged into the consulting room through the door Viktor held open. The two men clearly knew each other, but they certainly weren't on friendly terms. Then it occurred to Katja. Opening the desk drawer, she took out the bookmark she'd discovered on her first day at the clinic. *Levi*. This man had the same name as the one embroidered on the fabric. Could *Leisel Levi* be related? His daughter, perhaps? Could she also have been the doctor's assistant and, therefore, her predecessor?

Not long after, she heard raised voices. It was hard to concentrate on her typing, but she didn't have to wait long before the door opened once more. The doctor stood uneasily on the threshold as Herr Levi skulked out of the consulting room.

'No further consultations necessary,' the doctor announced, in a rather pointed way. He may as well have said: *I hope you never come here again*, thought Katja.

Herr Levi's limp hair flopped forward as he shook his head. 'Don't think this will be the last you hear from me,' he muttered before he left. It was a warning, or possibly a threat. Either way, the doctor seemed to take it in his stride.

'Odious man,' he mumbled, as he turned and stepped back into his office, as if he hadn't even noticed Katja's presence.

*

Over the next few days, Katja was able to continue the transcription with few interruptions. She was finding the more she read, the easier it became to decipher the doctor's handwriting. As well as his medical notes, the doctor had made personal observations on his patient. This she found particularly intriguing. She frowned as she read the closely written text.

They tell me this lance corporal is a troublemaker. A small group of men huddles round his bed most evenings to listen to his diatribes. He loathes Austria and says it is a corrupt and ineffectual country. He blames its woes on the Jews. Germany, on the other hand, is strong and virile. (Note to self: A possible sexual maladjustment? Perhaps a bad experience with a Jewish woman? To be explored.) Nevertheless, he also seems to blame the Jews for all of Germany's problems.

Whoever this man – this patient – was, he seemed utterly vile. He despised everyone who showed any sign of weakness, or even humanity. You didn't have to be a psychiatrist, Katja told herself, to understand there was some sort of deep-rooted bitterness inside this man's head. Presuming he was still alive, she supposed he would have joined the Nazi party by now and would be wearing his badge with pride, just like Fräulein Schauble and Dr Ulbricht. An urge to read on, in the hope that Dr Viktor had actually cured him of his affliction, took hold of her.

He wants to know why French pilots who had crashed their aircraft were given the same military honours as German pilots. He actually suggested their corpses should be left to rot on the battlefield.

There certainly was something inhuman about this mysterious patient. It was almost as if he was blinded by his own hatred. It seemed to make him incapable of understanding normal needs and emotions. And yet people listened to him, according to the doctor's notes. Was that out of curiosity or compulsion? Surely it couldn't be that they agreed with the vitriol spewing from his mouth? She shouldn't be asking such questions, she knew. No longer was she a student whose task had been to explore and question. A cruel twist of fate – and the rise of the Nazi party – had robbed her of that luxury. Now she was a humble secretary, trying to make ends meet. Hers was not to reason why, but the more she read, the louder her father's voice sounded in her head. 'Seek the truth in all things,' he would say. The trouble was the more she knew, the more suspicious she became.

*

It was the end of another working day.

'That will be all, thank you, Fräulein Heinz,' said Dr Viktor after she'd delivered another batch of typing.

Katja had just turned to leave when she saw the door open to her own office. To her shock, Dr Ulbricht was standing on the threshold, clutching a folder. He seemed equally shocked to see her. Even though she had every right to be there, his look made her feel like a burglar caught red-handed.

'You!'

'Dr Ulbricht.'

'What are you doing here?' he asked, his voice thick with disdain.

She swallowed hard. 'I work for Dr Viktor. I am his personal assistant.'

'Ha!' He looked heavenward. 'I should've known,' he muttered and, without knocking, he proceeded to barge straight into Viktor's office, slamming the door behind him. Katja edged forward and put her ear to the wood.

'I go away for a few days and all hell breaks loose in my absence!' cried Ulbricht.

'Your leave seems to have had little effect on you, if I may say, my dear fellow,' replied Dr Viktor, calmly. He regarded his colleague's bark worse than his bite.

'That girl! Who is she?' She heard the younger doctor cry.

Viktor's reply was measured. 'Come, come. You know very well who she is. You interviewed her yourself.'

'Don't play games. I saw her with you the other week in the café. Is she your latest whore?'

Katja bit her lip to stifle a gasp. *Latest whore?*

To her surprise Dr Viktor's voice remained calm. 'You know there was no basis to the allegations. As I told you before, I have been considering her replacement for some time. I am very behind with all my paperwork. I need someone efficient and organised to assist me.'

'We'll see about that,' Ulbricht shot back, clearly unconvinced. 'I would've thought after what happened, you'd have learned your lesson.'

A loud sigh came from Viktor then and exasperation coloured his reply. 'As I keep telling you, Ulbricht, and as I keep telling her father, nothing happened. It was unfortunate, but I was not to blame.'

The room fell silent for a moment before Ulbricht resumed. 'Levi. He was here the other day, wasn't he?'

'Yes,' replied Dr Viktor. 'The man's like a dog with a bone.'

'Well, he won't be troubling you anymore.'

'Why? What do you mean?'

'I've told Fräulein Schauble that Jews are no longer allowed in the building. Levi and his kind are barred from now on.'

'That's one thing I should be grateful to the Party for,' replied Dr Viktor sarcastically.

Katja tensed when she heard his remark and wondered how Ulbricht would take it, but if it offended him, he said nothing. The next sound she heard was a thud on the desk. Papers, she imagined. Dr Ulbricht spoke next.

'The minutes of the last faculty meeting.'

'Thank you,' said Dr Viktor. 'Perhaps we can go over them another time. I have an engagement this evening.'

Ulbricht sneered. 'I bet you do!'

Footsteps now stomped back towards the door, and Katja retreated to her desk. She moved around some papers to appear busy as the younger doctor thundered past her and out into the corridor. Dr Viktor followed as far as the inner door and placed his hand on the jamb, with a heavy sigh.

'You see, Fräulein Heinz,' he told her in a slow, steady voice, 'I have quite a few enemies round here. That man Levi, then Ulbricht. He sees himself as my successor, but he'll have to wait a while. Take no notice of our petty squabbles.' He turned to look at her, the lines round his eyes creasing. 'You and I must keep focused on the bigger prize.'

Katja nodded. *The bigger prize.* She presumed he was referring to the notes she was typing, but then she told herself she must not ask questions, even though it went against her nature. She must shut down her own curiosity. It was not her place to pry.

'The bigger prize,' she repeated, even though she had no idea what it might be.

Chapter 10

Hitler's eyes remained all-seeing, glaring from the huge billboard poster over the busy junction. It was twilight when Katja passed it again on the tram home from the university. Nowadays, swastikas were everywhere; on buildings, on houses and on armbands, but this was something else. She'd always snapped her eyes away before, but tonight she didn't, and the Führer's piercing gaze seemed to follow her along the street. Instinctively, she turned to look back over her shoulder. Sure enough, the unnaturally blue eyes were still upon her, boring into her mind. She shuddered.

By the time she alighted at her usual stop, it was almost dark, and she strode briskly into the street that led to her apartment. Dr Viktor's words – the words she had heard through his office door – were replaying in her mind as she walked home '*It was unfortunate, but I was not to blame.*' Blame for what? She guessed the visit of that man – that 'odious' Herr Levi – might have had some bearing on whatever it was too. Something had happened to his previous assistant, that much Katja knew. The incident had already left her feeling on edge when she thought she heard footsteps close behind, although they sounded quite soft. Not threatening. Then they began again. Walking on for a few paces, she suddenly turned to reassure herself there was no one following her. All she could see behind her was a small, hatless boy, who'd just bent down to tie his bootlace. Satisfied that she was in no danger, Katja clasped her coat collar around her neck to protect her from the cold and carried on.

Moments later, she was back in the foyer of her apartment block. She checked the pigeonhole for post. A bill for her mother's medication. She recognised the familiar envelope, only this time the demand didn't fill her with dread. This time she could pay in full and not beg for a delay. She'd just started to climb the stairs when she heard the main doors open and shut, and she turned nervously, to find the young boy she'd seen tying his laces.

'Can I help you?' she asked.

The child – she guessed he was about eight – shook his head vigorously.

'I have a message, but I am to talk to no one,' he said, his eyes wide with a mixture of fear and excitement.

Katja smiled: 'Then how are you to deliver your message?' she asked.

The boy frowned and looked confused. From under his cap, he held up a square of paper. 'I am to give this to Frau Cohen.'

Katja's smile suddenly disappeared, knowing the message could be from Aaron. After the visit by the Gestapo, Frau Cohen had come clean about her son. He was a graphic designer at an advertising company before he was dismissed for being a Jew. But his mother had been proud to broadcast that his talents were still in demand and that his many clients paid handsomely for his services. Katja had long suspected those services involved forging documents for hunted Jews and had been proved right.

She looked around. 'Come with me,' she said, and a moment later, Frau Cohen stood at her open door. Worry seemed to have aged her virtually overnight, but her eyes shone as soon as she heard there was a message for her. She snatched it from the boy and devoured its contents before raising her eyes heavenward.

'Thank the Lord he is safe. My Aaron is safe, but I warned him not to return for a while.'

'Do you know . . .?' started Katja.

'No.' Frau Cohen shook her head. 'And I don't want to know where he is.'

'Of course,' said Katja. Somehow the Gestapo had got wind of Aaron's underground operation – from Herr Becker, perhaps – and now the widow was left at their mercy. 'It's good to know he's safe,' she added, even though she knew Frau Cohen was now also in real danger.

'Is there a reply?' piped up the child, feeling ignored.

The widow's lip trembled. 'Tell him to be careful and that I love him.'

The boy nodded but loitered until Katja opened her purse and gave him a few pfennigs for his pains.

'Thank you,' she told him, before he skipped down the stairs and out into the cold night. *What has it come to when children risk their lives to become messengers?* she thought.

Chapter 11

The next time she took the tram to work, Katja looked the other way at the big junction, to avoid Herr Hitler's disturbing gaze. Even so, the mere thought of his eyes sent a chill down her spine. She'd heard how some women fainted at the sight of him and now she understood why. There was something so desperately compelling about his penetrating glare; a godlike, all-seeing stare, so powerful that it made you believe he knew what was in your heart.

'Ah, Fräulein Heinz,' Dr Viktor greeted her as soon as she arrived at the office. He was standing by a filing cabinet, haphazardly rifling through papers. 'You typed up those extra notes on hypnosis I gave you the other day?'

Katja nodded. She knew little about hypnosis, but she had quickly grasped the basic principles of it from the doctor's notes. She'd once seen an act at a theatre, where the showman had hypnotised members of the audience. He'd made them run around the stage like chickens, clucking and flapping their wings. It was hilarious, but, of course, Dr Viktor's work was no laughing matter. His hypnosis was undertaken in clinical conditions. Nevertheless, it seemed to Katja such a strange and curious thing to be able to induce someone to lose their own will and

64

make them responsive to another's. She wasn't sure she would feel at all comfortable about being hypnotised.

'Yes, sir,' she replied. Heading straight to an adjacent cabinet, without bothering to take off her coat and hat, she instantly laid her hands on the relevant file.

He smiled as she passed it to him. 'I am lecturing this morning, as you know, Fräulein Heinz,' he told her. 'So, you have enough to keep you going for a few hours.' He nodded at the notebook on his desk. 'Remember, it is not to leave your sight.'

'Yes, sir,' said Katja, as she took off her hat and put it on the stand. She was glad that she would be left alone for the morning. Dr Viktor's frequent need for coffee meant she regularly had to brave the kitchen where encounters with other staff, like the waspy Nurse Wilhelm, as she now knew her, or Nurse Blum – very young and with an irritating, high-pitched giggle – were more likely.

She settled down to work, knowing she would have at least three hours before Dr Viktor's return. The next few pages of the notebook beckoned. She began.

XX seems to have a split personality. Whether this is a clever ruse or a genuine condition, I have yet to discover. Whereas I have heard he is belligerent, and dictatorial, verging on maniacal, in the company of his peers, with his superiors he becomes completely subservient to the point of obsequiousness.

Katja shook her head. She'd come across a few people like that already in life. There were male students in her year who behaved similarly at university. But it was when she turned the following page that she read something quite troubling. This mystery patient was clearly a difficult, objectionable man. In her mind she loathed him already, but what she found on the next page made her shiver. She re-read it and shivered again. In Dr Viktor's hand were written the words: *he says his eyes 'had turned into glowing coals', and that 'it had grown dark' around him.* Whoever this patient was, he seemed deeply disturbed. Picturing the man's red-hot eyes sizzling in their sockets, she was suddenly reminded of Satan and an image she'd seen as a child in a church. The horned creature with its flaming eyes had disturbed her so much she'd screamed and hidden her face in her mother's coat.

The shrill ring of the telephone cut into her thoughts. It rang three times before she picked it up.

'Dr Viktor's office.'

'Who is that?' asked a woman's voice.

'Dr Viktor's assistant,' replied Katja.

'Are you, indeed?'

Katja was surprised by the tone. 'How may I help you?'

But the woman on the other end just made an odd sound, like a snort, and hung up.

The call, coupled with the transcription she'd just completed, puzzled Katja, as if something was out of kilter, but she couldn't quite put her finger on it. It left her with an unsettled feeling.

*

As Katja travelled home that evening, the tram slowed down once more at the junction with the huge poster of the Führer. Only this time, instead of averting her gaze as she'd done before, Katja stared at the image and, in particular, at Hitler's eyes. There was something about them: something mesmeric and disturbing. Whatever it was, it transfixed her, and a charge, like an electric shock, shot through her whole body. The wires connected and formed a circuit. Suddenly, in that moment, she knew.

Quickly, she rose from her seat and fought her way to the nearest exit. She had to leave the tram at the next stop. The door was just about to close but she stuck out her hand and jammed it open, managing to jump onto the pavement just in time. The road was busy with horses and carts, but she jinked across it, narrowly missing a truck that sounded its horn at her, until she reached safety on the other side. Pausing for a second to gather her breath, she turned right and hurried the few metres along the boulevard to Herr Wortzman's bookshop. A glance in the window told her all she needed to know, and she rushed inside.

Herr Wortzman himself was behind the counter. 'Fräulein Heinz. What a lovely surprise. I haven't seen you for a while,' he greeted her, a sudden smile on his face, but Katja was in no mood for pleasantries.

Brushing him off with a curt 'Good evening, Herr Wortzman,' she hurried over to the window and quickly picked out a volume, before presenting it for payment on the counter.

The bookseller's bushy brows shot up when he saw what she wanted to buy.

'You are sure?'

Katja could barely look him in the eye, feeling his disapproval seer into her, but she nodded as she handed over a note.

'Very well, fräulein,' he said frostily, wrapping the book in brown paper and tying it with string. A moment later, he was handing her the purchase, even though she saw the look of disgust on the bookseller's face. 'Here you are.'

'Thank you,' she muttered, snatching the book, and dropping it into her bag as if it were red hot. She knew what he was thinking – that her father would be turning in his grave – but she couldn't tell him the reason for her purchase. Not yet.

That night, after she had made sure her mother had eaten and helped her into bed, Katja went to her room. By the feeble light of an oil lamp, she cut the string and tore off the brown paper. The book's red cover with the Gothic type face, which had once repelled her, now beckoned her to open it.

'Forgive me, Vati,' she muttered as, with trembling hands, she swallowed down her disgust, opened the book at the first page and began to read *Mein Kampf*.

Chapter 12

For a second time, Katja's world changed suddenly and irrevocably. The following morning, her journey by tram remained the same, followed by the short walk to the clinic. Like every other staff member, she now saluted 'Commandant' Schauble behind the desk before going to her office to hang up her hat and coat as she had before. While outwardly nothing was altered, inside she was on fire. Her stomach was roiling, and her nerves were so inflamed that she was relieved when Dr Viktor summoned her straight away.

He was standing at a bookshelf, plucking out books, but didn't look at her when he wished her a cheery 'good morning'. She shut the door behind her and mumbled her reply, although as he headed for his desk, clutching an armful of books, Viktor seemed indifferent to her.

'I have some examination papers to look over today, Fräulein Heinz,' he told her, still not looking up as he lay the tomes on his desk. 'So, I won't disturb you in your endeavours. There it is.' He cocked his head towards the far edge of his desk, in the direction of the familiar notebook and proceeded to reach for a stack of papers in front of him.

Katja, however, remained motionless. Sensing her lack of

movement, the doctor looked up at her for the first time, to notice her eyes were fixed on him. He frowned.

'Is something wrong, Fräulein Heinz?' he asked, puzzled.

Katja heard the blood drumming in her ears and thought her heart might explode. 'Yes, *Herr Doktor*,' she replied. Her words cleaved to the roof of her mouth, but if she didn't get them out, she thought they might choke her. Last night, by the light of her oil lamp, she'd read how a young Austrian had joined the German Army and on October 15, 1918, while stationed near a small Belgian town, had claimed he was blinded by a British gas attack. His eyes, he'd written, were turned into 'glowing coals' and everything around him had grown dark. She knew then, what she had suspected in her heart a little earlier, that Dr Viktor's mystery patient was no ordinary soldier whose case was of interest to his fellow psychiatrists. Now, she knew for sure that this patient was none other than Adolf Hitler, the Führer, himself.

'Yes, something is very wrong,' she repeated, the words shaking from her mouth.

Viktor leaned back in his chair, his eyes clamped on hers, trying to gauge what lay behind them. After a moment, he took a deep breath, pitched forward and steepled his fingers, as if in prayer. 'Then, please share your anxiety,' he told her.

Katja tensed her body. She could tell from the doctor's expression, from the way the colour had drained from his face, that he already knew what she was about to say. She also knew her reply would leave her exposed. But the secret was too big to hide.

'You see, sir, the notes. The patient's notes. I think . . . I think . . .' Katja found it painful to say.

'What do you think?' Dr Viktor, clearly finding it painful to watch, tried to help her.

'I think I've found . . . I think . . .' Her courage was deserting her.

'You know, don't you?' the doctor broke in, putting her out of her distress.

Letting out a breath, she nodded. 'Yes, sir, I believe I do.'

Viktor was silent for a moment, his eyes dropping to his desk, before they lifted again. 'I was afraid you would guess. You are your father's daughter. Intelligent and inquisitive.'

'I didn't mean to. It was just . . .' Her voice trailed off, knowing she sounded pathetic. Her curiosity had led her down this path and now there was no turning back.

The doctor expelled a deep sigh and raised a hand. 'It is my fault. I shouldn't have placed you in this position. You understand this puts you in danger?'

Another nod. Of course she did. The very thought of it terrified her. The mystery patient Dr Viktor had treated all those years ago: the man whose hysterical psyche had blinded him; the man who had preached hatred; the man whose mental state was anything but balanced; the man who might be too dangerous to integrate into society, let alone govern Germany, was Adolf Hitler himself.

'If word gets out, I am in possession of the notebook, I am a marked man. You understand?'

Katja, momentarily too stunned to speak, remained silent, but nodded.

'You will say nothing?'

'Nothing,' she managed.

'I knew I could trust you.'

Katja understood what trouble looked like as far as Nazi politics were concerned; breaking down doors, dragging men from their homes, setting Jewish shops alight and beating up political opponents. She'd seen it happen with her own eyes and so had her dear Vati.

'I swear on my father's memory. I will not tell anyone.'

She noticed a smile crease the lines by Viktor's eyes then. 'He would be proud of you.'

An image of her father's anguished face, as he lay on his hospital bed, suddenly crowded her vision. 'It is the least I can do.'

The doctor fixed her with a disconcerting look and nodded.

'Now that you know, perhaps there is more you can do,' he suggested.

'Sir?'

This time, he chewed his lip in thought. 'You and I need to talk,' he said. 'Away from here.'

Katja was confused. 'But I—'

He broke her off and skewered her with a penetrating look. 'If you are serious about honouring your father's memory, perhaps it is time to act.'

By now the nights were drawing out. Winter still held the city in its grip, but at least the sun was making an intermittent appearance. When Katja arrived home that evening it remained light. She found her mother hunched over in a chair on the balcony, in the company of half a dozen pigeons. Her outline was silhouetted against a pinkish sky, and her head was drooping.

'Hello, Mutti,' called Katja through the balcony doors. 'It's cold. Why not come in now?'

When there was no reply, she moved swiftly to see her mother lift her gaze, distress lined her face. It was then that Katja saw the blood on her blouse.

'You're hurt, Mutti! What's happened?' She rushed forward to see her mother cradling something in her lap and quickly realised it wasn't her blood she'd seen. Moving closer, she saw it came from a bird; one of the feral pigeons that regularly congregated on the balcony. It was listless and obviously injured. There was blood on her mother's hands too. 'What happened?'

'A boy,' replied Hilde, her lips starting to tremble. 'He had a catapult and he shot it up here.' She suddenly dissolved into tears. 'Why would he do such a thing?' she asked pitifully.

Katja reached out and put a comforting arm around her. 'That is so cruel,' she said, looking at the pigeon, a patch of its pale grey breast feathers wet with crimson blood. It looked as though its flesh had been pierced by some sort of missile. Casting her eyes across the balcony floor, Katja saw a trail of blood – and something else. Lying in the corner was what looked like a rock. Leaving her mother still weeping, she crossed over to pick up the object. It was a rock all right, but it was also wrapped in hessian and bound with string. Why would anyone do such a thing, unless something was contained inside the sacking? She tugged at the string that bound it, but it was tied too tightly, so hurrying into the kitchen she cut open the strange parcel with a sharp knife. She was right. As the hessian fell away, a thin strip of paper dropped out and her eyes widened in alarm. A message.

'Kati! Kati, what are you doing?'

'Coming, Mutti,' she mumbled as she read the note, a smile suddenly replacing her frown. On the paper were printed in ink the words: *PLEASE GIVE TO FRAU COHEN*.

A laugh escaped Katja's lips then. She could barely believe what she had just read. The boy who had shot the rock was not the cruel bully she and her mother originally presumed, but a messenger. The hapless pigeon wasn't his target at all. It had just got in the way. Hurrying over to the balcony doors, she rushed to her mother and gently lifted the pigeon from her lap. 'We will look after it until it's better,' she said, 'but right now, Mutti, you and I have a message to deliver to Frau Cohen.'

Chapter 13

Paris

Daniel Keenan was already on his second drink in the bar off Boulevard Saint-Michel where he was a regular, and it wasn't yet noon. Through the window he could see the late February day held out a promise of spring. Despite the cool wind that blew along the Seine, in the sun it was warm. Lazy cats found themselves little patches on rooves to sleep and the pavement cafés were busy with smiling people. He'd once been one of them. But no longer.

He'd just stubbed out another cigarette in the overflowing ashtray next to him, when he was joined by a lean Jewish man with a receding hairline. Most people would guess Oskar Dreiberg was in his late forties, although he was only thirty-five. Life, or rather the Nazis, had not been kind to him. He'd fled Germany after the Burnings and now he stood at an angle over Daniel's table, propped up on a walking stick. In his free hand he held a glass of red wine.

'Oskar,' Daniel greeted him with a neutral expression. He preferred to drink alone.

'M . . . may I join you?' His eyes, framed by gold rims, swept around the bar. He was nervous and it wasn't just his stammer that gave him away.

Seeing his Jewish acquaintance on edge, Daniel gestured to the chair opposite him. 'How is life treating you, Dreiberg?'

'I can't complain,' Oskar replied with a shrug as he eased himself gently onto a chair and straightened his left leg in front of him. 'Considering what's happening in my country, I'm very l . . . lucky to be here.'

Daniel nodded. Everyone knew German Jews were suffering under Hitler. 'And Alfred? Is there any word from Spain?' Alfred Kantorowicz was one of the founders of the Library of Burned Books in Paris. It had been opened on the first anniversary of the Burnings in Berlin and contained thousands of volumes considered seditious and banned by the Nazis. After fleeing Germany, Alfred, a lawyer and intellectual, had gone to fight in Spain with the International Brigades the previous year, leaving Oskar in charge of the library.

'The last I heard he was in C . . . Córdoba. But that was a couple of months ago,' Oskar stammered.

Daniel raised his half-empty glass of whiskey. 'Then let's drink to his safe return.'

The librarian also raised his glass with a nod.

Daniel took another gulp. 'So, you have been left in charge of all those wonderful books.'

'Actually, that's what I wanted to talk to you about.'

'Oh?' Daniel looked surprised.

'Yes, I've been contacted by an old associate from Hamburg. He's got something . . .' He paused to search for the appropriate word. '. . . something important; a notebook he thinks will be of value to, shall we say, democratically minded people.'

Daniel noticed Oskar was looking around him as he spoke. He took out a packet of Gitanes from his breast pocket and offered him one. Oskar's hand was trembling as he took it.

'Sounds interesting,' said Daniel, striking a match and holding it to the tip of Oskar's cigarette. 'But if it's vaguely political, you know it's not of interest to *The Parisian*. The editor only wants gossip and fashion, and theatre reviews, these days.'

Oskar's head shot up. 'I didn't say it was p . . . political.'

Daniel dropped a knowing look. 'You didn't have to.'

Now he helped himself to a cigarette, cupped his hand around the flame and dragged deeply on the Gitanes. 'So why do you think whatever this associate has is of interest to me?'

Oskar took a first tentative puff of his cigarette and coughed. It was clear he wasn't a smoker. He inspected the lit end with the curiosity of a child, then leaned forward. 'I know your views on the Nazis,' he said, his voice barely louder than a whisper. 'And my contact seeks a p . . . publisher. I wondered . . . I hoped . . .' He leaned back.

Daniel's face split into a smile – something that didn't happen very often these days. 'A publisher,' he repeated, nodding his head slowly, before he flicked the cone of ash from his cigarette into a small dish. 'But surely you must know dozens.' He was playing devil's advocate.

Oskar shrugged. 'Of course I do. But this publisher needs to be . . .'

'Courageous, anti-establishment,' Daniel suggested, taking another drag on his cigarette.

'Precisely.'

'And you want me to have a word with her?'

For the first time during their conversation Oskar allowed himself a muted smile. At least they both had the same person in mind. 'You know Miss Beach very well.'

Daniel smiled too, while at the same time shaking his head. 'Publishing James Joyce's smutty novel, albeit a work of genius, is very different from publishing something, well, I don't know.' He shrugged and took another drag of his cigarette. 'Are you saying this work is anti-fascist?'

Oskar almost jumped out of his seat and his hand flew up

to his lips, as if begging his companion to lower his voice. Both men knew there were Nazi spies in the city, but the average Frenchman was more excited about the *Coupe de France* play-offs than worrying over Germany's intentions.

The librarian took another puff of his cigarette and coughed again. 'It is not an exaggeration to say it could bring d . . . down Hitler's government.' His voice was shaky, and his eyes remained lowered.

Daniel took a deep breath. 'Jesus,' he muttered.

'It's a delicate matter,' said Oskar, finally. 'Perhaps we can discuss it further, in private.'

Daniel let his gaze settle on the ashtray as he stubbed out his cigarette slowly and deliberately. 'So, this notebook is hot? That's what you're saying. And you're inviting me to get my hands burned.'

Oskar frowned. 'The whole of Europe risks b . . . burning if someone doesn't stand up to this mad man.' He spoke quietly but with a frightening intensity that made Daniel take him seriously.

'Is this work ready for publication, or does it need editing?'

The librarian's brows lifted simultaneously. 'I'm not sure.'

Daniel took a gulp of whiskey. 'I know Sylvia had a hell of a job with Joyce's manuscript. He wrote half of it at the printers, and she swore she'd never take on anything that wasn't – shall we say – completely polished ever again.' Daniel emptied the glass. He wasn't trying to be deliberately obtuse, but by now Oskar knew if he was to get any further, he needed to try harder.

'Doesn't it trouble you, Mr Keenan? This whole situation. Hitler.'

The Irishman's lips twitched. 'Any war, should it come, won't be fought in my name.'

Oskar's shoulders slumped and he realised he was probably wasting his time. 'Perhaps not, but it will affect you. It'll affect all of us.'

'I'll cross that bridge when I come to it, Oskar. Right now, I've got other things on my mind.'

Dreiberg knew Daniel was still dealing with his own grief. He stubbed out his half-smoked cigarette and stood. 'Of course,' he said. 'I'm sorry to have troubled you.'

'You're leaving so soon?' asked Daniel. 'But you haven't finished your wine.' He nodded at the almost untouched glass of red on the table.

Oskar returned a weak smile. 'I don't work well on alcohol. I'll see you around.'

'Yes. *À bientôt*,' said Daniel, reaching for the wine glass and raising it in the air as he watched the little man limp towards the door. Even before Oskar Dreiberg was out of sight, he'd downed the whole glass in one.

Chapter 14

Hamburg

As the late winter light faded, the lamps came on in Mönckebergstrasse, where Katja was to meet the doctor. It was the most elegant street in Hamburg, connecting the great Gothic town hall to the railway station. The crystal chandeliers in the jewellers and perfumeries were shimmering, and candles on restaurant tables were being lit. Just off the street, busy with both shoppers and commuters, another smaller street ran parallel, where the shabbier facades were peeling, and the plasterwork was black with dirt. Here the electric lights were also being switched on, over the night bells of hotels where rooms could be rented by the hour.

En route, Katja stopped to buy a copy of the *Hamburg Echo* from the kiosk on the corner. She'd heard some of the nurses talking excitedly about Hitler's visit next week. Nurse Wilhelm and Nurse Blum were in the kitchen when she gleaned the latter had been given time off to cheer the Führer's motorcade as it passed through the city centre. According to the newspaper report, Hitler was to visit the docks for the launch of a new battleship, named in honour of Germany's great former Chancellor *Bismarck*, where he would address the workers. A tour of the shipyard would follow. For the next few days, Katja knew the whole city would be in a frenzy of excitement. *God help any dissenting voices*, she thought.

For some reason, not entirely obvious to Katja, Dr Viktor considered a nearby coffee bar in this sleazy side street the ideal venue for a meeting. She found him seated in a corner when she arrived. The cold had misted the frames of his pince-nez and he was wiping the lens with a napkin. A glass of schnapps was already half empty. He rose when she approached.

'You're sure you were not followed?' he asked, pointing to the banquette opposite.

'I don't think so,' she replied, sliding into her seat. She was already nervous, and his question put her even more on edge. Dr Viktor had instructed her not to make mention of their secret within the grounds of the clinic. He'd already warned her to be on her guard at all times; especially at the clinic where enemies, like Dr Ulbricht, were happy to circle like sharks, ready to attack at the first scent of blood. She was to watch out for anything suspicious too; odd clicks on the telephone line, unexplained shadows, files out of place, but above all she was to say nothing. All conversations about 'the Austrian patient', as he referred to Adolf Hitler, were to take place at neutral locations where they could both blend in – hence the café in the city centre.

There was no need for Katja to be told how explosive Dr Viktor's notes were. Of course she had no idea what he intended to do with them once she had finished transcribing them, but she was sure he had plans. They could, she supposed, be used as some sort of bargaining tool, or, heaven forbid, for blackmail, although she was certain the doctor wasn't a criminal. There was another possibility too. Placed in the hands of a foreign power – an enemy of Germany, say – they could be used to destabilise the Nazi government. And now that she knew what the notes contained – in principle, if not in detail – those plans, whatever they were, necessarily had to involve her.

Katja told her mother she was working late. She wouldn't dream of asking the doctor what excuse he had given his wife, although she had the impression theirs was not a happy marriage. Viktor had made the odd throwaway remark about her: *Frau Viktor would not approve; Frau Viktor does not care for this or that.* In fact, every time he mentioned his wife, it was in a negative context. The more she dwelt on it, the more she thought the mystery female caller at the office the other day was probably her.

A waitress passed their table and Viktor snapped his fingers. '*Ein espresso, bitte,*' he ordered. His hat remained on the table, and he kept his coat on. Katja suddenly wondered if it was because he thought they might have to make a quick getaway. Even though it was warm in the café, she kept her coat and hat on too.

'I have much to tell you,' he said, hooking his pince-nez onto his nose. His eyes fixed on her and widened, almost as if seeing her clearly surprised him. The tables at the front of the café were all occupied, but at the rear they were the only customers. 'Of course, you know a lot already, but it seems I underestimated you.'

'Sir?'

'I thought there was a chance you'd guess the identity of my patient once you'd finished typing up my notes,' he told her, with a wry smile. 'But not before.'

Katja's mouth set into a tight line. Compliments wouldn't save her if she had a Nazi boot on her neck. She already knew that. Just then the waitress returned to set down an espresso in front of her, and gazing into her cup she said: 'Now I have opened Pandora's box, will you tell me the whole story?' She could afford to speak plainly because, ultimately, she held a good hand in this dangerous game of poker.

Taking his pipe from his pocket, Viktor proceeded to fill it with tobacco from a pouch as he began to talk. 'Very well,' he replied. 'If you are sure. I suppose it's only fair I tell you everything,' he mumbled before looking up at her. 'On reflection, I owe you an apology.'

'An apology?' Men never apologised to their secretaries, thought Katja. But then, perhaps because of what she had just discovered, he considered her more of an equal.

'Yes.' His gaze dipped again. 'I have handed you a poisoned chalice and I cannot ask you to drink from it.'

A realisation suddenly loomed over Katja like a pregnant storm cloud, poised to deliver a crushing torrent above her. Dr Viktor was giving her the chance to walk away: to dodge the deluge; to escape the drowning. She paused before she answered. What would Vati do? She did not have to think long. Her father would seize the chalice with both hands and drink from it, knowing that if he did not, more lives would be lost.

'Tell me,' she said emphatically. 'Tell me everything.'

'You are sure?' He was giving her a second chance. 'It's not too late . . .'

'Please,' replied Katja, straightening her neck, as if bracing herself for the impact. 'I am aware of the dangers.'

Viktor cleared his throat. 'Very well,' he said. 'I'll begin at Pasewalk, towards the end of the war.'

'Pasewalk,' she repeated, thinking of the smudged letter.

He nodded. 'A town about five hours east of here. In 1918 I was in the *Kriegsmarine – the* Navy – and stationed as a psychiatric doctor at the hospital. You already know that my patient had been diagnosed with hysterical blindness and that I was convinced his sight had not been physically damaged. You also know that I had received reports about his behaviour, citing his aggression, his pathological hatred of Jews and his absolute refusal to accept Germany's impending defeat in the war.'

'That much I know,' Katja agreed.

'By that time almost everyone had accepted that the Fatherland was on the brink of defeat. The Great War was lost. Our soldiers were dropping like flies. There were riots. People were starving. We were finished.'

One of Katja's most vivid early memories was seeing her

mother cry when she asked her for some bread. There was none. 'I remember,' she said with a nod.

'My patient, however, steadfastly refused to believe Germany could lose. I think he would rather have died than accept defeat.' He shook his head, as if reliving his dilemma. 'I thought long and hard how I should approach his treatment and I finally came up with a solution. Logical arguments were useless. There was nothing logical about this man's blindness, so reason would be wasted on him.'

Katja frowned. 'I'm afraid I don't follow.'

Viktor sighed heavily. 'I concluded that the only way I could cure him of his obsession was to pander to it.'

'Pander to it?' repeated Katja. 'You mean you would lie to him?'

She saw the doctor's eyes widen like saucers behind his lenses, delighted that she followed his argument. He leaned forward and his voice raised excitedly. 'The man was completely delusional. Oh, and an insomniac too. I needed to fight fire with fire. So that is exactly what I did.'

Katja looked about her, hoping his enthusiasm hadn't attracted attention. Aware he had been a little too loud, Viktor resumed in a half whisper. 'I had to make him believe his will was all powerful, and that if he wanted to see, then he could work a miracle on himself. Only he had the power to restore his own sight.'

'What did you do?'

'I sent for him one evening, so that we could talk by candle-light,' he continued, striking a match as if to illustrate his point, while dipping the flame towards the bowl of his pipe. 'I sat him down in a chair by the lit candles and examined him with my ophthalmoscope. Those eyes were an extraordinary piercing blue. I'd never seen anything quite like them before. Yes, they were inflamed, but that was probably due to lack of sleep, otherwise there was no reason why he could not see. The reflex on the retinas was normal. And yet . . .' He paused, reimagining the scene. 'And yet, his face wore a look of fear. His features were drawn, and tense, and I knew he was convinced I would reiterate what all the other doctors had told him – that his eyes were perfectly fine, that he was a liar and that he could see if he wanted to.'

Katja leaned even further forward. 'So, what *did* you tell him?'

'I blew out the candles and told him that his eyes had been badly damaged in the gas attack. I said he really was blind and that he – a good Aryan of unimpeachable character and a holder of the Iron Cross medal – should never have been doubted.'

'What did he say to that?' asked Katja.

'He seemed relieved at my diagnosis. Vindicated. But then I brought him back down to earth. I told him he would never see again, unless . . .' He sucked on his pipe and a cloud of smoke suddenly shrouded him.

'Unless what?'

'Unless he believed in miracles.'

'Miracles?'

'Yes. I suggested to him that while most people agreed miracles no longer happened, if they ever did, history teaches us there were a few extraordinary individuals who could bend nature to their will. I postulated these individuals were possessed of a truly special gift. I named Jesus and Muhammad as examples. Their powers, their wills proved supreme, and that only an exceptional person with limitless spiritual energy could hope to emulate them.'

Katja's response came out in an incredulous whisper. 'What?'

'I had been studying him, remember, for almost a month. I knew that he felt superior to everyone else; that he had been given a special gift of leadership; that he regarded himself as capable of having messianic powers. So, I suggested the opposite. I played the devil's advocate and told him that only a person with supreme spiritual qualities and a will of iron could overcome the darkness and regain the light.'

'Then what happened?'

'He turned his head towards me, and asked me, almost submissively, if I really thought he might be special. That's when I knew

I had him in the palm of my hand. He was placing his trust in me – he who reviled almost everyone else in the world, was showing me respect.'

Katja saw the doctor's own eyes grow watery. 'What did you do?' she asked.

'What did I do?' he repeated, his jaw suddenly trembling. 'I did the worst thing I have ever done in my entire life. It wasn't hard. He was very suggestible, and I *made* him believe in himself.

'I told him only he had the power to overcome his blindness. Over the next few minutes, I built up his ego. I managed to convince him he held Germany's destiny in his hands, but to exercise his power he had to demonstrate his will would conquer everything, including his own physical limitations.' He paused and shook his head. 'Then I struck a match and commanded him to open his eyes.'

Katja gasped. 'And?'

The doctor licked his lips. 'Almost instantaneously he said he saw something, but I told him "something" was not enough. I urged him to focus, to concentrate his mind. I reminded him that the Fatherland needed young men like him, with drive and energy. I relit the candle in front of me then, and I ordered him to see it. I told him he had the power within himself to work a miracle. I commanded him to see for the sake of Germany.' The doctor's voice was growing louder once more, and he was looking beyond Katja into the distance.

'And it worked?'

Katja's question brought him back into the moment, but with the recollection his eyes filled with tears once more. 'Yes, it worked. He started to regain his sight, as I knew he would. He told me he could see my face, my ring and the white coat I was wearing. And I . . . I told him . . .' He stumbled over his words. 'I told him he was healed.'

At the sight of a tear breaking free when he blinked, Katja was moved to reach out. Lightly she touched the doctor's hand.

'Please, no,' she said, looking around her to see if anyone else had witnessed the outpouring. 'You must be calm,' she urged.

Viktor shook his head and put down his pipe to reach for a handkerchief from his coat pocket. 'After that night something changed inside him. Hitler came to Pasewalk a broken man with a conviction, but he left my room a man possessed.'

'In what way?' asked Katja.

'Don't you understand?' he groaned. 'I must have unleashed a latent evil inside him, the likes of which I'd never seen before, nor since. After that night, his speeches became charged with a startling power and hatred. It was as if he had become an extreme religious fanatic, filled with an insatiable zeal, and no more so than when it came to the Jews.' He closed his lids and shuddered before he opened them once more. 'He thought he was the messiah.'

The words reverberated against Katja's lips in a whisper. 'The messiah?'

Viktor nodded once, then looking at her with urgent, red-rimmed eyes he said: 'Don't you see, Fräulein Heinz? I am the one responsible for what is happening. If it hadn't been for me, Adolf Hitler would have remained in some institution for the blind. No one would have ever heard his name. Now humanity will come to curse it and curse me too, because I was the architect of his success.'

Katja watched the doctor sniff back more tears. Her heart ached at the sight, while, at the same time, she tried to process the magnitude of what he had just told her. Adolf Hitler was not just a dictator. He was more than that. He believed himself to be some sort of saviour, with a destiny to lead the German people to the Promised Land.

'You must not blame yourself,' she whispered. 'You are a doctor. You have a duty to your patients. How could you have known what he would become?'

Viktor shook his head and lifted his eyes to hers. As well

as tears, there was something else in them. Katja recognised it instantly. His face was twisted with a look of remorse. 'I am Dr Frankenstein,' he told her flatly. 'I created the monster and now I must destroy it.'

His shocking confession unleashed his tears again and although he tried to stem them, Katja saw he was failing.

'Perhaps we should get some air,' she suggested, afraid he would draw attention to them.

They settled the bill and stepped into the darkness together. By now most commuters had scurried off to their homes, leaving the streets to drinkers and pick-pockets. They walked side by side, slowly. Some might have mistaken them for lovers; the doctor talking in a low voice and Katja leaning towards him so as not to miss a word, as they made their way to the central train station. But it was her father, he reminded her of. There was something about him; not in looks, but in his mannerisms. The way he chose his words so carefully. The way he seemed to battle with himself, as if he was holding a constant discussion in his head, weighing up the pros and cons of every situation.

'How long will it take you to finish typing the notes?' he asked Katja.

Her step faltered slightly. She wasn't even a quarter of the way through. 'Another four or five weeks, perhaps.'

It clearly wasn't the answer he wanted. 'I need you to transcribe faster.' He suddenly increased his pace as if the thought of urgency powered him.

Katja just about managed to match his step. He hadn't given her a concrete deadline. Now, all of a sudden, everything had speeded up. 'Has something happened?' she asked.

This time it was Viktor who stopped dead. 'I have a contact.'

'A contact?'

'In Paris. I spoke with him on the telephone a few days ago. He says he hopes to find someone willing to publish the edited contents of my notebook.' He began powering forward once more, as Katja digested his words. She could barely believe what she was hearing.

She caught up. 'Publish it?'

'Of course.' He stopped abruptly again. 'That's what this is all about. I want the whole world to know that Germany is in the grip of a megalomaniac.' Katja saw fire in his eyes as he spoke. 'Hitler must be stopped at all costs.'

She thought for a moment. What he was saying made perfect sense, but the prospect of unleashing the truth on to the world was also terrifying, and yet, even then, she found herself thinking practically. 'But I still have much to do,' she protested.

Viktor shook his head, as if brushing aside her objection. 'As I said, Katja – I may call you Katja?' he asked her, even though he didn't wait for her reply. 'If you continue with this mission, you will need to work faster. I need the typing finished by the end of next month.'

Now it was Katja who stopped abruptly in her tracks. Up ahead, a man reading a newspaper almost ploughed into her. '*Entschuldigung!*' she blurted apologetically. He threw her a dismissive look and walked on.

'But, sir, I have so many other duties,' she told him, switching to the doctor once more.

Ignoring her, he strode on. 'You must transcribe as much as you can, because I need something to show a publisher, should one express interest. Then we shall travel to Paris.'

'*We* shall travel?' she repeated, her eyes wide with incredulity.

'Yes,' he told her, his own eyes sliding away from her then, before he mumbled: 'My previous assistant always travelled with me.'

'Your previous . . .' Of course, Katja knew he was referring to Leisel. She refused to believe the rumours because the doctor always behaved in a proper way and his manners resembled her father's. 'You mean Fräulein Levi?'

Viktor frowned and swung round. 'How do you know about

her?' For the first time she heard a trace of anger in his voice, but she wanted to be truthful.

'I heard the nurses talking,' she replied.

'The nurses?' Viktor repeated.

'And then I found a bookmark with her name on it in my desk drawer.'

Without warning, he tucked his arm through hers and steered her into a shop doorway so he could speak without fear of intrusion. Above her pounding heart, Katja heard him say: 'A bookmark?' The discovery seemed to make him uneasy. Once more he closed his eyes, but this time he shook his head. 'No. No.' His voice rasped in his throat. 'Poor Leisel. I did nothing . . .' Another shake of the head. 'Whatever you heard, it wasn't like that.' His eyes were wide and his lips trembling, as if imploring Katja to believe him.

Katja wanted to know how it was. She *needed* to know, if she was going to risk her life for this man's work. 'So how was it?' she heard herself asking, even though she could barely believe her own nerve.

The doctor seemed taken aback too. 'I will tell you the full story,' he said. 'But not here. Not now. I am already treading on thin ice at the clinic. Such rumours only fuel the fire.'

Again, Katja nodded. 'I understand,' she replied.

Together they moved out of the doorway and resumed their journey to the station. Just outside the main entrance, Viktor stopped and turned to her. 'I planned to travel to Paris with Leisel, although she didn't know anything about the notebook. But now I have you.' A gentle smile spread across his face. 'Now I have you.' He tilted his head, looked deep into her eyes and, with a conviction that somehow startled her, he added: 'I know I can trust you.'

*

88

Katja couldn't sleep that night, too terrified to close her own eyes because all she could see were Adolf Hitler's staring back at her from the billboard. They were unfathomable, spellbinding and fascinating in a macabre and sinister way, like fingers that pressed her flesh and spidered down her neck. If only Dr Viktor hadn't worked his miracle; hadn't returned sight to his extraordinary Austrian patient by bolstering his self-confidence, by making him believe he possessed supernatural powers, how different things would be. The Book Burnings, the cruel laws against Jews and the labour camps for political prisoners – none of these may ever have existed. She would have finished her university degree. Her mother would be fit and well, and her dear Vati might still be alive. And now the threat of another war loomed and, as her thoughts pressed in on her, like the darkness of the night, she felt as if she were being consumed by the horror of it all. But then she remembered Dr Viktor's plan. It had offered a glimmer of hope, but it also brought with it danger.

Chapter 15

First thing, the following morning, Katja fetched Leisel's bookmark from her drawer and placed it silently on Viktor's desk. As soon as he realised what it was, the doctor's eyes clamped on it, but the moment he reached out to take it, Katja snatched it back. Overnight she had been thinking. If Dr Viktor was asking her to put her life on the line for his work, she needed something in return: respect. Right now, that respect should take the form of an explanation. He'd promised one last night, but she feared he might put it off. The look she gave him conveyed her frustration. He understood.

'You want me to tell you what happened, don't you?'

. She nodded. A question mark now hung in the space between them. Last night's revelations had given rise to a new intimacy between them because their lives now depended on each other. With a long sigh, Viktor gestured to the chair on the other side of his desk. He waited until she was seated to begin.

'I hired Leisel on her merits. I cannot deny she was a pretty young woman, but she was a good typist. Efficient too.' He shrugged. 'Not long after she arrived, I started noticing things.'

'What things?' nudged Katja.

'She'd bring me *leibkuchen* she'd baked herself, fresh flowers for my office. She seemed eager to please. I didn't think much of it until . . .' A sudden noise along the corridor caused him to break off abruptly. Katja heard it too. She retreated into her office to listen. More than one person was approaching. Two, perhaps three. Their treads were heavy, and they stopped outside. She made it to her desk just in time and her stomach clenched as the door opened without a knock.

Fräulein Schauble appeared before her in the doorway, looking officious and proudly sporting her Nazi lapel badge. Behind her loomed a broad-shouldered, high-ranking naval officer judging by his medals and brocade, accompanied by a sailor. Katja leaped up from her seat, as the sailor's arm shot out in front of him.

'*Zeig Heil!*' he cried.

Her right hand flapped in an almost involuntary response.

Fräulein Schauble looked as if she was about to burst with patriotic pride. 'Kommodore Flebert is here to see Dr Viktor,' she announced.

Knowing the officer had no appointment, Katja floundered. 'I will . . .'

She was about to give the diary a perfunctory look, even though she knew that might inflame the situation, when Dr Viktor flung open his office door.

'Kommodore Flebert!' he cried cordially. 'What a wonderful surprise. Please, come in.' He gestured the officer inside with a broad smile.

'Coffee, Fräulein Heinz,' he ordered, then leaning in mumbled something to her about knowing the officer from his days in the *Kriegsmarine*. He pulled back. 'And see if there are any *kuchen* too.'

At this, the kommodore, a ruddy-faced middle-aged man with a long scar down one cheek, let out a hearty laugh, reminding Katja of a foghorn. It came as a huge relief – and something of a surprise to her – that this seemed to be a social visit. For a moment she felt the tension ease until, that is, she remembered she'd already made a start on today's transcription. Half a dozen sheets lay in full view on her desk, not to mention the notebook, while several sentences had been typed onto paper clamped under the roller of her typewriter.

Fräulein Schauble had beaten a retreat, but the sailor was left standing to attention outside the doctor's door. He was staring straight ahead, but she imagined his eyes could wander and settle on the transcript at any moment. Quickly she returned to her seat and pressing the return key on the typewriter, wound the platen knob to retrieve the incriminating sheet of paper with a flourish, before quickly sliding the sheet under a file on the desk, along with the notebook.

In the kitchen, Katja poured out the coffee into the readied cups and set them on a tray, alongside a plate of gingerbread. On seeing her return, the sailor knocked and opened the door to Dr Viktor's office to let her pass.

The kommodore, she noted, was looking relaxed and seemed to be chatting amiably with the doctor.

'She's even happy to carry out her duties now,' he said. Katja caught him giving the doctor a wink.

Viktor snorted a chuckle in reply, but when his look snagged on Katja, the smile vanished.

'Thank you, Fräulein Heinz,' he said as she laid the tray on the desk and proceeded to pour the coffee. But Viktor waved her away. 'I shall see to it,' he muttered, and she retreated. 'I'm glad to hear she's restored to her former self,' she heard him say to Flebert.

There was another laugh from the naval officer. 'As dutiful a wife as a man could ask for,' he replied.

Katja returned to her desk and pretended to be fully occupied in the presence of the waiting seaman. She flipped through the desk diary and began to type a letter to a patient, dictated earlier by Dr Viktor.

Another twenty minutes passed slowly; with each one, the knot in Katja's stomach tightened as she questioned what the officer might want of Dr Viktor. As soon as she heard the scrape of chairs and footsteps approach, she too was on her feet and the sailor was once again standing to attention.

It was a relief to see Flebert emerge smiling. 'Until the launch, Viktor.'

The doctor gave a shallow bow. 'You honour me, Kommodore,' he said.

The officer was smiling, but when he turned to face Katja his smile dissolved into an odd look that made her stomach lurch. His eyes lingered on her face for a moment before dropping to her breasts. He returned to Viktor.

'And your secretary too,' he said.

Ignoring Katja's shocked expression, Viktor replied: 'You are most kind.'

The doctor escorted Flebert and the sailor out to the reception, leaving Katja alone to feel a creeping sickness travel up from her stomach. On his return, the doctor beckoned her into his office without a word and shut the door firmly behind him. His face had turned an odd shade of grey. Katja held her tongue as she watched him slump into his chair. It appeared he needed to compose himself for a moment. When he finally spoke, his head was in his hands and his words came out in a muffled breath.

'I've been invited to a reception for our illustrious Führer.'

Katja could barely believe her ears. 'Excuse me?'

The doctor lifted his head and put his hands to his temples. 'You heard me. The state visit, next week. The launch of the battleship *Bismarck*. There is a reception at the dockyard. Kommodore Flebert thinks he has given us the most enormous honour.'

Katja shook her head. 'But I don't understand. I . . .'

'I treated his wife for anxiety and depression.' He rolled his eyes. 'He believes I have cured her, and this is his way of repaying me.'

'But surely you won't go.' The thought of being in the same room as Adolf Hitler made her flesh crawl.

Viktor shook his head and rose from his desk. Opening the drawer to one of the filing cabinets, he pulled out a bottle of

93

schnapps and a glass and proceeded to pour himself a large glass. It was downed in one and a second was dispensed before he returned to his seat. She hadn't taken him for a drinker, and it shocked her, knowing that he, of all people, must be in turmoil to resort to alcohol to help him through his troubles. 'I have to go,' he said thoughtfully, as if he had been contemplating Katja's question all the while. 'If I refuse it will be seen as treasonous. I will be punished. I know it.'

Katja shook her head and frowned. 'But if Hitler sees you and recognises you, then surely he could put you in jail, or worse, because of what you know.'

Viktor tilted his head. 'Of course, but you see I have no choice.'

'But he could destroy you,' protested Katja, unable to hide her exasperation.

Slowly, the doctor shook his head, while keeping his gaze on her. 'The invitation was issued to you too.'

Katja recalled the kommodore's lecherous leer. 'What?!'

'He wants you to accompany me. I fear we are in this together.'

The thought of being in the same room as the man she held responsible for her father's death, made Katja dizzy. She prayed she would not be introduced to the Führer, because she could not be certain how she would react.

'You are prepared to risk your own life to do this?' she asked through clenched teeth, aware that hers would also hang in the balance if her complicity were ever discovered.

'I am,' he said with such conviction that Katja believed him. 'But not yours.'

'What do you mean?'

'I will concoct some excuse for you. It's not right to put you in harm's way. I would never forgive myself if anything happened to you. I owe it to your father to keep you safe. I will go on my own.'

His face had darkened, but in that moment, Katja knew that no matter how many objections she voiced about the madness of the idea, Dr Ernst Viktor had no choice but to go to the reception.

'No,' she blurted.

His head shot up. 'What do you mean, no?'

Katja stuck out her chin and felt a renewed energy surge through her body. 'You will not go alone,' she told him. 'Because I will come with you.'

Chapter 16

Paris

Daniel's apartment lay in a quiet block with an ornate facade in a residential quarter. He'd chosen it because, when the time came, there was an American school just around the corner for Bridie. It was on the second floor, well proportioned with a good-sized salon, and, most importantly, with two bedrooms. A floor-to-ceiling shelf was crammed with books stashed at all angles. Some even spewed out over the floor, alongside piles of magazines and newspapers. The walls were bare, as was most of the wooden floor, apart from an abandoned pair of slippers and a crumpled shirt. He'd made little attempt to make the place homely. What was the point? *Home is where the heart is*, and all that, but he'd lost his heart the day his wife and child died.

It was seven o'clock when he arrived back from work and the evening stretched ahead of him, long and lonely. Once, he'd pictured time spent on the little balcony. With glasses of red wine in hand, and Bridie tucked up in bed, he and Grace would watch the sun set over the rooftops. They'd talk about all the things they planned to do, like climb the Eiffel Tower and see the Mona Lisa, and maybe even have another child.

As he looked around the room he sighed. The rocking horse had been an impulse buy. He'd spotted it in a *brocante* shop near Shakespeare and Company and snapped it up for Bridie, imagining her sitting astride it, dressed as a princess or a warrior, playing some imaginary game. Now shoved into a dark corner, it was destined never to rock again. And as for the door on the far side; the one next to his bedroom, it would remain firmly shut for a very long time.

Flinging down his hat and coat on the sofa, he walked over to the large desk that dominated the room heading straight for the whiskey bottle on it. As he filled the glass, he studied the photograph of a beautiful young woman holding a baby girl. Grief was never good company and being surrounded by memories sometimes didn't help, especially when the wound was still raw. He raised his glass to the photograph in a toast.

'To you, my loves,' he whispered, 'wherever you are.' He then downed the whiskey, each gulp attempting to fill the hole left by their absence.

In the larger of the two armchairs in the room, a second glass of whiskey in hand, he sat in lonely contemplation. At first, he'd been angry. No. More than angry – incandescent with a rage so strong and unfathomable that he thought it would swallow him up and he'd be lost forever. His fevered mind had been in turmoil and his body an unexploded bomb. He'd even got into a fight in a bar when some clown had told him to 'cheer up'. His fury had boiled over then, and a left hook had dealt with the wisecracker but had done nothing to assuage his own anguish. Like the wooden chair he'd broken in the melee, his heart was splintered by grief.

After that incident, he'd sworn never to let his temper get the better of him again. His rage had finally subsided; slipping away like a snake shedding its skin. Sometimes it reared its head again, usually in the small hours, but he was able to keep it under control. Then had come the recriminations. He blamed himself. Of course he did. He should never have left Grace and Bridie in Ireland to start his job in France. They should have come with him right away; stayed in a hotel for a few days until he'd found somewhere suitable for them. Their savings would have been swallowed up, but they'd still be alive. They'd paid for his own caution and penny-pinching with their lives. Those ugly thoughts sometimes pushed through the fog of his depression but were not as constant as they once were.

The poetry had helped him. A slim anthology lay on the table in front of him. WB Yeats. His favourite poet and a true Irishman. His words had offered a lifeline when he thought he'd drown in the bog of his own grief, and still did. He was slowly coming to realise the drink was only a sticking plaster over his gaping wound. It made him feel foggy and heavy, and if he continued the way he was, he knew it would kill him. In his mind's eye, he could see Grace's disapproving look and hear her words, softly chiding him. She was always his rock, as well as his moral compass, but she'd be so disappointed in him if she could see him now. Her gentle admonition played in his head. 'I hate to see you like this. Feeling sorry for yourself. Who's it going to help, my darling? Not Bridie and not me, to be sure.'

In response to her voice, he found his thoughts drifting to the off-hand way he'd treated Oskar Dreiberg in the bar the other day. Through his alcoholic haze, he'd realised his associate was on edge. No, more than that. Afraid. He'd mentioned some sort of proposal. What was it again? There was something. 'Something important,' he'd said. A notebook containing information. That was it. He reckoned it would 'be of value' to 'democratically minded people.' Yes. The encounter and the words had bumped around at the back of his brain for a couple of days. They'd reminded him he wasn't the only one suffering. His was not the only tragedy. Perhaps it was time to cast his thoughts aside and lift his gaze. He was a hack, always on the lookout for a good story, but these days, he'd opted for the easy life; for reviews and society gatherings. Maybe it was time to re-enter the fight. To start being a real journalist again. To dig out the truth, dust it off and put it on show for everyone to see once more. He would contact Dreiberg again and find out more about this important notebook and what it contained.

By now the light had all but gone, and he was sitting in almost complete darkness, except for the dim glow from the apartments opposite. He reached out to switch on the table lamp before rising to close the shutters. As he stood by the window, he glanced down to the pavement below. The avenue was quiet. An old woman limped along. A boy with his hands in his pockets strolled past, while another elderly woman walked her small dog. All was relatively quiet, apart from the throb of distant traffic. All was relatively normal – except for one thing. In the pool of light cast by the streetlamp opposite the apartment, stood a man in a trilby, idly smoking a cigarette. At the sound of the closing shutters, he looked up quickly to see Daniel. Their eyes met and, in that moment, Daniel had the curious sensation that he was no longer alone. But it never occurred to him he was being watched.

Chapter 17

Hamburg

It was the day of the Führer's visit to the city, when the *Bismarck*, the pride of the *Kreigsmarine*, the German Navy, was to be launched at the docks. It had been raining solidly for most of the morning, but that didn't seem to dampen the spirits of the thousands who came out to greet their leader. As Hitler's motorcade passed, they waved their black and red flags as if their lives depended on it.

Just after one o'clock, Katja was relieved from her office duties to prepare herself for the afternoon reception. In the female washroom, she went into one of the cubicles, intending to change. She hadn't bought any new clothes for at least six years, but Dr Viktor had insisted. He'd told her to buy herself a special outfit from one of the city department stores. She was to charge it to his personal account. Naturally, she felt awkward, especially when it came to paying. Had she imagined it, or was the sales assistant's look judgemental, making her feel like a kept woman, a mistress.

Far from being alluring, the dark blue suit Katja had chosen was plain and simple – just how the Nazis liked their women.

So far, she had managed to squeeze into the tight-fitting skirt and had just slipped both arms into the sleeves of the well-cut peplum jacket. It was a top-quality suit, although not even the feel of the silk lining against her skin could override her sense of trepidation.

She'd had no choice but to accompany Dr Viktor to the reception at the dockyard. Apparently, Kommodore Flebert had been most insistent, and the way his eyes had played on her, just before he left, was unsettling, as if he was undressing her in his mind. If she refused the invitation, Viktor had pointed out, the kommodore would take it as a personal affront, while if the doctor himself refused, it would be seen as treason. Neither of them had a choice. That afternoon they would both be in the same space and breathe the same air as Adolf Hitler.

From the cubicle, Katja became aware of the washroom door opening, and two sets of soft-soled shoes shuffled in front of the basins. Over the sound of running water and a powder compact being snapped shut, she heard Nurse Blum, fresh from cheering the Führer's motorcade.

'You've never seen such a crowd. There were men clinging on to statues and lampposts just to catch a glimpse,' she gushed.

'Did you see him?' Katja recognised Nurse Wilhelm's haughty voice, although even she sounded impressed.

'Oh, yes. I saw him all right, and I swear on my life our eyes met.'

'He looked at you?'

'He did, and for a moment I saw what heaven must be like. He was inspirational,' Blum continued breathlessly. 'Dare I say – so virile?' This remark was accompanied by a girlish giggle, followed by the sound of running water for a second time.

Nurse Wilhelm spoke again. 'On that subject, what do you make of Dr Viktor's new girl?'

Katja had to stifle a gasp, but Nurse Blum let out a squeal of disgust. 'I can barely bring myself to look at her. She makes out she's so perfect. A hard worker when all the time you know she's—' She broke off, leaving it to her colleague's imagination to conjure up an image of Dr Viktor in the arms of his new mistress.

'It's his poor wife I feel sorry for,' volunteered Nurse Wilhelm. 'Everyone knows it'll end badly, like it did with that Jew, Leisel.'

Leisel. *That name again*, thought Katja. Dr Viktor would have been forced to dismiss her under the Nazi laws because she was a Jew, but it sounded to her as if his former assistant craved his attention. She still hadn't learned of the girl's fate. Kommodore Flebert's visit had interrupted his explanation. *So how did it end?* she wondered.

'I heard . . .' Nurse Blum began, her voice now a whisper, even though she'd no idea their conversation was being listened to, 'I heard he supplied her with the pills to do it.'

'No!'

A shock ran down Katja's spine. Was Leisel dead? It suddenly sounded as if she had taken her own life and now these nurses were alleging Dr Viktor helped her do it. It was tantamount to accusing him of murder. She couldn't stand by and remain silent. She had to defend him. Anger swelled inside her and spilled over as she flung open the cubicle door and marched straight out, her face like thunder. Glaring at the two women for a moment and seeing the mortified looks on both their faces, she decided to hold back. Her presence was enough. There was no need to say anything. Knowing that she'd heard all their vicious slights was enough. Both nurses simply stood open-mouthed as Katja, valise in hand, stalked out of the washroom and headed back to her office. Once inside, she slammed the door and leaned on it; her head tilting backward as she fought to calm herself.

'Something wrong, Fräulein Heinz?' asked Viktor, standing by his desk.

'No. No. Nothing's wrong,' she said, adding after a moment: 'I'm just a little nervous, that's all.'

The doctor was wearing a double-breasted suit with a red handkerchief in his top pocket. He'd also rubbed extra oil into his hair. For the first time, Katja found him almost attractive, but then the words of the nurses came flooding back to her and she pushed herself away from the door and set down her valise under her desk. Once again, the doubts crowded in. Could Dr Ernst Viktor be trusted? She was sure he wasn't a murderer, but could he be a philanderer?

'So, you are ready?' he asked, his eyes settled on Katja's new suit.

'Yes,' she replied, watching him closely.

'You look . . .' He smiled at her as he searched for an appropriate compliment, and Katja was relieved when he declared she looked, 'Very efficient'. The boundaries of their relationship were already blurred. It seemed he didn't wish to complicate them further. For that she was grateful.

*

Katja sat at the doctor's side on the back seat. The staff car had been sent by Kommodore Flebert to collect them. Once at the dockyard, they would be met by party officials and escorted onto the viewing platform created especially for *Kreigsmarine* officers and their guests to watch the launch of the *Bismarck*. Afterwards Hitler was scheduled to meet the high-ranking officers who'd been involved with the ship at a reception.

A glass screen separated Katja and Viktor from the driver so their conversation could not be easily overheard. The rain fell heavier by the second and Katja was glad the sound of the wiper blades made it even harder for the driver to hear what was said.

Viktor sensed something was wrong. 'You are nervous?' He was looking at her gloved hands on her lap as he spoke. Katja looked down too, and saw she was fidgeting, tugging at her fingers. Of course, she was nervous. Terrified, even. She turned suddenly to face him.

'You're sure Herr Hitler won't recognise you? I know it's been more than twenty years but . . .'

Viktor lifted his forefinger to his lips and pressed it against them, signifying she shouldn't be concerned. 'Of course I'm hoping he does not.' He continued with a shake of the head: 'And, naturally, I will do my best to avoid him, if at all possible.' He worked his jaw as he spoke, but Katja detected his fear.

The car drove on, down into the Elbe Tunnel that ran under the river for two kilometres. Although it was well lit, the very thought of being under a river with millions of cubic tonnes of water pressing down on them, only added to Katja's anxiety. It was almost a relief when the limousine slowed down as they emerged from the tunnel to approach the dockyard gates. Hundreds, if not thousands, of cheering people were lining the route. Everywhere there were swastikas. Banners were slung along railings and across buildings and on giant cranes. With the launch of this new battle-ship, Hitler was showing the world Germany would no longer be cowed and most people were ready to stand with him.

Entering the large dockyard gates, the car came to a halt on the quayside. The towering bulk of the *Bismarck* loomed over them. Katja's door was opened by a marine and she ventured out under a large umbrella which was held aloft for her. She and Dr Viktor were directed, alongside some other guests, up the stairs leading to a covered platform.

Once seated, they did not have long to wait before Hitler himself arrived, accompanied by his right-hand man Hermann Göring. Silence descended on the crowd the moment the Führer lifted his arm. A cold shiver rippled through Katja as he began to speak. There was something mesmerising about him. Mesmerising, yet terrifying at the same time, because now she knew what had happened to him, she could see that he truly believed he was the saviour of Germany – and so did almost everyone else.

When he spoke not a man moved. Hitler had everyone under his spell. The thousands who were assembled listened in complete silence to his speech, and when he finished the crowd broke into rapturous cheers. Everyone roared their approval as they raised their arms to salute as one. The sound was deafening, but the sight was chilling. One evil man held thousands in his thrall.

Dr Viktor leaned into her ear. 'Now do you understand why he must be stopped?' he asked.

Katja nodded. 'Yes. Yes, I do.'

It was then that Bismarck's granddaughter cracked a bottle of Champagne on the prow. At the signal, the forty-two-thousand-ton battleship slid effortlessly into the water, bringing the public proceedings to an end.

*

Shortly afterwards the guests were shown into the offices of the shipyard for the reception. They were led upstairs and poured into a huge room where everyone was to await the arrival of their leader. The noise was so loud it crashed into Katja's ears and made her want to turn and run. This was all a terrible mistake, she told herself. She should never have agreed to accompany Dr Viktor and was on the verge of slipping quietly away when a voice boomed the doctor's name over her head.

'*Heil Hitler!*' An arm lashed out in a salute. It was Kommodore Flebert. 'I am so pleased to see you, Dr Viktor,' he said. 'And delighted that you brought your assistant, Fräulein . . .'

'Heinz,' replied the doctor helpfully.

'Fräulein Heinz,' repeated Flebert, playing with her name on his tongue.

As the kommodore turned towards her, his undisguised leer made the hairs on the back of Katja's neck prickle. 'We expect the Führer at any moment,' he added.

It was too late to escape. She mustered a smile, but inside panic had already gripped her. Before she could say anything, an announcement was made, heralding the entrance of Hitler himself. The moment she'd been dreading with all her heart had arrived. Seconds later, the Führer – Kommodore Flebert now at his side – was progressing along the reception line of naval personnel and their wives, like a knife through butter.

As Katja watched Hitler move along, she understood these people were more than his supporters. They were his followers. Just as Dr Viktor had said, there was something messianic about his presence. If he'd fallen from his platform and into the sea during his speech, he wouldn't have drowned. He was unassailable. No one would challenge his power, and the thought chilled her to the bone.

Katja felt herself growing more light-headed with every step the Führer took. Stale body odour wafted down the line as he approached, until fear made her take a sudden step back. Shrinking behind the naval officer at her side, she was hidden from view as Hitler drew close. But Dr Viktor remained still until the moment was upon them. Katja glanced at him. Part of her wanted to pull him back, distract him, so that there was no chance of him meeting the Führer's gaze. But she could see the doctor was powerless to move, pinioned on three sides. His mouth was set firm; his eyes were blazing. His stare was locked on to the Führer's like a hawk on its prey.

'And this is Dr Ernst Viktor,' Katja heard the kommodore say.

'*Heil, mein Führer*,' came the doctor's reply, but she daren't look for fear of being turned to stone, for fear of the sky falling, for fear of something so terrible, so momentous, so biblical happening that she thought she would die of fright. She shrank back further still to watch the encounter from the shadows. But no, when she dared to look, she saw that Adolf Hitler, either because he recognised the name and deliberately chose to ignore it, or because his attention was simply elsewhere, did not blanch when he heard Viktor's voice. Nor did he meet his gaze as the two men pressed flesh. There were no sparks. No thunderbolts. No apocalyptic scenes. The Führer simply moved down the line to the soundtrack of excited murmurings and Ernst Viktor was left to retreat into the melee once more.

Katja felt her breath leave her in a rush of relief. She hadn't been certain what might have happened had the Führer's eyes met Dr Viktor's, just as Nurse Blum said they had met hers, but she remained puzzled. How could Hitler not remember the name of the man who restored his sight? And not only his sight, his self-belief too? If Dr Viktor was Frankenstein, then surely his monster should have acknowledged him? As soon as the Führer reached the end of the line Katja moved closer to the doctor. She saw he was trembling.

'Are you all right?' she asked in a low voice.

He turned, and she saw there were tears in his eyes, as he fixed her with a look so painful and tragic that her heart suddenly ached for him.

'He didn't look at me,' he muttered. 'Thank God. I think we are safe.' From his breast pocket he produced a handkerchief and dabbed at the sweat glistening on his brow.

Katja allowed herself to relax a little too. Hitler had not made eye contact; had not recognised the doctor who had given him back his sight. He was just another man in another crowd. 'There were so many people, that . . .' she began. She was about to tell Viktor that the Führer's attention had been diverted at the time, but something stopped her from finishing her sentence. From the corner of her vision, she spotted Hitler, now on the other side of the room. She caught him suddenly turn his head towards them and aim a look. It was straight and it was piercing, and it was targeted at them as surely as if it were a lance. He muttered something to Flebert, who was standing at his side. The kommodore also shot a look in their direction, and a current of dread coursed through her.

'Fräulein Heinz,' she heard the doctor's voice from somewhere far away. She pivoted. 'You were saying . . .'

She smiled on a sigh. 'Nothing. It doesn't matter,' she replied as a waiter offered her a glass of wine on a silver tray. An unsettling thought had suddenly seized her. What if Hitler had remembered

Dr Viktor from Pasewalk, but pretended he did not? There was something in that fleeting yet penetrating look that told her he remembered that night all too clearly. If that was the case, in her mind, it could only mean one thing.

Chapter 18

When Katja arrived at the clinic, the day after Hitler's momentous visit, Fräulein Schauble looked up, but instead of the usual Nazi salute, she glowered at her even more fiercely. In fact, her stare was so intense that Katja felt compelled to address her.

'*Guten morgen, Fräulein Schauble,*' she said, but her greeting went unanswered. Instead, the disapproving look simply latched on and followed her as she hurried swiftly past the reception desk towards Dr Viktor's office.

Katja walked down the long corridor with a growing sense of unease. Something wasn't right. Up ahead she saw Nurse Blum and Nurse Wilhelm huddled in conversation, but they suddenly stopped mid-flow as soon as she approached, then parted in silence to allow her to pass. She had never been so pleased to reach the sanctuary of her office, until that is, she walked in. Then the shock came. A large arrangement of flowers was standing on her desk. Resplendent red roses were interspersed with cascades of white gypsophila and spears of greenery. So, this was why Fräulein Schauble glared at her and why the nurses' chatter fell silent.

From his office Dr Viktor was watching her reaction to the blooms through the open door. He moved towards her and propped himself against the wall, as Katja grabbed the small card accompanying the bouquet.

'It seems you have an admirer,' he said, thrusting his hands into the pocket of his white coat.

Tearing open the envelope, Katja read the words on the card, and a sense of panic seized her when she saw the signature.

'Kommodore Flebert.'

She looked to Dr Viktor for his reaction. Mention of the name caused him to right himself and remove his hands from his pockets. He pursed his lips and shook his head. 'I feared this might happen,' he said, walking forward. 'May I?' He reached for the card, which Katja, still in shock, surrendered.

My dear Fräulein Heinz,
I was so sorry not to spend more time with you at yesterday's reception, but, as you no doubt realised, I had many duties which called upon my attention during the Führer's visit. I hope you did not think me neglectful and wondered if you would do me the honour of dining with me in the near future.
Your obedient servant,
Stefan Flebert (Kommodore, Kriegsmarine*)*

Katja's gaze remained on the doctor, a knot tightening in her chest. 'What should I do?' she asked, feeling like a snared animal.

Dr Viktor perched on the edge of her desk, his eyes playing on the roses whose scent had, by now, filled the office. 'You must stall him,' he replied after a moment. 'Tell him you cannot leave your sick mother.'

Katja nodded. Right from the start she'd known what sort of man the kommodore was; the sort who thought his professional power spilled over into his private life. What he wanted, he got. Yesterday, when Flebert had encountered her at the reception, she had seen desire in his eyes. He'd made her feel uncomfortable, and she'd deliberately avoided him. She'd gone out of her way to be cool towards him when he'd passed her during the reception. She had done nothing to encourage him and yet . . .

'Yes,' she replied weakly. 'Yes, I will do that.' Even though they both knew Kommodore Flebert was not a man who would take no for an answer. It was only a matter of time before an invitation turned into an order, with consequences for disobedience. Yet it was clear something remained on Viktor's mind. 'In my office, Fräulein Heinz, if you please.'

They had parted straight after yesterday's reception. There had been no time to discuss his brush with Hitler. Viktor kept his voice low as once again he perched on the edge of her desk. Slowly he looked at her and she saw the same fear from yesterday's encounter flicker in his eyes, but amid the residual anxiety there was something else.

'You remember I told you about my contact in Paris?' he asked.

'Yes. The person who might help with the transcript.'

The doctor stuck out his chin determinedly. 'I think it's time we met with him. The sooner the better. You've transcribed more than a quarter of the notebook. That should be enough to whet a publisher's appetite.'

'You still want me to go with you?'

'Of course,' he replied, as if he considered her question ridiculous.

'But won't people talk? Me going to Paris with you, it's . . .' She remembered Leisel and took her chance. 'You never finished telling me about your assistant.'

Her reminder brought Viktor up short. 'No. No, I didn't,' he acknowledged, rubbing his chin reflectively.

'Perhaps now would be a good time before we go any further?' she suggested.

The doctor sighed heavily. 'Very well,' he began. 'Right at the start, Leisel told me how her mother was dead and how her father mistreated her. Naturally, I showed concern for the girl, but she mistook it for . . .' He searched for a delicate word, '. . . interest.'

'I see,' said Katja.

'Apparently, she began spreading rumours about our relationship. All false, of course. And that is all there was to it. Of course, I dismissed her and never saw her again.'

'But she killed herself,' Katja reminded him.

Viktor's eyes suddenly turned glassy. 'Yes. Yes, she did. Most regrettable, but . . .' He pursed his lips and shook his head.

'What is it?' asked Katja, sensing he was holding something back.

'I cannot prove anything but . . .' He hesitated.

'But . . .' urged Katja.

'I suspect Ulbricht may have had a hand in it.'

'You think he encouraged Leisel to act towards you in the way she did?' It was a wild accusation, but from what she'd learned of Dr Ulbricht's professional rivalry with Viktor, it seemed plausible.

He shook his head. 'Perhaps.'

'And the pills?' Katja remembered Nurse Blum's accusation.

The doctor shrugged. 'Leisel wasn't a bad girl. Just easily led. Maybe she regretted what she'd done. After all, she'd tarnished my reputation.' He sighed. 'It would not have been too difficult for her to lay her hands on the pills from the clinic's pharmacy.'

Seeing his moist eyes and his slumped shoulders, Katja saw that, in his own way, Viktor was also a victim of Leisel's tragedy. 'Thank you,' she said. 'That is what I needed to know.'

Viktor nodded and Katja turned to leave, but as she did so the doctor rose and walked over to one of the filing cabinets. 'Wait,' he called, brandishing a letter. He cleared his throat. 'This was in my post this morning.' He laid it on the desk for Katja to see. 'There is to be a conference on psychiatry at the Sorbonne in two weeks' time. I've been invited to attend.'

'A conference,' she repeated, warily. She feared what may come next.

'Will you come with me? As my assistant? It's the perfect excuse.'

Katja suddenly felt the need to swallow hard. It was a relief to know what really happened with Leisel, and she certainly believed Dr Viktor's version of events, but she still had to consider Mutti. 'I'm sorry. My mother . . .'

Viktor, seeing her wavering, shook his head. 'Surely there is someone who can take care of her? It will only be for a short time.'

'But she needs me to see that she eats and takes her medication, and . . .'

Viktor turned as she spoke and walked over to the window, his hands clasped behind his back. After a moment, he said: 'I understand your predicament, but I've been given another chance, Katja, and I need your help, but if you feel . . .' His shoulders twitched, and he turned back to gauge her response.

'You know I want to help,' she protested, before she paused to relent a little. 'How many nights would we be away?'

'Three. We would travel by train and stay at a modest but adequate hotel that I know, a short walk from the Sorbonne.'

The doctor made it sound so simple. So routine. But Hilde's needs placed an added burden on her.

'Is there no one?' he asked.

Katja thought for a moment and a vision of Frau Cohen sprang into her mind. Now that Aaron was no longer living with her, perhaps she could ask her to look after her mother. She nodded slowly. 'There is someone.'

'Excellent. Does that mean you'll come?' Viktor asked, hooking his gaze under her downcast eyes.

She felt the pressure of the question and looked up. 'As long as I can make the necessary arrangements,' she told him.

His face burst into a smile. 'Thank you, Katja,' he told her. 'We are doing the right thing.'

'I know,' she acknowledged. There was never any doubt in her mind that what Dr Viktor was hoping to achieve was courageous, but she knew her own personal safety and that of her fragile mother was now also at risk. He was asking her to make more

113

sacrifices. In this unchartered territory the mines were primed and could detonate at any moment.

*

Katja forced herself to concentrate on typing out Dr Viktor's notes. Kommodore Flebert's flowers now sat on top of the filing cabinet, but their presence troubled her, and their perfume was a constant reminder that somehow she needed to rebuff him. She also knew that would be easier said than done.

At the end of the day, she decided she could no longer leave the bouquet in her office. It was a distraction, and a very unwelcome one. It made her stomach churn every time she looked at it because she was reminded of how Flebert had looked at her. The nurses who'd seen them had already jumped to the wrong conclusions. They would happily stoke the fires of rumour, assuming they were from Dr Viktor, no doubt. But if she were to throw away the fresh flowers at the office, that would be regarded with suspicion too. Rummaging in a cupboard, she found a large paper bag that had once held groceries, and taking the blooms by the stems, shoved them, flowers first, inside. She decided to dispose of them at home.

Dr Viktor was working late that evening as he so often did. She returned the typing and the notebook to his desk. He looked up at her and smiled.

'You have done good work today, Fräulein Heinz,' he told her. 'We have made progress.'

Katja knew he was referring to their Paris trip. 'Yes, Doctor,' she replied, even though the prospect of the conference and leaving Mutti still made her uncomfortable. She bid Viktor goodnight, and, picking up the large bag with the flowers, she started to make her way out of the clinic. Halfway along the corridor, Dr Ulbricht appeared from one of the consultation rooms and walked towards her. She moved to one side to let him pass and saw his nostrils twitch as he approached.

'Fräulein Heinz,' he said, his eyes narrowing behind his lenses as he peered at the bag she carried.

Realising he was trying to see its contents, she transferred it from one arm to the other, but it was too late. A stray rose petal broke loose and drifted to the floor. Ulbricht arched a brow.

'You have an admirer, Fräulein Heinz,' he remarked snidely.

'They are for my mother,' replied Katja.

The doctor looked sceptical. 'What a dutiful daughter,' he said. 'The Fatherland demands such duty,' he told her before letting her go.

*

Before she set foot in her own apartment that evening, Katja knocked on Frau Cohen's door to ask if she might be able to keep an eye on her mother while she was away. The widow agreed, and Katja felt less fearful about breaking the news of her short absence. She found Hilde on the balcony, feeding the pigeons, when she arrived home. It had been many years since they'd been able to afford fresh-cut blooms and she thought the flowers might cheer her up. Some of them hadn't travelled well on the tram and were crushed, nevertheless, she'd rescued the few that she could and arranged them in a glass vase.

'Here, Mutti,' she said. 'Aren't they beautiful?'

Her mother turned her head slowly, but her eyes lit up when she saw the roses.

'Oh yes!' she gasped in delight. Katja smiled at her reaction and was glad that she hadn't thrown all Flebert's tainted flowers away. She plucked a rose from the vase and handed it to Hilde. Her mother breathed deeply to take in its scent and Katja relished the simple joy it brought. But then she also remembered something else – the look, the leer Flebert gave her as both he and the Führer had turned in the doctor's direction. A current of dread coursed through her now, just as it had at the time, and it suddenly occurred to her that Flebert might just have laid a trap for her. Whatever she did next, she was already caught up in it. She could run from him, but she couldn't hide. Sooner or later, he would catch up with her, and the thought filled her with dread.

Later that evening, she penned the kommodore a note. She politely declined his offer of dinner, citing her elderly mother as an excuse. It would stall him, but for how long? As she came to the bottom of the letter, and wrote her signature with a flourish, she couldn't help but fear she might be signing her own arrest warrant.

Chapter 19

The sun had barely risen, but despite the early hour Hamburg's main train station was busy with commuters and those who, like Ernst Viktor and Katja, were travelling further afield. Katja had left her mother sleeping to rendezvous with the doctor at five o'clock. The train to Paris awaited them.

Inside, the *bahnhof* remained festooned with red and black Nazi banners, and SS guards were patrolling the concourse and platforms. Katja had packed lightly and carried a small valise with two changes of clothes and a hatbox. The doctor had two bags: a leather duffle bag and his briefcase. A young porter with a toothless grin approached with a trolley and offered to take their luggage to the train. The doctor agreed and watched as he hefted first his large suitcase then Katja's overnight valise and hatbox.

'Sir?' asked the porter, pinning his gaze on the doctor's briefcase.

'*Nein,*' replied the doctor firmly. Katja knew the papers it contained were more precious to him than his life and certainly more dangerous than a loaded gun. Her eyes dipped towards the case as they queued by the boarding gate to have their tickets checked. She had worked extra hours so that almost half of the transcription was now complete. That seemingly ordinary brown leather briefcase held a document that could see them both jailed, or worse. Not only was Dr Viktor breaking the Hippocratic Oath by intending to publish his former patient's records, what he was doing was treasonous. He planned to bring down the Nazi regime and she, Katja, was his accomplice. The whole situation seemed unreal to her.

Now the doctor was just ahead of her in the queue; his broad back less than a metre away. She looked about her; at the small boy in the cap selling bratwurst, at the porter pushing a trolley laden with luggage, at the two suited businessmen behind them in the line. There were people all around, yet she felt so isolated. She'd heard guilt did that to you; set you apart from society and made you live inside your own head, stranding you on an island of self-doubt and secrecy. It would be so easy for her to leave right now; to simply turn and walk away from Dr Viktor and from his mind-blowingly dangerous mission to expose the Führer. It wasn't too late to save herself and her mother. But then, glancing to her right, she laid eyes on the bookstall. Once again, the red cover of *Mein Kampf* dominated the display. Once again, she thought of her father, lying in agony in hospital, and the promise she made to him.

'Fräulein?' The guard was glowering at her. 'Your ticket.'

Katja shook away her thoughts. Vati would want this. Vati would be with her. She fumbled in her small handbag to proffer a ticket to the impatient official. He shot her a disapproving look then clipped the corner of the paper to let her follow Dr Viktor through the gate. He was waiting for her patiently, and his face broke into a wide smile as she approached, only she knew it was a mask.

'Don't look so terrified,' he told her through clenched teeth as they made their way along the platform. 'You'll only draw attention to us.' The corners of his own mouth lifted up even further, and he raised his homburg to a prim, elderly woman, who was passing.

Katja was too distracted to smile. Glancing down at her ticket, then up at the numbering on the railway carriages, she knew their compartment had to be nearby. Dr Viktor had told her to book second class to avoid standing out.

The gritty smell of coal was stronger on the platform and caught the back of Katja's throat as she walked. She passed a couple holding each other, the young woman sobbing into her lover's lapel. A mother and her young daughter walked ahead. A party of chattering children was shepherded by a harassed teacher. Life went on, and to everyone else, she and Dr Viktor were just ordinary people going about their ordinary, everyday business. Only now the ordinary had become extraordinary and the scar that had marked her ever since the Burnings had become inflamed again. The screech of a whistle suddenly split the air. Startled, Katja palmed her chest to still her heart.

'Twelve. Thirteen. Here we are,' she said, stopping by one of the heavy doors. The young porter stopped too and began unloading the luggage onto the platform.

'Relax,' mumbled Viktor, before forging ahead to climb the steep steps up to the carriage. He then turned to offer his hand and helped her up into the train.

Once the porter had deposited their luggage and left with a generous tip, Katja inspected the small compartment, knowing for the next twelve hours, this confined space with its faded red plush seats and antimacassars, marked by so many heads, would be their refuge. They sat opposite each other, both by the window. As long as they were alone, they would be able to talk freely. Viktor planned to proofread the typescript and Katja, unable to type, had brought along a companion to keep her company for the hours ahead; *Anna Karenina*.

When, ten minutes later, the guard's shrill whistle sounded, they swapped satisfied looks, both knowing they would have the space to themselves. The long journey now stretched ahead of them. All they could do was hope they would not be joined at a station further down the line.

119

The towering cranes and warehouses of the Hamburg skyline were soon behind them as the train headed south-west. Only when they'd crossed the border into France, would Katja feel able to relax into the journey. As she lost herself in her novel, the time passed quite quickly. Periodically, she would glance up to look at Dr Viktor, his eyes clamped on to the typescript, while she allowed herself the luxury of watching the sweeping landscapes fly by.

After a while, the countryside gave way to fine houses and elegant buildings. They were about to pull into Cologne. Moments after the train had come to a halt the carriage door slid open and a businessman popped his head inside to peer at the seat numbers. Satisfied he had the right compartment he greeted his fellow travellers.

'*Guten tag*,' he said with a suspiciously broad smile.

Dr Viktor returned his greeting and Katja nodded as the newcomer proceeded to take off his trilby to reveal a pale blond head of hair. He proceeded to slide it, along with his coat, onto the overhead rack. Taking a newspaper from his briefcase, he settled himself down in the seat opposite Katja. His presence immediately put her on edge. He was perhaps in his forties, quite tall with a bootlace moustache and a confident air. Katja guessed he might be a salesman or a banker, but whatever his profession, his being there meant she could not discuss the transcript with the doctor as planned.

Katja turned to *Anna Karenina* to distract her. Taking it out of her handbag, she had just opened the pages when her bookmark fluttered to the carriage floor. The stranger was quick to lean over and retrieve it. Too quick? He handed it back to her with a smile and glanced at the title of her book.

'Such a tragic young woman,' he remarked.

His eyes locked on to hers, as if there was a threat behind them, as if he was predicting her fate.

'An engrossing diversion,' came the doctor's welcome voice. His tone was light and broke the tension Katja felt.

'Yes,' said the stranger. 'You are travelling to Paris?'

'We are,' replied Viktor.

'On business?'

The question rang an alarm bell in Katja's head. It was probably perfectly innocent, but it may not be. Her anxious eyes slid over to Viktor's.

'Yes,' replied the doctor, adding: 'And you?'

'I, too, travel on business,' replied the stranger. His gaze dropped to Katja's book and then, to her horror, veered towards the typescript in Viktor's grasp.

'What a coincidence,' remarked the doctor, coldly, as if he, too, was suddenly alerted to a new danger, albeit a vague one.

From then on the tension in the compartment could have been sliced with a knife. Every cough, every shuffle of papers, every glance out of the window put Katja on edge. When a guard walked past the window, her stomach would clench and, fearing he was about to haul her and the doctor out of the carriage, she would hold her breath until he had passed. The next four hours were spent trying, but failing, to immerse herself in the world of Anna Karenina which, at that moment, seemed preferable to her own.

By the time the train steamed into the Gare de l'Est, instead of being rested, Katja felt as if she had endured an ordeal of silence where every word and every move had been scrutinised and interpreted by the stranger sitting opposite her. He had made two more attempts to engage her in conversation, but her reluctance had been apparent. That seemed to have amused him but had made her even more nervous.

When all three of them rose to gather their belongings, the stranger slipped into his coat and picked up his briefcase and trilby. He smiled at Dr Viktor and bowed to Katja, then said: 'I wish you both a successful conference.'

The throwaway remark, delivered with the casual ease of an assassin, came as a dagger from the dark, but Viktor kept his head.

121

'Conference,' he repeated, as the stranger was about to slide open the carriage door.

He turned. 'Yes,' he replied. 'That invitation from the psychiatric department at the Sorbonne.' His eyes slipped to a pile of papers on the seat next to Viktor. 'You left it in full view,' he said. 'One can't be too careful these days.' And with those chilling words he turned on his heel and marched out of the carriage.

Chapter 20

Paris

It was approaching six o'clock in the evening, and Sylvia Beach was considering closing her bookshop for the day. Business had been a little slow and she'd made plans for dinner with her writer friend André Gide. She was looking forward to an evening of good food and lively conversation, but just as she began cashing up her takings the little bell over the front door jangled and a familiar figure stepped inside.

'Daniel!' she exclaimed as the Irishman approached. She hadn't seen him for a few days and had started to make enquiries among his acquaintances. Since his tragedy, she worried about him. 'How good to see you.'

He made his way warily over to the counter where she stood, walking as if on a ship's deck in rough seas. She suspected he'd been drinking again. As soon as he reached her, he lifted his face towards hers and when she saw his eyes were bloodshot, she could see he had.

'Sylvia, Sylvia,' he said. His breath reeked of spirits and his lilting voice was halfway between talk and song. '*What light is light, if Sylvia be not seen?*'

She shook her head. He may be able to quote those Shakespeare lines to her – as so many of her male customers did regularly – but it didn't disguise the fact that he was four sheets to the wind.

'Daniel, dear Daniel. What have you been up to?' she asked, knowing full well that he must have spent the afternoon in his usual bar just a few doors away.

'I have been holding court,' he told her, now leaning on the counter. She could smell the whiskey on his breath. 'If only anyone would listen to me, the world would be a better place. We're all going to hell in a handcart, but no one will take any notice.'

Sylvia smiled. Drunk Daniel was no longer a threat. True, he sometimes had delusions of grandeur, but not aggression. Not anymore. In fact, he could become quite vulnerable, although, right now, it seemed he had entered his literary phase. This, Sylvia knew, so often saw him quote Shakespeare and poetry, and flirt with women, including, of course, herself, despite her own disinterest in men.

'I take notice of you, Daniel, but you must also listen to me.' Her tone had become maternal.

In response he jutted out his bottom lip, mimicking a child and, still leaning on the glass counter, replied: '*Oui, mademoiselle.*'

Sylvia, becoming just a little exasperated by now, said: 'You must go home, drink a glass of Evian water, and get straight to bed. Tomorrow you will have a very sore head, but you will still craft something marvellous, something uplifting and witty on the page, and people will take notice of what you write and not what you say. Now, off you go.'

Daniel was quiet for a moment, as if filtering what Sylvia had just told him through an alcoholic haze. 'But there's no one at home there,' he mumbled. Grace and Bridie had been his world and it was still short of eighteen months since his loss, but she'd thought he'd started to heal. Now she couldn't be so sure.

'I tell you what. I'll make you some strong coffee.' She gestured behind her to the little kitchenette at the back. 'Then you'll feel better and, in the meantime, go and have a browse.' But just as she turned, the bell jangled once more, and Sylvia pivoted back. 'I should have put the closed sign up.' She tutted under her breath as she hurried towards the door to turn away her potential customer.

A young woman, in her late twenties, perhaps, was standing in a charcoal grey suit and matching hat, below which cascaded shoulder-length blonde hair. Her large eyes were just visible beneath the brim of her hat, and she wore a sort of bewildered expression on her face, as if she'd just entered a beautiful church. She looked rather pale and thin, and not at all Parisian to Sylvia.

'I'm sorry. I was just about to close,' she told her in French.

The young woman now transferred her gaze to Sylvia. 'Forgive me,' she said suddenly. 'I did not know.'

The reply was delivered awkwardly, and from her accent Sylvia could tell immediately that her visitor was German.

By now Daniel had also turned to face the door. He leaned back against the counter and suddenly seemed to perk up.

'*But, soft! What light through yonder window breaks?*' he blurted, taking in the vision of Sylvia's customer. The setting sun was casting a glow on the pavement outside and backlit the young woman. With the door behind her, she was silhouetted in a perfect frame and her hair glowed like gold.

Sylvia shot Daniel a long-suffering look as he approached, then said to her customer in English, 'I'm sorry my German is not good, but I must apologise for my friend. He has had a long day.'

The young woman, clearly a little bemused by Daniel's greeting, smiled first at him, then at Sylvia. 'No matter. I'll come back tomorrow,' she replied in fluent English, even though her voice was tinged with disappointment. She lowered her head and was just about to leave when Daniel bounded forward.

'No, wait, please,' he called, suddenly sounding completely sober. 'I'm sure Miss Beach could stay open just a little longer for you.' His bloodshot eyes slid over to Sylvia, and he gave her the look of a beguiling puppy.

A little laugh escaped the bookseller's lips, but the young woman shook her head. 'I couldn't possibly . . .'

'I insist,' said Sylvia, gesturing inside. 'Please.' And reaching for the handle, she shut the door. 'Feel free to browse. Our novels are here, our poetry there and our non-fiction is over there.'

'Thank you,' replied the young woman, her eyes sweeping over the hundreds of volumes like a child in a sweet shop.

Daniel moved closer now, and Sylvia was concerned that the mere smell of alcohol on his breath would send her poor customer running, but when he next spoke there wasn't a trace of a slur. She supposed he no longer needed a coffee.

'What interests you in particular?' he asked, as the young woman, still looking overwhelmed, turned to face him.

'I like novels,' she replied. 'F Scott Fitzgerald is my favourite at the moment, although I've recently discovered DH Lawrence and I'm a quarter of the way through *Anna Karenina*.'

Daniel arched a brow. '*Anna Karenina*,' he repeated. 'You are a brave reader, and with Catholic tastes.'

She nodded. 'I'll read anything and everything,' she replied.

'So do I,' he said, suddenly looking very serious as he held the young woman's gaze for a moment longer than necessary. 'Perhaps you would allow me to recommend some authors?'

*

Once they'd checked into their hotel, Dr Viktor had told Katja he needed to rest before dinner. She, on the other hand, was too on edge to take a nap. The man in the train carriage had troubled her, and she knew she'd have to be wary, but she just couldn't resist making the most of her short visit to Paris and, in particular, to its bookshops. That was how she had ended up in Shakespeare and Company, being bombarded with novels and characters and short stories.

'Have you read Huxley's *Brave New World*?' asked the helpful man. 'Not very cheery, but interesting.' He picked out another novel. 'Or Orwell's *Down and Out in Paris and London*. Since you're in Paris it's surely a must-read?'

Katja had decided he must either be a writer or a poet who perhaps worked in the store in his spare time to make ends meet. She'd heard most writers were very poor. While the range of books in the shop dazzled her, it was this gentleman who impressed her most. He told her all about novels she'd never read and authors she'd never heard of. He was opening up a world of possibilities, introducing her to W Somerset Maughan and Agatha Christie – neither of whom were stocked in Herr Wortzman's bookshop. It turned out he even knew some authors personally, like that scandalous James Joyce and the American poet Ezra Pound. And while she could listen to his wonderful accent all day long – she couldn't quite place it, but it sounded as soft and rich as dairy cream – he'd asked her questions too. Did she enjoy adventure, realism, romance? Had she ever read any works by the Brontë sisters or George Elliot? But when he'd told her about Shakespeare and Company's wonderful lending library and how little it cost to join and that it had kept him sane for the past few months – although he didn't mention why he wouldn't be sane – Katja had told him her stay in Paris was only very short.

'I'm here on business. I'm afraid I must be gone in two days,' she said, finding herself apologising to a complete stranger for something over which she had no control.

The man's face fell, and a shadow scudded across it. Her revelation seemed to mute him almost instantly, like turning down the volume on a wireless. He looked so sad and that made her sad too. It was ridiculous, but she was just as disappointed.

'Well, I'm afraid I must go,' she said rather awkwardly. She brushed past him and headed for the counter to pay for the copy of an anthology by WB Yeats he'd recommended. But a moment later, he was beside her.

'Allow me to buy it for you.'

'I couldn't . . .'

'A souvenir,' he told her. 'From the city of light.'

Katja smiled then. 'Thank you so much, *Monsieur* . . .'

'Keenan. Daniel Keenan,' he replied, although strangely and disappointingly, he didn't ask for her name in return. He just pulled out a crumpled old hat from his jacket pocket and said: 'I wish you a pleasant stay, fräulein, even if it is far too short.'

A moment later, now much more subdued, he nodded at the bookseller and seemed to skulk like a sad dog out of the shop. Katja watched him go, her expression betraying her confusion about his behaviour. But the woman behind the counter gave her a knowing smile.

'Poor Mr Keenan is a broken man,' she told her wistfully. 'But I think you may have mended him just a little.'

*

In the bookshop Katja had felt safe. It had been a ten-minute walk along the Left Bank to reach it, over a bridge and down a windswept lane. All the while, she had been glancing about her, aware she might be followed. She'd feared the encounter with the businessman from the train might have unnerved her. Thankfully he was nowhere in evidence, and the only person she'd caught staring at her suspiciously turned out to be a priest, whose collar was obscured by a scarf.

Two hours after she'd first ventured out, Katja returned to the Hôtel du Roi, although it certainly didn't live up to its regal name. In fact, it was more of a *pension*, but with potted palms and a black and white tiled floor, that gave it an air of grandeur which didn't extend beyond the public areas. When she reached the reception desk, she asked for her room key. The concierge, a man with a bushy black moustache, handed it over with a mirthless smile.

Entering her modest room, papered in elegant stripes, but spoiled by a shabby carpet, Katja locked the door behind her. Moving over to the shutters she sat on her single bed, slipped off her shoes and slumped back on the fuchsia-coloured bedspread. Looking up at the ceiling, she pictured Daniel Keenan's face staring down at her and felt something stir. He'd been in his mid-thirties, she'd guessed, with a face that had witnessed much, judging by the lines on his forehead and around his green eyes. His sandy hair was a little dishevelled and he clearly didn't use oil on it. His expression had remained quite serious for most of the time, but when he smiled it was as if someone had struck a match. It seemed to light a fire inside her that took hold and blazed the whole time they were together. But then when she had told him she was in Paris for just a short visit, it was as if she had poured cold water on the flames. It was as if he had written off the possibility of ever seeing her again, immediately dousing any desire he felt. The stirring she'd had dissolved into a sort of sadness for what might have been, but any thoughts of self-pity were interrupted by a soft rapping on her door.

Immediately she sat bolt upright.

'Who is it?' she called, rushing over to the cheval mirror to check her appearance.

'Me. Dr Viktor,' came the low voice.

Unlocking the door, she opened it, although not fully. The doctor stood squarely in the corridor; his face marked by a frown.

'We need to talk,' he said, his brown leather briefcase clutched to his chest.

From his stance it was clear to Katja he expected to come into her room. Mindful of how the situation might look to a stranger, she poked her head out to look beyond her unexpected visitor. A maid approached, pushing a laundry trolley.

'Wait,' she hissed under her breath as the maid passed, then, sure she was gone, she opened the door wide, allowing the doctor inside.

Keen to hang up her clothes so the creases fell out, Katja had already tidied away her spare skirt and two blouses, along with a cocktail dress she'd bought on impulse last week – just in case. Thankfully her underwear was already in a drawer, but her cosmetics and toiletries were scattered haphazardly on the dressing table. She suddenly felt very exposed as Dr Viktor's eyes darted round the room, but he seemed totally disinterested in her belongings and concentrated his gaze elsewhere. As soon as he'd set down his precious briefcase, he strode over to the window and ran a hand under the inner sill. Next, he felt under the shade of the bedside lamp.

'What are you doing?' Katja asked. 'You said we must talk.'

Pausing for a moment, he put his forefinger to his lips and proceeded to examine the back of the cheval mirror.

'Hitler has spies everywhere,' he told her, as if she wasn't already aware, but then she understood what he was doing and was shocked.

'Surely you don't think . . .' Was he really implying there could be listening devices in the room?

The doctor nodded. 'You know as well as I do, Ulbricht will stop at nothing to discredit me and take my job as head of department.'

There was just one chair in the room and the only other place to sit was on the bed. Dr Viktor leaned towards a tall chest of drawers, his elbow taking some of his weight. He cleared his throat.

'But you still don't think anyone knows about the notes?' asked Katja.

This time the doctor shook his head. 'Even if that man on the train was a Nazi agent, he was probably just there to warn us not to step out of line. We should carry on as planned. You are my secretary and a necessary assistant at the conference.' He pushed away from the drawers to right himself. 'So, dinner,' he said, as if the prospect of food had suddenly cheered him. 'I shall see you downstairs at eight, Fräulein Heinz, but still we must be watchful. One can never tell who may be seated at the next table.'

*

130

The hotel dining room had a lofty ceiling and grand windows, but some of the floor tiles were cracked and the white cloths on the tables were frayed at the edges. Katja and Dr Viktor were the only ones dining, but still they kept their voices low as they drank an adequate but insipid *soupe à l'oignon from small tureens.*

Katja, however, spoke only when spoken to and seemed very preoccupied. Dr Viktor sensed something was wrong and tried to coax her out of her shell, but despite a large glass of Burgundy, by the end of the first course, she remained clearly uneasy. The encounter with the businessman in the train and the doctor's fears their rooms may be tapped, not to mention the man in the bookshop who was so unlike anyone she'd ever met before, all played on her mind, vying for her attention, until halfway through her coq au vin, Katja pushed away her plate.

The doctor peered at her over the rim of his wine glass. 'You must eat, my dear. You need to keep up your strength for the work ahead.'

She nodded but made no attempt to retrieve her knife and fork, seemingly content to watch the doctor eat alone. He, on the other hand, sought to fill the ensuing silence with small talk as he ploughed on. Wiping his chin with the napkin tied round his neck, he asked her: 'You have left your mother in good hands?'

Katja looked up, aware he was trying to take her mind off the notes. 'Yes. A neighbour is looking after her.'

He nodded. 'And her depression?'

She shrugged. 'There is no change.' The days stretched out endlessly in front of her mother, and life to her was one long, featureless road. But Katja knew that was the nature of depression, and she could not see an end to it anytime soon. Then something occurred to her. Thinking about her mother's condition suddenly reminded Katja that Viktor had treated Kommodore Flebert's wife, and the outcome had been such a success that the invitation to the ship launch was by way of a thank you. If the doctor had been able to cure Frau Flebert, then perhaps . . .

131

'The kommodore's wife,' she began. 'Was she suffering from depression too?'

Viktor coughed out a laugh. 'You know I cannot discuss such details, Fräulein Heinz,' he replied with raised brows.

Katja felt embarrassed. 'I'm sorry. I didn't . . .'

He winked at her and she understood he was mocking her. 'The kommodore came to me because his wife wasn't . . .' He shrugged. 'How can I put it? Obliging.'

For a moment Katja wished she had remained silent. Then, as the colour rose in her cheeks, her embarrassment gave way to shock. Surely Dr Viktor had not hypnotised the woman into acceptance. But, as if he could read her mind, he flashed one of his smiles.

'Have no fear,' he assured her. 'I do not believe hypnosis should be used to bend a patient to one's will. My method only suggests. Any actions come from the patient themselves, but in the case of the kommodore's wife, it was not necessary.'

'But then how . . .?' asked Katja.

Viktor's lips twitched and he leaned in towards her. 'I simply suggested the poor woman take a lover on the side.' He pushed back and chuckled. 'It seems to have whetted her appetite.'

Katja suddenly felt her cheeks burn and regretted having pried further. Doctor Viktor wasn't flirting with her, but he had a way about him that could easily be misconstrued. She thought about the nurses' gossip and what they'd said about Leisel. She hadn't believed their vicious lies then and nor did she believe them now, but she could see how the rumours had spread, and the doctor seemed quite content to fuel the flames of his own pyre. Still feeling awkward, she took up her knife and fork once more, even though by now her food had gone stone cold.

Chapter 21

The famous Sorbonne university occupied a vast, elegant building. It fronted onto a narrow road that was always crowded with students and teachers, carts and messenger boys, all milling around outside. The conference on psychiatry and its associated fields had proved a big draw for experts from all over Europe.

Once inside, Katja and Dr Viktor had joined the crowds and been carried along on a current of eager academics, all trying to pile into the vast auditorium. The lecture on the mass psychology of fascism was proving particularly popular. It was to be delivered by the controversial German, Dr Wilhelm Reich, a former student of Sigmund Freud, whose liberal views had landed him on the wrong side of the Nazis. He was now on the run from them. Dr Viktor suspected Ulbricht might have anticipated they'd be attending the lecture. It would have been reason enough to report him to the Party and track his movements while in Paris.

Katja sat nervously at Dr Viktor's side. She felt very small and helpless in such lofty surroundings, and a deep sense of anxiety made her mouth dry. As they waited for Dr Reich, her eyes swept the oak-panelled room, all the while looking out for the man on the train, when suddenly Dr Viktor jerked up from his seat, then down again just as quickly.

'And there he is,' he muttered, his head craning towards the doors. Katja froze, expecting to see the Nazi agent, but instead she realised the doctor was tracking a wiry, balding man with round-rimmed glasses and a walking stick, as he struggled up the steps.

The next thing Katja knew the doctor was waving a sheaf of papers in the air. Seeing the movement, the man with the walking stick looked up in his direction and quickened his pace as fast as he was able, given he dragged his leg. He did not smile when he greeted the doctor but took his hand to shake it and nodded politely at Katja.

'Fräulein Heinz, this is my good friend Herr Oskar Dreiberg,' Viktor said, even though Katja didn't think the doctor's associate seemed particularly friendly at all; rather nervous and furtive, in fact, as if he really didn't want to be seen in public with the doctor.

'We shall speak after the lecture,' Dreiberg assured him. 'Fräulein Heinz.' With a shallow bow he departed to the back row to join a group of Jewish students.

So, this was Doctor Viktor's contact, Katja thought, looking back over her shoulder to where the man sat. She only hoped his commitment to publishing the doctor's edited notebook would prove more solid than his apparent friendship. Glancing at the clock on the wall, she understood the lecture was due to begin in less than five minutes. Reaching for her handbag she took out her notepad and pencil so she could record any relevant sections for Dr Viktor. Just as she laid her hand on the pad, she caught sight of the slim volume of the WB Yeats poems Daniel Keenan had given her yesterday. The recollection sent a sudden tingle shooting through her. There was something so charming, yet so tragic about him, that she'd left the bookshop craving to know his own story and desperately disappointed that she could not.

At last, the noise in the lecture theatre died down, and Dr Wilhelm Reich strode confidently to the podium as the audience rose to applaud. The atmosphere was so electric it reminded Katja of the night her father took her to see the Berlin Philharmonic

Orchestra in concert. A hush descended like night on the place, and the stewards were about to shut the double doors, when Katja spied a latecomer sneak in to take his seat on the front row. She'd noticed five or six places had been reserved for members of the press. There was something about the man that was familiar; the sandy hair, the tweed sports jacket. She leaned forward and narrowed her eyes to focus on the back of his head, then leaned away. She must be mistaken. After all, what on earth would an Irish poet be doing at a lecture on the psychology of the Nazis?

Dr Reich was an electrifying speaker. Fascism, he told his audience, was not simply a political party. It was an ideology. A religion. And it was led by its very own prophet: Adolf Hitler. He spoke passionately for over an hour, and the applause he received lasted until he left the auditorium. Some people sat down again, while others began to file out. Katja watched Dr Viktor scan the back of the theatre, looking for Oskar Dreiberg. Lowering her gaze, she spotted the wiry little man standing below them. 'There he is,' she said.

Viktor's face broke into a smile and, sweeping up his brief-case and hat, he negotiated his way to the steps. Together they descended to the front of the auditorium, but Dreiberg's attention was suddenly caught by a gesture to the side. Katja did not see who made it, only that he disappeared into a huddle by the main door.

*

Daniel Keenan had heard about Dr Wilhelm Reich. He was an enemy of the Nazis and believed they were all sexually repressed. Chuck Patterson couldn't have had any idea, when he assigned him to cover the Sorbonne conference, that Reich's lecture would be so explosive and controversial. Here was a man, an inter-nationally famous psychiatrist, wanted by the Nazis, and what he'd said about fascism – and Hitler – was dynamite. No other publications had even bothered to send their journalists, thinking, as he had originally, that only puff stories, as they were called in the trade, or fillers, would be on offer. But what Daniel Keenan had noted down in shorthand was a scoop – a warning of the mystical hold fascism could have on the minds of its followers. This was headline news. As the adrenaline surged through him, Daniel hastily gathered up his things, intending to start writing as soon as he returned to the office, when he suddenly saw Oskar Dreiberg heading towards the exit. Remembering their last cryptic conversation, he called out to him. He'd been meaning to get in touch with him, but still hadn't quite got round to it.

Dreiberg's eyes widened in surprise. 'Keenan! I didn't expect to see you here.'

'I'm glad I came. Reich is some speaker!' said Daniel, fighting his way through the crowd.

The small man nodded. His usual wary expression had been replaced by something akin to excitement. 'It was fascinating, wasn't it? But it still didn't tell the whole story.'

'Ah,' responded Daniel, recalling their encounter in the bar. 'That transcript you told me about.'

Dreiberg jumped and raised his hands, looking about him nervously. 'Please. We do not mention such things in public.' He leaned in with a frown. 'Besides, I didn't think you were interested.'

After what he'd just heard, and coupled with his recent decision to dip his toe into the water of life once more, he certainly was, but he played his cards close to his chest. 'Perhaps I could be persuaded.'

The smaller man licked his lips. 'Well, in that case, I will let the author speak to you himself.' He turned round and craned his neck to look for Dr Viktor.

'You mean he's here?'

Dreiberg's head bobbed up and down. 'Yes. There he is!' He signalled with his walking stick at the doctor and Katja as they drifted towards the exit. On spotting him, they changed course.

'Doctor Viktor, I'd like you to meet Daniel Keenan, a respected journalist,' Dreiberg said, as the two men shook hands. 'He is very well connected.'

The doctor smiled broadly. 'In that case, I am particularly glad to meet you,' he replied. A young woman had followed on behind. 'And this is my assistant, Fräulein Heinz.'

Daniel's surprise was plain to see. So was the young woman's as she stood at Dr Viktor's side.

'You two already know each other?' asked Dreiberg.

'We have met, yes,' Daniel replied, his surprise tinged with embarrassment when he recalled the state he'd been in. 'In Shakespeare and Company, just yesterday, although I'm afraid we weren't formally introduced.' His eyes flicked up and brushed her with a knowing look. 'A pleasure, Fräulein Heinz,' he said.

She, in turn, appeared flustered, even though she had no obvious reason to be. 'Likewise,' she replied, her cheeks now flushing.

Dr Viktor's lips twitched in bemusement. 'Ah, then we all share a love of books,' he said, with a gentle laugh.

Addressing the doctor, Dreiberg ploughed on. 'Then perhaps we can meet to talk? Somewhere more private.' His voice dipped. 'My apartment? Tonight?' He moved closer and spoke low into Viktor's ear. Daniel heard him say: 'You will bring your document? Yes?'

Viktor nodded.

'Good, that's settled then,' said Daniel, dipping a bow and looking sheepishly at Fräulein Heinz. This young woman, this very attractive young woman, had seen him at his worst in the bookshop. He hated himself for having acted so boorishly and dreaded to think what she must make of him. Worse still, he felt he had betrayed Grace's memory. Yesterday, in the company of this Fräulein Heinz, he had felt alive for the first time in many months, but afterwards came the guilt. Like a terrible hangover after vintage Champagne. Was it worth it? He couldn't be sure.

'About yesterday. I . . .' he began. But the young woman interrupted him.

'Please. There is no need,' she replied.

Her gaze was direct and without pity. Daniel was tired of people feeling sorry for him when they knew about his tragedy. But this young woman didn't know and even though she had seen him at his most vulnerable, she didn't avert her eyes or walk away. He would go to Dreiberg's apartment tonight. Not so much because he was interested in some political cause, however noble, but because he wanted to find out more about Dr Viktor's assistant.

Chapter 22

The Dreibergs' apartment, so Dr Viktor had been told, lay on the edge of Le Marais, Paris's old Jewish quarter, where cobbled streets narrowed, and gables leaned over to almost meet in the middle. It was twilight when they hailed a taxi. The doctor had not wished, wisely thought Katja, to ask the hotel receptionist to order one. The fewer people who knew their destination the better.

Katja sat stiffly in the back of the cab, clearly on edge. As if reading her mind, the doctor ventured: 'If it makes you feel any easier, I only have the first few pages.' She followed his hand as he patted the breast pocket of his overcoat, then produced an envelope. 'In here,' he said. But it didn't really make her feel any better. How could it? No one else knew he was carrying only a few pages. The doctor could be beaten to pulp for one page or all of them. It made no difference to a Nazi spy.

'You left the rest in your room?'

His smile was a little on the smug side. 'Well hidden, of course.'

She held out her hand. 'Would you let me take them? They will be safer in here.' She looked down at the oblong clutch bag on her lap. The doctor knew there was logic in what she said.

'Very well.'

On the boulevards, the streetlamps were coming on and

every time they passed one of the beautiful wrought-iron posts, Dr Viktor's features were thrown into relief. Katja thought the shadows made him look older, drawn. Worried. He was doing his best to sound optimistic, for her sake, she guessed, as much as for his own, but the apprehension was still there in the way he tugged at his cuffs and coughed nervously between sentences.

'*Là-bas!*' snapped the rather unfriendly driver ten minutes later. He'd stopped the cab and was pointing towards a narrow street, lined with tall apartment blocks that sat uneasily side by side like squabbling neighbours. Some were elegant, others less so. The distinct smell of drains permeated the air, and Katja noted there were no *fin de siècle* lampposts here.

'Number eighteen,' said the doctor, checking the scrap of paper Dreiberg had given him. 'Here we are,' he said triumphantly, stopping in front of one of the shabbier blocks. It had a dimly lit hallway and there were bicycles stacked up by the entrance. There wasn't a concierge on duty, so they decided to walk up to the fourth floor. Viktor knocked and shortly afterwards a chain could be heard. A second later, Dreiberg's tense face appeared, unsmiling through a gap in the door.

'*Herr Doktor*, Fräulein Heinz,' he greeted them with a sombre face. 'No one followed you?'

With a shake of the doctor's head, Dreiberg admitted them into a cramped, drab room. A threadbare sofa was flanked by two equally shabby armchairs, with a low table in the middle. A small kitchen area lay to one side.

'*Bonsoir!*' greeted a woman with elfin-like features. Her dark hair was tied back in a casual knot, accentuating her large eyes. Her face was slightly flushed as she stirred a large pan of something that smelled delicious, as it bubbled away on a simple stove.

Dreiberg nodded at her. 'This is Monique, my wife.'

'*Enchanté, madame*,' said Dr Viktor with a bow.

Monique, slightly disarmed by the doctor's greeting, wiped her palms on her apron and held out a hand to be kissed. 'You are very welcome, sir,' she replied, then, darting a smile at Katja, she added: 'And you, also. Fräulein Heinz, yes?'

Katja smiled awkwardly. Venturing out at night with the transcript – even only the first few pages – wasn't such a good idea, in her opinion, but she'd agreed on condition that Dr Viktor allowed her to carry them in her evening purse. She figured she would be less of a target and besides, if she were honest with herself, the prospect of meeting Daniel again was not to be missed. But there was no sign of him, and now she wondered if he might not show. After all, he'd been drunk in the middle of the afternoon the first time she had met him, and the bookseller had inferred he was rather unreliable. Perhaps he had changed his mind. Perhaps he didn't want to be part of this dangerous conspiracy after all. She couldn't blame him. After the unnerving encounter on the train, she wasn't so sure, either.

'You will have wine, yes?' asked Monique, turning to reach for glasses from a cupboard.

'Thank you,' replied Katja.

Dreiberg leaned into the doctor, and asked in a half whisper: 'You have it?'

'It's here,' replied Katja, reaching into her evening purse.

'I left the rest in my hotel room, as a precaution,' explained Viktor.

'You are very wise,' Dreiberg agreed. 'Shall we?' He motioned towards the sofa, leaving Katja with Monique in the kitchenette.

'Oskar tells me you are just here for a couple of days,' said Monique cheerfully, as she returned to the pot on the stove. 'It is your first time in Paris?'

'Yes,' replied Katja, distractedly, watching the two men sit down. 'It is a beautiful city.'

'But of course,' replied Monique, just as a knock came. 'That will be Daniel,' she said, untying her apron strings and heading out into the hallway.

Katja felt her heart suddenly beat faster when she heard the familiar Irish brogue, then saw Daniel Keenan walk into the room, a bottle of red wine in his hand. The expression on his face was weary, almost as if he had come under sufferance. But as soon as he saw her, she thought she detected what seemed to be his version of a smile, a slight lift of the right side of his mouth. Or was she flattering herself?

'Fräulein Heinz.'

A thought dropped into her mind as he looked at her. He was a cross between Mr Dixon, the Irishman in Jane Austen's *Emma*, and Jane Eyre's Mr Rochester. In the bookstore he'd been quite charming and witty, although that was clearly down to the drink at the time, but now he appeared brooding and enigmatic. She couldn't quite fathom him out, but she found herself wanting to.

'Mr Keenan,' she replied, telling herself not to linger on his face too long.

He dipped a polite bow, but almost immediately moved on to join Dreiberg and the doctor.

Monique poured more wine into another glass and handed it to Daniel as he sat down in one of the armchairs. Katja remained watching him. This evening, he looked so serious and intense, as if he carried the weight of the world on his shoulders.

'Could you pass me the salt?' asked Monique a moment later, now returned to the ragout on the stove.

Katja whipped round. 'Sorry,' she replied. 'Of course,' and picking up a small pot, she advanced and handed it over.

'Oskar tells me you and Daniel met at Shakespeare and Company,' said Monique, seasoning the ragout. There was an edge to her voice, but a smile on her lips. Oskar Dreiberg had clearly been discussing yesterday's meeting with his wife.

'Yes,' replied Katja, leaning against a cupboard.

'He is what the English call a bookworm.' Monique laughed at the expression as she brought a spoon to her lips to taste the stew, but then followed on with a deep sigh. 'Poor man.'

Katja frowned as she remembered the bookseller's words. Miss

Beach had called Daniel a 'broken man' but didn't explain further. 'Poor? Why might that be?' she asked.

Monique reached for the pepper pot next to her and took a pinch from it. As she added it to the pan, she made sure Daniel was distracted and said: 'You don't know, do you?'

Katja drew closer. 'Know what?'

With a shake of her head Monique turned to Katja squarely. 'He lost his wife and little daughter a few months back. He is still mourning.'

Katja felt her lips make an 'o' shape, but no sound came out. Turning to regard Daniel, as he sat examining the first chapter of the typescript, she suddenly understood. His drinking, why the bookseller had described him as 'broken' and the melancholy expression he wore on his face like a shirt could all be explained by his tragic loss.

'I had no idea,' she said eventually.

Monique shrugged and reached for the plates. 'Why would you? You have only just met. But he is lonely. He needs companionship.'

Katja didn't understand why Monique was telling her this. 'You know I leave for Hamburg the day after tomorrow?'

Monique nodded. 'I know your stay is short, but perhaps . . .'

'*Chérie*,' Oskar called over just then. 'Our guests need more wine.'

'*Un moment*,' she called through, wiping her hands on her apron. 'I have an idea,' she whispered, reaching for a bottle of Burgundy.

*

'As I said, these are just the first few pages,' Dr Viktor made clear. He'd looked on nervously, scratching the palms of his hands while he waited for Daniel and Oskar to finish reading the first ten pages. 'Well?' he ventured, when both men finally looked up.

For a moment the two of them sat in stunned silence, as if

realising they had also just drunk from a poisoned chalice and were waiting for the after-effects to set in.

'Th . . . this is . . .' Dreiberg began.

'It's dangerous,' said Daniel, fixing Viktor with a glare. 'You heard Reich's lecture. You know what you are up against. The Nazis will stop at nothing until they dominate Europe.'

The doctor nodded slowly and expelled the breath that had been pent up since the men began to read. 'I am aware of that, but this is why it is so vital the whole world knows about their leader.'

Dreiberg seemed to freeze at the enormity of what Viktor had just said. Daniel appeared to take it in his stride.

'Naturally any editor would need to see the rest of the document before deciding whether or not to help you, Dr Viktor,' he said.

A nod. 'Of course. Only half of the entire manuscript is typed out.' He glanced unthinkingly at Katja. 'But I am hopeful there is enough for you to make a decision.'

Daniel arched a brow. 'Let me be the judge of that, doctor.'

Viktor raised a hand in surrender. 'I did not mean . . .'

'I know,' replied Daniel, frowning. 'You must understand that, from what I have seen, this document is extraordinary, but it will take a brave publisher to put it out.'

The doctor nodded again. 'But you will see what you can do?'

Daniel shot a glance over to the kitchen where Katja was talking with Monique. There was something about her that attracted him. Not just how much she loved novels and was so keen to learn more. Perhaps it was her smile or what lay beneath it. He sensed she may be a kindred spirit. Whatever it was, he wanted to be alone with her again.

Switching back to Viktor, he continued: 'As I said, I will need to see more,' he told the doctor, lifting up the corners of the pages before him. 'The rest of the typed pages are with you, in Paris?'

'Yes, in my hotel room.'

'Good.' Daniel clapped his hands on his knees. 'Then perhaps you could get them to me tomorrow,' he suggested. 'I will show them to my editor.'

As the conversation progressed, an idea emerged. Daniel would try to persuade Chuck Patterson to publish the medical notes in instalments, translated into English from the original German, of course. That way, Daniel argued, *The Parisian's* circulation would increase and all the major French publications, *Votr*, *L'Illustration* and the like, would come knocking at the magazine's door wanting to buy the rights. That was the theory at any rate.

Dreiberg, however, frowned. 'We n . . . n . . . need to handle this c . . . carefully. There are Nazi agents in the c . . . city.' His stammer suddenly re-emerged.

'True,' Daniel agreed. 'Perhaps it is best if you act as the middleman.'

Dreiberg looked horrified. 'Me?'

'It would only involve being a courier. Delivering the transcript where necessary, just to throw any potential dogs off our scent.'

'I'm not so sure,' Dreiberg replied with a shake of his head. 'It's risky.'

Daniel shot Viktor a look and then turned to face Dreiberg. 'My friend, after reading those pages, we are all in this now, whether we like it or not.'

*

'What they do is dangerous, yes?' said Monique, returning from pouring the wine with snippets of the men's conversation clearly ringing in her ears. Katja frowned. She didn't know how much Herr Dreiberg had told his wife, but she hoped it was very little. The more people who knew about the notebook, the more hazardous their mission to publish the notes would become.

'I think so. Yes,' she replied, gathering cutlery together, while trying to sound as vague as possible.

'And what about you?' Monique looked directly at Katja. 'Are you afraid?'

Katja thought for a moment. Ever since her world had gone up in flames in 1933 at the Burnings, she had known what it was to be afraid. In Hamburg she lived with fear. It was as natural to her as brushing her hair or cooking supper. Most times it was like a dull ache, but here in Paris, it was more like a sharp pain.

'No,' she lied. 'I know what we're doing needs to be done.'

Monique, a stack of plates in her hand, said: 'My Oskar feels afraid sometimes. He was a lecturer, in Berlin, you know. But the brownshirts gave him his limp and his stammer.'

Her shoulders heaved resignedly as she spoke of her husband, and Katja imagined the poor man being beaten up in some dark alleyway, simply for being Jewish. The thought dragged her back to the night her father was injured. Standing up against evil was always easier if you weren't alone.

*

They sat huddled round the small kitchen table to eat. Monique ladled out bowls of chicken ragout which she served with hunks of baguette. Daniel mopped up the thick tomatoey sauce with his bread as if he hadn't eaten a proper meal for days. When he realised Katja was watching him, he apologised.

'Forgive me,' he said, dabbing his chin with his serviette. 'It's not often I am treated to a home-cooked meal.' Daniel tilted his head. 'And in such company.'

Katja blushed.

'Daniel would rather devour a good book than a proper meal, wouldn't you?' Monique teased. 'You practically live in that bookshop.'

Daniel nodded. 'It's true I spend far too much time in there,' he confessed.

'Sylvia has a real, how you say, *soft spot*, for her Irish customer,' added Monique, patting him playfully on the hand while looking at Katja.

Daniel eyed Katja again. 'Miss Heinz knows that I am very fond of books,' he replied.

Monique twitched her full lips. 'Of course, Oskar told me you met at the bookstore,' she remarked with a wicked smile, wiping the corner of her mouth with her napkin.

'That's right,' said Daniel.

'So now you know all about George Orwell and WB Yeats?' said Monique, turning to Katja.

'Yes,' she replied, her eyes sliding towards Daniel. 'I was given a book of Yeats's poems.'

Dr Viktor looked up from his stew, and Dreiberg stopped chewing his bread, aware there was some sort of courtship playing out in front of them.

'Ah, Yeats,' reflected Monique, frowning, as if trying to pluck something from her memory. '"*Tread softly because you tread on my dreams.*" So beautiful, but not as beautiful as Baudelaire's poetry!' She tossed Daniel a playful smile.

The rest of the evening passed in conversation about books and poetry without further mention of politics. Katja was glad. It only made her anxious, but rather than open up over casual dinner party talk, Daniel remained a closed book to her. Monique was a superb hostess, keeping the chatter going, but the Irishman who sat opposite her remained enigmatic, and when a bell from a nearby church tolled midnight, and Dr Viktor took it as a cue to leave, Katja felt disappointed.

'Thank you for your hospitality,' the doctor told Monique.

'I'm afraid I need my sleep too,' said Daniel, his floppy hat in hand. Then, to Katja, he said, 'It was a pleasure to see you again, Fräulein Heinz. Another time, I hope.'

Katja wasn't sure if he meant what he said. And when would there be another time? She doubted if ever. Was there a conviction behind the smile he'd given her? She couldn't be sure because he didn't linger long enough to let her look deeper. Instead, he thanked his hosts, then just turned to leave. With his departure

Katja felt suddenly very flat. Part of her wanted to go after him and talk to him about Yeats, or Orwell, or any author he chose, just to hear the sound of his beautiful voice again. But the sensible part of her knew she was being absurd. How could they ever be star-crossed lovers if their situation had already dictated they may never see each other again?

*

Dr Viktor explained the plan to Katja as they walked back to the main thoroughfare to catch a cab, but she wasn't entirely convinced. She was also still disappointed not to be included in the discussions about the publication of the notes with the men, as if the risks she was taking counted for nothing. She kept her own counsel, of course, but when she heard that Daniel's proposed scheme relied on his editor's cooperation, the doubts set in. She'd flicked through *The Parisian*. There'd been a copy in the hotel lobby. It was full of fashion and reports from society parties. It was also a very conservative magazine, aimed at wealthy expats, most of whom probably thought Hitler was a good thing for Germany. Daniel Keenan certainly talked the talk – she'd heard all the Irish were good at that – but his plan wasn't without its faults.

Nevertheless, Dr Viktor seemed buoyed by the meeting. 'If all goes smoothly, the first piece could appear next month,' he said, as they made their way along the ill-lit street. Only a few more metres and they would reach the main boulevard to catch a taxi back to their hotel. But he was so engrossed in his thoughts that he didn't notice a man leaning up against the wall a little further ahead. As they drew closer, Katja saw he was wearing a trilby and she thought there was something familiar about him. But it wasn't until they were within a metre or less of him that he lit a cigarette, and she saw the flare from his match illuminate his face. At that moment he looked up and their eyes met. There was no mistaking. Katja suddenly grabbed the doctor's arm and pushed him off the pavement into the road.

'Katja, what are you doing?' asked Viktor, indignantly.

'Keep walking,' she hissed through her teeth.

They were only a few metres from the main junction, and Katja found herself wanting to break out into a run, but a quick glance over her shoulder assured her they were not being followed.

'What was all that about?' asked an irritated Dr Viktor, once they'd reached the comforting glow of a streetlamp.

'That man,' she said, her heartbeat only just starting to slow.

'What man?'

'The one we passed back there. It was the businessman. From the train.'

The doctor frowned. 'Are you sure?'

'Absolutely.' He'd shown his face deliberately. He'd wanted to let them know his presence, just as Katja had feared. Even in Paris they were not safe from Nazi spies. The businessman's appearance was a warning to them. From now on, every move they made could be watched.

Chapter 23

The encounter changed everything for Katja. It reminded her of the reception at the shipyard when, from the corner of her eye, she saw Hitler bend Kommodore Flebert's ear as he looked in her direction. She hadn't told Dr Viktor about the chilling incident, but kept her worst fears to herself, repeating over and over she'd been imagining that stare. Dr Viktor believed the businessman's presence served as a warning to them but had nothing to do with the transcript of Hitler's medical notes they were collating. He told her it was now standard procedure for academics to be followed on trips outside Germany, just to ensure they toed the Nazi party line. Katja wasn't going to convince him otherwise. Not for the time being at least. Only she harboured the fear: the existence of the notebook may no longer be a secret.

Dr Viktor telephoned Oskar Dreiberg the minute they arrived back at the hotel. It was past midnight. Perhaps half expecting trouble, Dreiberg rushed downstairs to the lobby as fast as his injured leg would allow and picked up the communal telephone before anyone else could reach it.

'Yes?' his voice was breathless.

'Dreiberg?'

'Doktor Viktor. S . . . something is wrong?'

'We were followed from your apartment.'

Dreiberg let out a muffled gasp. 'An agent?'

'Fräulein Heinz thought she recognised the man from our train journey.'

'But, surely, they can't know about the notes?'

'No. No, they can't, but if we are not careful, they will soon find out. I propose a change of plan.'

Originally, the doctor was going to deliver the remainder of the typed pages to Dreiberg at the Library of Burned Books early the next day, but that was now out of the question. Instead, an alternative plan was agreed. Katja had been a willing volunteer, especially knowing the mission would mean another encounter with Daniel. That was how she found herself once more in rue de l'Odéon the following morning. She'd slipped out of the hotel via the back entrance shortly after breakfast, a headscarf covering her blonde hair. In her hand she carried a hatbox, only instead of a hat, inside were the typed-up notes.

There was still a nip in the air, but a clearing sky held out the promise of sun as she arrived outside Shakespeare and Company. Taking a deep breath, she pushed against the door. According to the clock in the shop, she was two minutes early. The little bell signalled her arrival to the bookseller. Sylvia Beach was arranging books on a shelf nearby. She looked up and smiled broadly.

'Fräulein!' she said, surprise in her voice. 'How good to see you again.'

'And you,' replied Katja, her hatbox gripped tightly in her hand. She looked about the shop. No sign of Daniel.

'Are you looking for anything in particular today?' asked Sylvia, approaching.

Yes. Daniel, she thought but glancing up at the nearest wall, Oscar Wilde's photograph provided inspiration. 'Do you have *The Picture of Dorian Gray*?'

Sylvia smiled. 'I'm sure we do, somewhere.' She moved away,

towards the back of the shop, just as the bell tinkled again and in walked Daniel, right on time.

Whipping off his hat, his face looked pinched with concern as he spotted Katja. 'Dreiberg told me, Fräulein Heinz. Are you all right?' he asked.

'A little shaken, but I'm fine.' She shrugged. 'He didn't attack us, but he wanted us to know he was there. To frighten us, I suppose.'

Daniel nodded. 'But you don't think anyone . . .'

She cut him short. 'Dr Viktor says no one else can possibly know.'

'And you? What do you think?' His green eyes were fixed intently on her.

'I have my suspicions,' was all she would say.

He gave an understanding nod, then said quickly, in a low voice: 'You have the rest?'

Her eyes dipped to the hatbox. No one would suspect that a receptacle for toques, cloches or berets would hold Adolf Hitler's medical records. Moving away from the shop window, she placed the case on the only available empty surface, on the table in the middle of the shop. She opened it just as Sylvia returned with the novel.

'I've found a copy. It was at the back of—' She broke off mid-sentence when she saw Daniel.

'Well, *bonjour*, Daniel!' she exclaimed, with a broad grin. 'What a coincidence that you should bump into each other again.' Katja had just managed to shut the lid of her case before Sylvia noticed what was going on.

'I was just passing, and you know I can never do that without calling in to see you, Sylvia.' Daniel could switch on the charm like most people switch on a light bulb, thought Katja. She found it slightly disconcerting.

Sylvia held a novel aloft. 'Well, here it is. *The Picture of Dorian Gray*. I'll let you leaf through it, while I go and sort out a new delivery,' she told Katja, leaving the copy diplomatically on a nearby shelf.

Left alone, Katja and Daniel eyed each other, knowing what they had to do. The typescript was quickly transferred from Katja's hatbox to Daniel's briefcase in one smooth manoeuvre. He then secured the lock with a key.

Katja breathed a sigh of relief when she heard the lock click.

'It's safe with me,' said Daniel, trying to reassure her.

'I hope so,' she replied. 'I know you will take great care because . . .'

'Because lives depend on it?' he suggested.

Hearing him speak the truth out loud was even more terrifying than the thoughts in her head, as if his words seemed to make everything real.

'Yes,' she said, a tremble suddenly rippling through her.

Daniel kept his voice low. 'What you're doing is very brave, you know that?'

She nodded. What she did wasn't for herself. It was for her mother and her father and everyone else who was being persecuted in her homeland.

The jangle of the bell cut short their conversation, as a well-dressed woman and a small boy entered the shop. Sylvia, answering the sound, re-emerged from the storeroom to see if she could help her new customers.

'I better go,' said Katja. 'I am to meet Dr Viktor at the Sorbonne at eleven.'

Did his face fall slightly? She couldn't be sure, but her words sounded so final that she thought she noticed disappointment in his face.

'So, I suppose this is goodbye then, Fräulein Heinz,' he said. 'I wish you good luck.'

Was that it? So defeated? So final? Katja didn't want to leave him like this, tugging at her heart strings. As she made a move towards the door, something told her to seize the moment. She pivoted round. 'Perhaps you could walk me there? To the Sorbonne?'

The suggestion seemed to catch him completely off-guard. His reaction made her think she had made a mistake; misread the signs. He seemed puzzled, touching his temple absent-mindedly. Or perhaps he didn't know his own mind.

'Yes,' he said finally, his lips gradually lifting into a vague smile at the thought. 'Yes. I don't have to be in work until this afternoon. And, of course, it would be safer,' he added, as if he needed to justify his actions.

'Of course,' she agreed.

He frowned then. 'But what about . . .?' His eyed the hatbox.

'I can wait here, while you drop it back to your office, then you can see me safely to my destination,' Katja suggested.

He smiled then, a full, generous smile: the first proper one she'd seen from him after their first meeting, and his offer suddenly made her feel a little safer.

'It's settled then,' she replied. The breakthrough had been hard-won, but she regarded it as a small victory, nonetheless. To pass the time while she waited, she decided she would buy *The Picture of Dorian Gray* after all.

*

By the time Daniel returned, assuring her the pages were secure, the spring sun had dissolved the earlier thin fog that had run like a silver ribbon along the Seine. Looking up at the sky, he said: 'I want to show you something.'

Was she imagining it, or did his mood seem a little lighter, as if the fog that covered his eyes before had also lifted? He led Katja across the busy Boulevard Saint-Germain. Descending the old stone steps down to the quay, he paused so that she could take in the view of Notre-Dame on the Île de la Cité from across the river.

'I never tire of it,' he told her, as they stood before the majestic towers and the vaulted roof.

While Katja had to agree, she remained on edge. 'Surely this isn't the quickest way to the Sorbonne?' she said, after a moment. Dr Viktor had already given her directions.

Daniel blinked self-consciously. 'You're right. It's not,' he replied. 'It's just such a beautiful day and I wanted to show you these.' He pointed towards the green box stalls that lined the steep walls of the quay along the river.

As far as Katja could see, all along Quai de la Tournelle and beyond, there were stalls selling second-hand books. 'They say the Seine is the only river in the world that runs between two bookshelves,' he told her, his voice sounding lighter. 'They call the booksellers the *bouquinistes*. They've been here for around three hundred years.'

Katja had heard about the book stalls from her father, but never imagined she would actually see them.

'Can we take a look?' she asked, suddenly excited by the prospect of spending more time with Daniel as well as browsing books.

The transcript was safe, and she had over an hour to spare.

'Of course,' he replied.

A plump, older woman whose wispy grey hair had broken loose from a chignon, was standing behind one of the stalls as they approached. Wearing a dirty canvas apron and fingerless gloves, she waved at Daniel as he drew near.

'Yvette!' he greeted her, kissing her on either cheek. '*Ça va?*'

'*Oui, Monsieur Daniel. Et toi?*' Her eyes twinkled with sheer delight, before he turned to Katja. 'And your friend?' she enquired excitedly.

Daniel nodded. 'Fräulein Katja Heinz, meet Madame Yvette Lebrun, the most astute *bouquiniste* on the quays.' He leaned in towards her. 'And the most beautiful.'

The woman tapped him playfully on the arm. 'You are terrible,' she teased.

'Madame Lebrun used to work at one of the smart hotels until she had a clever idea.'

She winked at Katja. 'I sold any books the guests left in their rooms.'

Daniel shook his head. 'But you didn't rate novels written in English, did you Yvette?'

A chuckle then, as Madame Lebrun nudged Daniel playfully once more. 'Ah, Shakespeare and Company,' she giggled girlishly.

Daniel looked at Katja again. 'So, she sold them off to Sylvia very cheaply.'

'I 'ear some crazy American lady wanted to open ze bookshop,' she said, touching her head.

Katja smiled. 'Well, I, for one, am very pleased you did, Madame Lebrun.'

They walked on, stopping at each stall for a few moments. As she ran her eager eyes across the book spines, thrilling to the touch of the leather and breathing in the scent of old paper, Katja forgot why she was in Paris; forgot the need to look over her shoulder every few minutes. Daniel, too, seemed a changed man; more like the easy-going but knowledgeable – albeit inebriated – book lover she'd first met in the bookshop. Standing next to him, she thumbed through poetry anthologies and English novels by Virginia Woolf – something she could never dream of in Germany. She bought a copy of *Mrs Dalloway*, and Daniel purchased a slim volume of Irish poetry.

'I can never have enough Yeats,' he told her as they continued to stroll along the bank.

The April sun was now beating down through the horse chestnut trees, teasing out new leaves.

'You must miss it – your home country. Ireland, I mean,' Katja said suddenly. She'd been thinking about what Monique had said about the death of Daniel's wife and child, and even though she knew it was really none of her business, she wanted to find out more about his story. But he stopped in his tracks, and she suddenly realised she had hit a raw nerve. 'Did Monique tell you about Grace and Bridie?' The colour had suddenly leached from his face.

'Your wife and child?' She replied tentatively, afraid she'd overstepped the boundary.

Daniel opened his mouth to say something but thought better of it. Shoving his hands in his pockets, he began to walk on, but Katja knew the damage had been done. A large cloud passed over the sun and the lightness in his step also disappeared, along with his smile. She had spoken out of turn and was deeply regretting it. After that she held her tongue.

A few paces on, Daniel stopped by some steep steps leading up from the quay and patted down his jacket to bring out a packet of Gitanes from one of his pockets. He thrust it in front of her.

Confused by his sudden gesture, she pulled back. 'I don't,' she told him.

'Very wise,' he said, lighting one for himself. It was the first time he'd spoken since she'd revealed she knew about the deaths of his wife and child, and his anger seemed to have blunted. Katja, on the other hand, was still on edge, hating herself for being so insensitive. She watched as he cupped his hand over a match flame to light his cigarette.

'People have been kind, but they can't know,' he said. 'They can't feel.'

Katja didn't really know how to respond, but she thought of Sylvia, the motherly bookseller and of Monique. 'From what I've seen a lot of people care about you, Mr Keenan. They want to . . .'

But she could tell he wasn't listening. Instead, he took a hard drag on the cigarette and tilted his head towards the sky, deep in thought. Katja looked on, feeling wretched.

'It's . . . It's still raw,' he said finally, the smoke wafting above him in the still air.

'I'm sure,' she replied, knowing exactly how he felt, but unable to tell him her own circumstances. Besides, she could see he wasn't listening.

He just puffed on the Gitane and said: 'Thank you for your company, but I mustn't delay you any further, Fräulein Heinz. The Sorbonne is a few metres along the boulevard.' He pointed with his cigarette up the stairs leading from the quayside.

The bluntness of his statement knocked Katja off balance. 'I'm sorry, I . . .'

But her apology only prompted a shake of Daniel's head, and the sullenness she'd seen last night had suddenly turned to bitterness. 'I don't want pity,' he broke in. 'I want justice.'

'Justice?' she repeated, before grasping any further questioning would only make matters worse. 'I didn't mean to pry,' she told him. 'I never intended to . . .' She could tell she'd pressed on a wound that had barely begun to heal.

The smoke poured out as Daniel opened his mouth to speak, as he stopped her. 'I'm the one who should be sorry. I apologise for being so abrupt.' His words bled vulnerability, and yet again, Katja felt her heart ache as she studied his expression.

'There's no need for an apology,' she told him. 'Believe me, I understand what you're going through.'

Daniel looked deep into her eyes, as if searching for her meaning. He seemed to find it, because he nodded and said after a moment: 'I do believe you. I also believe you are a good person.'

It was an unexpected remark, but it seemed to Katja to be his way of declaring a truce, even though he was the one who had just disarmed her with his words.

For a moment they simply looked at each other, until Katja pointed to the steps behind her. 'I'll be late,' she said.

'Then we shall hurry.' After that, they walked side by side up the steps, although this time in silence. But it was an easy, rather than uncomfortable one, almost as if each step they took brought them closer to each other, until finally, after crossing a busy boulevard, they reached their destination.

'Here we are,' said Katja nervously, the Sorbonne rising behind them.

Holding her gaze, he nodded. 'Yes,' he replied, then surprised her by adding: 'Will I see you again, Fräulein Heinz?'

Katja's eyes widened, and she felt a lump rise in her throat. This beautiful, sensitive man was reaching out to her again, but all she could do was give him a helpless smile and shake her head. 'I'm afraid we leave for Hamburg tomorrow.'

He nodded. 'Of course,' he replied, touching his head to signify his mistake. His shoulders seemed to slump as he digested the news. 'Then I wish you *bon voyage* and good luck, fräulein.' He raised his hat, and it took all Katja's strength not to rush forward and fling her arms around him to cradle his broken heart. And as she watched him walk away from the entrance to the Sorbonne, she thought her own heart might break too.

Chapter 24

The memory of Daniel's forlorn face lingered long after Katja watched him leave: a solitary, sorrowful figure trapped in a world of his own. How she'd longed to hold out a hand to help him navigate the strange and harsh landscape of grief, but she'd missed her chance, and now she had to concentrate on the task in hand.

She'd arranged to meet Dr Viktor outside the seminar room. He was to attend a discussion at half past eleven and wanted her to take notes. She found the room easily. It was just a couple of doors down from the lecture theatre. But there was no sign of the doctor. A glance at the clock told her she was five minutes early. A woman, standing at the door of the seminar room, was taking names on a clipboard.

'Has Dr Viktor signed in, please?' Katja enquired in her stilted French.

After a swift check, the answer was as she feared. '*Non*,' Dr Viktor hadn't checked in. A quick scan of the room confirmed the doctor wasn't inside.

Katja waited on one of the benches in the corridor. Half past eleven came and went, and the doors to the seminar room shut as the session began. Katja rose and began to pace up and down, thinking about her next move. The minutes crept slowly around

the clock face, until at midday, she decided it might be best to
return to the hotel. Perhaps Dr Viktor was feeling unwell, although
he had seemed in good health at breakfast that morning. Of
course, she was fooling herself, but she hated to think of what
may have happened. Even though she'd tried to stamp on her fear
after last night, when he didn't show, Katja felt it rising again. That
same insidious menace that crept up from her gut and grabbed
her by the throat so often these days; the visceral fear that they
were being watched and that something bad had happened to
Dr Viktor re-emerged. As soon as she was out of the Sorbonne,
anxiety made her quicken her step and when she arrived back at
the hotel twenty minutes later, she was out of breath.

'*Numéro 23, s'il vous plaît*,' she asked the receptionist with the
bushy moustache. Looking at the board behind the desk where
the keys were kept, she noticed the hook for the doctor's room
next door was empty. Hopefully, that meant he was in, although
she didn't want to arouse suspicion.

'*Voilà, mademoiselle*,' said the receptionist, laying the key on
the counter.

She snatched it and, seeing the elevator was in use, took the
stairs, running up them as soon as she was out of sight of the
reception. Hurrying along the corridor, she reached Room 21
and knocked on the door.

No reply.

She knocked again, only this time with a clenched fist, not a
knuckle. Still no reply.

'Dr Viktor,' she called in a half whisper. She tried the handle.
It was locked. Keeping her voice low, she put her mouth to the
keyhole. 'It's Katja.'

The anxiety that had been growing since the Sorbonne now
threatened to bubble over as she imagined all sorts of terrible
scenarios. After last night's encounter, the threat had become a
reality. The doctor could be lying dead inside for all she knew.
Raising her clenched fist again, she was just about to knock one

more time before raising the alarm, when the door suddenly opened and there stood Dr Viktor.

'*Mein Gott!*' gasped Katja. 'What happened?'

The doctor's face was swollen and grazed on one side, and he held a white towel to the back of his head. She could see it was red with blood.

'Come,' he said, ushering her inside quickly. He slumped onto the edge of the bed and mumbled: 'I was hit from behind.'

She sat beside him to inspect the gaping wound at the back of his head. 'But you need this stitched.'

'No,' he snapped. 'I mustn't attract attention. The notes . . .'

'They're safe,' she told him, but mention of the transcript made her suddenly sweep the room. 'Your briefcase. They took it?'

The doctor, his head still in his hands, grunted, 'Yes.'

'But that means . . .'

Seeing the look of horror on her face, he tried to calm her fears. 'It doesn't necessarily mean they know about the notebook. It could have been a . . .'

'Please, Doctor, don't lie to yourself. They know. Perhaps not about what the folder contains, but that we have something to hide.'

Leaping up to hide her frustration, Katja stalked into the bathroom, filled a basin with warm water and grabbed a face flannel. Returning to the bedroom, she stood over him and began to dab his head. He winced and cowered away from her.

'You must at least let me clean the wound,' she told him firmly, squeezing out the flannel.

He sighed deeply and leaned forward, propping his head up with his hands. 'I'm sorry. Yes, of course.'

His scalp had been split a little way back from the temple, but although there was a lot of blood and some swelling, the wound did not seem too serious on the surface, although head injuries, Katja knew, should always be taken seriously.

'How are you feeling?' she asked, wiping away the blood.

'Like dancing a waltz.'

Katja stopped. 'How can you joke?' she asked. 'Whoever did this could have killed you,' She chided him, dabbing his scalp with renewed energy. Thanks to her, Daniel was in possession of the typescript, but that meant he might be in danger too. By now, whoever had attacked the doctor would know their mission had failed and they'd come away empty-handed. Katja knew they would focus elsewhere; on the doctor's associates. She had to warn Daniel that he could be a target. He must take extra care.

By now the water in the basin had turned a deep pink, but the wound seemed to have stopped bleeding. From behind a curtain that offered a little privacy from the bidet, Katja found another clean face flannel. Folding it in four, she placed it on the doctor's wound. Then, walking over to the bathrobe on the back of the door, she removed the belt and tied it round his head to hold the towelling square in place.

'Come,' she told Viktor, helping him to ease himself to the top of the bed. She plumped the pillows, so that he could prop himself up, before slipping off his shoes and helping him into bed. Finally, she covered him with the bedspread.

'You must rest now,' she told him, closing the shutters. She, of course, could not. She needed help. 'Oskar Dreiberg,' she said aloud. He had to know what had happened. Reaching for her evening purse, she scrabbled inside to find the scrap of paper Monique had slipped to her last night as she was leaving. 'Paris is a big city. Call us if you need anything,' she'd said. But any call would have to be placed through the hotel concierge. Dr Viktor's warning echoed in her ears. 'Listen for any clicks on the line.' It was a chance she'd have to take.

Hurrying downstairs into the foyer, she found the mirthless receptionist sulking behind the desk.

'I wish to place a call,' she said, trying to sound in control, even though inside she was quaking. She slid over the paper, and

163

the clerk arched a supercilious brow as he dialled the number. A moment later, Katja could hear a voice at the end of the line, but her black look made it clear she wanted privacy and the receptionist skulked through into the back office.

Swallowing down the panic, she held the receiver to her ear. 'Herr Dreiberg?'

'*Ja.*'

She recognised the voice and took a breath.

'It's Katja Heinz. Dr Viktor's assistant.'

'What's happened?' he jumped in.

'He's been attacked.'

A silence down the line.

'Is he hurt?'

She kept her voice low as a waiter passed carrying a tray. 'I think he needs a doctor.'

'You are at the hotel?'

'Yes.'

'At least the pages are safe,' she heard him mumble. She supposed Daniel had been in touch with him. 'Return to your room and I'll be with you shortly,' he added, trying to reassure her.

'How long . . .?' The line went dead, and Katja replaced the receiver and took the lift back upstairs to check on the doctor. Unlocking the door, she found him still sleeping soundly and decided to return to her room to wait for Herr Dreiberg's arrival. She sat down on the chair next to the bed and her gaze lighted on the poetry anthology Daniel had given her. It was hard to believe that just a few hours ago she had been happy for the first time in many years. Strolling along the Quai de la Tournelle on a spring morning, it felt so right to be in Daniel's company, just browsing books and feeling the spring sunshine on her back. But now every door that banged, every footstep in the corridor, was a Nazi agent coming to find the transcript that wasn't in the doctor's briefcase. For now, she had to come to terms with the fact that Hitler's power was reaching over borders and infecting neighbouring democracies. A Nazi agent had followed two German citizens into another country and could so easily have assassinated the doctor on foreign soil. Nowhere, it seemed, was beyond the Führer's reach.

Chapter 25

Katja left a message for Oskar Dreiberg at the reception, asking him to go directly to Dr Viktor's room. Less than half an hour later, she heard footsteps stop outside his door and prayed it was him. She raced to answer the knock at his door, but when she opened her own door, she was shocked to see not Herr Dreiberg, but Daniel.

'Mr Keenan!' Her stomach flipped at the sight of him. Less than two hours ago he had seemed so vulnerable, in need of care and understanding. Now the tables were turned. She was the one desperate for help.

'Fräulein Heinz, are you all right?' he asked, his face drawn with worry.

'Yes. Yes, I'm fine. How . . .?' She was relieved to see him, yet troubled too. He was being dragged even further into this spider's web.

'Dreiberg called me.'

'He's in here.' said Katja, ushering Daniel urgently into the doctor's room and making sure no one else saw.

The Irishman's eyes widened, then narrowed as he hurried over to the bed.

'He was hit from behind, on his way to the Sorbonne,' explained

Katja, looking down on the sleeping patient. She thought of the businessman in the trilby. It had to be him, or one of his henchmen.

Daniel's eyes locked onto the doctor's bloody makeshift bandaging. 'So, the attack wasn't random. It looks like the Nazis are already on to you,' he said in a low voice. 'He'll be all right, yes?'

Katja nodded. 'Let's hope so, but as you see, there was a lot of blood. He should have stitches, but he didn't want to cause a fuss. If this got into the newspapers . . .'

Daniel agreed. As a journalist he knew the implications and how such a story could put the doctor and Katja in even more danger. He looked at the chaise longue by the window. 'All we can do is wait. Let's sit, shall we?'

Katja nodded.

'You could probably do with one of these,' he suggested, passing the sideboard with a bottle of cognac on it.

Katja nodded and he poured out two brandies.

'What happened?' he asked, handing her a glass, and sitting beside her.

She frowned over the rim of her glass as she took a gulp of the brandy, and felt it burn the back of her throat and set her head on fire. 'After you left,' she began, 'I went to meet him, but he never showed up. I waited for half an hour then returned to the hotel. I found him in here, barely conscious.' She took another gulp. 'And you're sure the transcript . . .'

'In my office.' He sighed. 'But my editor was called away for a couple of days. A family emergency.'

Katja shot him a sceptical look. 'What?'

Daniel looked into the bottom of his glass, as if to avoid eye contact. 'His wife's broken her toe playing tennis and the nanny is sick, so she needs him to help with their daughter until she's back on her feet – literally.' He took a large gulp.

'So, he still doesn't know anything?' There was a touch of exasperation in her voice.

'I'm afraid not, but I'll show him the pages as soon as he's back. He might take the bait.' He shrugged. 'He might not.'

'Then what?' Katja felt herself growing more impatient. 'What if he refuses to publish it?'

'There are other, more political publications. It's just a case of finding one brave enough to throw their hat in the ring and run the risk of Adolf Hitler's wrath,' he told her plainly.

Katja took another large sip of brandy. 'But you still think your editor will be interested?'

Daniel nodded slowly, but she worried his conviction seemed half-hearted. 'As I said, if he's not, there will be others.'

'You don't seem convinced,' she replied.

The spring sun had disappeared behind rain clouds and the room was gloomy, apart from a small lamp casting a dim light in the far corner. She was glad she couldn't see the bright green of Daniel's eyes because she was afraid there'd be uncertainty behind them. 'We need to be sure,' she told him. 'Otherwise, we will be risking our lives for nothing.'

It must have been the swelling despair in her voice that made him suddenly reach out to her and put his hand on hers. At his touch, she looked down, as if wondering how to react, but in a heartbeat, she'd placed her hand over his. He looked up and put down his glass. 'Please believe me, Fräulein Heinz, I will do everything I can to expose Hitler. Remember I have read the first pages. The man is clearly unfit for office. Pure evil.' With his free hand he touched his forehead.

'I know,' she said. 'It's just, well . . .'

He tried to find her gaze, but she refused to look at him as tears welled in her eyes.

'There's something else, isn't there?' he said. 'Something you're holding back. I could see it in your eyes today as we walked by the quay. I'm listening if you want to tell me.'

Katja nodded and glanced at Dr Viktor, lying badly injured in bed. Seeing him like that reminded her of what had happened at the Burnings. 'My father,' she began.

'Did something happen to him too? Something bad? Is that what's driving you on?'

Katja hadn't grasped that although he barely knew her, Daniel seemed attuned to her distress. 'He was an anthropologist,' she said softly.

'He studied different cultures?'

'Human development and behaviour all over the world,' corrected Katja. 'Cultures, languages and, of course, people's physical characteristics.'

'Ah,' interrupted Daniel. 'And your father disagreed with the Nazi theory about the superiority of the Aryan race.'

Katja tensed. He was already one step ahead of her. 'Of course. It is completely false and without any scientific foundation.'

'Did he tell the Nazis that?'

She took another sip of brandy. 'He went one better. He wrote a whole book on the subject, debunking their vile racial theories and encouraging other lecturers to do the same. Of course, after that he was persecuted for his findings. He scientifically disproved one of their basic principles and they made him pay.' She stared into her glass as she spoke. 'When Goebbels announced the Book Burnings . . .'

Daniel nodded. 'Your father's book was burned.'

'Not just his.' A sob bubbled up in the base of her throat. 'All week, truckloads of books from shops and libraries and private studies and homes around Hamburg arrived for the bonfire. Everyone from the university was ordered to watch the Nazi students set light to it, and the flames burst into life against the black night sky. They just kept throwing book after book onto the blaze, feeding it like a ravenous monster. Every time the flames leaped, a cheer went up.' She wiped away a tear. 'Not everyone was happy, of course. A lot of us were watching in horror as all those years, and sometimes decades, of work and academic study went up in flames.' She paused and took another gulp of brandy. 'Then someone shouted my father's name. He was standing close by and looked to see a group of brownshirts holding copies of his book. One by one they started tossing them into the flames. A cheer for every book! He just couldn't bear it. He screamed at them. I tried to hold him back, of course, but I wasn't strong enough, and he rushed forward and began tugging the copies from their hands. They fought back, and one punched him so hard he lost his footing.'

She could picture it in slow motion yet again: her father's body toppling and falling backward into the flames. His agonising cry would forever haunt her.

'I rushed forward and pulled at his legs. Two or three others joined me, and we managed to drag him away from the blaze, but he was on fire.' She turned to Daniel, her own eyes alight with the memory of it and her voice cracking. 'His hair was . . . His hair was on fire! I took off my coat and flung it over him to smother the flames, but it was no use. The smell . . .' The awful, acrid reek of singed flesh stung her nostrils at the memory. 'We got him to hospital, but it was too late. He died in agony three days later. And my poor mother . . . she's never been the same since.' Inside she'd been trembling, but when she finished, and Daniel did not speak, there was a sense of unravelling. It was as if the ropes that had held everything together inside her had come apart and spooled out to lie in a messy, complicated heap before her.

When she turned to look at him, Katja saw there were tears in his eyes too. It was then that she felt his arm wrap around her shoulder. His touch was warm and soft, and for an instant, she wanted herself to dissolve completely into it; to be subsumed into him so that all the hatred and the madness would disappear.

'They say grief is the price we pay for love,' he said softly.

She bit her trembling lip. He understood her and his words

gave her the courage to fight off her despair. After a few moments, when she finally spoke again, she was surprised how confident she sounded, as if she'd drawn courage from telling Daniel her story. 'So you see why it's so important that the world knows about Hitler and what he's capable of,' she said, still not daring to look at Daniel because she feared she might lose control of her tears.

'Of course,' he replied, drawing closer to her. 'And I promise you, fräulein, I will do everything in my power to see that the world knows the truth and acts to stop him before it's too late.'

Katja nodded and this time her eyes found his, and she suddenly saw them shine brighter than before, as if someone had lit a fire behind them. He leaned in and she felt his breath soft and warm on her cheek.

'I've laid my soul bare to you. Now it's your turn, if you're ready,' she whispered. 'You can tell me,' she whispered.

A second passed. Then another, until much to Katja's dismay, Daniel pulled back, as if the spell had been broken. When he spoke, he sounded strangely formal.

'I'm sorry. Forgive me,' he said, shaking his head.

'Forgive you?' she repeated. It was as if he'd just touched a hot stove and got burned.

'I have to get to the office. I mustn't be late,' he told her. He stood abruptly. She remembered he'd told her he was working later that afternoon. Reaching into his breast pocket, he handed her his card. 'You can call me on this number if you need me,' he said, tugging at his jacket and sounding very businesslike.

She let out a faint laugh, then frowned. One minute she thought he might be about to kiss her, the next he was handing her his business card. It was as if she had taken off all her clothes to stand naked in front of him and he had simply stared at her. Her outpourings seemed to have switched off the light behind his eyes. Now his words brought her back to reality, reminding her she would be jumping from the frying pan of Paris into the fire of Hamburg. The heat in both was starting to become unbearable.

Right now, she felt as if Dr Viktor's attack had left her afraid of her own shadow. Nowhere was safe. It almost felt as if she was being deserted. She turned away from him, because his mood had shifted and this time, if he saw the fear in her eyes, he might not meet it with tenderness. She wasn't sure she was strong enough to bear that. Instead, her gaze settled on Dr Viktor. He hadn't moved for the last half-hour.

Sensing Katja's unease, Daniel made a vain attempt to ease her embarrassment. 'You still plan to leave tomorrow?' he asked her.

She took a deep breath to swallow the hurt. 'If he is no worse, yes,' she replied, looking at the sleeping doctor.

'You'll need help. I'll call round first thing,' Daniel said. He'd become a stranger again and his behaviour confused her.

She whipped round, a tear unexpectedly breaking lose with the movement. Quickly she brushed it away, hoping he hadn't noticed. 'Thank you, Mr Keenan,' she replied formally. 'That would be most kind.'

Chapter 26

Katja remained at Dr Viktor's bedside all night. At around eleven o'clock, he had woken and accepted two aspirin, washing them down with a little water, before promptly falling asleep again. She only wished she could sleep, but she was caught in a sort of no man's land between her fears for the doctor and the medical notes on the one hand, and her feelings for Daniel Keenan on the other.

One moment the Irishman was clever and charming, and the next gloomy and, worst of all, distant. He lifted her up with his talk of literature, his good manners and his commitment to fight injustice, but then he dashed her down just as easily with his quick temper and now, it seemed, his stiff, standoffish manner. From that first meeting in the bookshop, she had known there was something special about him. He'd excited her, thrilled her, and made her feel like a queen in his company. Yet some of the time, she'd had to question his behaviour. That evening, he'd been on the verge of kissing her; on the precipice of something beautiful, but it seemed he just couldn't make the leap. He'd held himself in check. Something had stopped him: guilt, she supposed, like a prisoner of his own conscience's making.

The shackles of his grief over his wife and child were still chafing, and perhaps she'd been wrong to long for his kiss. Sylvia was right. He was broken, but that didn't alter the fact that she knew she could love him. Maybe she already did, but there could be no future for them. At least, not until Daniel Keenan had come to terms with his own loss and that could take many more months, if not years.

The thoughts weighed her down and made her whole body heavy. Still seated on a chair, she laid her head on Dr Viktor's bed, and propped up on folded arms, she finally fell asleep just before dawn broke.

*

A while later, although she had no idea how much later, a tap on the door woke her. Her head jerked up and she let out a faint cry. A spear of sunlight was piercing through the shutters, lighting the unfamiliar room. Shaking the sleep from her head, she saw Dr Viktor lying in the bed. She looked at her own arms and was surprised to see she was still dressed. Then she remembered.

Another tap; this time accompanied by a soft call. 'Fräulein Heinz, it's me.'

Pulling herself up from the bed, she hurried over to let Daniel in, then shut the door behind him. She wasn't sure how to behave. She knew the best course would be to forget yesterday, and her revelations about Vati's death, had ever happened, but it wouldn't be easy.

As he marched into the middle of the room, Daniel seemed flustered, until he took a deep breath and cupped the back of his neck. 'How is he this morning?' he asked, glancing at the doctor.

Puzzled by his manner, she replied: 'He slept well.'

'Good,' he replied, before finally meeting her gaze. 'I said I'd help you get him to the train station.'

Daniel Keenan really was an enigma to her. She didn't understand him, but right now she didn't have to. She was just grateful for his help.

'I'm not dead yet, you know,' came a voice from the bed.

Katja's lips lifted. 'Good morning, Dr Viktor,' she said just as the doctor tried in vain to sit up. 'You must keep calm,' she soothed, hurrying over to his side. 'It's going to be all right.' She looked back at Daniel for support. 'Mr Keenan is here for us,' she said.

*

From inside the railway carriage, Katja stared down onto the platform below where Daniel was standing, looking up. Her hand was pressed forlornly on the window and her breath misted the glass. She dreaded the screech of the whistle.

Dr Viktor was slumped in the corner of the compartment. His head wound had left him drowsy and in constant pain. Daniel helped him dress, then accompanied Katja in a taxi to the Gare de l'Est to see him board the train. The doctor was unsteady on his feet and still dazed. Katja was grateful, too, that the typed-up pages of the notes were to remain in France in Daniel's office until she could retrieve them. It was one less thing she had to worry about.

It was hard for Katja to believe they'd been in Paris for less than seventy hours. So much had happened, it could have been seventy days. In her mind, images of the transcript, the bookshop, the Sorbonne, the Dreibergs' apartment and of Dr Viktor's bloodied head flashed by at breakneck speed. But above all there had been Daniel. She would cherish the memory of their brief walk along the quayside, browsing books in the sunshine, forever. When she boarded the train with the doctor, he'd refused to say goodbye.

'I prefer *à bientôt*,' he told her as they stood close on the platform. 'We will see each other again, soon.'

Not soon enough, she thought, as once again she hoped he might reach out to her. Yesterday, after she'd poured out her heart, there had been no immediate words between them; just an unspoken impression that Daniel appeared to understand the turmoil and heartache of losing an innocent loved one to tyrants; to appreciate the injustice of it all. Or was she misreading the situation? Perhaps he was just being sympathetic, although this time, when they parted, he leaned in, brushing first her right cheek then her left, in the French way. The gesture was rushed and slightly awkward, but it made her smile and gave her a little hope that he felt the way she did, only couldn't show it.

Just then a pompous little guard blew a short, shrill blast on his whistle, not five metres away. 'Tous à bord, mesdames et messieurs!' They both flinched at the sound, then Daniel's expression changed.

'You are a very special person, Fräulein Heinz,' he said, suddenly. 'I want you to know that.'

Katja almost wished he'd remained silent because he'd made her heart ache again. 'Thank you for listening to me yesterday,' she said, before screwing up her courage to add: 'I hope I can do the same for you sometime.'

He looked down, embarrassed, but she hooked her gaze under his, suddenly determined to press home her point. 'I understand, remember? I hardly know anything about your situation, but I do know it takes time.'

'Tous à bord, mesdames et messieurs!' repeated the guard, standing closer.

She'd turned then and now stood in a glass prison, separating her from Daniel, awaiting the start of a journey that would take her hundreds of miles away. She wanted so badly to be allowed into his world, to share in his grief and by sharing it, somehow ease it. But she still couldn't be sure he'd let her in.

When the dreaded moment came and the whistle sounded, Daniel took off his hat and raised his arm in a melancholy salute. He smiled then, and she took it to be a message. He was telling her everything would be all right; he would be there for her. The locomotive lurched, causing her to teeter slightly on her

176

heels before the train began to move off. Daniel moved with it at first, gathering pace alongside the train, but the speed soon defeated him and before long he was gone, swallowed up in a pillow of steam.

Managing to dam her tears, Katja took her seat next to the doctor. His hat remained firmly on his head, holding in place the makeshift dressing over the wound. His eyes were shut, and it was clear he simply wanted to be left alone.

Anna Karenina had now been joined by *The Picture of Dorian Gray* in Katja's suitcase. But there was another slim volume that caught her eye. She took out the anthology of poetry Daniel had given her in Shakespeare and Company. 'A souvenir. From the city of light,' he'd told her. For the next few hundred miles, in his absence, WB Yeats' moving verses would keep him in her heart on the long journey home.

*

It was late evening and not quite dark, when the train finally pulled into the main *bahnhof* at Hamburg. Dr Viktor slept for most of the journey. Even though Katja hadn't been able to stop herself scrutinising everyone who passed their carriage, she'd noticed no one vaguely suspicious. Only the guards checking tickets and passports, had disturbed them. Dr Viktor seemed a little better and was able to walk unaided to the station taxi rank when they arrived back in Hamburg. They went immediately to his home in the suburbs.

The Viktor residence lay in a leafy street in the north of the city, only a short tram ride to the clinic. The three-storey townhouse sat midway in an elegant early-nineteenth-century block and gave off an air of comfortable affluence. As soon as the taxi came to a halt, Katja alighted, leaving the doctor inside. She tugged on the bell rope. A moment later a maid appeared at the door.

'Is Frau Viktor in, please?' Katja asked. 'I need to speak with her urgently.' Standing to one side, she pointed to the car and added: 'Dr Viktor is in the taxi.'

The maid, a gangling teenage girl, looked terrified as she scuttled off to find her mistress. From somewhere inside, Katja could hear a harsh voice raised in anger, followed by a heavy footfall. A moment later a large woman, with her hair coiled over her ears and a frown on her face appeared.

'What has happened?' Gerda Viktor barked. 'Where is my husband and who are you?' Her heavily lidded eyes ran over Katja, sizing her up as if she were about to consume her.

'He is in the taxi,' Katja explained, pointing to the car. 'But there was an accident, and he is hurt.'

'Accident? Hurt?' repeated his wife, looking scandalised rather than worried about her husband. Barging passed Katja, she hurtled towards the cab and flung open the back door. Katja heard a groan.

'What have you done to him?' screeched Frau Viktor, turning back to Katja.

Katja tried to remain calm. 'He is injured. We need to call a doctor.'

A cross between a wail and cough was uttered, as Frau Viktor ordered the cab driver to help his passenger into the house. Bending low, the man managed to scoop the doctor from his seat and bring him inside, to deposit him on a small chair in the hallway.

Frau Viktor flapped around her husband like an anxious hen. 'What is the meaning of this, Viktor?' she clucked.

Ignoring her husband's cry of pain, she wrenched off his hat without the slightest care for his wound. At the sight of the blood-soaked dressing, her hands flew up to her flaccid face in shock.

'He needs a doctor,' Katja reiterated. But her advice was greeted with even more outrage.

'How dare you tell me what to do in my own house! I don't even know who you are!'

'I am Dr Viktor's assistant,' said Katja, hoping her explanation might calm the situation. It did the opposite.

'His assistant? Assistant? I know all about my husband's assistants!' she growled. 'The last one . . .' But before she could finish her sentence, her husband intervened.

'Munch,' he grunted, his head now in his hands. 'Call Munch,' he told his wife. There had been mention of a Dr Munch on the return train journey; an old friend from medical school, Katja learned. He would be discreet.

The order seemed to ground Frau Viktor in the moment. She jutted out her several chins and called the maid, who was standing nervously in the shadows. 'Ute! Telephone Dr Munch. Tell him to come immediately.'

Ute reached for the telephone handset on the hall table, while Frau Viktor turned to Katja, her face livid with rage.

'Now get out of my house!' she cried, flinging out her arm towards the still open door. 'Get out and never come back!'

Gerda Viktor's reaction shocked Katja. Nevertheless, picking up her cases, she obeyed, but not before she had called over to the injured doctor.

'I wish you a speedy recovery, Dr Viktor,' she said.

'Out!' screamed his wife, even louder.

A moment later, Katja heard the door slam behind her. She flinched at the sound then started to walk. With Frau Viktor's ravings still buffeting her ears, she'd been so disturbed by what she'd just witnessed it wasn't until she reached the end of the avenue that she discovered her last five Reichsmark note had gone to the taxi driver. Dropping her cases down on the pavement, she sighed heavily. After such a traumatic return, she would have to make her way back to her apartment by tram. Mutti would have to wait just a few more minutes to be reunited.

Chapter 27

Hamburg

Two clicks right, two clicks left. To her great relief, Katja found the Matterhorn painting seemingly untouched on the office wall on her return to the clinic on Monday morning. The lock on the safe gave a satisfying click on the fourth turn and a sigh escaped Katja's lips. While the typed chapters remained in France awaiting scrutiny by Daniel's editor, Dr Viktor's original notebook had been placed like the Holy Grail in a reliquary. It lay undisturbed as far as she could tell.

She was just shutting the safe door when suddenly she heard footsteps. Someone had entered the outer office. Straightening the painting over the safe as quickly as she could, she heard the door handle click, above the racing of her pulse, and open wide. Dr Ulbricht entered.

'Fräulein Heinz.' As usual the greeting was formal, without the trace of a smile. 'I heard about Dr Viktor.' Frau Viktor had obviously called ahead and told Dr Ulbricht about her husband's injury.

'Yes. A terrible ordeal,' Katja replied. 'Have you any news of him, sir?'

She was standing nervously by the doctor's desk, still trying to steady her quickened breath. She'd managed to look busy, rearranging pens and pencils, but she feared she didn't seem very convincing.

'I spoke with him last night. He has received medical attention and will need rest for another two or three days at least.' He was staring at her oddly, making her feel even more uncomfortable. 'Is there something you want to tell me?' he asked. He sounded like a priest about to hear confession, as he shut the door behind him.

Katja cleared her throat, already choked by nerves. 'I expect Dr Viktor told you what happened,' she said, knowing that any discrepancy in stories could prove dangerous.

Ulbricht nodded. 'He did, but I want to hear it from you too, fräulein.'

She shrugged nervously. 'A thief attacked him in the street. That's all I know.' It was the line she'd previously agreed with Viktor.

'Ah, yes, the thief,' Ulbricht repeated, pushing his spectacles back up the bridge of his nose.

Was that scepticism in his voice? thought Katja. 'He hit him from behind and stole his briefcase.'

'But when this thief found nothing of value in it, he tossed the case away,' added Ulbricht helpfully.

'Yes,' agreed Katja, nerves now dancing inside her stomach.

Ulbricht took three steps towards her, and she took three back. *He didn't believe her.*

'Are you telling the truth, Fräulein Heinz?'

Katja shot back with an indignant frown and looked into his eyes that now appeared even bigger and more penetrating through thick lenses.

'Why wouldn't I, sir? Besides, you heard it from Dr Viktor himself, didn't you?'

He nodded. 'I did,' he replied. 'But I also heard a different version from his wife.'

Two more steps towards her.

Two more steps back.

'His wife? I don't understand.' Ulbricht's questioning had just taken an even more sinister turn. *Why would Dr Viktor's wife not believe her husband's version of events?*

He tilted his head. 'But I think you do, Fräulein Heinz. You see, I think you are covering up for the doctor.' He was so close now that she could smell garlic on his breath.

She shook her head. 'I've no idea what . . .'

Ulbricht's finger suddenly drew level with her face and jabbed in the air. 'Frau Viktor believes it was you who attacked her husband.'

By now, Katja was almost against the wall, trapped by the doctor's advance. 'What? But that's absurd!'

Then she remembered. Leisel. Clearly, her predecessor had been disturbed enough to take her own life and there were those who blamed Dr Viktor for her actions. Frau Viktor would have probably discovered all about the unfortunate incident and convinced herself Katja was following in the desperate young woman's footsteps.

'She says you hit him because he resisted your advances!' Ulbricht remained directly in front of her, his magnified eyes boring into her brain.

The thought horrified Katja. 'No! No! That's not true. How could she think I would do such a thing?' She shook her head so vigorously that Ulbricht stepped back. Then he folded his arms, as if studying her.

'Why are you looking at me like that?' she asked.

His lips suddenly curled into a smile. 'I don't think it's true, either,' he told her.

Katja's brows shot up in surprise. 'You don't?'

'No. I don't.' Ulbricht uncrossed his arms and approached once more. 'I don't believe you would do such a thing.'

Katja snorted through her nose at the backhanded compliment.

'I believe you are a young woman of high morals.'

She nodded but was still uncertain as to where all this was leading.

Ulbricht narrowed his eyes and continued. 'That is why I think Viktor is the one to blame.'

'Blame? If anyone is to blame, it's the brute who attacked him in the street.'

Ulbricht shook his head. 'A flimsy story,' he said. 'No. Viktor tried to seduce you in Paris and when you refused him, he forced himself on you.' A nod. 'You had to protect your honour.'

Again, Katja's brows shot up. This time in disbelief. 'What? How can you say something so vile? Dr Viktor would never do such a thing. He is a gentleman. He has never behaved improperly towards me.'

Ulbricht barked out a laugh then; a sneering, horrid sound that made Katja's flesh crawl. 'That is where you are wrong, Fräulein Heinz. You are not the first, but if I have my way you will be the last.'

'What do you mean?' Shock was turning to fear.

'Dr Viktor's behaviour has been causing the university authorities concern for several months. It's time he was held to account and this latest incident, well . . .' He clasped his hands in front of him. 'It does not reflect well on his conduct.'

'But he was attacked, I tell you! By a thief in Paris. Why won't you believe me?' She felt like an animal caught in a trap.

Ulbricht shot her a sly look and leaned forward to tell her in a low, steady voice: 'The truth will out, Fräulein Heinz. With or without your cooperation. And in the meantime, you will say nothing of the affair. Nothing. You understand? Not if you wish to work in Hamburg ever again.'

*

Katja sat frozen at her desk, unable to move for fear of arousing suspicion; for fear someone might burst into her office at any moment with more unfounded accusations. She dared not even continue typing out the notebook. During an earlier trip into the kitchen to make a coffee, her presence had been met with silence by the nurses, although as she left the room excitable voices could be heard in her wake. In Dr Viktor's absence, she felt isolated and vulnerable, but not as isolated or vulnerable as him, apparently. She so desperately wanted to warn him that, as he suspected, the knives were out; that Ulbricht planned to bring him down as quickly as possible. But with his harridan wife, there was no way she could communicate with him.

There was no one else in the world Katja felt she could turn to; no one else apart from a certain Irish journalist in Paris who helped her see a way through the tunnel of her father's death to the light beyond. Searching through her purse she pulled out his business card. *Daniel Keenan, Chief Correspondent,* The Parisian, *Rue du Prévôt, Paris. Tele. 1 3672800.* She picked up the receiver of the telephone but paused, then set it down again. Her heart thumped wildly in her breast. Any communication she made would have to go through Fräulein Schauble on reception. What excuse could she possibly invent to make a long-distance call to an American magazine in Paris? No matter how much she longed to hear Daniel's voice; no matter how much she craved his wise counsel, she knew, that for now at least, she was very much on her own.

Chapter 28

Paris

When Chuck Patterson finally returned to the editor's desk at *The Parisian*, Daniel Keenan was ready for him. Holding the folder containing the typescript under his right arm, he followed his editor into the large glass booth.

'Good to have you back, Chuck,' he told his boss, watching the American take off his jacket to reveal a loud pinstripe shirt and red braces.

'Good to be back, Danny Boy,' he replied, patting down his pocket for cigarettes. 'Editing a magazine is a darn sight easier than playing *dollies* with a four-year-old girl! And I wasn't even allowed to smoke near her.' He threw the packet of specially imported Marlboro's onto the desk.

'And your wife's foot?' asked Daniel, making sure the door was shut behind him. All the other staffers could see inside the office, but, unless they were expert lip readers, they couldn't hear.

Patterson sat down at his desk and pushed back his shirt sleeves. 'Let's say she can get her shoe on now.'

'So, her toe's on the mend.' Daniel felt the need to make small talk; get his boss relaxed before he dropped the bombshell on his desk.

'Yeah.' The editor tilted his head to one side and scratched his neck. 'Which is more than can be said for our love life. It's not like you need to put weight on your foot to have sex, right?'

Daniel humoured him with a manly chuckle and sat down without being invited.

'So, what you got?' asked Patterson eagerly, rubbing his palms together, clearly raring to go. 'Shoot, I can tell it's something big, by the look in your eyes. A society wedding? A whiff of scandal?' He dipped his head in a mock soccer dive. 'Give me all you got.'

Daniel placed the folder onto the desk. 'It's big all right. Ten tons of dynamite,' he replied.

Patterson eyed him sceptically. 'Wow! After that intro, this better be good,' he said, pulling the file towards him and opening it at the first page. A moment later, he scowled at his chief correspondent. 'What the hell is this?'

Daniel leaned over the desk and spoke softly. 'It's what could rid the world of Adolf Hitler. Obviously, the document is incomplete, but . . .'

Patterson met his serious gaze, then leaned back, laughing. He slapped his belly. 'This has got to be a hoax. Someone's made this up. You've been had, Danny Boy!'

Daniel hadn't expected such a reaction. He shook his head. 'This is deadly serious.'

Patterson sat upright, reached for his cigarette packet, and took one out. Tapping the tip on the desk, he put it between his lips. Daniel could have killed for a Marlboro right then.

'Where did you get it?' asked Patterson, clicking a desk lighter and holding the cigarette to the flame, he lit it.

'A source,' said Daniel, breathing in the smoke as it wafted his way.

'Come on. You can do better than that.'

'I need to protect him.' Daniel bit his lip. He supposed his editor ought to be aware of the dangerous situation. 'He was attacked. Someone tried to steal it.'

Patterson threw his head back and snorted. 'Oh great! That's all we need. German spies sniffing around us!' He lurched across the desk. 'Which part of society magazine, do you not understand, Danny Boy?' he asked, putting the emphasis on *society*.

Daniel didn't try to hide his exasperation. 'This *society magazine*,' he mocked, 'is losing money, sir. Just think about it. If we were to publish something like this, then everyone would want to read it; not just bored rich housewives and golfing expats. You could publish it in monthly instalments. The circulation would go through the roof. Then, of course, there'd be world rights.'

Patterson narrowed his eyes. 'You taking a slice of this? A commission?'

Daniel shook his head. 'My source doesn't want money. He's putting his life on the line because he believes in democracy. He's got proof that Hitler is a madman, who'll stop at nothing until he's dominated Europe, if not the world, and if he's not stopped, there's a good chance your little Jeanie will be speaking Deutsche by the time she's in high school.' He slapped his hand on the desk in frustration, and a couple of other reporters outside looked in to see what was going on.

'Rant over?' asked Patterson, taking a drag of his cigarette and putting his feet up on the desk, one after the other.

The move irritated Daniel, as if Patterson was signalling he wasn't taking him seriously. 'Yes,' he snapped.

'Good, then leave it with me. I'll read it over and tell you if I want to see the rest.' He dragged long and hard on his Marlboro.

'But you'll keep it secure in the safe?' Daniel sought assurance.

'Sure will,' replied Patterson. He tapped the cover of the folder. 'This bombshell won't be exploding anytime soon.'

Daniel rose. 'Thanks, chief,' he said. 'I appreciate it.'

The editor nodded, but just as Daniel was about to open the door he called: 'Oh, and Danny Boy.'

'Yes?'

'Tell Peggy to bring me a coffee to have with my bourbon. I certainly need one after that!'

Daniel swallowed down his rising bile. He didn't reply.

As he left the glass booth and entered the main office, all eyes were trained on him.

'Wow. That looked like some meeting!' remarked Joe, a cynical sub-editor.

Daniel shrugged off his anger. 'I guess you could say that.'

He thought of Katja and of how she'd wept when she re-lived the night her father was burned in a Nazi bonfire. If he was truthful, he was doing this as much for her as for *democracy*. After what she'd been through – and was still going through – she needed to believe there was some good left in the world and, in reality, so did he.

Chapter 29

Hamburg

The clock was ticking. Katja knew the longer it took her to type up the remainder of Dr Viktor's notebook, the greater the danger to everyone involved. Not only had Hitler's spies tracked them down in Paris, but after yesterday's revelation, it was clear Dr Ulbricht had a big axe to grind and wouldn't hesitate to plant it in the back of Dr Viktor's already injured skull. Before the attack, she'd been given another few weeks to finish the project. Now, however, it seemed imperative to complete it in days. Overnight, she made the decision to continue as fast as possible.

As soon as she arrived for work at the clinic the following day, Katja went to the safe and took out the notebook, quickly slipping it inside an innocuous-looking accounts ledger. Seated at her desk, she forced herself to focus on the pages, even though her thoughts tugged and pulled in every direction. Dr Viktor's writing had become slightly easier to decipher, but the script was full of numbers and strange, scientific symbols which slowed up her progress.

Nevertheless, she'd managed to type out three more pages

before she smelled carbolic soap in the air. Waspish Nurse Wilhelm buzzed into the office without knocking and eyed Katja suspiciously. 'These patient records must be typed up as soon as possible. Dr Ulbricht said you needed to be kept occupied while Dr Viktor was away.'

Katja stifled the urge to swat her away by telling her to go to hell with her patient notes, but she did not.

'Of course, nurse,' she replied, biting back her irritation. 'Right away.'

It was a ruse, she knew that. Dr Ulbricht had clearly instructed Wilhelm to keep a watchful eye on Katja and make sure she was fully occupied with clinic business. She imagined the sour-faced woman reporting her findings to the doctor, taking great pleasure in pointing out any mistakes in the typing or ink smudges.

As for Dr Viktor's project, it had already occurred to Katja that the notebook and the completed typing may not really be 'safe' at all. She could take everything back to her apartment. She would need to keep the papers somewhere less obvious, somewhere they wouldn't be destroyed, and she knew exactly where. Before her father's death, the Gestapo had come looking for banned books. They'd searched the apartment and confiscated a few of his academic texts, but they hadn't found her precious novels. Jules Verne and HG Wells were kept safe from their evil hands under the floorboards. The transcript of Hitler's medical records could join them.

*

That evening, she folded the typed pages of notes in half and slipped them into her handbag. Surely no one, not even Dr Ulbricht, would dream of intruding into her personal possessions. Staring straight ahead, she strode confidently past Fräulein Schauble on the front desk. She bid her 'goodnight' as normal and walked out of the clinic.

At six o'clock, Katja took her usual tram back to her home district and walked the two minutes from the stop back to her apartment. It was still light, and the swastikas fluttered in a slight breeze blowing across the Elbe. The café on the corner had closed for the day, and the boy selling the latest edition of the newspaper was down to his final few copies. As she approached her apartment, she looked up to see the pigeons lined up on the balcony as usual.

Turning into the hallway of her block, she checked the post, as she always did. Today, among the bills, was an envelope, written in a masculine hand. As soon as she saw the French postmark, her heart missed a beat. It was from Daniel. It had to be. She desperately wanted to open it, but knew she had to check on her mother first.

Deep in thought, she climbed the stairs. She would hide the typed pages of the notebook under the floorboards. And now, alongside the incriminating typescript, she had this precious letter. At the top of the landing, she fumbled with the key in the lock only to find the apartment door was already open. Alarm bells rang as she hurried inside. What if the Gestapo had beaten her to it?

'Mutti! Mutti!' She rushed along the corridor.

'We're in here,' came a familiar voice.

Katja breathed a sigh of relief. 'Frau Cohen. How good to see you,' she said, arranging her features into a broad smile. 'Mutti.' She leaned over and kissed her mother's head as she sat in her usual chair.

Frau Cohen was nursing a coffee and there was a plate of lebkuchen on the table. 'I just dropped in for a chat,' she explained.

Katja stifled a sigh. 'I meant to thank you for looking after Mutti while I was away,' she said, sliding off her coat. 'Have you heard any more from Aaron?'

Frau Cohen shook her head. 'I don't expect to,' she said, then lowering her voice she added, 'But if there is an emergency, I have a contact at the pretzel stand on Müggenkampstrasse.'

191

Katja knew it was hard for Frau Cohen; hard for every Jew. 'That is good to know,' she agreed with a smile. At least her neighbour had someone to turn to if the situation became even worse. And now, thought Katja, thanks to Daniel, so did she.

Leaving Hilde to eat the supper she'd hastily prepared for her, Katja hurried into her bedroom and eagerly tore at the envelope's seal to take out a single typewritten sheet. It was signed *Yours, Daniel*. Hurriedly, she scanned through the rest of his letter, hungry for words of comfort after the last few wretched days when she'd felt so alone.

> *Dear Fräulein Heinz,*
> *(So formal, she thought)*
> *I trust you and Dr Viktor had a safe return to Hamburg and that the doctor is now fully recovered from his head injury.*
> *I have given the script to my editor who will read it over the next few days. As soon as he has made his decision, I will write to you again.*
> *Yours,*
> *Daniel Keenan.*

Katja held the letter to her chest, then re-read it one more time, looking between the lines for a word or phrase that might give her hope. At the railway station, when they'd parted, she'd dared to dream that he felt something more than friendship for her. She'd seen a light behind his eyes. There'd been an invisible thread drawing them together. *Or had she just imagined it?* But if that was the case, there was nothing in his letter that gave away his feelings for her. It was very businesslike. Courteous, but cold. Perhaps Daniel was being guarded because he feared the letter may be intercepted. His tone was, after all, very correct, but for now, his letter was all she had to comfort her. Folding it, she put it in her handbag. If the Gestapo were to get hold of it, Daniel could be implicated and investigated. For all she knew, he was already being trailed in Paris. He'd put his own safety on the line by escorting the doctor and her to the Gare de l'Est. He may well be a marked man too. But then, as she was just about to throw away the envelope, she spied another sheet inside that she hadn't noticed before. This time, when she unfolded it, she found the letter was handwritten on both sides of the paper. As her heart beat faster, she began to read:

Dear Katja (I hope you don't mind if I call you Katja),

I feel I owe you an apology. My behaviour towards you has been reprehensible. I took your kindness and threw it back at you when you first mentioned the death of my wife and child. Even after that, you were gracious enough to tell me of your own tragedy, and I felt honoured that you trusted me enough to share in your own grief. I, on the other hand, have been a useless coward, unable to face the fact that those I loved most are gone. As you know, I am a journalist, and find it so much easier to express my feelings on the page, rather than in words. So, here, in this letter, I am setting out my explanation, my apology and my intention for my own future. If you have no wish to read my words, then please feel free to rip the paper to shreds and dispose of it, but I truly hope you will bear with me and hear me out.

Katja gulped down a breath, barely believing what she was reading. Daniel was pouring his heart out to her on the page. For him the written word was a much easier way of expressing himself. More measured. Less impetuous. Now she understood. She tried to focus on the lines that swam in front of her.

When you told me how you had seen your own father suffer and die, I realised how lucky I was not having to witness the torn and broken bodies of my wife and child when they were pulled from the wreckage of the motor car. For that mercy, I shall be forever grateful.

After listening to your experience and seeing how you reacted, with dignity and courage, I understand the trauma has made you stronger. You have given me hope that I, too, can bear the brunt of my sorrows and channel my anger and my suffering into something positive.

You are honouring your father's memory by fighting against the tyrants responsible for his death. Grace and Bridie were also the victims of an oppressive regime. You've risen from the flames, literally. It is time I did the same. I, therefore, hope you do not think me impertinent if I tell you about my own situation. You have been so kind and generous to me; I feel an explanation is the least you are owed.

I wouldn't expect you to know anything about Ireland, but you may be aware my country was divided in two not so long ago. For centuries, the English tried to take away our culture and our wealth, and then not twenty years ago, the British government decided to cleave our land in two with their border.

Katja thought of the large landmass to the west of mainland Britain in her school atlas. The Emerald Isle, they called it, because the rainfall made the land so green.

There were mainly Protestants in the north and Catholics in the south, and hatred filled all the gaps in between. My wife, Grace, and our daughter, Bridie, lived just south of the border, in the new Republic of Ireland, while the north remained under British rule, but many families decided to leave the country to find decent work and a more hopeful future.

He was a bitter man. Katja could tell he was being eaten up by a resentment so deep it was reaching into the depths of his soul.

I came to Paris for a better life and a good job too, as correspondent for The New York Times. *I'd been in Paris*

194

for two months and had found a suitable apartment for the three of us. Grace planned to join me with little Bridie. She couldn't wait to come over and I couldn't wait to see them again. Only I never did.

She was staying at her mother's house in the north. Bridie was sick. There was no telephone in the house, but Grace called from the nearest town the day before to tell me our daughter was very ill. Then that night, Bridie couldn't breathe. She needed a doctor. The trouble was the nearest one was over the border, in the south. Grace bundled her into the car, wrapped in blankets, and drove to the crossing, but the guards refused to let her pass, even though she pleaded with them. They could see Bridie might die without help.

Katja tensed, fearing what would come next.

So Grace did what any mother would have done. She put her foot on the accelerator and drove through the checkpoint as fast as she could, but they fired their guns at the car.

Katja gasped as she read the brutal truth, cupping her hand over her mouth.

Grace lived to tell the tale in hospital but died two days later from bullet wounds. I never got to say goodbye. Bridie died outright. They were killed in cold blood.

When you shared with me your own pain over your father's death at the hands of the Nazis in Germany, I knew at once you would understand the grief I am going through. I wanted to tell you then and there, in that room, as Dr Viktor lay injured in his bed, but I could not. It was as if my tongue was still hobbled by sorrow, and I have regretted it ever since we parted. I hope this brief account of my personal tragedy will go some way to making amends for my apparent insensitivity towards you. If that is the impression I gave, I beg you to accept my sincere apologies. It is not that I didn't care. It is because your own story resonated with me so deeply that I did not feel it appropriate to show you how much it touched me. We have only just met and yet I feel as though I have known you for a very long time.

If you choose to ignore my apology, I will understand. If, however, I am forgiven for my boorish manners, and you accept my friendship, then I very much look forward to our next meeting, which I hope will come very soon. You are a phoenix, Katja. You have risen from the ashes of your father's death. For that you have my great admiration. I only hope by following your example, I can do the same.

I remain your obedient servant,

Daniel Keenan

As she read the last line, a tear dropped onto the letter, smudging the ink. How could she forgive when he had done nothing wrong? The tragedy he had endured was every bit as devastating as her own. What was it she'd read in *Anna Karenina*? '*There are as many kinds of love as there are hearts.*' Everyone's personal tragedy was different in many ways, but the same in others. Katja felt privileged that Daniel Keenan trusted her enough with his. She'd opened her heart to him and now he had done the same to her. He wanted to join her on the path to healing by holding out his hand. She would take it and together, she prayed, they could turn their personal tragedies into a force for good.

Kneeling by her bed, Katja drew back the rug and, taking a pair of pliers from her bedside drawer, prised up a floorboard, just as she'd done all those years back when the Nazis came looking for banned books. This time, she lowered in the transcribed pages of the notebook, and alongside those, Daniel's letters. They all needed to be kept safe. Their discovery by the Nazis would only lead to one thing.

Chapter 30

At first Katja wasn't certain what she was being asked to look at, or why. She'd been summoned to Dr Ulbricht's office around noon. A week had passed since her return from Paris, yet she'd still heard no word from Dr Viktor.

Ulbricht, in his white coat, was seated, wearing an expression even graver than usual. He hadn't looked up immediately but remained focused on something on his desk, as Katja waited nervously for his instructions. It was only when he told her to sit that she spotted the photographic prints.

Relieved he had spoken at last, Katja obeyed, clasping her hands on her lap to try and stop them shaking. The seconds had ticked by as she waited for the doctor to look at her, until finally, he spoke again. 'You remember our conversation the other day, Fräulein Heinz, regarding how Dr Viktor came to acquire his injury?'

Of course she remembered. How could she forget? She had replayed the incident over and over in her mind until her head pounded.

'Yes, sir.'

Ulbricht nodded. 'And you told me that Dr Viktor had never behaved improperly towards you. I think you said he was *a true gentleman*.'

Katja's stomach flipped. *Where is this going?* He had laid a trap for her and there was nowhere else to run. She was about to walk right into it.

Ulbricht flexed his fingers as he primed the snare. 'So how do you explain these?' he asked.

Photographs. Katja suddenly realised he'd been looking at two large, grainy prints. He slid them around and pushed them over to her side of the desk.

Katja heard the breath leave her chest in a horrified gasp as she stared down at the images. One shot was of Dr Viktor standing outside her hotel room as she spoke to him on the threshold. The other was of her leaving his room, a large, dark stain on the front of her pale dress.

Her head cracked up. 'No. No. This is all wrong. It wasn't . . .'

Snap!

The trap had just been activated and now she was caught in its steel teeth.

'Who took these? How did you get them?' She was half crying, half shouting.

'It doesn't matter who took them,' replied Ulbricht coldly. 'How do you explain them?'

Katja, still shaking her head in disbelief, suddenly felt sullied. Gulping down her outrage, she began falteringly.

'Dr Viktor . . . he . . . he called to see if I was ready for dinner, and here . . .' She pointed to the second image of her alone. '. . . I had just dressed his wound and left him to sleep. That was all.'

Ulbricht blew through his nose, flaring his nostrils. 'Surely you can do better than that, Fräulein Heinz. The chambermaid said your bed was not slept in the last night of your stay.'

'What?' Katja was scandalised. 'Dr Viktor was injured. I was keeping watch at his bedside.' Holding back tears, she told herself she had nothing to be ashamed of. 'It's the truth, Dr Ulbricht,' she protested. She straightened her back. 'And if you don't believe me . . .'

'What, Fräulein Heinz? What will you do? From where I am sitting, it is patently clear what went on between you and Dr Viktor in Paris. He kept making approaches to you for sexual favours and when you refused, he attacked you. You were merely defending yourself against his advances.'

She thought she might explode. 'That's a lie!'

'So, you welcomed his advances, did you, Fräulein?' he sneered.

'No!'

'Ah! So, he did proposition you?'

'No. He did not.'

'Then why did you attack him?'

'I didn't!' Her hands flew up to her mouth, to stop herself from screaming. 'I didn't. I swear.'

Ulbricht made an exaggerated sigh, sounding like a disappointed schoolmaster, whose star pupil had just failed an exam. 'This does not reflect well on either Dr Viktor or you, I fear. There will be consequences.'

Katja's head jerked up. 'What consequences?'

Ulbricht pursed his lips. 'Reputations are at stake. The good name of the clinic.'

'But nothing happened.' Katja groaned, trying to bridle her outrage. She shook her head again and edged forward to lean over the desk. But her exasperation resurfaced in her voice, as if she were trying to explain the situation to a child. 'Dr Viktor went to a conference on psychiatry in Paris, at the Sorbonne. I accompanied him as his assistant. I took notes at some of the lectures.' She jabbed the desk with her finger. 'I can show them to you, if you like. Pages of them. Please, you have to believe me.'

But Ulbricht made it clear he was no longer listening. He simply rose from the desk and coolly walked over to the door. Opening it wide, he told her: 'That will not be necessary. But I want you to think very carefully about your recollection of events. Working in a psychiatric clinic, you of all people must accept, Fräulein Heinz, that the memory sometimes plays tricks. When you have recalled what happened correctly, let me know.' Then glancing across to Nurse Wilhelm, barely able to conceal her delight at what she'd just heard, he instructed her to show Katja out.

Katja managed to control her anger until she reached her office. But once inside, hot tears of fury spilled onto her cheeks. Pacing up and down the small space, she knew she was trapped. She needed to speak to Dr Viktor; needed to warn him that he was in danger from his own colleagues. He'd always known that Ulbricht was after his job, by foul means rather than fair, but up until now it had been one man's word against the other's. Today, however, Ulbricht had produced evidence to back up his allegations. Of course the photographs weren't proof that she and Dr Viktor were having an affair, or that he had done anything unlawful, but the images could be misinterpreted. In themselves, they proved nothing, but someone in authority who was sympathetic to Ulbricht – the university *kurator*, for example – might regard them differently, with jaundiced eyes.

Katja was standing in the middle of the office, hugging herself tight, digging her nails into her arms, trying to stop herself shaking, when the telephone rang. The shrill sound made her jump, but sucking in her distress, she answered it on the fourth ring.

'Dr Viktor's office.'

'Katja.'

A rush of breath escaped from her mouth. 'Dr Viktor. It's so good to hear from you,' she gushed, but then, afraid their call might be monitored, she said: 'But Fräulein Schauble was told . . .' She knew the receptionist had been instructed not to put through any calls from Viktor.

'I disguised my voice,' he told her abruptly. 'I needed to talk to you, and I wasn't going to let that dragon stop me.'

'I'm so glad you called,' she said. 'How are you?'

His reply was subdued. 'I have been better, but I plan to return to work at the end of next week.'

'The end of . . .?' Katja couldn't hide the disappointment in her voice. It was only Friday. Was he really saying it would be another week before he was well enough to return?

'You have the typing to get on with, Katja.'

She did not reply.

'Katja!' he repeated.

'Yes. Yes, I do,' she said. 'It's just that . . .'

'What is it? What's happened?'

'It's Dr Ulbricht. He . . .'

'Yes?'

There was no delicate way of putting it. 'He has photographs.'

'Photographs? What photographs?'

Before Katja could explain, someone was in the room in front of her and a voice sliced through the conversation.

'Fräulein Heinz.' It was Nurse Wilhelm. Had she heard mention of the photographs, Katja wondered? If she knew Dr Viktor was on the other end of the line, news of his call would reach Ulbricht. She thought quickly.

'I'm afraid Dr Viktor is unwell and won't be back until next week, but if you'd like to enquire then . . .'

The doctor would not be put off. 'Katja, for pity's sake. What is going on?'

Katja smelled carbolic soap again. 'Thank you, sir. Good day.' She cut the call, put down the receiver and looked up at Nurse Wilhelm, who had just laid another file in front of her.

'By five o'clock this evening,' came the order.

Katja took a deep breath and prayed Nurse Wilhelm hadn't guessed who was on the other end of the line. Somehow, she had to warn the doctor.

*

Instead of returning to her home after work that evening, Katja took the tram out north, to the suburbs, to Dr Viktor's house. In

201

her handbag she carried a hastily written note, warning the doctor about Ulbricht and the incriminating photographs. *Forewarned is forearmed*, her father used to say. She wasn't sure what action the doctor could take, but at least, if she managed to smuggle a note to him, he wouldn't be caught unawares when he arrived back at the office. At least now there would be time for him to formulate a strategy to save his own skin and, she very much hoped, hers too.

At the townhouse, Katja rang the bell and to her relief the same maid – *Ute, was it?* – answered the door.

'*Ja?*' She greeted Katja with a frown, even though she clearly recognised her.

Katja put her finger up to her lips.

'Ute!' Frau Viktor's voice boomed from further down the hall. 'Who is it?'

Katja opened her bag and handed the maid the folded note, addressed to Dr Viktor.

Ute kept her gaze trained on Katja. 'A hawker, *meine Herrin*,' she replied.

Katja smiled and mouthed a '*Danke!*' before sloping off quickly into the twilight, a quiet sense of achievement powering her steps.

Chapter 31

Paris

Almost everyone at *The Parisian* had gone home for the evening when Chuck Patterson called his chief correspondent into his office. The editor stood by a filing cabinet, a bottle of bourbon in one hand and a full glass in the other.

'Drink, Danny Boy?'

'Sure,' said Daniel, shutting the glass door firmly behind him before he took a seat.

Patterson poured from the bottle then passed over a large glass, before settling back into his chair, cradling the tumbler on his stomach. Staring deep into the amber liquid, he said: 'You were right.'

Daniel rarely heard Patterson concede a point to anyone, let alone him, but he said nothing at first, sensing there was more to come.

'That transcript, well, it's got guts. I'll say that. I certainly wouldn't let this Hitler guy take my dog for a walk, let alone run my country. I'd heard he was too big for his boots, but he sounds like a real psycho.'

Daniel tried not to seem too eager. 'The man's certainly got psychological problems. A screw loose, as my mother used to say.' He shrugged. 'But then, I suppose, so have a lot of politicians.'

Patterson threw back his head, laughing. 'You're right there, but this guy, well he's way up there on the scale of megalomaniacs.' He lifted a hand up towards some imaginary graph.

Daniel watched and waited until his boss finally settled himself and turned to face him squarely. 'So, what's the verdict?'

Patterson took a large gulp of bourbon. 'Shoot. It's a great read but is it true? You're sure the story checks out?'

Daniel nodded. 'Of course.' He was a journalist. A hardened cynic. An old (or maybe not so old) hack. That's what he did. As soon as Katja and Dr Viktor had left for Hamburg, he had visited the Library of Burned Books and found references to the doctor's work in psychiatric textbooks and manuals. Another German psychiatrist at the Sorbonne, a Professor Stoebbel, had verified his credentials. Daniel had concluded that Dr Viktor was legitimate and every word he'd written in his account was, in all likelihood, true. If that was the case, given the situation in Germany, his life was very much on the line, although he didn't mention that part to Patterson. 'It all stacks up.'

'Well then, I'd like to see the rest.'

Daniel took a sip of bourbon to hide his surprise. He was never fully convinced Patterson would say yes. If he was being brutally honest, at the beginning he'd only feigned an interest in Hitler's medical records. All that malarkey he'd come out with about instalments and foreign rights had been made up on the hoof. On impulse. He'd pretended he could help get it published because he'd wanted to see Katja. Up until that meeting in the bookshop, he'd never imagined he'd meet anyone special again. But that first encounter with Katja made him re-think. At the dinner at Dreiberg's, he'd played it cool, but it had only confirmed to him that she was different. Then, of course, there'd been the walk by the Seine. After Grace, he'd told himself he would never give his heart to anyone else. It would be a betrayal of her memory, but those few hours he spent together with Katja seemed to bring him back to life. It may only be eighteen months since his loss, but this beautiful German stranger had blown into his life like a warm spring breeze, and he couldn't stop thinking about her. He'd acted hurt when she'd made mention of Grace and Bridie that day by the Seine to mask his own guilt. It wasn't right that he should feel so happy in another woman's company. But in punishing himself, he'd punished Katja too. Her train had barely left the station before he'd started to miss her. It was ridiculous, he knew, but it was as if he'd been sleepwalking for the last few months and she'd awoken him to his surroundings, to new challenges and to what it meant to be alive. That's why he had written to her; poured out his own tale of tragedy onto the page, so that, if she chose to, she could share in his sorrow and his truth, just as she had allowed him to share hers.

'When can you get it to me?' asked Patterson.

'Sorry?' Daniel had to force himself back into the moment.

'The rest of it, of course.'

'Soon,' he replied, even though he hadn't really bargained for this scenario. 'In the next couple of weeks,' he said, knowing that Katja still needed to type out the final half of the manuscript.

An American calendar on the wall displayed an image of the White House taken from behind a cherry tree in full blossom. Patterson squinted at it. 'How about by the end of the month?'

Ten days. Daniel had no idea if that would give Katja enough time. He nodded.

'Deal,' said Patterson, raising his glass, then draining it. 'It's a good story. Power, madness . . . Any sex?' He glanced at Daniel hopefully as he stood to leave.

'Not that I know of,' he replied with a shrug.

'That's a shame. Sex sells, but, hey, let's see, shall we? But no guarantees right now.'

Daniel mustered a smile and nodded, but inside he was afraid that he just might have made a commitment that Katja and Dr Viktor couldn't keep. But more than that, he'd just taken them a step further into the minefield of publication. He'd fallen in love with Katja, even though he wasn't going to profess it yet. But Patterson's initial enthusiasm meant her life was in even more danger. Once the story of Adolf Hitler's psychosomatic illness and self-delusional behaviour was out, he feared even more for her safety.

Chapter 32

Hamburg

Someone was in Dr Viktor's office. His door was ajar. A knot tightened in Katja's chest as soon as she entered the anteroom and heard footsteps inside. She'd arrived early at the clinic, even before Fräulein Schauble, and planned to do an hour's transcription before Nurse Wilhelm piled more patient records onto her desk. Now, however, she knew she needed to rescue the original notebook from the safe before it was too late.

Edging forward as quietly as she could, she put her ear to the door. A drawer opened, then shut. Another sound then. A creak. *Not the Matterhorn painting. No!* Had someone discovered the secret that lay behind it? She peered through a small crack in the door and to her horror saw the safe was wide open. Flattening her body against the wall, she closed her eyes, the options flashing through her mind. She had to confront the intruder.

Grabbing a paper knife from her desk, she lunged through the door. A man, his back to her, was opening the safe. She had to stop him. Hearing her enter, the intruder turned.

'Dr Viktor!' she cried.

'Katja!' His eyes widened in alarm when he saw the knife in her hand, poised to strike.

'Oh, Dr Viktor!' She looked at the blade with equal horror, and dropped it on the desk, as she rushed forward. 'What are you doing here? I thought you'd been told to rest.'

Viktor palmed his chest and closed his eyes for a moment to recover from the shock. 'I have,' he conceded after a moment. 'My head still has an oompah band playing inside it. But your message . . .'

Katja nodded, then hurried over to shut the door.

'Ulbricht is out to get us.'

The doctor frowned. 'Us?' he repeated. 'But he can't know about the notes.' The safe door was open, and he brought out the notebook as he spoke and walked over to his desk.

Katja shook her head. 'I don't believe he does, but the photographs . . .' She felt a sudden wave of embarrassment wash over her, even though she'd done nothing wrong.

'Ah, yes.' Understanding spread across the doctor's face like a shadow, as he slumped in his chair. 'They are indeed compromising,' he said, nodding in thought. A moment later he snapped his fingers. 'The chambermaid!'

'The maid? I don't . . .' Katja was confused.

'The one with the laundry basket in the corridor. I thought it odd at the time. I wondered what she was doing there in the late afternoon, when beds are usually changed in the morning. Ulbricht must have paid her to take the shots.'

Katja paused for a moment. It would be the same maid who reported her bed wasn't slept in on the last night of the stay. 'However it was done, there are photographs that make it look like we are having an affair. Ulbricht has made up this story about you and me, and . . .'

Viktor jerked up his head. 'Story? What story?'

Katja now sat opposite him. Her voice was low and measured and her eyes were fixed on the desk in front of her. 'He says he thinks you tried to seduce me and when I refused, you wouldn't take no for an answer.'

'What?' Viktor's brows shot up.

'So, I hit you in self-defence.' Her own words shocked her as they left her mouth, but Viktor seemed oddly prepared for them.

A smile flickered on his lips. 'Of course,' he said with a nod, then with a faraway look in his eyes, as if he was slowly piecing together some imaginary jigsaw. 'An interesting plot,' he said, after a long pause. 'Naturally, I knew he wanted to be director of this clinic, but to go this far . . .' He shook his head. 'The man's determined to ruin me. So that makes it all the more important that we step up our efforts.' The doctor leaned forward confidentially. 'I had a call from Mr Keenan last night at my home.'

At the mention of Daniel's name, a pang of longing stabbed her as she remembered his letter. His private letter.

'What did he say?'

'He told me his editor wants to see the rest of the transcript, and could we get it to him by the end of the month?'

Katja's eyebrows suddenly shot up. 'But that's . . . that's less than two weeks away.'

Viktor nodded. 'It's a tall order, I know. How much more do you have to type?'

Katja thought for a moment. She'd managed another thirty pages since she'd returned from Paris, but she had at least another hundred to complete. 'I'm not sure . . . I . . . Nurse Wilhelm has been giving me extra work since you've been away and . . .'

Dr Viktor shook his head and waved a hand. 'I will deal with Nurse Wilhelm. You are my assistant, not hers. From now on you will type up my notes. That will be your sole job. You understand?'

'Yes, doctor.'

'I am back now, and you will concentrate all your efforts on finishing as soon as you can.'

'Yes, sir.' Thinking the doctor had said his piece, Katja rose from her seat. But there was more.

'We can do this, Katja. You just need to crack on,' he told her, as if he'd just asked her to make him a coffee or run to the shops for more tobacco. He tilted his head to gauge her mood. 'You do not have second thoughts? You still believe we are doing the right thing?'

Katja flashed him a wounded look. Of course, she still believed. How could he question her commitment to the cause, especially after witnessing how her own parents suffered and how Mutti still did? 'Yes. Yes, I do,' she replied, bridling the hurt she felt at being doubted.

'Good,' said Viktor with a nod and pointing to a pile of pristine copy paper in front of him. 'Then perhaps you'd like to continue.'

Katja stood and scooped up the notebook from the desk. Come hell or high water she would type out the words that would condemn Adolf Hitler in the eyes of the world. At the end of the line, waiting for her precious delivery, would be Daniel. She wondered if he was as anxious to see her, as she was to be with him.

*

For the next five days, Katja typed frantically, stopping only now and again to rub her tired wrists, or pull back her stiff, rounded shoulders. With Dr Viktor back in his office, there was less chance of being interrupted by Nurse Wilhelm. But all the while she was expecting Dr Ulbricht to ask to see Dr Viktor to confront him about the photographs. She'd been ordered to say nothing about them to Viktor on pain of dismissal. But Ulbricht had remained silent, clearly biding his time. But for what reason? *When did this viper propose to strike?* she wondered.

Apart from his first day back at work, there had been little cause for the two men to meet. Now and again, they would pass each other in the doctors' rest room and nod to each other, but that was all. Katja knew this was the calm before the storm, but what was Ulbricht waiting for?

The answer came when she was walking along the corridor and was forced to stand aside to allow Fräulein Schauble to pass. The receptionist had left the door to Dr Ulbricht's office slightly open, and Katja could hear him speaking in an agitated way on the telephone. Making sure no one was around, she moved closer and purposely dropped one of the sheets of paper she was carrying to cover her tracks should she be caught eavesdropping.

'But we have the evidence. I don't understand why . . .'

Was he talking about the photographs, she wondered? And who was on the other end of the line?

'I can find witnesses too. Everyone has their price.'

Witnesses? thought Katja. Witnesses to what? But then it dawned on her. Was Ulbricht implying he could pay people to tell lies? To bear *false witness*? It certainly sounded that way, and a growing unease flooded her body.

'Very well. I shall wait until then, but I'm sure you appreciate, sir, the sooner we convene, the sooner I can act.'

Footsteps then, coming along the corridor. Katja picked up the sheet of dropped paper and straightened herself. Nurse Wilhelm was approaching.

'So clumsy,' she mumbled disdainfully as she passed.

Katja returned to her office. What had she just heard? As soon as Dr Viktor returned from his lecture later that morning, she told him everything she could remember. To her surprise, the doctor didn't seem at all shocked by what she said and the conclusion she had drawn. He'd carried on packing the bowl of his pipe with tobacco without even looking at her.

'I know there are plans to set up some kind of enquiry into my alleged behaviour. They will try and nail all sorts of misdemeanours on my door.'

Katja suddenly thought of what he had told her about his previous assistant and how she had taken her own life.

'You mean Liesel?' she asked. She'd said the name he'd forbidden her to say and waited for his reaction.

The doctor's shoulders sagged submissively, and he nodded. 'Liesel.'

Resting his pipe in an ashtray, Viktor fixed Katja with a contrite look. 'My wife has always been the jealous sort. Our marriage was a mistake from the start. If I even smiled at another woman, she would accuse me of infidelity, and rumours spread quickly.'

'So everyone here, at the clinic, assumed you were having an affair with Leisel?'

He nodded. 'With hindsight, the more I think about it, the more convinced I am that Ulbricht put her up to it. So, when she took her own life, everyone blamed me.'

Katja held his look for a moment, assuring herself that he was speaking from his heart. Their working relationship was never a straightforward one. The lines had been blurred from the start. But she'd always regarded Viktor as more of a father than a philanderer. Charming, yes, but not an adulterer.

'I believe you,' she said.

'Good,' he replied. 'Because we both need to trust each other.' He picked up his pipe once more and, striking a match, lit the tobacco.

Katja rose to go.

'Just one more thing,' said Viktor.

'Yes?'

'Mr Keenan's editor needs the rest of the script by the beginning of next week. Something about altered deadlines.'

She felt her chest constrict with the mounting pressure. Dr Viktor noted her anxious expression.

'That's good news, Katja. It means he's seriously thinking about publishing it. He has arranged for me to meet with the editor next Monday.'

'Next Monday? But that doesn't leave me—' interrupted Katja.

'I have every confidence you will finish the task and I truly appreciate what you are doing,' said Dr Viktor with a disarming smile. 'Now go and get some fresh air and some food. To keep your strength up, eh? Then you will come back refreshed.'

Katja nodded. Once again, he was asking her to work harder, and once again, she agreed. She had no choice. Of course she would continue to work all the hours God sent to complete the transcription, but right now, she felt she had to take advantage of the doctor's offer.

'Thank you, Doctor,' she said, just as the telephone rang in her office. Dr Viktor nodded, and she walked through to answer it. It was Fräulein Schauble.

'I have Frau Flebert here to see Dr Viktor,' she boomed down the line.

Katja balked at the name. Kommodore Flebert's wife. The woman Dr Viktor had treated; whose husband was close to Hitler and wanted to seduce her. Glancing at her open diary on the desk, Katja's voice remained calm, even though inside she was churning. 'Frau Flebert? There is no appointment.'

'She says it is very urgent that she sees Dr Viktor now,' came the reply.

Viktor, hovering on the threshold, overheard. He frowned, also wondering what might be so urgent, then nodded.

'I will see her,' he told Katja, returning to his desk. 'But you must still go to lunch now, Fräulein Heinz. I can manage here.'

In a moment Fräulein Schauble appeared, standing beside a well-groomed woman in her forties, dressed in a peach brocade jacket and matching hat.

'Frau Flebert to see Dr Viktor,' she announced.

Through the thin veil that covered her eyes, Katja could see the kommodore's wife was wearing heavy make-up but her glossy lips were turned down at the corners. She dismissed Katja with an icy look and ploughed straight through to Dr Viktor's office. The doctor rose as she entered and, walking to the door, addressed her like an old friend.

'My dear Frau Flebert. How wonderful to see you again. What brings you here?' he asked, before shutting the door firmly behind her.

Katja went to lunch, even though she was no longer hungry at all. A visit from the kommodore's wife had left a strange sense of foreboding in the pit of her stomach.

*

Frau Flebert did not reciprocate Dr Viktor's enthusiastic greeting. In fact, she barely acknowledged him, as if she was in his presence under sufferance. Instead, she sat down before being invited, crossed her long, elegant legs, and looked everywhere except at the doctor himself. Ignoring his question, she pulled off her silky gloves.

'May I offer you a schnapps, Frau Flebert?' asked Viktor, watching her staccato movements. Did he detect a shaking of the hands? He couldn't be sure.

'That would be most welcome,' she replied, in her low, husky voice. She reached for her bag, took out a cigarette holder and proceeded to fit a Sobranie into it.

At his drinks cabinet, the doctor poured out two schnapps into small glasses and set one down by his patient. Seeing her searching for something in her bag – he presumed a lighter – he held out his own to her cigarette.

'Thank you,' she said, her breath juddering as she inhaled deeply. There was an uncomfortable pause as she considered the glass of schnapps in front of her, then reached for it, downing it in one.

Viktor sat at his desk and studied her a moment longer before he said: 'Forgive me for saying so, Frau Flebert, but I sense that something is troubling you.' The doctor leaned back in his seat. 'Given our previous sessions together, I hope you can trust me enough to be frank with me.'

She slid him a furtive glance, before her gaze returned to the

214

floor. Her reply was not immediately forthcoming, but she lifted her head. Dr Viktor followed her eyes to the clock on the wall.

'That girl,' she said suddenly.

'Girl?' Viktor thought for a moment, recalling she must have passed Katja on her way in. 'Oh, you mean my assistant? Fräulein Heinz.'

'She will be away long?'

Viktor pursed his lips, then smiled broadly. 'I shouldn't think so. I told her to take a break, but she is very conscientious.'

Frau Flebert's lips twitched. 'And are you, Doctor?'

'Conscientious?' He frowned. *Why was this woman playing games with him?* 'I like to think so,' he replied. 'I pride myself on my commitment to my patients, if that is what you mean, Frau Flebert.'

'I know you can be very thorough in your examinations too.' She was inspecting her manicured nails as she spoke, puzzling the doctor even more by her behaviour. 'I think I would feel more comfortable lying down,' she said next, eyeing the couch.

Viktor nodded. 'Of course, if that is your wish.'

She rose and slowly took off her hat, placing it on the nearby hat stand. Her hair was dark, almost ebony and the effect against her milky-white skin was quite striking. The doctor's professional mask slipped momentarily as his eyes betrayed an attraction, but he recovered quickly and clearing his throat said: 'Please.' He was motioning to the leather-covered couch.

Slipping off her shoes, Frau Flebert sat on it before lifting her legs to lie down.

'You are comfortable?' Viktor asked, standing over her. Once again, he followed her gaze to the wall clock, but when he looked back at her, he noticed she had reached for her blouse.

'I will be in a moment,' she replied, slowly undoing the buttons.

As soon as he grasped what she was doing, Dr Viktor's brows shot up. Frau Flebert had just revealed her silk camisole and a large expanse of pale flesh above her breasts.

'I'm not sure that is nec . . .' he began, but before he could stop her, she reached up, grabbed him by the lapels of his jacket and pulled him towards her. 'What are you . . .? Please? This is most irregular!' protested the doctor as she took his hand and held it to her left breast.

She looked at him in the eye then, for the first time, her hand still cupped over his. 'I am so sorry. He made me do this,' she whispered.

'What? Who?' The doctor was still trying to pull away from his patient when Fräulein Schauble, sent by Dr Ulbricht to deliver some papers, arrived at the doorway to see Viktor in a compromising pose.

A high-pitched shriek signalled her alarm, and Frau Flebert scrambled quickly from the couch.

'You filthy beast!' she cried, promptly slapping the doctor across the cheek, in full view of the scandalised receptionist. 'No! Leave me alone.'

Dumbstruck, Dr Viktor rubbed his jaw and could only watch in bewilderment as his patient fumbled with her buttons, and Fräulein Schauble shot him a furious scowl.

A moment later, who should also appear but Dr Ulbricht, blocking the nurse's exit from the office.

'What is going on here?' he exclaimed, his face the very model of righteous indignation.

Frau Flebert, by now hurriedly replacing her hat, was clearly in great distress. Tears were streaming in rivulets of black mascara down her face.

'You know very well,' she mumbled to Ulbricht as she brushed past him on her way out of the door. 'I hope you both rot in hell.'

Chapter 33

'They're suspending me pending a disciplinary hearing,' said Dr Viktor, as he sat stony-faced at his desk, later that day.

Katja sat opposite him. She knew something had happened while she went out for a break, because when she returned, after less than half an hour, it seemed all hell had broken loose. Dr Viktor was nowhere to be seen, although she could hear raised voices from Dr Ulbricht's office. She'd caught sight of Frau Flebert leaving the building in tears, and when she'd asked Nurse Wilhelm where everyone was, she'd been told in no uncertain terms to mind her own business. Now she understood why.

The whole unfortunate incident had been reported all the way to the top. The *kurator* of the university had been informed and, after learning of events from Ulbricht, had ordered a disciplinary hearing as soon as possible. Apparently, Dr Viktor was not the only one who had been compiling a dossier. Ulbricht, it seemed, had also been gathering incriminating information about his rival for some months.

Frau Flebert's visit had been a trap and Dr Viktor had walked straight into it. Fräulein Schauble had witnessed what she thought was a sexual assault on the kommodore's wife. Herr Levi, Leisel's angry father, had also given a written statement to Ulbricht, implicating Viktor in his daughter's death, even though it was now almost certain the girl was also in on the plot to discredit the doctor. The case against him was serious. It was also cut and dried. And today Ernst Viktor wore the weary expression of a man already defeated. It seemed to Katja he was almost accepting his fate.

'Have they said when the hearing will be?' she asked.

'Shortly,' he replied. 'But no. They haven't given me a date.'

'And until they do?'

'I am to leave the premises by this evening.'

'It's so unfair,' said Katja wanly. But then life wasn't fair. She'd learned that at a young age, after her father's death.

'Fairness doesn't come into this. This is politics,' remarked the doctor with a wry smile. 'And it's brutal.'

'And me?' asked Katja. 'What am I to do?'

His shoulders rose and fell as he exhaled. 'As you know, you will probably be called as a witness against me.'

Her head span as she pictured the photographs. Ulbricht would put pressure on her to lie; to say Viktor had tried to assault her, just as he had allegedly assaulted Kommodore Flebert's wife. She would be forced into an impossible position. But first she had something she needed to show the doctor and lifted a brown paper parcel onto the desk.

'It's in here,' she said.

The doctor was silent for a moment, then said: 'You've finished it?'

'Yes.' She kept her voice low. She'd worked late last night to complete it.

'May I?' He lifted his hands.

Katja nodded and watched nervously as Dr Viktor opened the brown paper to reveal a smart buff-coloured folder. The finished transcript sat in all its terrifying glory with the front cover proclaiming in bold capitals: *Notes & Observations on the Serious Mental Disorders of Adolf Hitler.*

Katja had typed the last sentence that afternoon, having smuggled the rest of the document into the clinic earlier, before the incident with Frau Flebert. But what would happen now? Surely all their hard work wouldn't go to waste. All the risks they'd both taken had to pay off somehow.

Two pairs of eyes focused on the folder sitting between them as if it were some religious relic. Silently, they contemplated its power. If kept in the right hands, Katja knew it could work a miracle and bring down an evil tyrant. But if it fell into the wrong hands . . .

'You must take it to Paris,' said Viktor suddenly, his words splicing through the air like an arrow.

'What?' Katja was alarmed. 'Me?'

The doctor huffed. 'It's obvious I cannot go again. I will be trailed. I doubt if I'd be able to leave the country. You, on the other hand . . .'

Katja shook her head. 'You want me to take the transcript to Paris. Alone?'

Dr Viktor flagged up a hand and fixed her with a look that was halfway between stern and apologetic. 'I hate to have to do this to you, but you know it's the only way.'

Katja lifted her bowed head that was suddenly filled with thoughts of the man in the trilby, of her poor mother and of the sight of Dr Viktor lying bloodied in his bed. But then she thought of Daniel and her breath steadied.

Viktor carried on. 'Mr Keenan said he would make the necessary arrangements with his editor,' he told her, trying to reassure her, even though he sensed her reticence. 'It's more important than ever that the script is published as soon as possible.'

'But what about my mother?' Katja protested, knowing she would be unhappy about being left again so soon.

Viktor shook his head. 'You found someone before.'

Her thoughts turned to Frau Cohen once more. 'Yes. But . . .'

The doctor remained adamant. 'I'm afraid there's no alternative.'

Even though the prospect of seeing Daniel again was a great comfort, she still felt uneasy. 'Won't Dr Ulbricht be suspicious if I don't come to work?' she asked, trying to hold down her rising disquiet, but seeing only problems ahead.

'You will fall ill. One of my last acts as your employer will be to grant you sick leave. You will stay in Paris for two nights, but there must be no communication from you at all while you are away.' He glanced at his telephone. 'You never know who might be listening. Mr Keenan will help you. You understand?'

'Yes, *Herr Doktor*,' she said, even though every sinew of her body screamed no!

Silently, she watched Viktor produce several notes from his wallet and lay them in front of her. 'For your expenses,' he told her.

She took them and rolled them up to fit neatly into her hand.

A sharp stabbing pain shot through Katja's chest at the thought of what lay ahead. As much as she longed to see Daniel again, travelling to Paris with the transcript on her own terrified her, even more than the thought of having to leave her mother alone once more.

'I'm so sorry,' he said, reading the dread on her face. 'It's the only way.'

Katja nodded and picked up the folder from the desk. 'I know,' she replied softly. She now had sole charge of the most explosive transcript in the whole of Germany.

Dr Viktor rose and held out his hand to her. Katja was surprised by the gesture until she understood how uncertain the doctor's future was.

'But we will see each other again soon,' she insisted.

Viktor nodded. 'Of course, but we don't know when that will be and, in the meantime, I want to thank you for all you have done.'

Her eyes stung with the delayed tears she was fighting back. 'I have only done my duty,' she replied, her voice trembling.

Viktor shook his head. 'You have gone beyond and are about to go much further.'

Something in his voice made her frown. Reaching into his

desk drawer, he pulled out his notebook. 'Take it, please,' he said, thrusting it in front of her. 'It is no longer safe here. It would be better kept at your apartment.'

Katja stared at the notebook in horror. It had been risky enough hiding the transcript under her floorboards, but this, the original, was a smoking gun. Thoughts crowded her head, but she forced down the panic swelling in her chest. What she was being asked to do carried with it so many risks, but she knew it was only logical. She reached out to take it.

'Yes. You're right,' she replied, her throat suddenly rock-hard.

Cupping her hand that took the notebook in both of his, Dr Viktor looked her squarely in the eyes. 'Take care, Katja,' he told her. It was the first time he had ever called her Katja.

'I will,' she said softly, trying to stem her tears. 'I will get word to you on my return,' she told him, adding, 'Somehow.'

She'd no idea what the next few days would bring. All she knew was that she would face challenges, some of them extreme, and she would have to face them without Dr Viktor. From now on Daniel would be her rock. All her trust would have to be placed in him. Holding back her tears, she was just about to open the door back into her own office when he called to her.

'And remember, Katja,' he said, with the same generous smile that had first made her warm to him, 'your father would be proud of you.'

*

That evening, Katja broke the news to her mother. As soon as she arrived home, she'd prised up the floorboard in her room, and Dr Viktor's notebook, alongside the completed transcript, had joined Daniel's letter. Then later, over a bowl of boiled potatoes and sauerkraut, she said: 'Mutti, I have to go away again for work.'

Hilde's fork stopped midway between bowl and mouth, and she looked up at her daughter with childlike eyes.

'Why?' she asked. She set down her fork, as if she'd suddenly lost what little appetite she had.

Katja found it hard to swallow. She'd feared this would be her reaction.

'For work. Like before. Only this time it's just for two nights.' She spoke lightly, as if Mutti would barely notice she was gone. 'Frau Cohen is going to come in three times a day, to see you are well and comfortable and to make sure you take your pills.'

Her mother pushed away the bowl. 'Must you go, Kati?' she asked. 'I hate it when you go.'

Katja hated it too, but she knew she had a duty to fulfil. Her father would have done the same, and now she must honour his memory by risking everything for her country.

'I'll be back before you know it,' she replied, grasping her mother's cold hand. But as she began clearing away the supper dishes, she knew her words were hollow, because there was a chance, albeit a slight one, that she might not make it back at all.

Chapter 34

Paris

The locomotive pulled into the Gare de l'Est at 18.34. As she stepped off the train and onto the platform in Paris, Katja was overcome by a strange apprehension. There may not have been any armed guards, or snarling dogs or red and black swastikas draped from every pillar and post, but it didn't make her fear any less real. She looked down at the hatbox she clutched in her right hand. Inside lay the finished transcript she had promised Dr Viktor she would guard with her life. She may have escaped Germany unscathed, but she knew to her cost that in Paris there were also people who would kill her for what she carried.

Leaving the platform, she headed straight for the main entrance, while her eyes roamed around the station. It was early evening, and the concourse was busy with commuters. Every one of them might have been sent to spy on her. The man with the wooden leg leaning on the lamppost, the newspaper seller, the woman with the poodle under her arm; suddenly they all looked suspicious to her. Arriving at the taxi rank slightly out of breath, she asked the driver to take her to rue de l'Odéon in the 6th *arrondissement*. She was going to Shakespeare and Company.

*

'Katja, dear!' said Sylvia, kissing her visitor on both cheeks, embracing her like an old friend.

'It's so good to see you,' she replied. She really meant it.

The comforting sight and smell of the books seemed to envelop Katja like a warm blanket and she couldn't help looking around her, taking in the bulging shelves, and drawings by William Blake. It was wonderful to see everything just how she remembered it, but something was missing.

As if answering Katja's wordless question, Sylvia told her: 'Daniel should be along shortly. He asked me to prepare a room upstairs for you, so in the meantime, let me show you.' She began to walk towards the back of the shop. 'I'm afraid it's nothing special, but I expect you're tired after your journey,' she said, bending down to pick up Katja's suitcase and the hatbox. She was immediately prevented.

'It's fine. Thank you,' Katja said. 'I can manage.'

They took the stairs. The concierge was an old lady, who wore a black dress and a black lace cap. She was sitting, dozing, in a sort of cubbyhole between the floors. A spool of dribble reached from the corner of her mouth to her whiskery chin as she snored quite gently, like a contented cat.

Sylvia cleared her throat and the old woman's eyes snapped open. 'Madame Duprés, I am expecting Monsieur Keenan to visit shortly. Please show him up,' she said in French.

Madame, slightly indignant at being caught napping, agreed with a brusque nod.

So, Daniel would arrive soon, Katja told herself. The thought of seeing him again lightened her step as she followed Sylvia up a narrow wooden staircase to her apartment on the second floor. Like the shop below, what it lacked in grandeur, it made up for with good taste. Sylvia had painted the walls of her small salon an elegant grey and adorned them with carefully chosen paintings. Silk throws and cushions covered two large sofas and a Turkish rug lay on the wooden floor. There were pot plants in corners and, of course, books. Lots of books. Sylvia showed Katja into the bedroom next to a small kitchenette. The shutters were closed but Katja could make out a double bed draped in a cream brocade bedspread and a chest of drawers in dark wood.

Walking to the window, Sylvia flung open the shutters on to a spring evening.

'*Et voilà!*' she exclaimed with laughter in her voice.

Katja was hard on her heels and smiled broadly when she looked at the view. Rising indomitably above the rooftops stood Notre-Dame Cathedral.

'It's so beautiful,' she whispered.

Sylvia nodded. 'Isn't it?'

'It's certainly a sight for sore eyes,' came a familiar voice from behind.

Both women pivoted towards the door to see Daniel Keenan standing on the threshold, vainly attempting to smooth down his ruffled hair after quickly removing his hat.

'Ah, Daniel! You made it,' said Sylvia, offering her cheek to one of her favourite customers as he drew close.

'You couldn't keep me away,' he said, although he was looking at Katja as he spoke. He stepped closer and Katja felt drawn to him. She had pictured their meeting ever since she'd read his letter, wondering how he'd react to her; how she'd react to him. 'It's good to see you again,' he said. His expression was serious, intense even, as if he, too, were trying to gauge her feelings towards him.

'And you,' she replied, glancing at her hostess, but feeling strangely awkward in front of her.

Sylvia, sensing her presence was not entirely welcome, tactfully volunteered to make some tisane. 'I'll be in the kitchen if anyone wants me,' she said, even though she doubted anyone would.

Left alone in the little bedroom, Daniel fingered the brim of his hat. The space between them seemed to shrink as soon as Sylvia left, but uncertainty remained.

'You got my . . .?'

'I got your . . .'

Their words came out simultaneously, before they both broke into smiles.

'Yes,' said Katja, relieved at his reaction. 'Yes, I did.' But she hadn't replied, fearing her letter might be traced and could put him in danger. 'I wanted to tell you how grateful I was – I am – that you took the time to explain, but it really wasn't necessary,' she told him.

'You mean that?' His breath left his chest in a sigh of relief.

'Of course I do,' she replied. 'I'm the one who should be sorry. I was . . .' she searched for a word but shook her head. 'Everyone mourns in their own way, and I shouldn't have goaded you.'

'Goaded me?' he repeated. 'I never felt you did that, but let's draw a line under it, shall we? Start afresh?'

'I'd like that,' she said, her stomach turning cartwheels.

'Thank you, Katja,' he whispered.

She'd forgotten how she loved the way he said her name in his Irish accent. He made it sound light, like thistledown. Since her return to Hamburg, the thought that she might see Daniel again kept her going while Ulbricht tried, and succeeded, to sully Dr Viktor's good name. He was the one bright light in her darkness. Now, she dared to hope that her feelings might be reciprocated. She was standing on tiptoe on a precipice, and she wasn't sure how the moment would end. His lips lifted at her comforting words, and he moved closer and swept up both her hands in his. 'That means so much to me,' he said, his eyes on hers. His touch was warm and soft, and sent a shock through her body. She looked down at his hands cradling hers. But then Sylvia called through.

'The tisane is ready.' Her voice broke them abruptly apart.

'You have it?' asked Daniel quickly, suddenly looking grave.

Katja's body shuddered as she snapped out of her trance to draw a deep breath. Her eyes shot to the hatbox on the floor. 'In there.'

'Good,' he replied. 'My editor wants to meet you tomorrow, first thing.' He took a step back then. 'Shall we?' He gestured towards the door, and Katja led the way back into the salon where Sylvia was sitting at the table with a glass teapot full of herbal infusion.

'You'd probably prefer a whiskey, Daniel,' suggested the bookseller, pouring out the tea while snatching a sideways glance.

'Actually no, thank you,' replied Daniel, his eyes on Katja. 'Tea will do me nicely.'

Sylvia followed his gaze and noted the look that rippled between them. 'Daniel tells me you have an important meeting with a publisher,' she said.

Katja frowned. Daniel was sworn to secrecy, but then he intervened.

'Sylvia knows you are a literary agent. Your client's going places, isn't he? He just needs a break.'

Katja's stomach flipped when she grasped she was being drawn into a web of deceit. In Paris her mission was known only to Daniel and the Dreibergs – and, of course, to Daniel's editor. The deception was spawning more lies, but Sylvia could not know the real reason for her stay.

'Let's hope so,' she replied lightly.

Sensing a slight awkwardness between them, Sylvia intervened once more. 'So, you have plans for this evening?' she asked, indifferent as to who answered.

Daniel was quick to jump in and took Katja by surprise. 'Yes,' he said decisively. 'I thought we'd go to Michaud's tonight.'

'Ah. You might bump into James,' Sylvia replied.

Katja frowned.

'James Joyce,' explained Daniel, turning to her.

She really didn't want to see anyone Daniel knew. She imagined he might become embroiled in some lengthy conversation about prose or syntax, or worse still, might be asked to join the writer at his table. Tonight, she wanted Daniel all to herself.

'I hope not,' he replied to Sylvia, at the same time darting a smile at Katja. It seemed he wanted her to himself as well.

*

Sylvia insisted on lending Katja her black lace cocktail dress for the occasion. 'And I could put your hair in a French pleat,' she suggested, sweeping her guest's tresses back and away from her face.

Katja was sitting in front of the small ornate dressing table, with Sylvia standing behind, talking to her reflection in the triptych mirror.

Katja replied, nodding her approval. 'If you don't mind.'

'It would be my pleasure,' Sylvia replied, opening a small drawer to reveal hairpins and combs. As she began to brush Katja's hair, she said: 'He's a different person when he's with you.'

The remark, clearly referring to Daniel, took Katja off-guard, but she matched it with a surprise of her own. 'I know about his wife and child,' she said, watching the mirror for Sylvia's reaction.

'You do?' she replied, raising a brow. 'Who . . .?'

'Monique Dreiberg. It must have been terrible for him.'

By now the sun was setting just above the rooftops, casting the room in a golden light. 'Oh, it was,' Sylvia replied thoughtfully, running a comb gently through Katja's hair. She raised her gaze and regarded her straight in the mirror. 'And it still is. He just needs time,' she said with a sigh. 'And the right person to spend it with.'

*

An hour later, freshened up from her journey, wearing Sylvia's dress and her blonde hair secured in an elegant pleat, Katja was ready for a night out.

Outside the bookstore, Daniel, now quite debonair in a smart dinner suit and with his sandy hair slicked down with oil, offered her his arm, and she felt so right to take it. They started down the road and made small talk as they walked. Daniel asked her about her journey, and his manner reminded her of the easy, affable man he'd been when they'd browsed books on the Quai de Tournelle back in early spring.

Michaud's stood on rue des Saints-Pères. It was stylish and rather chic with an air of luxury that was mirrored in the prices on the menu. Mercifully, there was no sign of James Joyce, although a broad-shouldered man with a fat cigar came over to talk to Daniel, as did an elegant older woman, dripping in diamonds. She touched him lightly on the arm and whispered something into his ear that made him smile. At the sight, Katja suddenly felt a pang of jealousy.

'You must know a lot of people,' she remarked as the waiter flapped out her napkin.

He shrugged. 'It's my job,' he replied, settling himself down opposite her. 'I write about Parisian society; the rich and the very rich. But you know the best part?' he asked, leaning over the table, looking earnest.

She shook her head.

'I don't have to like them.'

He leaned back as he let out a laugh. Katja laughed too, especially when she noticed a dimple appear on his cheek that had never been apparent before. When he smiled his whole face lit up. She wanted to see him happy more often, but more than that, she yearned to be the source of that happiness.

Daniel ordered a whiskey for himself and suggested Katja try a martini – she'd never had one before – and when their drinks arrived, he lifted his glass and asked her: 'What shall we toast?'

She thought for a moment about the rocky start to their relationship and how she prayed it was behind them. 'How about to new beginnings?' she suggested.

'To new beginnings,' he said, then lowering his voice slightly, he added with a smile: 'And to friendship.'

'Friendship,' she repeated, blushing slightly as their glasses clinked. She would settle for friendship, if she could have nothing else, but she still longed for more.

From the menu Daniel ordered rare tournedos while she ate salmon *en paupiette* which tasted like heaven on a plate. Their conversation was light at first. Simply to hear Daniel's voice brought her pleasure. She found him both knowledgeable and amusing, but shortly after the hors d'oeuvres, the evening took a serious turn when he mentioned the medical notes. They spoke about it cryptically. Like partners dancing a quadrille, they skirted around it, not mentioning it specifically, but both knew exactly what each other meant. Daniel seemed more engaged than he'd been before, reminding her of the enormity of the task she faced. His company, the food and the ambience may have been perfect, but underneath it all, Katja's happiness remained tempered. Not only was she risking her life; not only was she worried about Hilde and Dr Viktor, the thought of the meeting with the editor of *The Parisian* the following day was also unnerving her.

As if reading her mind Daniel said: 'You've got nothing to worry about with Chuck, you know. He's a ladies' man. One look from you and he'll be eating out of your hand.'

She smiled. 'You think so?'

'Sure, I do,' he said, and his gaze lingered on her long enough to say that she'd already had that effect on him.

Chapter 35

The offices of *The Parisian* lay on a chic street not far from the Hôtel de Ville. Even though it was a relatively short walk from Shakespeare and Company, Katja had decided to take a taxi. The transcript may have been well concealed in her hatbox, but she couldn't afford to run the risk of being attacked on the street like Dr Viktor.

A display of previous covers graced the office's large plate-glass window like brightly wrapped lollies in a sweet shop. There were several portrait shots of elegant women dripping in jewels or fur or both, posed against famous Parisian landmarks. A woman in a blue silk suit with her back to the camera looked up at the Eiffel Tower. Another wore black and white polka dots and gazed down at the Seine. There were action shots too. Stick-wielding men on horseback played polo or sat grinning behind the wheel of sports cars.

Katja gazed at them in awe, suddenly feeling like a poor country cousin. Hamburg was a city of the sea, of ships and merchants. It was rich, but real and solid too, yet right now, Paris seemed like a fairy tale where every street was enchanted, and every young Frenchwoman a princess.

'Don't be fooled,' said someone behind her.

Katja switched round quickly at the sound of Daniel's voice. He was standing close and leaned in to peck her on both cheeks. She was feeling nervous before, but when his lips brushed her skin, she tensed as an electric current pulsed through her body.

Together they looked at the display. 'It's all smoke and mirrors,' he told her, nodding towards the bright covers. 'We create the myth and the magic so that people can aspire to the dream, but the reality is rather different.' He shouldered the heavy glass door and held it open for her.

A fashionable young woman sat behind a large reception desk. Her hair was cut short like a boy's and at her neck was a string of pearls – the very opposite of Fräulein Schauble at the clinic in Hamburg, Katja thought.

'*Bonjour, Monsieur Daniel.*'

'*Bonjour, Jacqueline,*' he replied, crumpling his hat and slipping it in his pocket. 'Anything for me?'

Jacqueline's large, curious eyes slid towards Katja, then back to Daniel.

'You have a message from Miss Stein.' She handed Daniel a small square of paper. 'And Monsieur Picasso asked you to call him.'

'Picasso,' repeated Katja, as they walked across the lobby. 'You know Pablo Picasso?'

Daniel shrugged. 'It's my job to know people.'

They stopped by the elevator cage where a young boy in a double-breasted tunic slid back the concertina door. They stepped in.

'Impressed?' asked Daniel, as they glided up to the second floor.

'Yes,' she replied, as the lift juddered to a halt.

'Good. You're meant to be,' he replied. 'But here's where the glitz ends, and the hard graft begins.'

He held open an old wooden door, badly scuffed at the bottom where it had been continuously kicked. Katja walked through.

The room was large and square with a sort of glass booth at

the end of it and Katja saw what Daniel meant. The contrast between the effortlessly chic image of the reception area and the reality of what he called the press room was enormous.

'This is the engine house,' he told Katja, raising his voice above the clatter of typewriters as they walked past rows of desks. 'And here is the editor's office.'

A well-presented middle-aged woman with tortoiseshell glasses sat at a desk just outside.

'Peggy,' Daniel called.

She looked up and snatched off her spectacles, as if she didn't want him to see her wearing them. 'Yes, Mr Keenan,' she answered with a smile.

'Where's the chief? We've got a meeting with him in five minutes.'

Peggy shot Katja a flustered look and reached for a notepad on her desk. Holding it at arm's length, she narrowed her eyes, trying to focus, and paraphrased what she'd written.

'Mr Patterson says he's sorry, but the American ambassador invited him to play golf at Le Touquet at short notice.' She brought down the pad to peer cautiously at Daniel before she added by way of an apology: 'He wants to reschedule the meeting for Friday.'

The news hit Katja like a slap to the face. Couldn't this man comprehend that blood had been spilled and lives risked bringing Hitler's medical notes to his attention? He clearly had no idea what life was like in Germany; that Jews could be imprisoned for owning a wireless or taking the tram or that anyone who refused to salute the Nazi way could be sent to a detention camp. In Paris, it seemed people didn't care what went on just over the border. It may as well have been on a different planet as far as they were concerned.

'Friday,' repeated Daniel, with a frown.

Katja thought of her mother. She'd imagine she'd been abandoned. 'I need to be back by—' She started to protest, but Daniel cut her off.

233

'Thank you, Peggy. Can you reschedule for the same time?'

The secretary cast Katja a disapproving look. 'Sure will, Mr Keenan,' she replied.

Katja seethed in silence as Daniel led her back out of the office and down to the lobby. When she glanced once more at the framed cover shots in the window, they had suddenly lost their lustre. What was it Daniel had said? Smoke and mirrors. How right he was. All the Parisian chic, all the *bonhomie*, all the *joie de vivre* or whatever the French cared to call it, couldn't hide their indifference to what was going on in Germany.

Katja let out a groan as soon as she set foot on the pavement. 'I came all this way. I risked my life for this,' she cried, looking at the hatbox.

'I'm so sorry,' said Daniel. 'This is what my editor is like. He's nigh on impossible to pin down. All we can hope is that he keeps his appointment for Friday, then you'll be home on Saturday.'

'Saturday,' she repeated. He may as well have said next year. Saturday was four days away. Mutti would be worried sick, not to mention Dr Viktor. 'If only I could get a message to—'

'You can use my office phone,' Daniel offered as they started to walk along the boulevard.

'It's not that simple,' she replied, thinking of Dr Viktor's warning. 'I will need to reach him at home, in the evening.'

Daniel smiled. 'The office is open until late. You mustn't worry. Everything will work out.' He stopped then to hook his gaze onto her face to add: 'Trust me, Katja.'

Looking back into his eyes, she saw a dynamism she hadn't noticed before. A conviction and a purpose seemed to be shining through, as if he'd just opened a window that had been shut to her before. Placing her trust in him seemed natural and right. He was willing to guide her through the minefield that lay before her, and for that she would be forever grateful.

'Yes,' she replied. 'Yes, I do trust you.'

'And besides,' he said, 'while you wait to see my boss, it means

I can show you some more of the sights.' He lifted his arm in a grand gesture towards the splendour of the Luxembourg Gardens ahead of them.

His suggestion coaxed a smile. The thought of spending more time with Daniel filled her with excitement and hope, but the fate of the transcript still hung in the balance and not even he could guarantee her safety.

Chapter 36

Hamburg

In the dining room of his Hamburg townhouse, Dr Viktor sat at the table and waited for his wife to join him. It was a ritual they had performed every day for the past twenty-eight years. Ever since their wedding, Gerda Viktor had ruled the roost. Her father had been a leading psychiatrist and Ernst was his protégé. The former had insisted on the match and the latter regretted it every day. From the very beginning, Gerda was most insistent that when his work did not take him away, her husband should dine with her. It didn't matter that hardly a word ever passed between them or that the silence was sometimes so frosty it might freeze their soup.

On this particular evening, when the telephone rang in the hallway, Dr Viktor heard Ute answer in her best high German.

'The Viktor residence.'

Of course, what Dr Viktor could not hear was the voice on the other end.

'Ute. Ute, it's Dr Viktor's assistant. Katja.'

Katja knew she shouldn't be calling, but she needed to update

Viktor on the situation, and, most of all, she wanted him to assure her mother that, although she would be back three days later than planned, she'd come home just as soon as she could.

'Oh!' was all Ute managed to say before she heard Frau Viktor's quick footsteps approach from the dining room.

'Who is it?' her mistress barked from the door.

'No one, *meine Herrin*,' snapped Ute, thinking on her feet.

'No one?' echoed Frau Viktor. 'Give me the telephone.'

On the other end of the line, Katja listened in horror as the footsteps grew louder.

'Give me that,' commanded Frau Viktor, her face taut with suspicion as she approached the maid. But all she could hear as she put the receiver to her ear was a click on the line as it went dead.

In the dining room, Ernst Viktor had been listening intently to what was passing on the other side of the wall. He suspected he knew exactly who had just called. Katja could be in trouble, but he feared there was nothing he could do.

*

The following day, Dr Ernst Viktor was allowed back to his office at the clinic. He'd had to deal with an emergency on the day of his suspension – a patient threatened suicide and he'd been obliged to attend – so there hadn't been time to pack away his personal effects. He was only glad that Katja had relieved him of the burden of the notebook and hidden it in her apartment. It was one less thing he had to worry about.

With a heavy heart he began to collect his belongings. There was a signed volume of Freud's *The Interpretation of Dreams*, a marble ashtray he'd received after ten years' service at the clinic and a framed photograph of his wife, which had lain face down in a drawer for at least the past fifteen years.

He'd made a good start clearing out a cupboard when, a little later, he heard footsteps pounding along the corridor. Expecting

237

a knock, he braced himself, but there was none. Instead, his mystery visitors didn't bother with such courtesy. Two seconds later, he understood why.

'Dr Viktor?' A man, in a black leather coat and peaked cap, and flanked by two guards, confronted him on the other side of his desk.

'Yes.' He saw immediately his visitors were Gestapo.

'We have been given authority to search this office,' the officer informed him.

'What? But this is university property,' protested Viktor. 'You have no jurisdiction here. There is no need for—'

The Gestapo cut him off. 'I have my orders. I am to escort you from the building to your home.' He turned to his men. 'Proceed.'

'Wait!' urged Viktor. 'Where is your warrant?'

The officer sneered. 'The Gestapo does not need a warrant.'

One soldier proceeded to rip through the filing cabinet like a rabid dog, tossing files and papers onto the floor as he went. The other began to look behind the paintings on the wall. It was clear he'd been tipped off about a safe. At the third attempt he found what he was looking for behind the Matterhorn painting.

'The combination,' snapped the officer.

Beads of sweat were gathering on Viktor's forehead. He mopped them away with his handkerchief.

'Nine, seven, five, three.'

The dial finally clicked, and the door opened to reveal a small bundle of letters and a folder. One of the men retrieved them and laid them on the desk in front of the officer.

'This is all?' he asked, thumbing through the papers.

The folder contained page after page of figures. It was the department's annual budgetary report. Viktor exhaled deeply, silently thanking Katja for being true to her word. The notebook was safe with her. He fixed the Nazi with a glare. 'What were you expecting, offizier?' he asked, feigning innocence.

The Gestapo officer worked his jaw in frustration. 'My orders are to escort you to your home, *Herr Doktor*,' he said. It was clear he had been informed there might be something of great significance in the safe. But by whom? It was the question that played on Dr Viktor's mind as he went to shut his briefcase.

'Not so fast!' The officer clamped a gloved hand on the brass clip. 'Open it.'

So Viktor pulled open the two sides of his briefcase, like the jaws of an animal, to reveal a few books, the ashtray and the photograph of his wife. Seemingly suspicious of the doctor's efforts, however, the officer's eyes bored into the case and his gloved hand rummaged around a little until he appeared to come across another item. An oblong fountain pen case. Opening it immediately, he scanned the pen's silver barrel to read the inscription aloud. 'To Ernest, all my love, Leisel.' As he did so, he smirked. 'Interesting,' he said, snapping the case shut and pocketing it.

'What?' Viktor's eyes jerked wide open in shock. 'I've never seen that before in my life! You . . .'

'Out!' ordered the Gestapo, pointing to the door. And with that Dr Ernst Viktor's fifteen years at the University of Hamburg's Clinic for Neurological Disorders came to an abrupt and undignified halt. The forthcoming tribunal would decide if he would ever return. In his heart of hearts, he knew there wasn't a hope in hell.

*

Later that evening, Katja returned to the office of *The Parisian* with Daniel. He lit a cigarette at his desk, while she sat at his shoulder, as they waited for the long-distance operator to put them through to the Viktor residence. As soon as they were connected Daniel stubbed out his cigarette. Ute answered as Katja had expected.

'*Guten Abend*,' Daniel greeted in his best German. 'May I speak to Dr Viktor?'

After a slight pause, Ute came back with: 'Who is it, please?'

'My name is Daniel Keenan. I'm calling from Paris on a work-related matter.'

Ute was not alone as she stood in the hallway that evening. Hearing the telephone ring, Frau Viktor had, once again, made it her business to stand by the maid to hear who was at the other end of the line. Satisfied that the call was of a professional nature, she nodded to Ute to fetch her husband, who was in his study. Gerda Viktor had greeted the news of his suspension from the clinic with a mixture of embarrassment and relief. She was embarrassed by what the neighbours would say, but relieved that she could now keep an eye on him. As long as her disgraced husband remained under their roof, there would be no more unfortunate encounters with the fairer sex.

Like a beaten dog, Ernst Viktor trailed through from his study to take the telephone call under his wife's watchful eyes.

'Viktor speaking,' he said, then looked so forthrightly at his wife that she decided to allow him his privacy and waddled away.

'Dr Viktor.' Daniel knew he would have to speak in riddles for fear of incriminating Katja's mother and inadvertently putting her life at risk too. 'I understand it may be hard for you to talk freely, but I have a message from a young woman who is concerned for her mother.'

'Nothing's wrong, is it? Nothing . . .' Daniel could hear the anxiety in the doctor's voice.

'All is well, but I'm to tell you there has been a delay.'

'A delay?'

'Yes. Everything is going to plan but you will now have to wait until Saturday.'

'Saturday,' repeated Viktor.

'That's right. If you could convey this to the lady in question, it would be appreciated.' There was a pause on the line. 'Doctor,' repeated Daniel, thinking the connection had been lost.

Viktor cleared his throat. 'I fear I cannot,' came the eventual reply. 'I am suffering from a bad back and am housebound for the foreseeable future. I regret I cannot assist you. Goodbye.' And with that, he returned the receiver to the stand, nodded to Ute and walked back to his study without a word.

'Well?' Katja had been waiting silently, listening with growing anxiety to the direction of the conversation. 'Can he get word to my mother?'

Daniel shook his head slowly. 'I'm afraid it sounds as though the doctor is being watched. His phone might be tapped too, Katja.'

'It's as we feared,' she replied.

Just when she thought everything was going her way; that she could make it home to her mother the following day with a signed publishing contract, the news hit her hard.

Chapter 37

The sun was setting on another cloudy day and the sky could only manage a pink tinge rather than anything spectacular. Nevertheless, Hilde had spent the last half-hour with her pigeons, while her thoughts had been with Katja. She hoped her daughter was safe going about her business. Her work was important, she was sure, even though she didn't understand what Katja's job entailed to take her away from her for so long. She missed her so much that her heart ached in her chest. Her only consolation was that she knew her daughter wouldn't stay away a moment longer than she had to. Her Kati had promised she would be home tomorrow. And Katja never broke her promise.

The last of the breadcrumbs lay scattered on the balcony. The pigeons had eaten their fill, and now it was her turn to dine. She'd promised Katja she would drink the broth she'd made while she was away. Frau Cohen would come to check on her later that evening, so it was only right that she should try to gulp down a few spoonfuls.

Closing the shutters behind her, she shuffled into the kitchen to heat up the broth. Ten minutes later she was ladling it out into a bowl when a knock came at the door. She tutted and wiped her hands on her apron.

'*Ja! Ja!*' she bleated, thinking Frau Cohen had come a little early to check on her. But instead of her Jewish neighbour on the doorstep, she found a man; a youngish man with glasses that made his eyes look enormous. He made no attempt to smile.

'Frau Heinz?' He took off his hat to reveal dark, greased-back hair and a high forehead.

She regarded him warily. 'Are you a friend of Katja's?' she asked, her eyes now narrow slits.

'Not a friend. I am from the clinic, where she works.' As he spoke, his gaze strayed above her head to look beyond her into the apartment. 'Your daughter has not been in the office. She was reported to be sick, and I wanted to check on her welfare. May I come in?' He took a step towards the threshold, but Hilde looked puzzled.

'Who are you, again?' she asked.

'I am Dr Ulbricht from the clinic where your daughter works,' he told her, his tone growing more rasping, like an iron file on stone. 'It would be best if I came inside.' This time he lunged forward, barging past Hilde before surging down the corridor.

'No!' she called after him, annoyed. 'Katja isn't here.'

Ulbricht pivoted quickly. 'Not here? But she is supposed to be ill. Dr Viktor reported her absence to the clinic two days ago.' He glared at her.

Hilde's face puckered with fear. 'But she has gone away,' she mumbled.

'Gone away? What do you mean, old woman?' he demanded.

Shocked, Hilde shrank away from him. 'She said it was for work. She said she would be back in two days.'

Ulbricht nodded. The tension in his face relaxed. 'Of course,' he said to himself. 'The bird has flown.'

'Bird? What bird?' asked Hilde, instantly thinking of her pigeons.

Ulbricht's eyes now focused on the beaded bowl and an elaborate necklace displayed on a shelf. 'These . . .' He was unsure as to how he should describe the objects. 'These trinkets,' he said. He picked up the bowl, then laid it down immediately on the table when he spotted something he regarded as more interesting. His eye had been caught by the photograph of Katja's father, and a memory flickered across his face.

'Your husband?' he asked.

She nodded tentatively. 'My late husband.'

'Yes.' Ulbricht nodded. The photograph triggered a memory. The professor's face was familiar. Suddenly it all made sense. He had just finished his doctorate at the time of the Burnings. Reinhart Lemmerz's lingering death had been the talk of the university. He'd had no sympathy for the man. He'd brought his suffering on himself. His so-called 'principles' led to his downfall. And they would lead to his daughter's too.

Ulbricht turned once more to face the old woman, wringing her hands anxiously behind him. 'Frau Lemmerz,' he addressed her. 'That is your real name, is it not?'

Hilde's eyes widened in shock. 'How did you . . .?' She suddenly looked hopeful, as if she'd just found an ally, one of Reinhart's old friends or students, who would want to reminisce. 'You knew my husband?'

'Yes,' replied Ulbricht. 'And I know your daughter is planning to follow in his footsteps.'

'What do you mean?' Hilde shook her head.

Reaching for the shelf, Ulbricht picked up a photograph of the professor. He was pictured with a tribal chief, and the doctor's lips signalled an obvious disgust as he scrutinised the image.

'Your husband was a traitor, Frau Lemmerz,' he announced shaking his head. 'His life's work was studying savages. He did nothing to glorify the Aryan race, but rather denigrated it.' He placed the photograph face down on the table to show his contempt. But the move angered Hilde. She leaned over to right the frame, as if her own husband's memory had also just been denigrated.

244

'Reinhart was a good man,' she growled, suddenly finding strength from somewhere deep inside.

Ulbricht shook his head. 'He was a traitor, and he is gone, Frau Lemmerz, and now it appears your daughter has left you too.'

'Left me?' repeated Hilde. Her gnarled hands shot up to her chest.

Ulbricht shrugged, his eyes now settled on a small photograph of Katja that had sat beside her father's. 'She is not coming back,' he told her, reaching for the frame.

'No. That's not true!' wailed Hilde, snatching the photograph from Ulbricht's hands. 'What are you saying?' This time there was little trace of frailty in her voice – only anger.

Ulbricht's nostrils flared in disdain. 'Do you really think your daughter gives a damn about you?'

Hilde took a step back, her forehead puckered in a frown. 'What? Of course she does. I'm her mother.'

Ulbricht snorted. 'She told us all about you at the clinic. How you suffer from anxiety and depression. How you drag her down. You are a burden to her, old woman.'

Hilde clamped her hands over her ears. 'No!' she bleated. 'This is lies.'

Ulbricht was unrelenting in his assault, and he knew, as she sniffed back tears, she was walking right into his trap. 'I'll tell you something.'

'What?' said Hilde, her eyes widening. 'You know where she is? Where is my Kati?'

Slowly he shook his head. 'Your precious Kati is working for an enemy of the Reich. I can't tell you where she is, but what I do know is that she has deserted the Fatherland and she has deserted you, old woman.' He leaned forward and suddenly jabbed Hilde in the chest, pushing her backwards. 'I can also tell you this. You will never see your precious daughter again.'

Chapter 38

Paris

It was the end of another day of waiting. Katja walked with Daniel, side by side down the street, in the cool air as the sun went down, although she was careful not to touch him. Not to brush his arm, nor tap it in a playful gesture. It was up to him to make the next move, if he made a move at all. As much as she longed for him, she knew her heart lay at his feet. He could kick it again, like he did at Dr Viktor's bedside, or he could pick it up gently.

The dinner at Michaud's had been wonderful, but there had been no longed-for kiss at the end of the evening when he'd escorted her back to Sylvia's. This evening, she really couldn't be sure what he'd do. She wanted so much more than friendship, but she still couldn't be absolutely certain Daniel wanted the same. Nor could she blame him for guarding his heart against any feelings he may harbour for her. After all he had been through, and knowing the dangers, not to mention the distance that lay between them, she could understand.

He'd called for her at Sylvia's, suggesting a stroll. Some of the shops were still open, their windows brightly lit and enticing.

The delayed meeting with the editor had left Katja even more anxious sand although, now and again, Daniel would helpfully point at a building and tell her its history and she would nod appreciatively, they both knew things weren't right. Thoughts of the notes, of Dr Viktor's fate and of Hilde's anxiety cast a long shadow over everything.

As they continued to walk along a wide boulevard, past a pavement café and a fruit seller, Daniel said suddenly: 'It's funny.'

'What is?' asked Katja.

He kept looking straight ahead. 'I used to see Grace everywhere in the city, even though she never came here. There'd be some young woman drinking coffee, or buying vegetables, and I'd think it was her, then when she looked round and I saw her face, she'd be completely different.'

There was a silence, and Daniel, worried he may have revealed too much, turned to her. 'I'm sorry, I . . .'

'No. No need to apologise,' she replied, aware he had just entrusted her with his innermost feelings. Katja understood. At first, she'd seen her dead father in the park, on the tram or in cafés. Grief so often played tricks on vulnerable minds. 'It's hard,' she said. 'So what changed that?'

Whether he didn't hear her question, or he simply chose to ignore it, it went unanswered as they began to walk again.

'But recently . . .' he went on, before stopping in his tracks.

'Yes?' said Katja, her heart suddenly beating faster. 'What has happened recently?'

He was looking at her intently, before suddenly raising his gaze to the shop directly behind her and leaving her question hanging. Instead, he said: 'There's someone you must meet.'

Katja turned to see a bow-fronted bookshop – one that sold French books – and an elderly man standing by the door, just about to turn the sign from *ouvert* to *fermé*. Daniel waved his hand and rushed forward.

'*Monsieur Gaillard.*'

The elderly man, with white sideburns and a waistcoat that protested over his large belly, suddenly recognised Daniel. Smiling broadly, he unlocked the shop door.

'*Monsieur Keenan*,' he greeted, embracing Daniel enthusiastically. '*Comment allez-vous?* You look well.' Putting his arm around Daniel's shoulder, he studied his face. Daniel rolled his eyes. 'Better than the last time you saw me,' he replied, trying to extricate himself from the old bookseller's grasp.

'And I presume this is the reason for your good health.' The bookseller's twinkling eyes were fixed on Katja. She felt the colour rise in her cheeks.

'Fräulein Heinz is from Germany and a book lover like us,' explained Daniel.

'Then you have come to the right place,' said the old man nudging Daniel's elbow.

Daniel smiled. 'Tonight, we shall just browse, Monsieur.'

Gaillard nodded sagely. 'Ah, *le* browse,' he said with a mischievous smile, touching his nose knowledgeably. 'It is ze best zing in ze world.'

'It is, indeed,' agreed Daniel, throwing a wry smile at Katja and shepherding her inside the shop.

'*Et voilà*,' announced Gaillard, gesturing to the shelves that lined his shop, all groaning with books. 'You have novels there and autobiographies there.' He pointed vaguely in various directions. 'Histories and the arts.' Then he cast a mischievous look at Daniel. 'But, of course, the most precious books are in ze cellar,' he said, with a wink as he turned his head from Katja.

There were only two light bulbs in the basement, so the bookseller gave Daniel a torch and told him to watch his step on the way down. The rickety stairs led to a large, shambling space, festooned with cobwebs and full of boxes that overflowed with books.

'Well,' said Daniel, looking at Katja. 'Where shall we start?'

He shone the torch beam on one of the piles, as Katja tilted her head to read the titles on some of the spines. There were fables by La Fontaine, collected letters by Rousseau and Voltaire, plays by Molière and poems from Lamartine. The volumes were all leather bound, some with gold lettering and many looked so fragile, she was afraid they might fall apart if she opened them.

'These are collectors' books,' she said. 'More for admiring than for reading.'

'But they're very beautiful, aren't they?' Daniel had picked up a volume of works by eighteenth-century poets and blew the dust from its cover. Inside the leaves were as brittle as tissue paper.

'Like butterflies' wings,' suggested Katja.

'Like butterflies' wings,' repeated Daniel, looking up to meet her gaze. 'Yes,' he agreed as the moment suddenly stopped them both in their tracks and held them suspended in the lamplight.

Why is he doing this? thought Katja. Why was he torturing her with his looks and gestures. He was drawing her to him like the little moth currently dancing around the bulb above their heads, and it was killing her. She didn't think she could stand much more.

'And look at this pile,' said Katja lightly, suddenly breaking the spell. 'These seem to be novels. Dumas and Hugo.'

Daniel moved closer to her so that she could feel the warmth of his breath on her cheek.

'*The Count of Monte Cristo*,' he said, squinting at one of the spines in the pile. 'A story of cruel injustice and revenge,' he announced dramatically.

The bulb flickered on his face as she turned, and Katja knew if she didn't say something then, the moment would be lost. 'Is that what you want, Daniel? Do you think revenge against the English will bring back your loved ones?'

Her question seemed to shock him. He was silent for a moment as he looked deep into her eyes. 'No. No,' he repeated, before he began to nod. 'You're right,' he said finally. 'I let myself be eaten up by anger. As I told you in my letter, it's time for me to focus on something positive. That's why I'm here. With you.'

Half expecting him to add 'and the transcript' she waited a moment. She couldn't be sure of his next move, until he said: 'You remember I told you how I used to see Grace everywhere? And you asked me what changed that?'

'Yes,' she replied, her heart racing again.

'Well,' he said slowly. 'The answer is you.'

The words took a moment to sink in.

'Oh,' was all she said at first. For a split second she closed her eyes then opened them again to make sure she wasn't dreaming.

'I've thought long and hard since you left for Hamburg,' Daniel continued. 'And I just can't get you out of my mind. There's something . . . a connection between us, Katja.'

A connection. She repeated the words in her head and realised he had taken a step closer towards her. He was right, of course, and she'd known all along she couldn't rush his feelings. No one had ever accused her of being impetuous, but perhaps she'd been too impatient. Perhaps it was because she'd never felt for any man, the way she felt for Daniel.

He took a deep, steadying breath. 'We share something special, don't we?'

The question hung in the air between them, until Katja smiled. 'Yes. Yes, we do,' she agreed, trying to give him the space to say more.

He shrugged. 'It's been well over a year now since . . .' His eyes gleamed in the torchlight's beam. 'And I've been angry all that time. Angry and bitter.'

Katja nodded. 'You had every right to be at the time. There's no need to explain.'

His hand brushed her cheek, sending a charge through her. For a second it was just the two of them. She wanted so badly to kiss him, but still she checked herself because he had to feel the same longing for her. He had to be ready to make the first move.

'Grief blinded me, Katja, but now, thanks to you, I'm starting to see things clearly again.' He leaned forward, but they didn't kiss right away. Instead, they just dived into each other's eyes before

Daniel's arm wrapped around her and his lips suddenly pressed tenderly against hers. Her whole body dissolved into his to be lost in another place, another dimension.

She had no idea how long the embrace lasted because time seemed to stand still, but when their lips finally parted, she just rested her head on Daniel's shoulder. A wave of contentment washed over her.

'That was . . .' he said slowly, his face still half in shadow as he remained holding her.

'Wonderful,' she told him, raising her head, and looking at him once more.

'Yes, it was, wasn't it?'

'*Monsieur Keenan. Je vais fermer le magasin dans cinq minutes.*' The bookseller's voice boomed down the stairs.

'Poor Monsieur Gaillard wants to shut up shop – again,' Daniel relayed with mild embarrassment.

Katja retuned his sheepish look as she opened her handbag and checked her lips in her small compact, just in case the kiss had left any tell-tale signs.

'You are perfect,' he told her, picking up the torch and holding out his hand to hers. She was about to take it when she suddenly had a thought.

'Wait,' she told him. 'We ought to buy something.' She picked up the first book on top of the nearest pile and led the way back upstairs.

'So, you did *ze* browsing,' remarked Monsieur Gaillard to Daniel, his tongue firmly in his cheek.

'We did, thank you,' replied Daniel. 'And now we'd like to buy.' He turned to Katja who handed him a hastily snatched book.

The old man examined the title and raised an eyebrow. 'An interesting choice,' he observed.

Daniel paid him five francs, but it was only when Monsieur Gaillard returned it to him and he had a chance to look at the cover that he understood why he'd been a little shocked.

Katja waited until they'd both left the shop and the door was shut behind them to ask why the bookseller's eyebrows had arched when he saw their choice.

Daniel laughed heartily – something she'd never seen him do before – as he showed her the title.

'*Madame Bovary*,' she read. '*Madame Bovary*. But wasn't the author . . .?'

Daniel nodded. 'Yes. Poor old Flaubert was tried for obscenity.'

'No wonder your Monsieur Gaillard looked shocked.'

'No wonder,' replied Daniel, laughing and suddenly pulling her close to him.

She didn't want the evening to end, but she knew it must. As they strolled arm in arm down the Quai de la Tournelle, Katja thought she might burst with happiness. She was in the city of light and wherever she looked, there was romance. Whereas before she had only seen spies on every street corner, now she saw lovers kissing on benches or strolling hand in hand. And that night, after her longing and her waiting for her feelings to be reciprocated, she had finally joined them. Suddenly the dangers ahead of her over the next few days had just become bearable because she no longer faced them alone.

Chapter 39

Hamburg

Ute was about to draw the shutters for the evening when she saw the car pull up outside the Viktors' townhouse. It was an official car; the sort with blacked-out windows; the sort favoured by the Gestapo. Flustered, she flew to the nearest mirror and made sure her hair and cap were straight, then listened as car doors slammed and footsteps beat a path to the door. A loud knock came next, three Gestapo stood before her.

'We are here for Dr Viktor,' announced the officer.

The stunned maid didn't get the chance to ask them to wait in the hall because they simply barged past her.

'Who is . . .?' Frau Viktor's voice preceded her from the salon, but as soon as she ventured into the hall and saw the Gestapo, her tongue seemed to cleave to the roof of her mouth.

'Frau Viktor.' The officer greeted her with a Nazi salute before whipping off his cap. Thrusting it under his armpit, he said: 'We will talk with your husband.'

Gerda Viktor fingered the gold cross at the base of her flabby neck as if silently asking for divine protection. 'Yes. Yes, of course,' she replied hesitantly. 'Ute, go fetch your master,' she instructed the frightened girl, hovering by the door.

Confident that Ute was out of earshot, Gerda leaned forward towards the officer and kept her voice low. 'Is this about the . . .?' She couldn't bring herself to give her husband's alleged sexual misconduct a name.

'I am not at liberty to discuss such matters,' came the reply, just as Ernst Viktor appeared at the top of the stairs.

He walked down unhurriedly, but realised, as he grew closer, it was the same officer who had searched his office at the clinic. He didn't address him until he had reached the bottom.

'Yes?' His voice remained measured, but his expression was bemused. 'Is there a problem?'

The officer fixed him with a cold stare. 'Ernst Viktor, you are to accompany me to headquarters for questioning.'

The doctor shook his head. 'There must be some mistake. I am awaiting a tribunal, as you know. It is a university matter.' But his words only seemed to inflame the situation. 'I have my orders.' This time they came out in a shout. There was to be no argument.

Viktor turned to his wife, whose expression was already a mixture of loathing and disgust but said nothing. Instead, he simply took his coat and hat from an agitated Ute who stood nearby, on the verge of tears.

'I am ready,' he told the officer and, flanked by the two armed men, Dr Ernst Viktor was escorted out of his home and into the waiting Gestapo car.

Chapter 40

Paris

When she awoke the following morning and remembered Daniel's kiss, Katja thought she might have been dreaming. Had he finally managed to make a leap of faith and trust her with his broken heart? Had he really chosen her to mend it? But then her blurry eyes settled on the copy of Flaubert's *Madame Bovary* and she knew what had happened was real. Stretching lazily, she recalled the strange, wonderful stirring somewhere deep inside her as he'd held her close.

Outside, the day threatened rain, but everyone was in carnival mood in anticipation of the *quatorze juillet* celebration to commemorate the storming of the Bastille during the French Revolution. Afterwards, they would head off for the mountains or the beaches for their paid holidays, thanks to a new law that made all the workers happier. According to Sylvia, many would take with them the new bestseller from America, *Autant en emporte le vent*.

'*Gone with the Wind*,' said Katja, venturing into the shop shortly after breakfast. The front window was piled high with copies.

'The Nazis don't like this one either, do they?' commented Sylvia, busily tweaking the display.

'No,' replied Katja. 'They say it's all about individualism and survival against the odds.'

'The very opposite of what they stand for,' remarked Sylvia, on her knees and reaching into a far corner to right a wayward copy.

'Yes,' agreed Katja.

'Well, I'd root for Rhett Butler over Adolf Hitler any day,' replied Sylvia, before adding with a laugh, 'if I found the opposite sex the least bit attractive.'

Katja smiled but remained looking at the shelves. She was at a loss. With Dr Viktor's attacker still at large, she didn't feel safe out on the streets alone and yet inside, in the four walls of the shop, she felt quite useless.

'It's a shame your meeting was delayed,' said Sylvia, retreating from the front window and brushing down her skirt. Katja had explained that she needed to extend her stay for two more nights and the bookseller had kindly agreed. 'But I can always use some help,' she said. 'Especially in the lending library. I'll show you how it works, if you like.'

'I'd like that very much,' replied Katja, her mood suddenly lightening.

For the rest of the day, she busied herself in the smaller room off the main shop, returning borrowed books to their shelves and logging them out to members of the library. Time passed slowly, but at least she felt safe in the sanctuary of Shakespeare and Company.

Towards six o'clock Sylvia came through to the lending section. No borrowers had visited for the past hour.

'I think you may as well call it a day,' she told Katja. But just as she'd spoken the tinkle of the doorbell could be heard. Sylvia rolled her eyes. 'Isn't it always the way?' she said, turning on her heel. A moment later she returned with a big smile planted on her face – and Daniel following behind her.

'No visitor to Paris should spend an evening inside when the entire city beckons!' he declared.

'I, but . . .' Katja turned to Sylvia, as if silently asking her permission to go out for the evening.

'It wouldn't do to keep such a handsome guide waiting. Off you go now,' she said, waving her arm towards the shop door.

Katja grabbed her jacket from the back vestibule and glanced at herself in the mirror. Her eyes were bright, and her skin was glowing, and she suddenly felt she could take on the world.

'Shall we?' said Daniel, offering her his arm as they stepped into the Parisian evening.

They crossed the Seine to Notre-Dame and Katja marvelled at the architecture and the carvings, including the famous gargoyles that warded off evil spirits.

'Magnificent, isn't it?' said Daniel, as she gazed up at the towers. 'And timeless. Victor Hugo would have stood here to take in exactly the same view, dreaming up that character of Quasimodo.'

The very thought thrilled her, and Daniel caught the excitement in her eyes and drew her closer to kiss her on the top of her head. But just as he did, Katja thought she noticed someone – a man in a trilby – standing near the main entrance to the cathedral. She switched round.

'What is it?' Daniel asked, looking down at her and seeing her frown.

'That man.'

'What man?' he asked, his gaze darting around the building's facade. But when Katja looked again, he was gone.

Daniel put his arm around her. 'You're nervous. I understand. Come on, let's get something to eat.'

They settled on a little bistro, tucked away in a back street where they were the only diners, and sat with a good view of the door so they could see any comings and goings. After a glass of wine, Katja felt her nerves ease.

'You're safe here,' said Daniel, stretching over the table to take her hand in his. The memory of seeing Dr Viktor after the attack was fading but he knew her anxiety remained just below the surface. 'I've been thinking about the doctor,' he said suddenly.

Katja put down her wineglass. 'Yes?' The other day she had told him about the trumped-up charge of gross misconduct involving both herself and Kommodore Flebert's wife. It was clear to Katja that the kommodore had engineered the incident, forcing his wife to act as he had. Dr Viktor told her Frau Flebert even apologised to him afterwards, blaming her husband for forcing her to act the way she had.

Daniel nodded. 'It's clear he's in real trouble.'

Katja agreed. The misconduct hearing could only go one way, as far as she was concerned. Her memory flashed to the reception after the launch of the *Bismarck* and the finger pointed to one man. Adolf Hitler.

'What if Dr Viktor could get a visa for the United States?'

'A visa?' Katja repeated. The words sliced through her uneasy thoughts.

'It would make his life a lot easier,' continued Daniel.

The prospect was certainly enticing, but surely implausible. But then Katja remembered Dr Wilhelm Reich, the anti-fascist lecturer. The Americans were granting him one, so why not Dr Viktor?

'You could do that?' she asked.

Daniel nodded. 'I reckon my editor could pull a few strings. He goes to embassy parties and is pals with the new ambassador. If Dr Viktor has helpful information, then it shouldn't be too hard to make his case.'

'But that would be wonderful,' Katja replied. Her thoughts snagged on Frau Viktor for a moment, although she doubted the doctor would hesitate to leave his wife. 'I shall ask him,' she said, before remembering that communication with him was off limits while he was confined to his home.

'Good,' replied Daniel with a smile. 'Then, assuming Patterson says "yes" tomorrow, I can start the ball rolling.'

Tomorrow. She felt her stomach clench. 'And you think he will?'

'I do, yes,' he replied. 'He seemed positive the last time we spoke.' He lifted his wineglass, still half full, and toasted. 'To tomorrow,' he said, looking deep into her eyes as she raised her glass to his.

'Tomorrow,' she replied, her stomach cramping once more.

Chapter 41

The morning of the meeting at *The Parisian* finally arrived. Together, Katja and Daniel took the elevator up to the press room. With their new intimacy had come a new sense of purpose. They were undertaking this mission together.

Clutching her hatbox containing the typescript, Katja followed Daniel as he led the way, running the gamut of chattering typewriters. He announced their arrival to Peggy. This time there were no excuses. Chuck Patterson could be seen hunched over his desk in his glass booth, but even before they'd been ushered inside, Katja could read the editor's expression. Something was wrong. His face was contorted in a grimace as he spoke on the telephone. When he put down the receiver, he remained staring at it, deep in thought.

'Good morning, chief,' greeted Daniel.

Patterson looked up, and seeing Katja, rose quickly to lean over the desk and shake her hand. He gestured to the chairs in front of him.

'Sorry about the other day,' he said. 'When the ambassador says "jump" you jump.' He shrugged. 'Or play golf in my case. But . . . hey.' He sat down again, with his hands clasped. 'Drink? Coffee, Fräulein Heinz?'

He was stalling. Katja could tell. 'No, thank you,' she replied.

If it was bad news, she wanted to be put out of her misery as soon as possible.

Patterson grimaced again. 'I'll level with you,' he said, suddenly slapping the desk with his palm. 'It's not looking good for your precious medical notes, Fräulein Heinz.' He pointed to the thin pile of pages in front of him.

Katja shuddered.

'Wait a minute,' Daniel barged in. 'You've only read the first three chapters. We've got the rest here,' he said tetchily, as Katja laid the folder on the desk.

'Shoot, you know I read what you gave me,' Patterson replied, flapping a hand. 'I was all for running with it, in instalments, but then ...' He slumped back in his chair, letting out an exasperated sigh and pointing to the telephone. '... then I get a call from the editor of the *Nouvelle Revue Française*.'

'And?' said Daniel, knowing the *Revue* was a well-respected publication with a circulation a hundred times bigger than *The Parisian's*.

'And, the long and the short of it is, he's been threatened with court action by the French Foreign Ministry if he publishes any article unfavourable to either Hitler or Mussolini. They won't hesitate to threaten us either.'

Katja took a moment to digest the news, but Daniel dived in.

'What are you saying, Chuck?' he snapped, knowing exactly what the reply would be.

Patterson rubbed his jaw and looked at Katja. 'I'm saying I can't publish this folder, Fräulein Heinz,' he told her, jabbing the notes. 'Because if I do, the French government will come down on me like a ton of bricks and I could end up in jail.'

Daniel slammed his fist on the desk, making Katja jump – the anger she'd seen before suddenly returning. 'But you know Hitler is a dictator. You know he's hell-bent on war.'

Patterson threw both his hands up in mock surrender. 'I agree. I agree, but you know the Foreign Minister is an appeaser and,

261

quite frankly, so are many of the French. They want the quiet life and after what happened in 1914, who can blame them?'

'So that's it?' asked Katja bluntly.

Patterson nodded as he looked at her. 'I'm afraid it is, Fräulein Heinz. My hands are tied.'

It took all Katja's strength not to follow Daniel's lead and beat the desk with her fists. She wanted to rail against the injustice of the situation. She wanted to scream a warning not just to the whole office, but to all of France about what the future held if they didn't act against Hitler before it was too late. But she did not. Instead, she reined in her fury, turned to the editor and simply said: 'Then there is no more to be said. Thank you for your time, Mr Patterson.' She stood. 'Goodbye.'

She picked up the pages from the desk and, with her head held high, marched out of the glass booth. Daniel, also suppressing the urge to vent any more spleen, cast an angry look at his boss and followed Katja out through the main office, watched by a dozen pairs of curious eyes.

Katja waited until they were out on the street to give full rein to her wrath, and she didn't care who heard her.

'What shall I do now? I've failed. What do I tell Dr Viktor?'

'Jesus, I'm sorry,' mumbled Daniel, taking her by the arm and gently pulling her towards him. 'It's not your fault. I should've known.' But his words did little to calm her. 'It's all right,' he soothed, as he held her, feeling her body shake with fury. 'Nothing will be wasted. We can still warn the world about Hitler. We just need to find another publisher.'

She looked up at him, as if he'd just said something that hadn't occurred to her before. 'Another publisher?' she repeated.

'Yes. There will be someone brave enough to do it. We just have to find them.'

Katja swallowed back her anger. 'You think someone like that exists? In Paris?' she asked. 'You think someone might take that risk, even though they could be arrested?'

'There are some brave people in France, and I will find them,' he told her with such sincerity that, for a moment, any misgivings she had melted away. But then she thought of Dr Viktor's uncertain fate and how the responsibility had shifted onto her shoulders. Doubt stalked her once more.

'Let's go back to Sylvia's,' Daniel suggested. 'We can talk in private there.' He held out his hand and she took it. Together they walked in the late spring sunshine back to rue de l'Odéon. Around Katja the pulse of Paris beat as strong and vibrant as ever, but her own heart was leaden. Only a few hours ago, it had felt as light as a feather. She'd almost forgotten what happiness was until Daniel had come into her life. Now, after the editor's refusal to publish, it was only knowing he was there for her that gave her the courage to continue.

The ringing of the bell above the door at Shakespeare and Company alerted Sylvia to their unexpected arrival. Katja had told her they weren't due to return until early afternoon. Seeing the glum expressions on their faces, she emerged from behind the counter to greet them with a frown, suspecting something was awry.

'What's happened?' she asked, her eyes flicking from Daniel to Katja and back again. 'What's wrong?'

Daniel was quick with an excuse. 'The publisher rejected the manuscript. There's no reason for Fräulein Heinz to stay on,' he replied, convincingly.

Sylvia's small mouth parted before she switched to Katja and said earnestly: 'I'm so sorry, but you'll try others, surely?'

Seeing Katja was in no mood to invent excuses, Daniel came back again. 'Of course, just not right now,' he said with a shrug.

Katja managed a brave face. 'I'm sorry too, Sylvia, but I need to collect my things,' she explained.

'Of course. Of course,' replied the bookseller, just as a customer walked through the door. 'Madame Duprés will let you in,' she said, pointing upstairs.

Madame Duprés, unusually awake, duly obliged and let them both into the apartment to collect Katja's belongings. As soon as the door was shut and they were alone, Daniel cupped her face in his hands and kissed her long and hard once more. It was the confirmation that he needed her, just as much as she needed him. Flinging her arms around him, she held him close. When they eventually broke apart, he smiled gently.

'I knew I wouldn't get another chance,' he told her, looking deep into her eyes. 'Patterson is expecting me back at work this afternoon.'

She touched his hand as it remained on her cheek. 'When will we see each other again?' she asked, the tears threatening once more.

'Soon,' he reassured her, but they both knew they couldn't be sure when. 'And in the meantime, I'll write.' He reached for her hand and softly kissed her wrist. 'And I'll do all I can to find a publisher.' He touched his breast pocket to the folded first chapters of the notebook.

With the rest of the transcript now back in her hatbox, and her goodbyes to Sylvia said, Katja left the shop with Daniel to hail a cab on the corner of rue de l'Odéon.

'Goodbye,' she told him as a taxi pulled up, her voice cracking as she spoke.

'Not goodbye. À bientôt, remember? It's so much nicer,' he replied.

She smiled at that remark. 'Yes. À bientôt,' she repeated, as Daniel opened the cab door for her, and she eased herself onto the back seat. 'Gare de l'Est,' she instructed the driver.

As the engine started, Sylvia ran out of the shop. 'Bon voyage, Katja,' she cried, with a wave.

Katja waved back half-heartedly, all the while holding her tears in check. She didn't want them to fall until she was out of Daniel's sight because, despite what he told her, she had the horrifying feeling that having just found love for the first time, their parting meant she might now lose it forever.

Chapter 42

Hamburg

Ernst Viktor sat shivering in a cold, windowless cell. A metal bench was screwed to the wall and there was a bucket for his slops, but no blanket. A few times he'd heard boots stomping along the corridor and the screech of cell doors as they opened and shut. There'd been other sounds too: of men moaning or crying and once a terrifying scream, followed by an even more terrifying silence.

When he'd first arrived at the Gestapo headquarters, he'd told himself his questioning would be a formality and that he would soon be allowed back home. The officer had, after all, been quite courteous. There'd been no manhandling. No violence. That had been twenty-four hours ago, and in that time, he had eaten little and slept hardly at all. He supposed his captors were playing a game with him. He was, after all, a psychiatrist. A man's mind was often very suggestible and malleable. Thoughts could be imprinted – he'd proved that to his cost with Hitler – just as they could be obliterated; ideas implanted, just as they could be corrupted; answers to questions extracted without the subject being aware. But if they wanted to play games, then he surely had the upper hand. He could always be one step ahead of them because he would undoubtedly know their tactics, wouldn't he?

A deep sigh, then, *Who am I trying to fool?* he thought. *Only myself*, came the answer. He wasn't shivering through cold, but fear. With every hour he was made to wait alone, his sense of dread grew.

To distract himself, he focused his thoughts on Katja. He trusted her implicitly, but he now knew he'd asked too much of her. And yet, like her dead father, she'd willingly put her own life in danger for the sake of her principles, for the notebook. She was so strong and clever and brave. He doubted poor Leisel would have acted the same in the face of such adversity. The dead girl's name would undoubtedly be raised during his questioning. What led to her death? Who supplied her with the pills? They'd planted that pen with the incriminating inscription, too. And there he was again, sinking down into a murky quagmire of despair. Now, all his hopes rested in Paris with Katja.

*

Katja was grateful to have the train carriage to herself for much of the return journey to Hamburg. The hatbox containing the folder would remain on the rack opposite until she planned to close her eyes, then it was taken down and kept by her side. There had been a priest and two nuns at first, but they had disembarked before the train crossed the border. It was only then that, left alone with her thoughts and a dull ache in her heart, that her tears had flowed freely once more. When she finally managed to grab three hours' sleep, she dreamed of Daniel. They were walking by the Seine, browsing the book stalls as they had done on that wonderful spring day when she'd fallen so helplessly for him; the way he could be vulnerable at times, then make her laugh with a single phrase; the way his smile could melt her troubles. But waking to the sight of sunlight on the flatlands of Belgium, it didn't take long for her heart to sink when she recalled hundreds of miles now separated her from the man she loved.

When the train next stopped, it was in Germany. An elderly woman boarded and shared the carriage. With her rounded shoulders and slight frame, which looked as though it might snap in a strong wind, she reminded Katja of her mother. She prayed Mutti had managed over the last few days. Having Frau Cohen keep a watchful eye on Hilde was such a relief, but she still fretted over her wellbeing. Nevertheless, the mere thought of seeing her again was a comfort for the last two hours of the journey. Finally, at just after eight o'clock on Saturday morning, the train pulled into Hamburg Central Station.

With the sight of the huge familiar swastika banners festooned on every public building, the feelings of fear returned. They'd faded in Paris when Daniel was by her side. In his company, she'd felt bolder. She clasped the hatbox tightly to her chest as she climbed on the tram to take her home. If the Gestapo were to board now, as they were doing routinely these days, looking for Jews, and found the folder, she would be interrogated and executed. The thought caused beads of sweat to break out on her forehead. A man sitting next to her noticed her agitation and looked at her curiously. He reminded her nowhere was safe. She disembarked at the next stop.

Within five minutes, she had turned into Müggenkampstrasse and even her suitcase felt lighter as she powered down the street and up the stairs to her apartment on the first floor. She couldn't wait to see her mother, even though it was such a comfort to know that Frau Cohen had been keeping an eye on her.

Arriving on the landing, Katja paused to catch her breath before looking for her key. But when she turned her head to the left, towards Frau Cohen's apartment, she let out a muted gasp. On the front door someone had daubed the Star of David in blue paint and written the word *Juden* underneath.

Diving across the landing, Katja banged on the door. 'Frau Cohen!' she called. 'It's Katja. Are you all right?'

No reply.

She tried the handle and the door opened. 'Frau Cohen,' she cried again, hurrying along the corridor, glancing into each room as she went. But there was no sign of her elderly neighbour; only a scarf and a single stocking on the bedroom floor and open drawers and cupboards, as if she had left in a hurry. Had she gone through fear or was she forced to leave? Katja had no idea, but she hoped Mutti would be able to shed some light on what had happened. She hurried back across the landing to her own apartment and unlocked the door with shaking hands.

'Mutti! Mutti! I'm back,' she called, setting down her cases and scurrying towards the salon.

Startled by her voice, the dozen or more pigeons on the balcony flapped their wings in a frenzy and scattered. A familiar draft hit her in the face, and she felt reassured that her mother had been outside. She was right. The shutters were open, and the pigeons had evidently been on the balcony as usual, but Hilde wasn't with them. Stepping further into the room Katja suddenly saw her, sitting in her favourite chair, facing the French windows. Her eyes were closed, but her mouth was wide open. Katja smiled and laid a gentle hand on her shoulder to nudge her awake.

'Mutti, I'm home.' But there was no response. 'Mutti?' She knelt down beside her. 'Mutti.' This time there was panic in her voice. An empty box of pills and a half-full bottle of schnapps lay on the table beside. Lunging forward, she grabbed her mother by the shoulders and shook her. 'No! Mutti, no!'

She felt for a pulse in her neck, but her mother's skin was as cold as *kachelofen* tiles, and as pale as the ivory carvings. After the terrible moment of realisation came the tears. They welled up as she slumped by her mother's side on the sofa, drawing her frail body to hers in a final, tragic embrace.

'Surely you knew I'd come back, Mutti? I've never let you down before. How could you think I would, Mutti? How?' she asked over and over, cradling her mother in her arms. She rocked her back and forth like a baby, and as she rocked, her guilt re-emerged. She should never have agreed to go to Paris with the transcript. There had always been an element of doubt over the timings. Deep in her heart, she knew that not being able to get a message to her mother had been the final nail in her coffin. Hilde had felt abandoned by the one person she could trust in a world where evil and ugliness had stalked her. Her only comforts had been found in her daughter and her pigeons. And her daughter had let her down. If she hadn't gone to Paris to deliver the transcript, Katja told herself, Mutti would still be alive.

Rising from the sofa she trudged along the corridor to where she had set down her luggage. She starred hard at the hatbox and suddenly felt nothing but hatred for what it held inside. It couldn't remain in the apartment a moment longer than necessary. Like one of the shamanic talismans her father brought back from his travels in Africa, the contents of the folder took on a life of their own, as if Hitler himself had cursed them. It suddenly became the focus of her pain and anger. Bending low, she opened the hatbox and took out the folder, then hurled it along the corridor in disgust; it landed with its pages splayed a few metres away. It was pure evil. It had led to her mother's death. It couldn't stay in the apartment another day. She wanted it out of her home and out of her life.

*

Dr Spier certified Hilde's death. He also said he would arrange for her body to be removed for burial. It was clear, he said, she had taken her own life. After all, it was not the first time she had tried.

'Thank you, Doctor,' said Katja, showing him to the front door. As she opened it, the blue star opposite reminded her of Frau Cohen.

269

'Do you know what happened?' she asked, aware Dr Spier had also treated her neighbour in the past.

He shrugged his indifference. 'They've been rounding up Jews for the past few weeks. They're sending them to Neuengamme,' he told her in the same way a teacher might tell a parent their child was going on a school outing. It seemed of little consequence to him, but Katja understood its significance. A labour camp had been built nearby the previous year. No one spoke about it, but Katja knew Frau Cohen's fate was virtually sealed.

*

Later that same day, after the undertakers had removed her mother's body, Katja knew what she had to do. The folder belonged at Dr Viktor's house. It was cursed. Taboo. After what had happened to poor Frau Cohen, it would be safer in his home rather than hers too. At least that is what she convinced herself.

Clutching the hatbox with the transcript inside, she took the tram to the Viktors' townhouse in the twilight. Inside was a note she'd penned, explaining what had happened in Paris. In it she'd tried to replicate Daniel's optimism, assuring the doctor this was not the end of the mission. It would continue, but it must be without her. Her mother was dead, and she felt responsible. There were other avenues the doctor could try to bring the free world's attention to Hitler's dangerous mania. *But from now on,* she wrote, *I regret I want no further part in it.*

The shutters at the townhouse were closed, but a light burned in the front room. Someone was in, although this time Katja would use the tradesman's entrance. Taking the steep steps down to the basement, she tapped gently at that door. No reply. Moving to her right, she peered through a grille to the kitchen window to see Ute, stoking the fire. She tapped again, only louder this time. Seconds later, when Ute finally opened the door, her eyes widened in surprise at seeing Katja, before she began to shut the door in her face.

'Ute, please,' she pleaded, stepping quickly over the threshold. Wedging herself against the doorjamb and keeping her voice hushed, she said: 'You've got to help me.'

'I . . . No, I . . . Frau . . .' Flustered, the maid looked behind her, as if expecting her mistress to appear at any moment.

'Just see that you put this in Dr Viktor's study. He'll know what it is,' she said, taking the parcel out of her hatbox and handing it over. 'Please, Ute,' she added, thrusting the package under the maid's nose. 'For Dr Viktor. I will telephone him as soon as I can.'

Another glance over her shoulder assured the maid they were still alone. 'But the doctor . . .' she began with a frown, when suddenly . . .

'Ute! Ute, is that you? Is someone with you?'

The maid tensed then took the parcel from Katja's hands.

'*Nein, meine Herrin,*' she called up to Frau Viktor then resumed scowling at Katja. 'Now go.'

'Thank you,' mouthed Katja, pressing her palms together and leaving the kitchen in haste to make her way back up the steps and safely out onto the street.

It felt good to be rid of the folder, like casting off a hex, but it also felt bad. She had just passed the poisoned chalice back to Dr Ernst Viktor, cursing the day she'd ever agreed to help him.

Chapter 43

Time had collapsed around Ernst Viktor. Without any natural light in his cell, he had no idea whether it was day or night. All he did know was that he could hear footsteps echoing along the corridor and they had just stopped outside his door. It clattered open.

'Get up!' shouted the guard.

Stiffly he lumbered to his feet and, after being handcuffed, he was pushed out into the corridor and marched up a flight of steps into a small room. It was furnished with a table and two chairs.

'Sit!' came the order.

Left alone, Viktor understood he was awaiting an interrogator. He would, no doubt, be asked about his relationship with Katja, as well as Kommodore Flebert's wife. They'd definitely drag up Leisel's suicide too. But he had witnesses: friends who would surely testify in his defence. Katja for one. He knew he could rely on her to stand up for him in the face of these bullies. Although try as he might, after Katja, he really couldn't think of anyone else who might speak in his favour.

Sounds in the corridor. The clicking of heels. An officer was approaching. The door swung open, and a guard gave the Nazi salute, as in walked a man wearing the uniform of a high-ranking naval officer.

'Stand!'

Viktor's expression betrayed his shock.

'You are surprised to see me, my dear Doctor,' remarked Kommodore Flebert. The observation was followed by one of his hearty laughs. 'Please take a seat and, guard . . .' He gestured across the room. 'Uncuff him.'

Another guard pulled out a chair to allow Flebert to sit opposite the doctor. Clasping his hands on the table, he smiled broadly. 'I am sure you would like something to drink, *Herr Doktor*. Coffee, perhaps. Or a schnapps.'

'Water, please,' replied Viktor through parched lips.

'Of course.' Flebert clicked his fingers. 'I trust the Gestapo have not been too inhospitable. They do have quite a reputation. In the *Kriegsmarine* we are much more civilised.'

A cup of water suddenly appeared on the table and, as Viktor gulped most of it down, the door was shut. 'Good,' Flebert said. 'Now we can start our little chat.' He made it sound as if they were sitting by the fire in a gentleman's club. The doctor suddenly felt a little less troubled. 'You know why you are here?'

Viktor frowned. 'I'm assuming there has been some sort of misunderstanding. I was told my alleged' – he emphasised the word *alleged* – 'misconduct was an internal matter and that I would go before a tribunal, Kommodore,' he pointed out.

Flebert nodded. He seemed to be acting reasonably. 'And that might still be the case.'

Viktor allowed himself to release a little of his breath in a sigh. *Was his former colleague proposing some sort of trade-off?* he wondered.

And then it came. Flebert pressed his fingers to his lips as if priming his weapon, then fired. 'This business with my wife.' He leaned forward, putting his elbows on the table. His stale breath wafted across it when he exhaled. 'We both of us know she is a highly strung woman, prone to mood swings and hysteria, which of course is not uncommon in her sex.' Viktor, although not agreeing, remained silent. 'She may, of course, have imagined the unfortunate incident she alleges happened in your clinic.'

The doctor's brows shot up simultaneously, hoping for a moment that the kommodore might take his side. Such a suggestion would certainly work in his favour. He took advantage, leaning forward eagerly. 'If you'll allow me to explain. As I said, a misunderstanding. Frau Flebert may have problems with her recollection of events.'

But his plan backfired. 'Are you calling my wife a liar, Doctor?'

Viktor retreated. 'No. No, of course not.' He shook his head vigorously. 'But she may have been pressurised.'

Flebert shot back. 'By whom?'

Viktor took a deep breath. 'I have enemies at the clinic, Kommodore. Professional enemies who want me out of the picture. The charges against me are invented. Surely you know, as a fellow former naval officer, I would never touch your wife inappropriately.'

'But others most certainly have,' Flebert continued, his mouth now a flat line across his florid face.

'I don't understand,' replied Viktor, trying to disguise the fact that he understood all too well.

Flebert tilted his head. 'Last week, I discovered her in bed with a much younger rating.' He paused before pulling his lips into a taut smile and deferring to Viktor. 'He's since been dispatched, by the way.'

Suddenly feeling his mouth go dry, Viktor reached for the last of the water and drained the glass, telling himself he mustn't dwell on the fate of the young mariner.

'But it was what my wife told me afterwards that I found particularly interesting,' Flebert continued.

'Oh?' said Viktor, remembering with dread the advice he had

274

given to Frau Flebert, half-jokingly. Now it seemed it was not only his career on the line.

'Yes. She told me it was you who told her take a lover to help her overcome her frigidity with me.' His mouth twitched a smile. 'Surely that cannot be true. Tell me she was making that up, dear Doctor?'

Viktor thought quickly and coughed out a laugh. 'As you said, your wife is prone to mood swings which, in turn, can affect recall.'

Flebert leaned back in his seat. 'That is reassuring to know. I am glad we have cleared up that matter, at least.' He looked at the empty cup. 'More water, Doctor?'

Viktor shook his head. 'No, thank you.'

The kommodore nodded, then, still looking at the cup, added: 'But I fear there is something even more pressing.' His delivery carried a sharp edge to it, cutting through any previous courtesy. Viktor sensed more trouble and shifted on his chair. 'The last time I saw you was at the launch of the *Bismarck*.' Flebert licked his lips.

Viktor nodded, wondering what calibre of torpedo was being aimed at him.

'The Führer noticed you too, of course.'

So, there it is, Viktor thought, his stomach suddenly convulsing at the mention of Hitler's name. The kommodore had launched his torpedo and it was locked on to him. Viktor thought he might vomit.

'It was an honour to see him again,' he replied, remembering Hitler's reaction at the meeting and how his demonic blue eyes had shifted away rather than dare look into his. 'But he seemed not to remember me.'

Flebert threw his head back and a hollow laugh rang round the walls. 'Not remember you? On the contrary. True, the Führer did not acknowledge you, but I can assure you, your presence was noted. In fact, seeing you reminded him that you might have something of his in your possession.'

The torpedo was on target. Viktor tried to take evasive action, even though he knew it was futile. 'Really? And what might that be?'

Leaning forward, Flebert said in a low voice, 'Why did you and that pretty little secretary of yours go to France?'

Viktor shot him a shocked look. It was all making sense now. It was the kommodore who sent his spies to Paris and took photographs.

Flebert's shoulders heaved in silent mockery. 'You see, the Führer believes you have something of his – something very personal – and he wants it back.'

A direct hit. 'I don't know what you're talking about,' said Viktor, turning his head away from his inquisitor.

'Oh, but I think you do,' came the reply. Flebert lifted his wrist to look at his watch. 'About an hour ago, the Gestapo went to your house to search it. They should be back any moment now.'

'What?' For a second Viktor allowed his anger to show, before he said with more confidence: 'They certainly won't find anything belonging to the Führer in my house.' He'd remembered that Katja had the folder. As long as it was in her possession, together with his original notebook, both remained relatively safe. And so did he.

A knock at the door came then. 'Ah, the search party returns,' said Flebert smugly. 'Come.'

In marched a Gestapo officer carrying a brown paper parcel. He saluted the kommodore and set the package down on the table, then stepped back. It was clear it had been opened.

'Well, well,' said Flebert, his head angled to inspect the parcel.

The seal on it was already broken, but the kommodore approached it with the focus of a surgeon, delicately prising the brown paper apart to reveal the folder, then opening it to uncover the first page of the document.

'What have we here?' he asked, staring gleefully at the typing on the front.

Ernst Viktor didn't reply, even though he knew only too well what Flebert had just seen. His mouth was so dry, no words could escape. Instead, he simply stared at the sheet of white paper on the table on which Katja had typed the title – centred capitals in twenty-point Brokenscript font – *Notes & Observations on the Serious Mental Disorders of Adolf Hitler.*

He also knew he was a dead man.

Chapter 44

Katja's Sunday was spent making funeral arrangements with the church. Her mother had been a devout Catholic and it hurt deeply that she would not be buried in sacred ground with her husband. But she had taken her own life and that meant she could not be reunited with her beloved Reinhart in the next.

Hilde's death was not the only thing that pressed heavily on Katja that Monday morning. Returning to the clinic would not be easy either. She would have to account for her week-long absence, and being unable to speak directly with Dr Viktor only made matters worse. Nor did the icy stares and glowers from Fräulein Schauble and the nursing staff do anything to ease her worries. She had left the clinic as an employee, but it seemed she was returning as an outcast. Did they suspect what she had been doing? Or did they know?

She had just reached for the handle of the office door, when Dr Ulbricht ambushed her.

'Fräulein Heinz,' he called. 'My office, now.'

Katja felt a vice clamp round her chest. Something had happened in her absence. She stood before Ulbricht's desk, trying, unsuccessfully, to stop herself shaking.

'Sit,' he told her, making her feel like a dog. 'You are recovered?'

She wasn't sure if he was being concerned or sarcastic. She decided to tell the truth.

'My mother died yesterday,' she said. The words hurt her as they tumbled from her mouth. After Dr Spier and the priest, Ulbricht was only the third person she had told, and she found it painful. But instead of offering his sympathy, Ulbricht appeared unmoved.

Leaning back in his chair, he said: 'A woman in her condition shouldn't have been left on her own, should she?'

Katja shot him a horrified look. 'What do you mean?'

He continued high-handedly, arching his brow: 'Surely, Fräulein Heinz, you must accept responsibility for your mother's death. After all, you did leave her alone.' Blood was pounding through Katja's ears so hard, she found it difficult to think, let alone hear. 'You lied when you reported sick. Or rather Dr Viktor lied for you.'

Suddenly Katja's mind flew to the photograph of her father, which she noticed had been moved, along with the beaded bowl, plucked from its normal place on the shelf and left on the table. The realisation suddenly dawned.

'You went to my apartment to check up on me. You visited my mother.' She tried to keep her voice even, but she was struggling against the tide of rage sweeping through her veins.

Ulbricht nodded. His voice was also measured. 'I left her in a most distressed state. She thought you'd gone for good.'

The anger that had bubbled up inside Katja's chest now cracked the surface. She leaped up. 'No!' she insisted. 'How dare you say that? She knew I would never leave her.'

'Oh, but you did, didn't you?' Ulbricht let his words sink in for a moment before he reminded her of his power. 'I could easily dismiss you without a reference,' he said.

Katja paused, then slumped back down into her chair, holding her breath. Work was hard to come by. She wouldn't be able to pay her rent, let alone eat.

'But I will not, if you do as I say.'

And here it comes, she thought. The bargaining, or rather the blackmail. He had those photographs. He would require her to lie about her relationship with Dr Viktor at the tribunal in return for keeping her job.

'As you know, there is to be a disciplinary hearing for Dr Viktor on Friday. He is a man of low morals and a lover of Jews, and no doubt more about his sordid past will come out. And you, being of good character, will testify against him.'

It was what she dreaded most. 'And if I refuse?'

Ulbricht leered at her. 'Then I will see to it that you will never work again.'

*

Later that evening, Katja travelled back to the suburbs to see Dr Viktor, but she'd only taken a few steps down the tree-lined street towards his townhouse when she stopped dead. Two Gestapo were stationed outside the front door. Daniel was right when he said he feared the doctor was being watched. It seemed his suspension had escalated to house arrest, but why had Dr Ulbricht not mentioned anything? Why had the Gestapo become involved? Puzzled, she decided not to interfere by trying to see him. She was about to turn round when she stopped to make sure her eyes weren't deceiving her. A man in naval uniform was emerging from the front door. A tall man. An officer. As the two guards flung out their Nazi salutes, she recognised the imposing figure stepping into a waiting limousine straight away. It was Kommodore Flebert, and his presence at the Viktors's house could only mean one thing.

Panic pressed against her chest as she grasped what she had just witnessed. Ulbricht may not know about the medical notes, but the kommodore just might. That was why Dr Viktor was under house arrest. But why hadn't he been taken into custody? He was, after all, guilty of treason and the Third Reich showed no mercy to traitors. She doubled back and this time took the tram straight to the train station. On arrival, she hurried to one of the telephone kiosks on the concourse. With a trembling hand, she lifted the receiver to make an international reverse charge call to Paris, to the offices of *The Parisian*.

'Daniel Keenan speaking,' came the voice down the crackly line when they were finally connected.

'Oh Daniel, thank God.'

'What's wrong, Katja?'

'I just went to Dr Viktor's house and there are Gestapo outside.'

A short pause on the line. 'But you still have it, yes?'

She took a deep breath as she thought about the folder. Regret had set in the moment she saw the guards at the doctor's door. Regret and fear. 'That's just it, Daniel. He has it! When I returned from Paris I went to his house and gave it back.'

The sound of a sharp gulp travelled down the line. It was another moment before Daniel said anything again, as if he'd needed to think through his next move.

'It's going to be all right,' he soothed, playing for time.

'But it's not, Daniel. It's not going to be all right because she's . . . she's dead.' Another sob strangled her words.

'Who, Katja? What are you talking about?'

'My mother, Daniel. My mother is dead.' She wiped away her tears with the back of her hand.

'Oh, God! I'm so sorry. What happened?'

Katja sobbed out her reply. 'She took pills. She killed herself because . . .' She gave in to tears again. 'Because she thought I'd abandoned her.'

'No. No. You mustn't blame yourself.' His voice came concerned down the line.

'I don't know what to do, Daniel. If they've found it, then they'll execute him. They won't even give him a trial.'

'Listen, Katja. Listen to me,' he pleaded. 'I spoke with the US embassy yesterday. I had to do an interview and I managed a word with the ambassador's deputy. He said if Dr Viktor can get a couple of sponsors, his application could be speeded up.'

'But he's under house arrest, Daniel. There are guards at his door.'

'When is the hearing?'

'This Friday, I think.' She could barely breathe, let alone think.

'You must find witnesses who will speak up for the doctor.'

She shook her head. It was hard to explain that fear held so many in its grip. 'Everyone is afraid, Daniel. I've been told I won't ever get another job if I don't tell lies about him. Don't you see, I . . .'

'Then you need to find out if the Gestapo have found it.' His voice was more forceful, and she knew he was right.

'And what if they have?' she muttered.

'Then you must leave, Katja. Get out of there while you still can. War is coming soon. Maybe next week. Maybe next month, but it'll happen, and you need to escape from Germany while you can.'

He was well meaning, but there were so many obstacles to overcome before she could reach Paris. Guards were now stopping people who wanted to board cross-border trains. They would never let her leave Germany.

'What about Dr Viktor?'

'If they have the folder, then I'm afraid there's little hope, Katja.'

'But what if I can help him escape and get him to Paris?'

'You couldn't do that. It's too risky.'

'Risky?' she repeated, her mind whirling at the thought. 'But it could be done.'

'You need to save yourself, Katja. I'll do all I can to find another sponsor for the doctor's American visa if the Gestapo do release him, but don't put yourself in any more danger. Please, Katja.' He was pleading down the line. 'Call me again as soon as you know more.'

'Yes. I will,' said Katja.

'Whatever you do,' he told her, 'I have faith in you.'

The words that had been hovering on her lips finally surfaced.

'I l . . .' she began, but before they could all come out, the line went dead.

*

Katja needed to clear her head. She walked back from the *bahnhof* towards her apartment and had just reached the busy junction where Hitler's image still glowered down, when she suddenly spotted a food cart on the opposite side of the road. At the sight, Frau Cohen's words came flooding back. 'The pretzel stand on Müggenkampstrasse,' she'd said. In the event of an emergency, her son could be contacted via the stall. She dreaded to think what had happened to the old lady, but maybe, just maybe, Aaron was still safe and forging documents somewhere in the city. She crossed the road. A young man with greasy hair and pimples was manning the stand.

Taking out her purse, Katja handed him a few coins. 'I'd like a pretzel,' she told him. 'And I'd also like to find out how I can get in touch with Aaron Cohen.'

The youth gave her a stealthy look. 'I don't know any Aaron Cohen,' he told her, reaching for a warm pretzel.

'I think you do,' Katja insisted. 'He was my neighbour. They took his mother last week.'

The young man dropped the pretzel in a paper bag and handed it to her, all the while looking nervously around.

'I'm in trouble. I need documents. Quickly.' She searched his face but found no recognition.

'I'm sorry,' he replied with a shake of his greasy head. 'I don't know what you're talking about.'

*

Returning to the apartment was hard for Katja. It was empty and yet her mother remained. Outside on the balcony, the pigeons

283

still congregated, expecting the doors to be flung open at any moment and breadcrumbs showered down. Hilde's slippers sat at her bedside. Her smell too, a sort of musty yet comforting scent with a hint of lavender, lingered in the bedroom.

Katja reached for a blouse that lay crumpled on the bed and held it close, breathing in its perfume. 'Why did you leave me?' she whispered, tears trickling freely down her cheeks.

At first, she thought the soft tapping she could hear was made by a pigeon and ignored it, but when it grew louder, she walked over to the balcony and realised the sound was coming from the hallway. Someone was at the front door. Wiping away her tears in the hall mirror, she opened the door on the chain and peered out warily. But it didn't take long for her to fling the door wide.

'Aaron!' she said, as soon as her visitor was over the threshold and safely inside. 'It is so good to see you. But your mother . . .'

As soon as he took off his hat, she saw his face was pinched and thin. But when she looked down at his hands and saw his fingers were stained with ink, she knew he was still working.

'Yes. They took her,' he said, resignedly. 'I heard she went to Neuengamme.' But he seemed reluctant to talk about her. 'I was told you need documents.'

'Yes. Yes, I do. Come,' she said, leading Aaron through to the salon.

'How is your mother?' he asked, his eyes on Hilde's empty chair.

Katja bit her lip. 'She's dead, Aaron,' she replied, not wanting to catch his eye or explain.

'I'm so sorry,' he said. 'She was a good person.'

'Yes, she was,' Katja agreed. 'And so are you,' she added, offering him a seat.

She sat opposite him. 'I'll come to the point.' She was wringing her hands as she spoke. 'My boss at the clinic where I work needs to leave the country and so do I, but I know we will be stopped. We both need false passports to get to Paris.'

Aaron nodded. 'You have come to the right person. You have photographs?'

Katja went to a nearby drawer. 'Here is my Reichpass. I'm supposing you can use the photo from that, but as for Dr Viktor . . .' She continued to rummage in the drawer. 'What about this?' She handed him a brochure, opened at a page entitled 'Clinical Staff'. Ernst Viktor's face stared out at the top of the page. 'Could you do something with that?' she asked, pointing to the doctor's face.

Aaron nodded. 'Leave it with me,' he said, starting to tear the page from the brochure.

'I am grateful,' said Katja reaching for her purse and unfurling the remainder of the bank notes Dr Viktor had given her for the trip to Paris. 'Here,' she said, pressing them into Aaron's palm.

Seemingly satisfied, he nodded, but then handed back the notes. 'For your mother,' he said with a shake of his head. 'The passports will be waiting for you at the pretzel stand the day after tomorrow.'

Katja smiled as a glimmer of hope suddenly returned. 'Thank you so much. Your mother is proud of you, you know, wherever she is.'

He nodded at her remark, then making sure he wasn't being watched, left as quickly as he had come.

Chapter 45

Ernst Viktor sat alone in his study, gazing around him at the wonder of it all. Since his escape from the jaws of hell, it had struck him how there was beauty in even the simplest things, like his silver inkstand, or the small painting of a woodland scene by the door. Every stick of furniture now became an icon; every book in his library a treasure. He hadn't expected to see any of them ever again; hadn't expected to return to his refuge alive. He'd anticipated a firing squad at best, or at worst beheading. But here he was – released from the clutches of the Gestapo and back home.

His former naval comrade, Stefan Flebert, had shown him mercy, even though his freedom had come at a price. The kommodore may have handed him the lighted match, but it was he who had done the deed. Being forced to burn the typed notes in front of Flebert, had been the hardest thing he'd ever done; like killing his own child. It had cut him like a knife, but the only alternative, he'd been warned, was execution without trial. The transcript was already in their hands. His death would have served no purpose, so a bargain was struck. In return for his silence, he, Viktor, would appear in front of the disciplinary panel and be found guilty of gross misconduct. He would be struck off as a practising psychiatrist – he had, after all, violated the Hippocratic Oath – be stripped of his pension and would live out the rest of his life in disgrace. But at least he would be allowed to live. Given what he knew of the Nazis, that was all he could hope for.

Flebert insisted the Führer would remain forever grateful to Viktor for showing him how to cure himself of his blindness, and as a mark of his gratitude, his life would be spared. Of course, he hadn't believed anything the kommodore had said until he'd finally been allowed back into his own home. Now, it seemed Flebert's word just might be his bond – now, at any rate – and Ernst Viktor was luxuriating in his freedom.

Since his return, even Gerda seemed almost bearable to him, although he knew the feeling wasn't mutual. His professional disgrace reflected so badly on her that she planned to return to live with her parents in Potsdam. Ever since she'd learned of the hearing, there'd been no doubt in her mind that her husband was guilty of gross misconduct. She'd been in a murderous mood for the past few days. Nor had she seemed overjoyed to be reunited with him when he was delivered home safely by Kommodore Flebert, although the Gestapo would remain outside his house until the tribunal on Friday, to ensure he didn't try to flee beforehand.

It was, therefore, of little surprise to the doctor when Gerda stormed into his office that morning like a tornedo.

'What is the meaning of this?' she demanded to know, holding up a pannier of pretzels and a baguette. 'Is cook's bread not good enough for you now?'

Ernst Viktor offered his wife a perplexed look, eyeing up the bread with a frown. 'I'm not sure . . .' he began. But she cut across his words.

'Look,' she scowled, pointing to an invoice in the basket. *Four pretzels and a large Parisian loaf.* 'Of course the guards helped themselves to two of the pretzels, but can you explain the order?

It's not our usual baker, but it has your name on it.' Her fat finger tapped the handwritten note.

Intrigued, the doctor shrugged. 'No, dear. I have no explanation, but since it is here . . .' He took the loaf from the basket and broke off one end before popping it in his mouth. His wife's eyes followed his hands in disgust.

'You are impossible!' she exclaimed, and tutting to herself, she exited the room, taking the rest of the bread with her.

It was the word *Parisian* that struck a chord. All baguettes were French in origin, Viktor reasoned, so why call it Parisian, unless there was some special significance? And why did the order have his name on it? He scrutinised the bill and suddenly recognising the handwriting, felt a surge of adrenaline course through his veins. Eagerly, he examined the long, golden loaf, and noticed a strange bulge in the middle. When he tapped the underside, it made an odd sound, so using both his hands, he broke it in two. Something was inside; something square that was wrapped in baking paper. Quickly tearing it off, Viktor could barely believe his eyes when out fell a French passport. Opening it, he saw his own face, but under it a different name. Not only that. There was a note. It said simply: *Platform 5. Thursday. 19.03.*

Viktor paused for a moment. The date was the day before his hearing and the train for Paris always left from Platform 5. He had just been thrown a lifeline.

'Katja,' he whispered.

*

The day of Dr Ulbricht's ultimatum to Katja finally arrived.

'So, you have come to a decision?'

The doctor had ordered her into his office, as she'd anticipated, and now she stood before him. She guessed that by now the Nazis would have the transcript in their possession. They would surely destroy it. Thank God she still had the original notebook.

'Yes, sir.' Her eyes dipped to the desk. She didn't want him to see the contempt in them.

'Well?'

She swallowed, choking down her true feelings. She had thought long and hard about what she was going to say. 'Yes. I will testify against Dr Viktor.'

Ulbricht's normally solemn face lifted in a smile. 'Good,' he said. 'You have made the right decision, Fräulein Heinz. Men like Ernst Viktor are a scourge on our profession. Sexual impropriety will not be tolerated.'

There was a certain conviction in his words that led Katja to wonder if he knew anything about the medical notes. If he had been told of its existence, he hadn't mentioned it. Perhaps he was being kept in the dark. After all, the fewer people who knew about Hitler's mental disorders, the better. What if – and she knew she was jumping to conclusions – what if Hitler himself had ordered Flebert to be the puppet master? After all, his wife was one of Viktor's accusers. Maybe it was the kommodore and not Ulbricht who was ultimately pulling the strings that would inevitably lead to Dr Viktor's downfall?

Ulbricht drummed his fingers on the desk. 'So, the statement?'

'I have it here, sir,' Katja replied, handing over three sheets of paper, neatly pinned together.

She had written her testimony in the apartment the evening before, knowing it would be required of her. It was a work of pure fiction, of course. It stated that when the doctor had first made advances to her, she had rebuffed him. When he persisted in Paris and had come to her room to seduce her, she had been forced to defend herself against his sexual advances. Under attack, she had fought back. She had grabbed a vase and hit him. That was how he had sustained his head injury.

Ulbricht scanned it. 'Good,' he said, as if the statement was simply a schoolgirl's essay and not a colleague's character assassination. 'You have done well, Fräulein Heinz, and now you may go. Oh, and . . .' He nodded at a pile of papers on his desk. 'Please take those notes with you. They need to be typed up by this evening. From now on, you work for me.'

*

That evening, Katja finalised arrangements. She purchased two one-way tickets to Paris from the train station. But even more important, was the notebook that now lay under her floorboards. It was all that remained, but it was enough. In truth, it was only when she was halfway to Dr Viktor's house to warn him that she'd remembered that it still lay under the floorboards in her bedroom and berated herself for not returning it too. But then catching sight of Flebert had shocked her so much that she was suddenly thankful she'd kept the precious original. Now, she was determined to leave it untouched in its secret hiding place until the last possible moment. It was her death warrant, but it was also her lifeline.

Finally, she inspected the forged passports. Aaron had done a wonderful job on them both. She'd asked for French forgeries, believing it might smooth their journey to Paris. Aaron had given them French names and they would travel on the same train but in separate compartments, pretending not to know each other in case either was arrested. She would keep the original notebook in her hatbox.

Once in Paris, she hoped that an American visa might be waiting for Dr Viktor, while she was sure she could prevail upon Sylvia to accommodate her until she could get a work permit.

An image of Daniel popped into her head and her heart skipped at the thought of seeing him in just over twenty-four hours, if all went to plan. The WB Yeats' book of poems lay on her bedside table; the one Daniel had given to her. Reaching for it, she kissed it. It would sustain her on the journey to Paris.

By the time she had checked and rechecked everything it was

late. After work the next day, she would collect her belongings and travel straight to the train station to rendezvous with Dr Viktor. Somehow, probably with Ute's help, he would have managed to slip from his home unnoticed. It was a huge gamble she was taking, but she was sure he'd find a way of escaping from under the Gestapo's nose if he knew a ticket was waiting at the train station for him. Together, she and the doctor would catch the 19.03 to the Gare de l'Est and, if all went to plan, eight hours later they would both be starting new lives.

Chapter 46

Ernst Viktor stared hard into the bathroom mirror. The air was so chilly that his breath hazed the glass and he had to grab a towel to wipe it clear of the condensation. While he was still happy to be home, he'd had a troubled night, kept awake by thoughts of the forthcoming tribunal and his undoubted professional humiliation. He took out his pince-nez from his dressing-gown breast pocket and hooked them over his nose.

With both hands planted on either side of the handbasin, he sighed heavily as he studied himself in the mirror; the hair that stood stiffly like grey tree trunks from his scalp, the deep creases on his broad face and his less than taut jawline. With a look of resignation, he told himself age was catching up with him, and that, given the deep vertical furrows above his large nose, he'd obviously frowned far too much over his fifty-five years. But at least now, after his bargain with Flebert, there was a chance he might reach old age.

As he opened the bathroom cabinet door to reach for his shaving brush, his thoughts turned to Katja. He could trust her. At least he knew she wouldn't betray him at the tribunal, although he couldn't blame her if she changed her mind. She was young and her whole life lay before her. He, on the other hand, was finished. The most he could hope for was to be left alone to live out his life in the shadows. But whatever his hopes – and fears – that morning, less than two minutes later, they'd disappeared, splattered, along with his brain, all over the bathroom's white tiled floor and walls.

The doctor's last blurred view in the mirror was not of his own bloodshot eyes nor of his stubbled chin, but of a silent assassin aiming a loaded pistol at his head before the fatal shot was fired.

*

'Ernst!' called Gerda, as soon as she heard the deafening bang. Her husband – her clumsy, useless husband – must have dropped something heavy on the floor. She hoped he hadn't broken anything of value. Struggling out of bed as fast as her bulky frame allowed, she drew her dressing gown across large breasts and lumbered over the landing.

'Ernst, what have you done?' she bellowed. She'd already lifted her hand to bang on the door when she noticed it wasn't fully shut. It was only after she'd pushed it open and stepped forward that she froze, and her gaze dropped to see she'd stepped in something warm, sticky and bright red.

Downstairs in the kitchen, Ute had also been alerted by the noise. She'd been about to carry up a breakfast tray to Frau Viktor, but, thinking either her master or mistress might have fallen, she set it down immediately to rush upstairs. In her haste and concern, she failed to notice someone in the shadows, hiding below the treads as she ascended, although she did feel a rush of cold air around her ankles before she reached the landing. Looking down towards the back door at the foot of the stairs, she was just in time to see it shut. Confused, she continued to the top of the flight to witness Gerda Viktor's eyes open wide in horror and a chilling cry escape her lips. A second later, Ute found out the reason. Her mistress had just realised why her bare feet suddenly felt warm. Looking to the floor, she'd seen they were planted in her husband's blood.

*

Sleep had not come easily to Katja that night. Her mind had ticked like clockwork, trying to synchronise timings and plan for eventualities, so that when the sun rose over Hamburg on the morning of 30 August, she found herself wide awake. Dressing quickly, she decided to take an earlier tram into work.

It felt odd making the journey for what she knew would be the last time. Past the junction with the pretzel stand on the corner of Müggenkampstrasse she went. Past the huge poster of Hitler and the enormous black and red banners fluttering in the fresh breeze from the Elbe, past Herr Wortzman's bookshop where she and her father spent so many happy hours. She prayed he would watch over her and Dr Viktor and guide them both in what they were about to do.

It was not yet eight o'clock when Katja arrived at the clinic, but the main entrance was open, even though Fräulein Schauble was absent. Walking along the corridor, Katja glanced to her left to see Nurse Wilhelm busy filing documents at the desk, and somewhere in the distance a telephone began to ring. Approaching Dr Viktor's office, she realised it was his phone. Hurrying through the door, she dived for the receiver to pick it up, then taking a deep breath she answered as professionally as she could: 'Dr Viktor's office. How may I help you?'

'Fräulein Heinz. Fräulein Katja Heinz?' The words, spoken by a woman, came out shakily.

It was as if a stone had dropped onto Katja's chest, sending ripples of anxiety throughout her body. Something wasn't right. How did the caller know her name? Fear suddenly gripped her. Clearing her throat, she asked: 'Who's speaking, please?' She didn't recognise the clotted voice at first, although it became clear soon enough.

'He's dead, you filthy whore!' A sob strangled the woman's voice for a moment before she added: 'My Viktor is dead from a bullet through his head, and it's all your fault!'

The caller's vitriol continued to spew down the line. A torrent of vile accusations and lies threatened to drown Katja, although after Frau Viktor's first few words she did not listen. Although they swarmed around her like angry bees, she didn't bother to fend them off. News of the doctor's death blanked out everything else as a sense of dread settled upon her. Viktor had warned her this might happen. He'd told her the authorities would say it was suicide. Or that he'd had an accident. But never the truth. Never that they'd ordered his murder.

After a moment, the telephone clicked, and the line went dead. Slowly, mechanically, Katja replaced the receiver in its cradle. Silence settled on the room once more. The clock still ticked, and in the next office Nurse Wilhelm's nimble fingers continued to flick through files, but in her head Katja heard the doctor's words echo: *I am a marked man.* He had prophesied his own death.

The focus shifted. And now, alone at her desk, across the room from where the doctor usually sat, a thought struck her like a sharp blow to the jaw. Dr Viktor had been in possession of the folder containing the typed notes. With his death would come its inevitable discovery – if the Gestapo hadn't already found it – and undoubted destruction. Only she knew about the original notebook. That meant that she, Katja Heinz, was now the sole keeper of Ernst Viktor's secret – the secret that had led to his death.

Chapter 47

News of Dr Viktor's death spread like wildfire around the clinic. Throughout the morning, Nurse Wilhelm had to break up huddles of junior nurses as they neglected their duties to peel off and gossip in corners. Most talked of suicide. The doctor couldn't face the shame. Some said he'd done *the honourable thing*.

Katja found it impossible to concentrate on the pile of typing Dr Ulbricht had loaded on her desk the previous evening. Her trembling hands had no strength to press down the keys of her typewriter and tears kept springing without warning from her eyes. She was just wiping her cheeks dry when Nurse Wilhelm sneaked into her office, a look of malicious glee on her face.

'Look what you've done,' she hissed. 'You drove him to it.'

Katja returned a horrified glare. 'What?'

'You may as well have pulled the trigger.' She narrowed her eyes. 'Perhaps you did.'

Panic filled Katja's hollowed chest. 'How can you say that? I had nothing to do with the doctor's death.'

The nurse coughed out a mocking laugh and folded her spindly arms. 'Come on. Don't play the innocent. Everyone knows you two were having an affair.'

Of course, Katja was aware that's what the nursing staff had thought for a while. She'd ignored their whispers and insinuations because they were baseless. But now that Dr Viktor was dead, they took on a new significance.

'I'm sure you've got better things to do than spread false rumours,' countered Katja, trying to keep calm. She started to insert a sheet of paper into her typewriter roller. 'Now, I have work to get on with.'

Nurse Wilhelm uncrossed her arms. 'Not for much longer,' she sneered, before walking off. Katja could have crumpled then, but she told herself to hold things together, just until the evening. A few more hours and she would be shot of the clinic and all the despicable people who worked in it. But then she heard a voice; a familiar laugh boomed outside in the corridor.

Kommodore Flebert.

'Good morning, Ulbricht,' Katja heard him say.

She put her ear to the wall to eavesdrop on their conversation but found she could snatch only the odd word, like 'fool' and 'suicide' that rose above the rest. They were talking about Dr Viktor all right, tearing his character to shreds like slavering hounds, and about her. She felt sick and she felt numb until, five minutes later, she heard the scrape of chairs on the floor and a door open.

The kommodore was leaving, but instead of turning right down the corridor towards the reception, she heard footsteps approach her door and saw it open without warning. Flebert's large frame filled the doorway.

'Fräulein Heinz, I wish to speak to you.'

Katja leaped from her seat to see two uniformed mariners were with him, but he stepped inside and shut the door behind him. A feeling so ominous descended on her that she could barely stand under its weight. It was a relief when the kommodore gestured her to sit down.

'This morning's news,' he began, taking the chair opposite

297

her and laying his gloves and cap carefully on her desk. 'It must have come as a . . .'

Katja was anticipating him to say *shock*, but instead he said, '. . . relief.'

'I'm sorry,' she replied, thinking she had not heard the kommodore correctly. He merely smiled.

'Come, come, Fräulein Heinz. Please don't pretend the doctor's predicament over the misconduct charges didn't leave you in a difficult position. After all, you were going to have to testify against your former lover.'

Katja shook her head. 'The doctor and I were never lovers.'

His lips twitched in a half smile. 'You're a beautiful young woman. Viktor warned me off you. He wanted you to himself.' He leaned forward and lowered his voice. 'That's why he confided in you.'

'Confided?' The accusation sent alarm bells ringing in Katja's head. 'I don't know what you're talking about.'

Flebert's broad shoulders lifted. 'I think you do. Someone had to type out all the Führer's medical notes and it had to be you.'

The four walls of the office suddenly seemed to collapse in on her. It was hard to breathe.

'I've no idea what . . .'

Flebert shrugged. 'I just thought you'd like to know that the doctor destroyed the folder containing his typed notes. He burned it himself before my very eyes and told me he'd left the original at the hospital in Pasewalk. He also assured me no copies were made.' He tilted his head. 'Can you assure me of that too, Fräulein Heinz?'

Katja's body went rigid as she imagined Dr Viktor setting a match to the very papers he'd risked his own life for; the flames licking at the evidence he had spent more than twenty years guarding. He would never have set light to them willingly. The misconduct charge was just a smokescreen for something much more serious. Katja was certain Dr Ulbricht had no idea about the folder but simply played along with the disciplinary hearing, hoping to further his own career. He'd no notion it was the Führer himself who had ordered Kommodore Flebert to ensure his medical notes from Pasewalk were never made public. First Dr Viktor had been cornered with the misconduct charges, then driven into submission. At that point, he'd have been of more use to Hitler alive, but once he'd been forced to destroy the folder, it was safer to dispose of him. And now – seeing as Flebert thought she was the only person alive to share his secret – of her. This only confirmed that Ernst Viktor's murder was carried out on the orders of the officer who sat in front of her. Underneath the desk, Katja clenched her fists. She wanted to punch this evil brute dressed up in his fine uniform and tell the world he was a murderer.

Fixing Flebert with a glare, she took a deep breath, aware that a single blink might betray her. 'There were no copies,' she said.

He rose and stalked over to the window, before turning to stare at her, stony-faced, for an excruciating few seconds until, finally, he said: 'Good. Because I can assure you, Fräulein Heinz, if any original notes exist, just like the transcript, they will be burned.' He moved back to where she sat. 'And we both know when paper is burned it can sometimes lead to accidents,' he reminded her, leaning in towards her ear. 'Just like it did with your father.'

Katja's eyes widened with outrage as the memory of the flames at the Burnings flashed before her. She'd tried to put them out. Tried to save her beloved Vati. She wanted to scream as she felt Flebert's hot breath on her cheek, but she forced her jaw to remain shut. Retaliation was not an option. Not yet, at any rate. She simply nodded her cooperation and stood as the kommodore retrieved his cap and gloves to deliver one final, chilling warning to her.

'I'm glad we understand each other, Fräulein Heinz,' he told her. 'And to further that understanding, I will send a car for you this evening to bring you to my residence. I trust you will keep the appointment,' he said, suddenly reaching over the desk to lift her chin and look into her eyes. 'It would be too bad if that pretty face of yours got burned.'

*

The threats only made Katja more determined than ever to escape. She'd been given no choice. She'd left the clinic that evening and returned home to collect her things. She had to leave before Flebert's car came for her.

Mounting the stairs quickly at first, she slowed as she caught sight of the door to her apartment from the first-floor landing. Reining in her breath, she trod carefully up the stairs as fear started to creep through her. Someone had been in the apartment. Lurching from room to room, she saw the place had been ransacked on the kommodore's orders, she guessed. She didn't care so much about the smashed china ornaments or the torn books. It was what lay beneath the floor that mattered. Dashing to her own room, she prised up the board underneath her bed and her shoulders heaved with relief at the sight. There it lay. Dr Viktor's notebook. Reaching down into the dusty void, she grabbed hold of it. It was safe. She held the thick leather book close to her chest as her breathing steadied, then placed it in her hatbox.

Casting around the salon for what she knew would be the last time, she saw the intruders had flung open the French windows to the balcony. Outside the pigeons cooed above the hubbub of the trams and motorcars on the street below. She pictured Mutti, talking to them, throwing them crumbs. She reached forward to shut the doors, but her footsteps startled the birds and nearly all of them flew off immediately. But there was one – the one they'd nursed back from injury – that remained. It made no attempt to follow the others. With tears in her eyes, she held it aloft. 'Go, little one,' she whispered, adding ruefully: 'Time for us both to fly.'

*

The tram journey to the central *bahnhof* had seemed interminable. All the time Katja was fearful of arrest. All the time she kept the hatbox clasped to her, afraid to breathe, afraid to move. War was coming and the station concourse was chaotic as the tram pulled up nearby. The sound of screeching sirens scored through her head and from the window, she could see two Gestapo cars disgorging leather-clad men.

As she walked into the station, the noise from thousands of desperate people bounced off the high walls and domed ceiling and echoed all around, making it hard to think, let alone hear. Trying to keep out of the Gestapo's clutches, she'd stopped to buy a newspaper. It was then she'd heard the vendor tell a customer she was wanted for Viktor's murder. The news had come as a shock, but deep down it only confirmed her worst fears. Flebert intended to have her arrested and convicted. The death penalty would be a convenient outcome to mask the real reason for her execution.

With her head pounding and weighed down by her suitcase and hatbox, Katja staggered clumsily through the crowd. She made it to Platform 5 just before the gates closed.

'Ticket, *bitte*,' Katja heard a guard snarl.

She hoped he didn't notice her shaking hands as she presented him with her documents. As she waited for them to be checked, her eyes swept the concourse, scanning for trouble. There was a commotion further down the platform. Black-capped heads bobbed like gulls through the sea of commuters. The Gestapo were stalking along the waiting train.

'*Danke, fräulein*,' said the guard, seemingly satisfied.

Handing her ticket back, he let her pass, but then . . .

'*Reichpass, bitte!*'

A customs official was glaring at her. Fixing her lips into a smile, she handed over her French passport with all the charm she could muster. But her mouth went dry as the official studied the document carefully. Could he tell it was fake? Could he see where the photograph has been pasted, or the stamp forged? She held her breath.

The official skewered her. '*Französisch?*' he asked with an arched brow.

'*Oui*,' she replied with a smile.

'Off!' He tugged at her headscarf to reveal her blonde hair. Its revelation made her feel vulnerable. Naked even, as the guard scrutinised her features with critical eyes.

A grudging nod signified Katja could proceed. The passport was returned. She breathed again. With her head held high, she marched down the platform as fast as her heavy luggage allowed.

The Paris train was packed with people wanting to leave Germany before Nazi jackboots mobilised. Not only were all the seats full, so were the corridors. Old men crouched on suitcases. Women squatted on the floor, with children squirming on their laps and babies crying. Fighting her way through the crowded, smoke-filled corridor, she found her third-class compartment and settled in the one remaining seat. Taking out Daniel's book of poems, she placed it on her lap. The other seats in the carriage were occupied by a family. A mother and father, two children and an older woman – a grandmother, she presumed.

Together, all six of them sat in silence; no one daring to move. Eyes clamped to the floor. Too fearful, even, to draw breath. It seemed to Katja she was not the only one hiding a secret, but the more she studied the adults' drawn faces, the more she understood. Their shoulders drooped, weighed down by some unseen burden and no amount of neat patching could hide the wear in their clothes. Set against gaunt cheek bones, dark shadows only accentuated what she could see in their eyes when the parents cautiously raised their gaze. Fear.

The station clock on the platform told Katja there were just two minutes before the scheduled departure. Time stood still until, from somewhere outside, came a shout. The father turned his head towards the window. A second later, a Gestapo appeared outside, to be joined swiftly by another.

The mother and father traded terrified glances. Boots tramped along the corridor. One of the children, the little girl, began to whimper, as a figure appeared at the sliding door. A passing Gestapo glanced inside. Katja's eyes darted to the book of poetry, just as the door slid open. For a heartbeat she froze.

'You!' thundered the Gestapo.

Katja's head shot up to see the policeman lunge at the terrified man and heave him up by the lapels. 'Out. You Jewish swine!'

By now the little girl was screaming, and her brother joined in as their father pleaded with the brute.

'But we have papers,' he protested, fumbling in his coat pocket.

'Out,' shouted the Gestapo, as his colleague began yanking the grandmother's arm.

'Out! Now! You old Jew!' he yelled, suddenly drawing a gun and pointing it at her.

'Please. No,' cried the mother, pulling her daughter close.

The other Gestapo drew a cosh and hit the father's trembling hands, sending his papers flying. 'Out, I say!'

After the frail old woman was plucked easily from her seat and flung into the corridor, it was the turn of the little boy, but he proved harder to budge, biting down hard on the Gestapo's hand. The brute growled and replied with a slap across the face that sent the child hurtling backwards. His distraught mother dived screaming into the corridor, while her husband was finally bundled out of the carriage by the other Gestapo. One by one they were manhandled onto the platform.

Inside Katja was screaming too, but she held her tongue. Only a few more seconds. She had to keep it together, as her own heart broke silently and unseen.

Somehow, she managed to hold her nerve, although it wasn't until the express was well clear of Hamburg station and en route to Paris that she allowed herself to relax a little. She tried to shut out the memory of the Jewish children's screams by escaping into her book of Yeats' poems. She imagined Daniel reading them, his voice soft and soothing. But there was still the French border to cross. For the moment, however, she could breathe easier and even get a little rest. She laid her hands on the precious hatbox on her lap and finally closed her eyes.

*

Shortly after midnight, the train stopped with a jolt just before the border checkpoint with France, and Katja's nerves were pulled taut yet again. Doors slammed, and there were shouts as the German guards swept through the train one last time, looking for Jews and other 'undesirables'.

'Papers!' they boomed as they advanced along the corridors. Through blurry eyes, Katja saw a guard approach and kick a sleeping man's suitcase. The man woke with a start and hastily produced his documents. Next the guard slid open her compartment door.

'*Reichpass, bitte,*' he told her.

Katja handed over her travel documents, her heart in her mouth.

The guard looked at the carefully forged French passport and then back at her, before returning it to her without a word.

A few moments later, the French guards also boarded the train to check documents. Once more, Katja held her breath as one examined the fake.

'*Bienvenue, mademoiselle,*' he greeted, touching the peak of his kepi.

'*Merci, monsieur,*' she replied in her best French accent.

Only after he'd left the compartment did she allow herself to breathe again. Now, just five hours remained between her and Paris where the man she loved was waiting and where together they could carry on the fight to honour Dr Viktor's legacy.

304

Chapter 48

Paris

At the sound of the bell over the door, Sylvia looked up from her accounting ledger. She set down her pen to see a young blonde woman stagger into her shop under the weight of a suitcase in one hand and a hatbox in the other. But it took her a moment to fathom this was no ordinary customer.

'Katja!' she exclaimed, rushing forward to greet her, then stopping in her tracks at the sight of her face, she cried: 'But my dear, you're so pale. What's happened?'

Whether it was exhaustion, extreme stress or simply the sheer relief of having made it safely to Paris with the notebook, Katja could not answer the bookseller. Instead, stars danced in front of her eyes, her legs began to buckle, and she felt herself falling down a bottomless pit. Everything went blank.

The next thing she knew she was waking up in a large armchair in the office behind the shop. There was a stove in the corner, and Sylvia was pouring boiling water into a teapot.

'You poor, dear thing. You're exhausted.' She handed Katja a steaming cup of herbal tea just as the shop bell tinkled once more.

'Ah, good,' she said with a smile, as if she was expecting someone.

At first Katja thought she was dreaming; especially when, through a haze of blurred images, she saw Daniel stride towards her. But when he took her hand in his and spoke, the mist that had fallen in front of her eyes began to fade, and she could see him clearly. He was real, but he looked concerned.

'Katja. Katja,' he whispered. 'Thank God, you're safe.' He turned to Sylvia. 'What happened?'

Sylvia poured more tisane into glass cups. 'As I said on the telephone, she just turned up and fainted, poor darling.'

Daniel stroked her forehead and looked worried. 'We better call a doctor.'

'No. No doctor, please,' said Katja, suddenly finding her voice. 'I'm just so happy to be here.'

'But you must rest. I'll see to your room,' said Sylvia, smiling at her guest. 'Then Daniel can bring you up to my apartment when you're ready.'

As soon as they were alone Katja could hear Daniel's breath leave his chest in a sigh of relief. 'It's so good to see you. I've been worried sick.' He clasped her hand firmly, then finding each other's lips, they kissed tenderly.

'Is Dr Viktor with you?' Daniel asked, breaking away a moment later.

His words hit her like a wall of water and the painful memories flooded back in a rush. Her silence signalled bad news.

'He didn't make it, did he?'

She stiffened. 'No,' she replied. 'No, he didn't. He's dead.'

'Jesus,' gasped Daniel. 'How?'

'They killed him. I know they did.' The threatened tears broke loose and cascaded down her cheeks.

'Oh, my love,' he said, holding her to him. 'I'm so sorry.'

'They shot him. At first they made it look like suicide, but then they went after me. They wanted to arrest me for his murder.'

'Oh God,' he whispered. 'And the notes?'

'They made the doctor burn the transcript.'

'What?' A look of horror swept his face.

'But I still have his original notebook,' she replied, her eyes casting over to the hatbox. 'They suspected I'd made a copy, so they ransacked my apartment. I'd already planned to escape with . . .' She broke off as her voice cracked. 'I'd got rail tickets for us both. Dr Viktor should have come with me.'

Daniel stroked her head. 'I know. I know. His US visa was granted just yesterday,' he told her.

She pulled away from him at the news. It was so ironic, but it also meant that she couldn't let Viktor lose his life for nothing. 'It's not too late to get the notebook published, is it?'

Daniel shook his head. 'Not too late. No.'

Katja detected hope in his voice. 'What is it? You've found another publisher?' She tugged at his jacket.

He cocked his head. 'Perhaps. It's a magazine called the *New Diary*, run by German émigrés. Dreiberg suggested it. The editor doesn't shy away from publishing anti-fascist articles.'

'We have to try everything,' Katja said, suddenly slightly cheered.

'And I think we should tell Sylvia,' Daniel suggested. 'She's on our side.'

Sylvia had been so good to her. So kind. And, what's more, she also hated Hitler. 'I understand,' she replied. 'But we still need to be careful. I'm a wanted woman, and you know this city is crawling with German spies and—'

She broke off when she saw the way he was looking at her.

'I'll take care of you,' he told her, kissing her gently on her forehead. 'But first you must rest. Everything will be all right, my love. You're safe now.'

Chapter 49

Three days after Katja's arrival in Paris, Hitler invaded Poland. Two days later, Prime Minister Daladier delivered the news the French had been dreading, over the wireless. France and Britain were at war with Germany.

'Of course you must stay here,' said Sylvia the next morning, dipping her baguette into a large bowl of coffee. 'I need help in the shop. You could be my assistant.'

The declaration may have brought France into the war, but the French, it seemed, had no appetite for it. Katja didn't have much of an appetite either. She toyed with the croissant, from the baker three doors down the street, on her plate.

'Eat up,' scolded Sylvia, looking disapprovingly at her guest. 'We may be at war, but we must enjoy our food while we can. They're talking about rationing. Can you imagine telling a Frenchman he can't have his filet mignon?'

Katja, sitting opposite her, didn't find her remark very reassuring, but she did appreciate Sylvia's offer. With a warrant probably out for her arrest, and both Dr Viktor and her mother gone, it would be madness to return to Germany, even if war hadn't been declared. Sylvia's observation also reminded her of Daniel's words. It was only right to tell her the truth. Now seemed as good a time as any.

Pushing the croissant away from her, Katja said: 'Sylvia, I have something I want you to know, but I must have your word that you will not tell another living soul.'

Sylvia's neat head whipped up from her baguette. 'A secret,' she repeated, her eyes burning brightly, like a child about to be told a mystery story. 'I love secrets.'

Katja shook her head. There had to be no question about the gravity of what she was about to divulge. 'This is very serious,' she began. Sylvia, noting her tone, pushed away her plate and leaned in as Katja continued. 'My friend, Dr Viktor, died for this secret, so I will not tell it to you lightly.'

Sylvia's expression had changed too. She frowned and fixing Katja with a solemn stare, suddenly appeared older. 'If it concerns defeating that monster Hitler then, my dear, consider me up for a fight.'

*

'How did the meeting go with the *New Diary*?' asked Katja, as soon as she saw Daniel the following day.

They'd agreed to meet for dinner and were headed for a little bistro with chequered cloths and candles in old wine bottles, just around the corner from the bookshop.

'In principle he seemed interested,' he replied, as the waiter handed them menus. 'At least he wants to see the notes for himself. If he feels it's for him, he'd like me to write an article on it.'

'But that means he wouldn't publish the notebook in full?' asked Katja, disappointment tingeing her question.

'No, but the magazine is very influential.'

They sat at a table in the corner. So much had happened since they first met; so many terrible things. But that evening Daniel had still managed to strike a positive note. Katja watched him thoughtfully. A single candle flickered between them, casting his face in part shadow. It was a good, honest face, she thought, even though tragedy and whiskey had both left their marks on it.

After a pause, she said: 'Do you think I'm wrong to want to carry on? To try to get the notebook published?'

Both Daniel's brows lifted. 'Of course not,' he replied, his sudden exhalation making the candle flame flicker. He reached for her hand across the table. 'The French need to be persuaded to put their heart into the fight. Knowing they're up against a demonic madman who'll stop at nothing until his glorious Reich triumphs, could just turn them.'

'So, perhaps it should be translated into French,' she suggested.

A pained look scudded across Daniel's face. 'Yes. No. Let's cross that bridge when we come to it, shall we? For now, we must wait and see what the editor of the *New Diary* decides.'

Katja carried on looking at the menu. 'I told Sylvia about the notebook,' she said suddenly.

Daniel looked up from his bread roll. 'How did she take it?'

Katja smiled. 'She's a remarkable woman. We can trust her. She wants me to work in the shop. The American girl who helped her has just left for home.'

'Because of the war?'

'Yes,' she replied. 'A lot of foreigners are leaving Europe, so I'm to take charge of the lending library.'

Daniel's eyes widened. 'The lending library! But that's wonderful news.' He beamed. 'And it means you'll stay close by.' He reached across the table to take her hand. 'I missed you so much when you went back to Hamburg, Katja. I don't want to lose you again.'

*

The war in Poland raged. Each evening for the next few weeks Katja sat by Sylvia's wireless growing increasingly anxious until, on October 6, following days of bombardment and destruction by both German and Russian troops, the brave Poles finally conceded defeat.

Sylvia, a glass of Burgundy in her hand, stood up to turn off the wireless in disgust.

'Will you leave?' asked Katja, knowing a victorious Hitler would surely turn his attention elsewhere. France could be in his sights.

Sylvia looked shocked. 'Leave?' she repeated indignantly. 'And go where? Paris is my home.'

Katja had picked up snippets of quiet conversation in the bookstore and knew several expat writers and artists had already returned to America, or Britain. More were considering leaving while they still could.

'Besides,' added Sylvia, clearly emboldened by the wine, and suddenly sounding like a French politician, 'Hitler would never attack our mighty Maginot Line. France will be safe.'

Katja wished she could agree. She'd heard the previous day that the editor of the *New Diary* no longer required an article about Dr Viktor and Hitler's medical records. 'The time has passed,' was the excuse he'd given to Daniel.

As if following her thoughts, Sylvia asked: 'What news on the notebook? Have you found an editor to run the story?'

'No. No, we haven't.' She shook her head and carelessly picked up the book she'd been re-reading from the seat of her chair. Hemingway. *A Farewell to Arms*. Ironic, she supposed.

'What will you do?'

Katja sighed. 'I'm not sure.' She flashed a smile at Sylvia to reassure her of her determination. 'But I won't give up.'

Sylvia laughed lightly. 'Oh, my dear, your resolve has never been in doubt.' She took another sip of wine. 'I just wondered if I might be able to help you.'

'Help?' repeated Katja, snapping shut her book. 'How?'

Chapter 50

Even though Katja now had Daniel to protect her, the fear remained like a dull ache. Time had flown by since she'd escaped Germany by train. Almost eight weeks had passed, and the horror of what happened to Dr Viktor and her mother, although still lurking at the back of her mind, had begun to feel more distant. But while the notebook was still in her possession, she knew she couldn't rest.

During the day she worked in the lending library at Shakespeare and Company, but at night she focused on Sylvia's proposal of help. The most famous bookseller in Paris had offered to publish Dr Viktor's notebook herself.

'I did it with Joyce's *Ulysses* and I can do it with Hitler's medical notes,' Sylvia announced over dinner a few days ago. She even proposed to raise the money herself. Ever since then, Katja and Daniel had spent their evenings translating the original two hundred pages of barely legible German text into English.

They were halfway through the translation when, one morning in November, as cold winds whipped all the leaves off the horse chestnuts in the boulevards, the telephone rang in the shop. Sylvia, in the midst of stocktaking and surrounded by unruly piles of books, answered it. One of her best customers, a rich

American widow, was requesting a copy of *David Copperfield*. For some reason she said it was urgent, but then everything Mrs Wannamaker asked for needed to arrive instantly.

Moments later, Sylvia called over to Katja in the lending library in the adjoining room. 'Could you take a book over to Mrs Wannamaker at rue Soufflot?'

Katja appeared from around the corner to see Sylvia brandishing a small book-shaped parcel wrapped in brown paper.

'She's asked for it right away.'

'Of course,' Katja replied. Her morning had been slow and spent rearranging shelves. She was glad of the excuse for some fresh air and set off immediately for the widow's residence, about a twenty-minute walk away.

Sylvia returned to her stocktaking, and another half-hour passed before the doorbell jangled again and in walked a tallish middle-aged man in a dark overcoat and a trilby. Peering around a shelf to greet her customer, Sylvia gauged the man was on business. He had an air of formality about him, but when he came closer and removed his hat to reveal a bootlace moustache and a head of pale blond hair, she thought he looked more German than French or British. Something told her to approach him with caution.

'*Bonjour monsieur. Puis-je vous aider?*' she greeted. French was always her first choice of language until she was certain of a person's nationality.

'You have a fine shop. Yes?' replied the customer in stilted English.

Sylvia was right. From his accent she could tell he was German. So what was he doing in Paris when his homeland was at war with France? Nevertheless, she accepted the compliment.

'Thank you.'

The German stalked towards the counter. 'I trust you can give me help.' He advanced on her with an arrogance that Sylvia found vaguely disconcerting.

'I will try, sir.'

He laid his hat on the counter. 'I look not for a book, I fear, but for a person.'

Sylvia arched a brow. 'Oh?'

'She is the daughter of a friend of mine. A German naval officer.' Reaching inside his coat, he produced a small photograph. 'She is believed to have travelled to Paris just before the war began. I own a business here and offered to help. Naturally, her parents fear for her.' Flipping over the photograph, he held it up level with Sylvia's face. It was a picture of Katja.

The shock showed in Sylvia's eyes, but she bit her tongue to play for time. 'No,' she said with a shake of her head. 'I'm sorry.'

'She is not one of your customers? I know she is a real book lover and this is, after all, the most famous bookshop in Paris.'

Again, Sylvia acknowledged the compliment, but remained resolute. 'As I said, I do not know the young woman, but if I see her . . .'

'Her name is Katja Heinz. Her father is most anxious to find her, as am I.'

'Of course,' replied Sylvia, forcing a nervous smile, knowing Katja could return at any moment.

'I shall call again.'

Another false smile from Sylvia.

Seemingly satisfied, the man nodded.

'Good day, sir,' she said, anxious for him to leave the shop.

Lifting up his hat from the counter, he held it to the side and gave a shallow bow. 'Good day, Miss Beach,' he said, before turning as he replaced his hat on his head and walked out of the shop.

Sylvia's smile quickly disappeared. A chill prickled her skin as she watched him go. He knew her name. Of course, so did many of her customers, but this man was no ordinary customer. He was after Katja and he was a German spy, she was sure of it. After hearing everything that Katja had endured for the sake of the notebook, she knew this visit was a frightening development.

Still trembling, she dropped into a nearby chair and remained staring into space until the doorbell awoke her from her daze. Katja had returned from her errand.

'Are you all right?' she asked, seeing Sylvia's troubled expression. Hurrying over, she knelt by the chair. 'Is something wrong?'

Sylvia turned to look at her with a frown. 'Oh, my dear,' she replied. 'I fear it really is.'

*

Katja was no longer safe in the shop. The protective blanket wrapped round her by Daniel and Sylvia had been torn away. Ever since she'd escaped to Paris, and Sylvia had offered her a bed and a job at the bookshop; ever since Daniel had taken her in his arms and told her he would protect her, she'd been given a security that she hadn't enjoyed since her father's death. But now Kommodore Flebert had sent his spy to trail her once again. He'd had Dr Viktor murdered and he wouldn't hesitate to do the same to her.

'I'm so sorry, my dear,' said Sylvia, reaching out to clutch Katja's hand across the table later that evening. The soup she had served her guest remained untouched. 'But it's not safe here any longer.'

Daniel sat next to her at the table.

'But what shall I do?' pleaded Katja, her head in her hands. 'Where can I go?' There was a pause and looking up at Sylvia, she followed her gaze as it settled on Daniel.

'It's been agreed,' he said, pushing away his soup plate and leaning over to touch her arm. 'You will stay with me.'

Katja shook her head. 'I couldn't really. I . . .'

'I have a spare room,' he said gallantly, before adding: 'And I make the best Irish stew in the whole of Paris.'

'But I—'

'Daniel is right,' interrupted Sylvia. 'You say this man sounds like the one who followed you and the doctor before. If he was

315

sent by this Nazi kommodore, then it's because he suspects you have the original medical notes.'

Daniel nodded, his green eyes latching on to hers. 'You have to lie low for a while. Please, Katja,' he pleaded. 'Do this for me.'

'For me too,' chimed in Sylvia.

Katja knew they were both making sense. She had their safety to consider as well. Harbouring a wanted fugitive certainly put Sylvia in danger. She sighed heavily. 'You're right. I know.'

Daniel sighed too. 'Good,' he said. 'Then we shall leave tonight, while it's dark.'

Sylvia agreed and now it was she who reached out across the table to Katja. 'You know this is best, my dear. For all our sakes.'

*

Under cover of darkness, Daniel hailed a cab to take Katja and her luggage to his apartment. On arrival, he ushered her quickly up to the second floor and let them both inside.

As he switched on lamps and closed the shutters, Katja looked around. There seemed little attempt to make the place homely, let alone habitable. It was clear to her it lacked a woman's touch. The room was dominated by a large writing desk and her eyes were immediately drawn to a photograph on it, of a beautiful young woman holding a baby girl. Grace and Bridie, she presumed.

'I'm sorry about the mess,' said Daniel, bending to pick up a discarded cigarette packet. 'I try not to spend much time here.' He shrugged. 'You know.'

Katja did know, but she pretended not to notice the disarray; the film of dust that covered every surface, or the unwashed coffee cup on the desk. 'It's a very nice apartment,' she told him.

He appreciated she was being gentle on him, and a muted laugh made his shoulders heave before he glanced over at the far side of the salon. 'Allow me to show you your room,' he said, leading the way across the floor. Opening a door, he held it

316

open wide and bade Katja go in first. She smiled before edging forward, but the moment she set eyes on the room she couldn't help but gasp.

Daniel flinched at her reaction. 'I'm so sorry. I should've warned you,' he said, rushing inside to scoop up a stuffed rabbit and a ragdoll from the pink coverlet on the single bed. It was a shrine. A child's bedroom. A little girl's. 'It's been a while since I was in here. I've been meaning to . . .' He began to gabble out his excuses as he stripped away the coverlet from the bed, then reached up to grab a painting of a fairy from the wall.

Katja shook her head. She hated to see him so rattled. 'No, please.' She stayed his arm. 'There's no need.' Snatching at his other arm, she looked at him squarely. 'It's all right, Daniel. It's all right to hold on; to keep remembering the good things.'

'I . . . You know . . .' In his distress, his tongue was tied.

She lowered herself to sit on the bed and patted the space beside her, inviting him to join her.

'Don't you see?' she said, taking his hand in hers, as he sat beside her. 'Your memories of Grace and Bridie are part of you.' She lifted her gaze. 'Like the colour of your hair, or the shape of your lips. You shouldn't ignore them. I don't want to ignore the memories of my parents either. I need them to give me strength.' She palmed her chest. 'They're still part of us. They make us what we are.' She lowered her gaze, as well as her voice. 'They make me love you, Daniel,' she said, and when she looked up again, his eyes were filled with tears.

'Katja.' Her name left his lips on a whisper, and he said it so sadly, she thought her heart might break. He reached out for her then and wrapped his arms around her to nestle his head on her neck. His tears felt hot on her skin. She wound her arms around him, too and with each of his sobs, she felt the pent-up pain leave his body, until a few moments later, his breathing had relaxed into an easy rhythm.

'Forgive me,' he said finally, pulling away from her. 'That was the first time I . . . well . . .' He pinched the bridge of his nose with his thumb and forefinger.

Katja could tell he hadn't fully released his grief before. It had lain dormant for all this time. 'It feels good, doesn't it?' she said.

'Yes. Yes, it does,' he replied. 'Like being born again.' He sniffed back his final tears while keeping his gaze on her face. 'Will you lie with me?' he asked, suddenly.

There was no hesitation. 'Yes. Yes, I will,' she replied and together they lay back, their heads on the pillows on the single bed, Katja's head in the crook of Daniel's arm, her right hand draped over his body. Lying there, with him, she felt as if she'd been born again too. There they stayed in silence for a while, watching the moon rise against the dark oblong of the open window.

It was Daniel who spoke first. 'I never thought I could love anyone again, but you . . . you've brought the light back into my life,' he told her. He kissed her head softly. 'I am so grateful to you.'

'We should be grateful to each other,' she told him. She twisted round, then tenderly kissed his lips, losing herself in his touch. And there they continued to lie until sleep released them both.

Chapter 51

It was Christmas Eve and despite the freezing weather, the prospect of spending her first Christmas Day with Daniel put Katja in a festive mood. She had bought him a gift – a book, of course – and he planned to take her and Sylvia to a restaurant for a special meal. 'The chef's goose is legendary,' he'd told them.

There'd been no sign of the German 'businessman' for several weeks, and Katja was beginning to think that the war might have diverted his attention. The previous week she had returned to work at Shakespeare and Company, to help out with Christmas orders in Sylvia's office at the back of the shop, and away from customers. That was why she was determined to enjoy herself and had agreed to Daniel's suggestion.

In the shop there'd been an early rush on last-minute gifts in the morning, but custom in the afternoon had tailed off.

'I need to nip out for some brandy,' announced Sylvia. 'I always have it in my coffee this time of year. You'll be all right?'

Katja, who was parcelling up books in the back office, and having trouble with a heavy volume on Dostoevsky, replied unthinkingly.

'Of course,' she said, continuing to wrestle with the book.

Only a few moments later, Katja heard the bell tinkle again

and footsteps progressing towards the front counter. At first, she thought Sylvia might have forgotten something and retraced her steps, but no. As she straightened herself and moved through to the shop, Katja could see a well-dressed customer. He rang the little gold bell on the counter for service, before turning to face the door once more.

'*Bonjour, monsieur,*' she greeted in French. '*Never assume your customers are native English or American speakers,*' Sylvia had advised. '*The French don't like that.*'

'*Bonjour, mademoiselle,*' came the reply, as the customer removed his trilby. Until that moment he had his back to her. Now he turned to face her. 'Or should I say, fräulein?' he responded.

Katja's heart missed a beat. There'd been something vaguely familiar about him, but now, seeing his blond hair and his thin moustache, she recognised the man and instantly took a step back from the counter.

The man smiled. 'You seem alarmed, Fräulein Heinz. But Kommodore Flebert will be delighted to hear you are safe and well.'

A shiver was travelling through Katja's body. She opened her mouth to speak, but the words deserted her. There was a cold menace behind the man's smile as he spoke.

'While I'm here, I would like to see if you have a copy of a very special book that I can't seem to get my hands on in Germany.'

She cleared her throat, but her mouth remained so dry it was hard to speak. 'What m . . . might that be?'

He lowered his head and fumbled in his coat pocket. 'I have written the title down here,' he told her, producing a crumpled piece of paper. 'Ah, yes,' he mocked, as if he needed to be reminded of the name. 'It is called *Notes & Observations on the Serious Mental Disorders of Adolf Hitler.*' He tucked the paper back in his pocket. 'The author was a Dr Ernst Viktor. Now deceased, I believe.'

Katja grabbed at the edge of the counter to stop herself shaking, all the while praying someone, anyone, would walk through the shop door and the Nazi would flee. 'I am not familiar with the book, sir. We do not stock it,' she replied.

The man cocked his head. 'A pity. I was told you did,' he said, reaching into his overcoat to suddenly pull out a Luger. Katja watched in disbelief as it was pointed straight at her. 'Are you sure you don't have a copy? Perhaps you could close the shop and look in the storeroom for me,' he suggested, keeping the pistol trained on her.

Fear was invading every sinew of Katja's body. Slowly she nodded. 'I will shut the shop,' she said, and she started to edge from the counter towards the front door. He followed her close behind and when she reached the window, he jabbed the gun into her back.

'No false moves now,' he told her as she turned the shop sign to *fermé*. A hundred scenarios started running through her head, as the adrenaline coursed through her body. What could she do? She wasn't strong enough to overpower him. Sylvia would be another ten minutes at least. Would anyone come to her aid? A customer, perhaps? It was then Katja's prayers were answered. From the corner of her eye, she caught sight of a familiar figure approaching along the street. She had to think fast.

'I've just remembered,' she said suddenly, glancing at the wall clock. 'I'm expecting a client to pick up an order any minute now.'

Behind her she could see the German's reflection in the shop window, as he held the gun to her back. He narrowed his eyes suspiciously. 'Then they will be disappointed,' he replied, ramming the muzzle of the pistol hard into her ribs. 'Now lock the door!'

But it was too late. Ignoring the sign, Daniel was just about to try the door, when Katja flung it wide open and screamed. 'He's got a gun!'

Without hesitation, Daniel instantly hurled himself at the German, grabbing him around the neck and trying to prise the gun from his hand. 'Get away, Katja,' he shouted. 'Get back!' just before the shot rang out and a crimson firework exploded.

A second of silence was followed by an odd sound. A gurgle. Time stood still until Katja dropped to her knees, her head hitting the floor hard. The German bounded out of Daniel's grasp and through the door. Daniel fell to the floor too, landing on his knees, next to Katja's limp body, just as her blood began to pool.

*

It seemed all of Europe was in the grip of the coldest, cruellest winter. Water pipes froze, and supplies of fresh food were hard to come by. At Shakespeare and Company, Sylvia kept the stove burning throughout the bitter weeks, although fewer people ventured from their apartments. Many writers were, however, drawn to the warmth offered by the store's heating, but all the talk was of Katja.

After the operation to remove the bullet from her chest, it had been touch and go. Daniel kept vigil by her hospital bed. As well as a bullet wound, she'd also suffered a fractured skull as her head hit the floor. She remained unconscious. Sylvia was a frequent visitor too. A week after the shooting, when there was still little sign of recovery, she found Daniel seated by her bedside, holding her left hand and looking at it intently. Sitting opposite him, she realised he was studying a diamond ring on the third finger of Katja's left hand. He looked up at her then, and she could tell he'd been crying.

'I'd planned it all,' he said, his voice thick with tears. 'I was going to propose on Christmas Eve, after we got back from the restaurant.'

'Oh, you dear man,' said Sylvia, her eyes fixed on the solitaire on Katja's pale, limp finger. 'I know she'll say "yes" when she's feeling better.' She reached across the bed to offer him a comforting hand. Still clutching on to Katja's, Daniel took Sylvia's into his free hand, so that the three of them were connected. 'Katja will make it,' Sylvia assured him. 'She knows you're here for her, giving her your strength, willing her to live. It'll just take time.'

Daniel nodded then looked up, his moist eyes glinting in the dim light. 'I've already lost two people I loved, Sylvia. I can't lose another.'

Chapter 52

The miracle happened one day in mid-February, as almost everyone was starting to lose hope. Madame Duprés was convinced it was down to the special prayers she'd had said in a side chapel in Notre-Dame, and Daniel wanted to believe her, even though he'd lost his faith long ago. But miracle or no, Katja had regained consciousness. It was a voice she'd heard first. A man's? She'd tried to open her eyes, but her lids were heavy.

'Katja.' The voice again. Smooth and cool as moss.

This time she managed to open her eyes to slits, to see light and shade. Colours followed. Blue, yellow and green, then the touch.

'Katja, it's me.'

The hand closed around hers, warm and comforting, and she knew.

'Daniel.'

'Yes, I'm here, my love. It's all right. You're going to be all right.'

Now her eyes managed to focus on his face, and she saw his smile.

'What happened?' she whispered, her throat feeling full of glass.

'It doesn't matter. The thing is you're safe now,' he replied.

A sharp pain stabbed her somewhere inside her rib cage. She winced. 'I was shot, wasn't I?'

Daniel's expression darkened.

'And the notebook?' she tried to move, but the pain beat her back.

'It's safe. You mustn't worry about anything.'

She relaxed a little at the news, but then another memory returned.

'The agent. The man in the trilby.'

Daniel took a deep breath and shook his head. 'Forget him.'

'But what happened to him?'

Daniel shook his head. 'As I said, forget about him, my love.' How could he tell her that the French police seemed unable, or unwilling, to put any meaningful resources into tracking down her attacker?

'He escaped, didn't he? He . . .' Horror widened her eyes, but another sudden pain made her words trail off.

'All that matters now is that you get better,' Daniel told her, lifting her hand to his lips. It was then that she saw the solitaire sparkling in the light.

'A ring,' she whispered. 'Daniel?' She gazed at him for an explanation.

He nodded thoughtfully, then rising from the bed, without a word, he knelt by Katja's side. Puzzled, she frowned, but then, taking her by the hand once more, Daniel looked deep into her eyes, and said in his low, lyrical voice: 'Katja, my love, my darling, will you marry me?'

*

When the thaw finally set in at the end of March, it was as if, like Katja, Paris had woken from a long sleep. As soon as the sun made its presence felt, the pavement cafés were bustling once more, accordion music wafted on the warm air, and Katja was finally ready to leave hospital. Shakespeare and Company beckoned once more.

325

'Welcome back.' Sylvia smiled, her arms outstretched, ready for an embrace.

Katja leaned forward gingerly. She remained shaky on her legs and simply took her friend by both hands. Her torso was still tender.

'Of course,' said Sylvia, suddenly reminded of the injury. 'Your room is ready, my dear. Daniel will get you settled, then I'll bring you up some tisane.'

It had been agreed that until Katja was fully back on her feet, Sylvia's apartment above the bookstore would be the safest place for her to stay. As far as her assassin knew, she'd died that afternoon. Daniel had pulled strings and managed to keep the attack out of the newspapers. It suited Katja. No one could get through the bookstore without being seen. With Daniel working all day and unable to care for her, Madame Duprés was tasked to check regularly on the patient, between her own naps, of course.

While Katja was in hospital, work on translating the notebook had ground to a halt at first, as Daniel tried to shake off the shock of almost losing her. He'd focused all his energies on her recovery, but as soon as she'd regained consciousness, he'd redoubled his efforts. There could be no more excuses. Now, more than ever, the notebook had become a dangerous liability. The sooner it was published, the sooner the danger would recede. Sylvia remained enthusiastic about the project, and had somehow raised sufficient capital to fund it, while a deadline to send the copy to the typesetters had been agreed. The final document was scheduled to go to press in the next two weeks, although it was nowhere near ready. Besides, Katja had other ideas.

'I've been thinking,' she told Daniel when he visited her after work the following day. He'd brought her a cup of herbal tea and slices of apple on a tray. She'd put the hours spent recovering in her hospital bed to good use and had decided on a new strategy. Sylvia's plan to publish the translated notebook was generous, but after the shooting, Katja believed publication would take too long. Even then there was no guarantee bookshops would stock it. She needed to act swiftly.

From reports on the wireless, it appeared Britain was the only country prepared to stand up to Nazi tyranny. What's more the British government had committed to the fight by sending over thousands of troops to Europe. The idea of delivering the translated notebook into the hands of the British had come to her after listening to one of Mr Churchill's speeches on the wireless. He'd warned that while everyone in Europe hoped the storm would pass before it came to their turn to be devoured, he feared it wouldn't. What was it the prime minister said? Something about raging *'ever more loudly, ever more widely'* and he'd warned about France and Britain making *'a shameful peace'*. His words had only spurred her on.

'I think we should take the translation to the British Embassy,' said Katja suddenly.

Her suggestion took Daniel by surprise. 'What?' He looked startled as he sat down beside her on the bed.

'Perhaps their government might be interested in knowing more about the enemy.'

Daniel paused. The suggestion clearly took him by surprise. After a moment, he nodded. 'You might have something there. It may well be useful to know the way Hitler's mind works. And it's all there, in black and white. Dr Viktor certainly did a thorough job on his profile.'

Katja looked into her teacup. 'The notebook would be safer in their hands too. The more I thought about it in hospital, the more it makes sense.'

Daniel nodded. 'Sylvia has good contacts with the British Embassy.'

'That's because they're all her customers,' Katja replied with a smile.

'The translation is almost ready. I began working on it again as soon as I knew you were . . .' His voice began to crack, and he took a moment to compose himself. 'But I need your help to finish it.'

Katja reached for his hand. 'Then we'll make our move. The British are sure to want it,' she said.

But Daniel was no longer listening to what she was saying.

Putting the pad of his finger to her lips to stop her talking, he told her: 'It's so good to have you back.' And with that he kissed her long and tenderly and the war seemed a million miles away to them both.

Chapter 53

An appointment was arranged with the deputy ambassador – a Mr Herbert Horner – at the British Embassy. He was a personal contact of Sylvia's and, apparently, a fan of Anthony Trollope. Sylvia said he'd complained he couldn't understand all the fuss about Hemingway. After that she'd admitted cooling towards him, although she still kept him on side.

Since the shooting, Dr Viktor's notebook had been kept locked in a safe at Shakespeare and Company and only brought out when Daniel, or Sylvia, were working on it.

'I guess this means I don't get to publish that nasty little tyrant's medical records after all,' Sylvia mused, handing over the thick folder of the translated notes into Daniel's outstretched arms. 'It would've been a bestseller, I'm sure.'

Katja didn't hide her disappointment. She and Daniel had both spent many hours working on translating and typing the notes, preparing the copy for the printers, but the circumstances had changed dramatically.

'We appreciated your offer. We really did, but it's safer for everyone this way,' Katja explained. Knowing her German attacker was still at large had left her on tenterhooks. Only when they had delivered the translation, alongside the original notebook, to the

British would she feel more at ease again. That same feeling of knowing she was handing over a poisoned chalice to someone else was hard, but she knew that this time she'd be delivering it to an organisation, not an individual. It would feel so good to be rid of it after all the misery it had heaped, not only on her, but on all those connected with it. Enough blood had been spilled. Dr Viktor was sacrificed for it and, indirectly, so was her mother. Katja could never live with herself if anything happened to either Daniel or Sylvia. They had both risked so much. It was time to put an end to it all.

Daniel had called the notebook a 'millstone' round her neck. He'd said as long as it was in her possession, she could never be free. He was right, of course, but curse, chalice or millstone, whatever name was given to it, Hitler's medical notes would shortly be out of Katja's hands, and she and Daniel could feel liberated from the source of all their evils. At least, that was the plan.

A car was ordered to take them to the British Embassy – a short trip to the other side of the Seine. The driver, Pierre, was one of *The Parisian's* regulars. Daniel knew him to be reliable. The saloon arrived on time and Katja settled herself for the ride, the notebook and the typed translation cradled on her lap. Daniel sat at her side.

'Tell me I'm doing the right thing,' she said as they passed through the Place de la Concorde. The square looked majestic in the spring sunshine. Paris had emerged from its winter cocoon into the spring, seemingly oblivious to the war just a few hundred miles away. It was as if, like a troublesome child, Hitler was best left to his own devices. And, maybe, just like a troublesome child, he would go away if he was ignored.

'Of course you're doing the right thing. It's what Dr Viktor would want too,' Daniel assured her, squeezing her hand. 'His voice will finally be heard by the people who can act on his work.' He lifted her hand to his lips and kissed it. She was about to return his tenderness, to lean over and kiss him on the lips when the car suddenly swerved, sending both of them lurching to the left.

'What the . . .?!' cried Daniel. But the driver didn't answer straight away. He was far too busy looking in his rear-view mirror. A black Mercedes had just shot out of a side road and narrowly missed hitting them. Now it was on their tail, speeding behind them along the Place Vendôme. Yanking the steering wheel suddenly to the right, Pierre turned down another street and hurtled full pelt to the far end. Another left turn took them towards the Tuileries Gardens, before he slammed on the brakes and came screeching to a halt behind a hedge.

Katja switched round to see the Mercedes speed passed them. She took a deep breath.

Pierre lifted his gaze to the rear-view mirror. 'Someone is angry with you, Monsieur Daniel,' he joked, before cranking the car into reverse gear.

'You could say that,' replied Daniel. 'Perhaps we ought to walk from here. It might be safer. We're only a few minutes away on foot.'

Pierre gave a Gallic shrug. 'As you wish.'

Daniel helped Katja, still clutching the folder, out of the car. They kept close to the edge of the gardens, all the time looking over their shoulders for the Mercedes to return. When it did come crawling slowly along the kerbside, they flattened themselves against a tree until it passed, then soon after found themselves on rue du Faubourg Saint-Honoré. Katja looked up to see the union flag fluttering above a magnificent building. A long line of people were queuing outside it. Desperate Jews, seeking help, she assumed. The Nazis were on the move. They'd reached the refuge of the British Embassy not a moment too soon.

*

Herbert Horner was a goggle-eyed old Etonian with a waxed moustache and a well-behaved gun dog. The animal, lying at his master's feet, looked up as soon as Katja and Daniel entered the deputy ambassador's office.

'All right with hounds, are we?' Horner asked when he rose to greet them.

'Retriever,' said Daniel, knowingly, bending down to pat the dog.

'Yes, indeed. Shoot, do you?' replied the Englishman.

Daniel aimed a knowing glance with Katja. He was tempted to say 'Only game, not innocent Irish citizens.' But for Katja's sake, he checked his cynical tongue and diplomacy prevailed.

'No, sir, but I'm a countryman at heart.'

'Hmmm. Irish from the sound of you,' said Horner, resuming his seat.

'That's right, but it is my fiancée who has something of interest for you.'

'Ah, yes. The folder, according to our mutual friend, Miss Beach. Of course, Miss Heinz, technically you are an enemy, so your visit needs to be kept hush-hush. Is that clear?'

Katja nodded. It had not been easy gaining access to the embassy, and she was grateful for the meeting.

The deputy leaned forward. 'You have the item with you?'

Katja laid the notebook on the desk, together with the transcript in the folder. 'This is the original, in German,' she explained, pointing. 'And this is the English translation.'

Horner hooked on his spectacles and reached for the file. 'My German is a little rusty,' he said, with a smile, ignoring the notebook and picking up the translation. As soon as he lowered his head to read the cover of the English version, however, he shot up again almost immediately.

'Good God!' he exclaimed. 'Adolf Hitler's medical notes!'

Katja felt vindicated by his reaction.

'Yes, sir. They were compiled by his psychiatrist Dr Ernst Victor. He treated Herr Hitler for a mental disorder during the Great War.'

Horner cleared his throat and circled his shoulders inside his jacket, as if he found the revelation most unsettling. 'I see,' he said, as he thumbed through the first few pages, shaking his head as he did so. 'This material is . . .' He searched for the right word. 'Extraordinary.'

'But is it of use to the British?' asked Daniel.

Horner nodded. 'I imagine it would be.'

Katja frowned. 'You imagine, sir?' It was not the vague reply she was expecting, especially given the official's immediate reaction.

Horner whipped off his spectacles and sighed. 'I must be honest with you, Miss Heinz.' His eyes darted from Katja to Daniel and back. 'In the event that Hitler decides to move west and invade France and – heaven forbid he makes it to Paris – then we have instructions to burn all the papers that we hold to prevent them from falling into enemy hands.'

Daniel narrowed his eyes. 'I don't understand. What are you saying?'

Horner elbowed his desk, tented his fingers and looked down at the folder. 'What I'm saying, Mr Keenan, is that no matter how valuable this intelligence may be, it could shortly end up on a bonfire if we take custody of it here.'

Katja's heart sank. That was not what she had expected, or wanted, to hear.

'What do you suggest we do?' she asked, cracks in her patience now beginning to show.

'If you really want this to reach the right hands – and I'm sure British intelligence would be most interested – the only way is to take it yourself.'

Katja waited for a moment to make sure the official wasn't joking, but Daniel, taking his words literally, raked an exasperated hand through his hair.

'You aren't serious?' asked Katja.

Horner nodded. 'I don't joke about such matters, Miss Heinz,' he told her. 'We have agents. Good agents up near Calais. They could see that it arrives safely on the right desk.'

Daniel snorted at the thought. 'I don't believe this,' he muttered under his breath, prompting the retriever to sit up suddenly and look alert. He leaned over the desk to look Horner in the eye. 'We've risked our lives to get this far. My fiancée was even shot for this.' His finger prodded the folder. 'And now you tell us we have to go even further?'

Afraid Daniel might go too far himself, Katja threw Daniel a reprimanding look. His temper could unravel everything, she knew.

'It would be most helpful if we had a name, sir,' she said, her tone remaining even.

Herbert Horner shook his head. 'I'm afraid I can't pass on the names of agents, especially . . .' There was an embarrassed pause. '. . . if you'll forgive me, to an enemy citizen.'

At this remark, Daniel threw back his head towards the ceiling as if to appeal to some higher authority. Katja saw his fists clench, but, once again, she stepped in to soothe the troubled waters.

'I understand, Mr Horner. We are most grateful for your time and . . .'

A knock came suddenly at the door and the retriever's head snapped round. A woman in a shapeless suit appeared. 'I beg your pardon, Mr Horner, but Sir George is on the line for you.'

The deputy looked relieved that he had been rescued by a telephone call.

'If you'll excuse me,' he said, picking up the receiver on his desk. 'A call from the War Office.'

They were being dismissed. Katja picked up the folder and the notebook from the desk and the two of them headed for the door, now held open by the woman in the suit.

'Meldrum,' Horner called after them suddenly. They both

334

turned. 'The contact is Meldrum. Only you didn't hear it from me,' he said, picking up the telephone. 'Oh, and good luck,' he added, cupping his hand over the receiver, and looking at his dog to add under his breath: 'They'll need it.'

Chapter 54

'So, what do we do now?' Daniel sank into an armchair in Sylvia's apartment after pouring himself a large glass of whiskey. Even though he barely drank spirits these days, he'd made an exception under the circumstances.

Katja, perched on the chair's arm, was taken aback by his question, as if there should be any doubt. She stiffened. 'We go to Calais, of course.'

Daniel spluttered and coughed out his response. 'You're not serious?'

'I most certainly am,' she replied, tapping her fiancé playfully on the shoulder. 'We can take the train. It won't be easy. I know most of them are full of troops going back and forth to the frontline these days, but there will be a way.'

He looked at her wide eyed, leaning forward with his elbow on his knees. 'And what then? What after we reach Calais? How do we find this Meldrum, or whatever his name was? Is he a British agent, or an officer in the Armed Forces? We just don't know.' His voice was tinged with exasperation.

Katja shrugged. 'It can't be too difficult. There will be networks. Connections. After all, it's what you do, Daniel. You said to me once that if good journalists mix with the right people, then good stories will follow.'

He laughed and shook his head. 'Did I say that?' he asked, looking deep into his glass.

'You certainly did,' she insisted, arching her brow and leaning over to wrap her arm around his neck.

He squared up to her then. 'And if I agree to go to Calais, what will you do for me?'

The remark seemed to knock the wind from her sails, and she sat upright. 'I'll, well . . .' She shook her head and looked deep into his eyes. 'I can't lie to you, my love. It will be dangerous, and I'll understand if you don't come with me. I'm being mad and reckless, but if I don't do everything in my power to get the notebook into the right hands, then I won't be able to live with myself.'

Daniel shook his head and said bluntly: 'If things go badly, you won't be able to live. Full stop.'

They were both aware that whether or not they managed to deliver the notebook was a roll of the die. But Daniel also knew the woman he intended to spend the rest of his life with would go to Calais with or without him.

After a moment, he said: 'Of course I'll come with you, my darling.' A sudden kiss was planted on her lips, and he reached for her left hand to look at the engagement ring he'd slipped on her finger in hospital. 'But only on one condition,' he said reflectively.

'What's that?' asked Katja, puzzled.

Lifting his gaze again, he said with a smile: 'That our trip to the French coast is also our honeymoon.'

*

'You look so beautiful,' said Monique, gazing at Katja's reflection as she sat in front of the triptych mirror in Sylvia's apartment. Her blonde hair was swept back from her face and was secured with fresh flowers fixed to an antique ivory comb.

'Something borrowed,' added Sylvia with a wink.

Katja's eyes were moist in the light of the late spring sunshine. As a child she'd always imagined her own wedding day, but she'd never pictured it being like this. Happy, yes, but tinged with great sadness, and a sense of urgency. It was less than a week since their meeting with the deputy ambassador at the British Embassy and she and Daniel were agreed. The mission to Calais could not wait. An appointment at the *mairie* was hastily booked. As well as Sylvia, Monique and Oskar, all the staff at the Library of Burned Books were invited to the ceremony, as were a handful of Daniel's colleagues from *The Parisian*, including Chuck Patterson and his wife, and, of course, Madame Duprés.

Rising from the little stool by the dressing table, Katja stepped over to the cheval mirror to inspect her dress. Monique had kindly donated the floor-length ivory gown she'd worn five years before at her own wedding. The sight of herself as a bride was too much for Katja and the threatened wave of emotion washed over her.

As she gave way to tears, Monique rushed over. 'Oh, *ma chérie!*' she soothed, wrapping her arms around her. 'You are emotional. It's your wedding day. It's only natural.'

'Oh Monique,' cried Katja, grateful for a friendly shoulder, but there was no way she could tell her how she was really feeling. Yes, it was her wedding day, and she had no doubts that Daniel was her soulmate. For that she felt truly blessed. Yet alongside her happiness, she was sad that neither of her parents had lived to see this day. But more than that, overshadowing everything, was the thought that her wedding could also be her final farewell. If something went wrong in Calais – really wrong – today could be the last time she would be together with the people who mattered most to her. How could she explain to Monique that the feeling hovered over her like a black bird? 'I'm sorry,' she said finally, pulling away. 'You're right. It's only natural to feel like this.'

The reception was held at Michaud's where Katja and Daniel had first dined *à deux*. The war meant it had been designated a meatless day by the government, but no one seemed to care about meat-free canapés as long as the Champagne flowed. Few of the guests knew of the notebook's existence, of course, but they all understood that Katja had escaped from a murderous regime.

When the time came for the speeches, Sylvia insisted on making one. When she rose, the whole room seemed to fall under her spell. 'If ever there were star-crossed lovers, they are here,' she told her hushed audience, tilting her head graciously towards the newlyweds. 'Their love of literature brought them together and, it's safe to say, they are some of my best customers, so I hope they will continue to be for many years to come.' Her words lightened the mood. Chuck Patterson's laugh could be heard above everyone else's, while the merriment even kept Madame Duprés awake.

When it was Daniel's turn, he stood to remember those who should have been with them to celebrate; Dr Viktor and, of course, Katja's parents. 'They would have been so proud of their daughter, had they been here today. Proud of her sense of duty and of justice, and her willingness to sacrifice herself for what she believes in.' He looked down on her, sitting at his side as his wife, and said: 'I only hope I can match her courage.'

That night, for the first time, Katja slept in Daniel's double bed. In the single bed, with just a thin wall separating their two rooms, she'd sometimes lain awake for hours listening to the sound of his breathing. Occasionally, she'd heard him talking. She'd supposed he was dreaming about Grace and Bridie. Perhaps he had nightmares about them, just as she had nightmares about her father in the flames. Once, when she'd heard a cry tail off into a sob, she'd hurried to be by his side and lain on the bed to cradle his head in her arms. He hadn't really woken and didn't seem to be aware that she was there, but he appeared to take comfort from her presence and soon settled once more.

She had desired him like no other man, and now that her desire had been officially blessed, she could let it engulf her. Daniel felt the same. Barely was the door to the apartment closed behind them, than they fell into one another's arms, tearing frantically at each other's clothes, hurrying to the bed – the double bed. There was madness at first. Katja was caught up in a tornedo that spun her around and around, leaving her breathless. But then came the tenderness. As she felt the naked softness of Daniel's skin on hers, he stroked her hair and reached into her heart.

'Thank you,' he said softly.

'For what?'

'For waiting for me.'

Chapter 55

'Let me get this straight.' Chuck Patterson sat with his feet up on his desk, listening to what his star correspondent was proposing. He rubbed the back of his neck as he mulled over the idea. As the weeks of war had passed, he'd finally understood he could no longer ignore it. It was affecting his readers' lives, restricting their yachting holidays and their formal banquets. He'd also come to the conclusion he needed a war correspondent.

'So, you'll write the words, and your lovely new bride will take the photographs?'

At first, Daniel had been horrified at the plan Katja had hatched the previous day. But now he'd come round. The newlyweds would be fully accredited war journalists, travelling on a troop train and given carte blanche as far as the frontline. There they would somehow find this Meldrum who could be trusted to take the folder to MI6 or Whitehall, or whoever it was in Britain who would find it helpful. It was madness. Dangerous too. But with Daniel at her side, Katja had the courage to see through the mission she'd undertaken with Dr Viktor. She would do it in his memory and for her parents too.

'So, your wife is a photographer?' quizzed Patterson.

'No,' Daniel replied truthfully. 'But she's a fast learner and, if

I know Katja, she'll find a way of coming with me anyway, so you may as well get some snaps out of her while she's about it.'

*

The mood among the troops on the train to Calais was mixed. From the carriage where she sat, pressed against Daniel, Katja could hear some of them singing rousing songs. Others were more reflective.

There were two other journalists in the carriage, along with a photographer, who was yet to open his mouth, but Katja saw from his papers he was French and his name was Gerard Joubert. All male, all smoking and what's more, all bona fide, accredited magazine, newspaper or press agency correspondents. And her – sitting with an unexploded bomb in the shape of a folder, in a rucksack on her lap. She felt such a fraud, masquerading as a seasoned photojournalist when in reality all she had ever shot were ducks at a fairground attraction. Daniel, on the other hand, had covered a war before. He hadn't gone into detail about what he'd seen in Spain four years back, but she knew from his expression that the very mention of it put him in a black mood.

News of the German advances came two days after his meeting with Patterson. Katja had given Daniel the chance to back out – to retreat. 'Looks like they're heading our way,' she'd told him. But she had come this far, and she'd continue until she'd accomplished what she set out to do, with or without her new husband.

About twenty kilometres away from Calais, she almost started to have second thoughts. Peering through the carriage window into the distance, Katja could see plumes of black smoke rising against the blue sky, feathering the gritty horizon. She looked up at Daniel, who was also squinting against the sunlight to process what he saw. They'd been travelling for two days because of delays on the line that had forced them to spend a sleepless night on a platform at Lille. They were out of touch with the news too.

Ironic, she'd thought. So, when the train made a stop, an hour later, one of the journalists – a big Canadian named Flanders with at least three days' stubble on his chin – went to find out the latest. When he returned grim-faced, ten minutes later, he delivered the startling news.

'The Germans have made a breakthrough and the Brits are on the run. It looks like they might have to evacuate Calais.'

'What a scoop!' said a shabbily dressed Englishman with red hair and a glass eye from a news agency.

Katja looked at Daniel to see the shadow of fear settle on his face. This was not what they had planned. A few days ago, Calais wasn't even that important strategically to the British. Now it had suddenly become crucial for supply lines. Even if they wanted to, they could no longer turn back.

When they eventually made it to the port of Calais and stepped out of the railway station, the ramparts of the old town loomed above them. Ahead lay the sea, as grey as the forbidding fortifications. A loud crack from a gun somewhere nearby disturbed the roosting pigeons, and for a fleeting moment, Katja thought of Mutti, but then she saw a moustachioed soldier heading straight towards them. It turned out Brigadier Wareham was the army press liaison officer, although Katja decided he was clearly in the wrong job because he didn't disguise his dislike of the press.

'You lot couldn't have come at a worse time,' he said, as his adjutant herded the five of them into a Land Rover. 'It's going to get dashed difficult round here.' He tapped Joubert's camera. 'No unauthorised photographs,' he said before switching to Katja and asking patronisingly, 'Think you can handle it, young lady?'

Katja opened her mouth to protest but Daniel squeezed her hand surreptitiously. 'This *young lady* is my wife,' he said with a false smile. 'She'll be just fine.'

The officer's driver took the press corps to join the British encampment, passing hundreds of French soldiers on the way. They were guarding the bastions and ramparts that buttressed the old town. Their faces were tired and drawn. Katja could tell they were only soldiers in name. Their hearts were back tending their fields or with their families. They had no stomach for a fight.

As the Land Rover reached the port, more troop ships were disgorging their cargo of reinforcements. Scores of young khaki-clad men poured down gangways and headed for the town to make camp. The noise of trucks and machines was almost unbearable, and barked orders were being lost amid a cacophony of Royal Air Force planes overhead.

'Jerry's on his way with a few dozen Panzer tanks,' shouted Wareham over the rattle of the engine.

Daniel put a steadying arm around Katja as they bounced along the uneven road to the British encampment. His eyes slid down to the rucksack that she still clenched on her lap. Nudging her ear with his mouth he told her: 'As soon as we find this Meldrum, we'll be shot of it, then we can get the hell out of here.' His voice registered a certain disdain. He'd come to loathe the folder, blaming it for getting them into this mess in the first place.

Katja nodded. With the rapid German advance, she knew that as soon as they'd put the file in safe and reliable hands, they needed to somehow return to Paris before it was too late.

Once at the headquarters, Wareham showed them into the press room, a makeshift office with two tables, three typewriters and two field telephones.

'Is this it?' asked Flanders, who didn't seem to care who he offended.

Wareham's moustache twitched. 'It's not much, but it'll have to do,' he told them.

Katja's eyes swept the room. 'And if we need anything, sir?' she asked.

'I'm sincerely hoping I won't be troubled. I've got better things to do, but if you have an issue, you should take it up with Colonel Meldrum. He'll sort you out.'

'Thank you,' said Katja, unable to believe her luck. Brigadier

Wareham had just helped them cut through an awful lot of red tape by pinpointing the contact the British diplomat had given them. Waiting until he'd gone out of earshot, she turned to Daniel excitedly. 'Then tomorrow we shall pay Colonel Meldrum a visit,' she said.

That night, as they lay side by side on camp beds listening to the pounding of heavy guns just a few miles inland, Katja remained restless. As if sensing she was troubled, Daniel propped himself up on his elbow and reached for her in the darkness.

'Enjoying your honeymoon so far, Mrs Keenan?' he asked. A beam of light from outside the tent caught the whites of his eyes.

Reaching up, she hooked an arm around his neck and, pulling him towards her, planted a soft kiss on his lips. *Mrs Keenan*, she repeated in her head. Her new name still sounded wonderful but strange at the same time. She almost told him then. Almost told him her secret, but she managed to quell the urge. It was safer for him, if he didn't know. Lacing her fingers through Daniel's, she went to sleep comforting herself that if they both died that night, at least it would be as husband and wife; as one in life and in death.

Chapter 56

Calais

The blue sky turned an ominous grey the following morning with news that a German tank division, halted the previous day, had begun to advance once more on Calais. A battle was raging less than forty miles inland. The Luftwaffe was out in force. There were at least one hundred and fifty enemy tanks, according to intelligence rumours Daniel had picked up, and over fifteen thousand men.

'That means the Brits and French are outnumbered three to one,' said the Canadian. 'Don't fancy their chances.'

'Their chances? What about ours?' asked the red-headed reporter in the crumpled suit, who Katja now knew as Sharples. 'I just heard the Germans repulsed an attack on the road to Dunkirk and the Brits have had to pull back. We're going to get cut off.'

He painted a dire picture and Katja knew time was running out. 'We need to see this Meldrum right now,' she told Daniel as he sat typing up a dispatch in the press room. 'He's at the headquarters in town.'

'How did you find that out?' asked Daniel.

She patted the Rolleiflex camera hanging in a case round her neck. 'I got talking to a captain who wanted a souvenir photo,' she replied. 'I promised to send it to his sweetheart if he could tell me where I might find the colonel.'

Daniel nodded. 'So, what are we waiting for?'

They hitched a lift into the old city where the ancient walls loomed dark and solid all around. The French were manning them, their big guns jutting from the ramparts, aiming out across the sea.

'Meldrum's office is in a cellar. It's somewhere along here,' she yelled. Her voice sounded husky, as if she'd smoked a hundred cigarettes at once. Jumping out of the Land Rover, she landed with a thud, with the folder in the rucksack strapped to her front.

Dodging trucks and weaving in and out of columns of troops, they made their way to rue Léon Gambetta. All around it was chaos. The sound of heavy tank fire grew louder by the hour and there was an acrid tang on the breeze. Rag-tag queues of civilians and wounded personnel snaked their way towards the Gare Maritime, to board the evacuation boats that were coming under fire as they entered the harbour.

They fought their way along the street, flattening themselves against walls now and again as lorries passed laden with supplies. Men were shouting at each other above the drone of engines. A line of vehicles moved slowly out of the city to block the roads in advance of the anticipated German tanks.

Suddenly Katja spotted a handful of officers emerging from a building. 'This must be it,' she shouted, hugging the rucksack to her chest. Hurrying towards the main door, she felt her heart quicken. She'd no idea how she was going to gain access to this Colonel Meldrum, let alone persuade him to take the folder to safety, but she knew she had to try. Daniel was a few steps behind her as she forged her way towards a staircase.

'Miss! Miss!' A guard dashed in front of her. 'Authorised personnel only,' he snapped.

347

'But Colonel Meldrum asked to see me,' she replied, flashing her press pass. 'I'm to photograph some sensitive documents.'

The soldier's eyes bulged as he inspected the pass. 'Oh, right you are then, miss,' he conceded, standing aside, but then seeing Daniel also wanted access to the colonel's office, he barged in front of him. 'Just you, miss.'

Katja took a deep breath and shot Daniel a look. She'd have to go it alone. Scurrying along the corridor, weaving her way through the maze of passages, she came to what she assumed was Colonel Meldrum's office. Chaos confronted her. The air was thick with dust. Boxes were piled high. Papers were being packed and maps torn off the walls.

Ambushing a passing squaddie, she pointed to her camera and said breathlessly: 'I'm here on Colonel Meldrum's orders.'

The squaddie paused to look her up and down. 'If you say so, miss,' he replied, then cocked his head towards a middle-aged man in a regimental beret, shouting loudly down a telephone line. As soon as he replaced the receiver, Katja dived in.

'Sir. Colonel Meldrum, sir.'

The officer scowled. 'How the devil did you get in here?' he exclaimed.

'Sir, I have something very important to give you, but it's secret.' Her eyes slid to another officer who was watching.

'Will it help me stop almost two hundred German tanks from wiping out most of my men?' he barked.

Katja wavered. 'No.'

'Then I'm not interested.' He stood up abruptly, but Katja blocked his path.

'Please, sir. It may not stop the tanks, but it could help you win the war. You have to listen.'

The colonel was scandalised. 'I don't have to do anything you say, young lady. Out of my way.' He continued to stride towards the door.

'But please, sir. Mr Horner from your embassy in Paris gave me your name.'

'What?!'

Now that she had his full attention, Katja reached into the rucksack to produce the folder. 'Look, sir.' She thrust it under his nose.

'What the devil is this?' he asked, glancing at it.

Katja drew breath. 'The mental health records of Adolf Hitler. They prove he is psychologically dangerous, sir.'

Meldrum grabbed hold of the file and stared at the cover sheet. 'Good God! Hitler's medical notes. Well, I suppose that *is* something,' he said. Was he relenting? Katja prayed he would, but then he dashed all hope by handing it back to her. 'But we may be evacuating the town within the next few hours, and it's likely a lot of us won't make it out of here. So, young lady, if I were you, I'd hang on to something so important and see if you can find another way of getting it to England, because right now, I'm not sure I will.' He barged past her and out of the room, leaving her still clutching the folder.

It was over.

A minute later she emerged from the building where Daniel was waiting. He could tell from her expression she had failed to persuade the colonel to accept her precious delivery. She looked up at him, her eyes full of both frustration and fury.

'He said "no"?'

She balled her fists. 'I've been so stupid,' she growled through clenched teeth.

'Let's get out of here,' said Daniel, shepherding her into the growing mayhem of the street. A silent column of exhausted troops, the shattered remnants of companies, trudged passed them towards the harbour.

'There has to be another way,' she fumed. 'If we could just . . .'

Daniel grabbed her then and clamped his hands over her shoulders, forcing her back against a wall. 'You had to try,' he told her through parched lips. 'We had to try, but . . .'

Just then a lone Messerschmitt appeared overhead and started

349

to spit bullets, strafing the troops below. Men flung themselves on the ground, others dashed for cover. Daniel shoved Katja down behind a nearby wall as the plane's assault was answered with a volley of anti-aircraft fire from somewhere near the port. But the shots missed, and the German pilot lived to kill another day.

Daniel pulled Katja to her feet. Undeterred, her head jolted up again. Her right cheek was smeared with dirt, but he noticed something else about her; a wild look in her eyes.

'You don't understand, do you?' she cried, her voice now scratchy and harsh.

'What?' Daniel took a step back as if she'd just lashed him with a belt.

'I'm not giving up. I can't,' she shouted over the sound of exploding shells.

Daniel grabbed her by the wrist. 'Don't be so ridiculous. It's no use.'

She struggled from his grasp. 'I'm going to take the folder to England myself.'

Daniel found the idea so ludicrous that he let a laugh escape his lips, but his smile soon vanished when he realised his wife was deadly serious.

'What? But how? The Germans are surrounding us. We're all that lies between them and the British and they're certainly not going to let us go willingly.'

'There are ships. We've seen them ourselves. They're taking the wounded. They could take me.'

Daniel scratched the back of his neck and turned around in a circle, as if by doing so he could make his wife's hare-brained scheme disappear. From the scowl she still wore, it had no effect.

He jabbed at the rucksack she was clutching. 'So, you want to take it to England? To Whitehall? Or Westminster, or wherever the British top brass hangs out. Or why not give it to Mr Churchill himself?' He was waving his arms around in frustration. 'I tell you it's madness, Katja!'

Throughout his tirade, she'd remained silent, just watching him tell her it was time to abandon the mission that had brought them together in the first place.

Slowly, she shook her head and searched his eyes. 'Oh Daniel,' she said, in a more measured voice. 'If I gave up now, I would never be able to live with myself.'

'Even if it means you die trying?' he asked exasperatedly.

Another nod. 'Yes. I would rather die trying than live a failure.'

He sighed heavily, then pulled her to him, but the rucksack got in the way, so he slipped the straps off her shoulders and kissed her on the lips. 'And that is why I love you,' he said.

She broke away; her eyes on fire. 'Good,' she cried, snatching back the rucksack. 'Then we have a boat to catch!' and, taking his hand, she began to storm off in the direction of the harbour.

*

As darkness fell that night, the German tanks roared up to Calais' ancient gates. Under cover of heavy artillery fire, they scissored out to the south and south-west of the town. The detachment powered towards the advanced positions held by a British battalion, and the exhausted men had to be pulled back. The Germans quickly captured a bridge and breached the outer perimeter walls, swarming over them like cockroaches and gunning down everyone in their way. By dawn it was clear they'd opened the jaws of hell. From up above, shells started to rain down on the ships that were loading the wounded, but still they came; some on crutches, some on stretchers, all trying to dodge the relentless bombardment.

Now in the old city, thunderous bangs and ear-splitting screeches shredded the sludgy air, and the ancient walls that once repelled privateers and invaders, threatened to crumble like sandcastles.

'We've got to get to the docks,' cried Katja, above the deafening roar of gunfire, her voice struggling to overcome her dry throat. Although just how they would, was anyone's guess. The gun emplacements were fixed and pointing out to sea, not inland at the enemy. Despite coming under heavy fire, a few of the soldiers seemed to be holding the line, but their numbers were dwindling as more German shells hit their target.

Katja and Daniel were at the edge of town, just east of the harbour. Nearby, soldiers were piling into trucks and, without warning, Daniel snatched at Katja's hand. They clambered aboard one just as it began to move off, heading for the docks. Dodging exploding shells on the way, the truck arrived five minutes later to find a mass of soldiers and civilians swarming around the quay; terrified, aimless and needing orders. A senior officer suddenly clambered onto a Land Rover bonnet and took charge, ordering the troops to adopt positions in the houses on either side of the bridge.

'Fight like bloody hell,' Katja heard him yell.

Meanwhile, Katja and Daniel made it to a warehouse at the eastern edge of the port, where they were forced to take shelter. To their amazement the other two journalists were also holed up in the same building. Part of the roof had collapsed, and they had to pick their way over jagged beams and shattered glass to an area that remained unscathed. They found a pile of empty sacks stacked in a corner to keep them warm. There was no sign of Joubert; Sharples, the agency reporter, said he thought he might have been hit.

In the town, the fighting raged and overhead Stukas dropped their deadly cargo. Bombs pounded the port and the old town indiscriminately. Calais was on fire. Whenever there was a slight lull in the shelling, Flanders and Sharples dashed out to look for food and water – and, most importantly, information. But as night fell, the Canadian staggered in, clutching a bleeding arm and bearing grim news.

'The swastika's flying above the Hôtel de Ville, and the Germans

352

sent the mayor to request the Brits surrender,' he panted. 'If they don't, they'll raze Calais to the ground.'

'And have they surrendered?' asked Katja, rushing forward to inspect his wound.

'All comms with London are cut, but that crazy brigadier of theirs, Nicholson, he told the Hun if they want Calais, they'll have to fight for it.'

Over the next few hours, the battle intensified. Katja blocked her ears to try and grab some sleep on top of some sacks, but it was useless. Any chance of escape was ebbing away with the Calais tide. That's when she decided to act.

'You can't really be serious about taking photographs, can you?' asked Daniel, seeing her open her camera case.

'I'm just checking it's not damaged,' she said, keeping her back to him. A moment later she turned with a smile on her face. 'Who knows? The film may still be developed.'

'And that's another reason I love you,' said Daniel. 'You're so stubborn.' He kissed her head and led her down to sit on the floor, their backs resting against the wall. 'I may not like the British, but they're bloody good fighters. They don't give up,' he told her, pulling a sack over them both for warmth.

A moment later, yet another shell landed nearby. It shook the floor beneath them, sending more chunks of masonry crashing down, just as the door was flung open. Sharples stood in its frame, blood pouring from a head wound. Katja leaped up to help him.

'That'll teach me to go outside,' he joked weakly.

Daniel sat him down, while Katja dabbed the wound with a bandage she'd salvaged from her hospital stay. 'You're going to be all right,' she said. 'It's a nasty cut, but you'll live.'

'They're running out of ammo,' he groaned. 'It's no use.'

By midnight, except for the fires burning around Place d'Armes, all was eerily quiet. The guns had fallen silent.

Inside the warehouse, Katja was shivering and drew the sacking under her chin. 'I don't like this,' she said, afraid that almost everyone else had evacuated, and fearful they'd been left to face the enemy alone.

Daniel edged his way towards a blown-out window. Straining his eyes in the darkness, he could see nothing but black, but could hear the faint sound of men talking nearby. And even, perhaps . . . Was that a ship out there? There was the faint thrum of an engine. Were they still evacuating? It was impossible to tell.

Crawling back across the floor, he told Katja: 'We're not alone, but I can't tell how many Brits are left.' He pulled her towards him.

'I'm so sorry,' she mumbled after a moment, as he held her, shivering, in his arms.

'Sorry?' Daniel stiffened. 'What have you got to be sorry about?'

'For dragging you into this. For making you come here.'

'You didn't make me do anything,' he told her. 'You know I'd willingly follow you to the ends of the earth, but we're going to need all our wits about us to get out of here.'

She could tell he'd had to stop himself from adding 'alive' to his instruction, but she knew it was what he was thinking. Looking up at him, she traced the outline of his cheekbones with her finger. 'Will we make it?' she asked.

He squeezed her tight. 'Of course we will,' he said.

Katja wished she could be so certain.

Chapter 57

As dawn broke, bleak and grey, the Germans launched their final attack. They came from the air where Stukas were joined by Junkers, and they came from the ground with their precise mortar fire. But the British were facing them without tanks or artillery support. Yet even though they were being driven back, they refused to give in. Sporadic bursts of gunfire split the fume-filled air, and the situation grew worse with each passing hour.

Daniel kept watch. Flanders had a pair of binoculars with him. Now and again a handful of British troops would scramble to a new position, further towards the harbour, and by late in the afternoon, through the acrid smoke, he thought he could just about make out a vessel off the coast.

'I'm going down to where the boats may be,' said Daniel, suddenly rising. 'I think they're still getting them off.'

'You crazy?' moaned the injured Canadian, his back propped against the wall. 'You'll be full of holes before you make it there.'

'We've got to try,' said Katja, rising to join Daniel. 'Mr Sharples?'

The Englishman was clutching the bloody dressing on his head. 'Yes,' he said slowly. 'Yes. I'll come.'

'Good luck,' Daniel said to the Canadian.

Flanders just smiled and said: 'It's you who'll need the luck, Irish.'

The three of them braved the outside, keeping close to the warehouse wall and edging towards the waterfront. A shell suddenly whistled past them and exploded about fifty feet up ahead. They waited a few seconds until the smoke cleared then ploughed on.

Skirting the remains of a burnt-out hulk of a truck, they took shelter under a wagon as another wave of bombers flew over like bats on giant wings. There were more explosions, and all the while bursts of artillery fire crashed into the surrounding warehouses. Night was falling once more and with the fading light went hope of rescue.

Katja, Daniel and Sharples had been crouching down behind a wall for the past hour, pinned down by the constant heavy shelling coming from the town. Sparks peppered the air like fireworks, yet still the British wouldn't surrender. Daniel guessed there could be fewer than fifty men, although there was no way of knowing. But then came the sound of heavy footfall, punctuated by shouts. British voices. Cautiously peering above the wall, Daniel could make out about three or four dozen troops, including walking-wounded, some with their uniforms in shreds, and men being carried on stretchers, heading towards the port. He dipped down.

'This is our last chance,' he panted. 'We follow them. Quick.' He helped Sharples to his feet and nodded to Katja. 'Come on.'

They tagged on behind the motley column of soldiers as they moved from building to building, progressing slowly towards the port.

'There'll be a ship to take us off,' Daniel told Katja, still hefting most of Sharples' weight as he dragged him along.

Ten minutes later, the men stopped ahead of them, beams of field lights chasing across the horizon. But still Katja couldn't see any ships, just a black void in front of them where she knew the sea lay. Then she realised what was happening.

'Oh God!' she cried, as she watched the desperate troops struggle down the harbour wall and edge onto a breakwater that jutted out across the sand as the waves crashed below. She pulled back.

'It's suicide!'

The tide was rushing in, and the seawater lapped the ladder, but one by one the men climbed down and slowly made their way out along the breakwater. When they could go no further, they packed themselves tight like sardines, huddling together against the cold. They were sitting targets for the rapidly advancing German troops.

Katja hesitated and looked back. The raging fires seemed to be drawing closer and the howling shells falling faster.

'We've got no choice!' yelled Daniel above the roar of artillery fire. 'Come on!' He clambered onto the breakwater, then helped her down the ladder. 'Steady now,' he said, guiding Sharples next onto the slimy pier. Seaweed covered the wooden planking, making it treacherous under foot. One slip and it would mean a fall into the rising sea below.

Daniel led Katja and Sharples closer to the troops. Now and again the sky would light up like day and he could see something had caught the men's attention. He followed their gaze. A large white shape was looming out of the darkness.

'Oh Christ,' he said suddenly, squinting into the blackness. 'There's a boat coming in.' Then a moment later: 'A bloody German boat.'

'We're done for,' moaned Sharples.

Katja clung on tight to Daniel, her body convulsing each time she coughed as the smoke threatened to suffocate them. She began to pray.

The troops braced themselves, as well. Too numb to move, too exhausted to cry out, they waited for the enemy boat to open fire; to put an end to their torment. But then . . .

'She's ours!' A cry went up. 'She's bloody ours!'

'What? Oh, thank God,' cried Katja. She flung her arms around Daniel.

The German artillery saw the ship too. They had it in their sights and began firing a moment later. A shell whistled then exploded in the sea nearby, sending up a huge plume of icy water that drenched them. The force knocked Sharples off balance. He lost his footing and slipped into the sea, but Daniel managed to grab him by the arm and haul him back to the breakwater, just before his head disappeared.

On the harbourside, fire was raging. The flames lit up part of the breakwater and they lit up the men too, ranged like sitting ducks to be picked off one by one by German snipers. But still the British vessel advanced, and Katja could make out it was towing something. A barge. When it came within reach, they could try and fling themselves onto it and be towed away to safety. Adrenaline flooded her body. Soaked to the skin and shivering with cold, she told herself she had to hold on for just a few more minutes.

'It's going to be all right, isn't it?' she asked Daniel, as she felt his arm around her.

'Yes, my love. It will. Remember you're a phoenix. You'll rise.' He kissed her then and tightened his hold as once again he made her feel safe.

Just a few more seconds and the vessel, a motor yacht according to Daniel, had manoeuvred into place and the propellers slowed. Above the mayhem, someone barked an order, and the troops began jumping off the breakwater and up onto the barge. The injured went first. There were three stretchers, and Daniel pushed Sharples to the head of the queue.

'I can't thank you enough,' said the reporter as he shook Daniel's hand.

'Buy me a pint of Guinness sometime,' he replied.

From the shore, the hail of machine-gun fire continued. The sky still flared with artillery rounds. Worse still, as more explosions lit up the night sky, German troops were spotted advancing with rifles on the rocks. Shots were fired from close range. They were sitting targets. Two men were hit by snipers just as they made it onto the barge. The seawater was lapping round Katja's knees now, chilling her to the bone. All the while she'd kept the folder safe in the rucksack, holding it aloft when the waves threatened to consume it. The shells fell around them, sending spray high into the air. Someone screamed. Another man had been hit by sniper fire. Katja, who'd started to edge forward, looked round. Daniel was still behind her and his lips were moving, as if in prayer. Tilting her head nearer his mouth, she suddenly understood what he was saying. He was reciting one of Yeats's poems from the volume he'd given her a lifetime ago.

'*The blood-dimmed tide is loosed, and everywhere . . .*'

She joined him in the next line. '*. . . The ceremony of innocence is drowned . . .*'

But not us, she prayed. *Please, God, not us.*

At last, it was their turn to board.

'Hurry it up!' cried a voice in the darkness. Just a few more steps to the barge. From somewhere above her in the void, a hand appeared. She tried to extend her arm to meet it, but the bulk of the rucksack prevented her.

'I'll take it,' shouted Daniel from behind and she felt him unhook one of the straps, while she ripped off the other and handed over the burden. Freed of the extra weight, she was able to reach for the stranger's arm. It was joined by others, that dragged her up roughly onto the barge. Scraping her shins on the side, she yelped in pain, before turning to Daniel, as he held the rucksack towards her. Her shaky arm reached out as far as it could to take it from him, as the barge pitched and rolled.

'I can't get . . . closer!' she yelled.

This time he managed to sling one of the straps round his neck and raised his arms to grab hold of the gunnel to hoist himself up.

'Coming over!' he cried, heaving himself up from the breakwater, but just then his body seemed to flinch. Katja lurched towards him but suddenly realised he was looking at her with unseeing eyes. For a moment his limbs seemed frozen until a split second later he lost his grip and sank back into the dark waters, the weight of the rucksack dragging him down.

'Daniel!' she screamed. 'No. God, no!'

The barge veered to the left as fumes coughed loudly from the yacht's motor.

'No. We can't leave him. My husband! Please!'

Flinging herself towards the side, Katja stretched out a hand, frantically crying out Daniel's name. Gulping down desperate tears, she lunged forward clawing at the water, straining to snatch him up, but then she felt hands on her body, pulling her back onto the barge.

'No!' she screamed. 'Daniel!'

Even though her anguish blinded her, she could still see enough to know that her husband was no longer there. The angry sea kept churning, swirling all around. There was no sign of him as the furious shells hurtled all around and the vessel gathered speed to escape them. No hope remained. Daniel Keenan had been swallowed by the sea. And so had Adolf Hitler's medical notes.

Chapter 58

London

Katja sniffed as she sat in the soulless Whitehall waiting room. The smoke on the air reminded her of Calais, only this time it came from cigarettes, not artillery fire. Nevertheless, the acrid smell triggered memories of her escape from the blazing citadel just forty-eight hours before. On the dingy wall opposite, a poster urged everyone to '*Keep Calm and Carry On*'. She was doing her best, but without Daniel at her side, she was struggling.

Since the rescue, she'd barely stopped shaking. She hadn't been able to eat, or sleep, and the clothes she'd been given by the Red Cross at Dover offered little warmth. The only thing she'd manage to salvage from the wreckage of Calais was now wrapped in a bag made of khaki canvass. She clung on to it like driftwood as she sat in the waiting room, but still a pang of guilt jabbed at her conscience. She'd hidden the truth from Daniel and that made her feel even more wretched.

The last thing her beloved had done before he'd hit the water on that fateful night was to free her by taking the rucksack and slinging it over his own head. Then the bullet had struck, and as he dropped below the waves, the weight of the bag dragged him down into the cold depths. She grimaced as she remembered he'd once called Dr Viktor's notes 'a millstone' round her neck. With hindsight, how prophetic that remark now seemed. If only she'd told him before, things may have worked out differently. But she'd kept her secret for his own protection, or so she'd thought, and now he was gone.

The journey back to England had been a waking nightmare that kept repeating itself over and over. Her brief time with Daniel strobed through her mind; fragments of past conversations, the sensation of his touch, their first kiss and later, how she'd clawed at the waves in vain to reach him. She recalled, too, her first interview at the clinic; how she'd likened her mother's depression to a huge wave that hit you and barrelled you round to finally drag you down. *How ironic that Daniel should die in such a horrible way*, she thought.

She'd been wrenched back on board the barge by the other rescued troops. Her screams had melded with the shrieks of the artillery shells exploding all around and sending plumes of water high into the air. The explosions rocked the flimsy barge as it was towed behind a motor yacht. Strong men had clamped their arms around her as the small vessel rolled and dived through the black swell. It was just as well because, in that moment, all she'd really wanted to do was throw herself overboard to join Daniel.

They headed away from the French coast at full speed, but the yacht that was towing the barge – she now knew it was called HMS *Gulzar* – slowed as soon as it was out of artillery range. For the next hour they cut their way through the waves until dawn broke and she could see clearly for the first time. Battle-weary men surrounded her, huddling up to each other for warmth. They'd escaped death by moments and yet their faces were etched with pain and exhaustion, just as she knew hers must be. The stench of their uniforms mixed with the diesel of the motor yacht's engine had made her want to retch. But then . . .

'Dover!' came the call. Bowed heads jerked upwards. Bodies twisted round to get a view. Sure enough, on the horizon, with the rising sun turning them a pale shade of pink, were the famous white chalk cliffs of England.

Those who had enough strength cheered. Even some of the injured men raised a smile. Others cried tears of relief, but Katja felt only a crushing pain inside, as if every mile she'd travelled had taken her further away from Daniel. Even though he was gone, she still couldn't believe what had happened. Despite knowing that her own safety was within reach, a terrible urge, like a strong current, was pulling her back towards the shore where he was lost.

There was mayhem at the quayside as the motor yacht docked. It landed its passengers safely at Dover just before six o'clock in the morning. All fifty-one of them. *There should have been fifty-two*, thought Katja. A kindly sergeant directed her on shaky legs to the reception centre where, wrapped in a warm blanket, she managed to force down a cup of sweet tea. Yet despite reaching safety and the kindness of strangers, a jab in the ribs reminded her, as if she needed reminding, that her own personal war was far from over.

The shrill ring of the telephone on the War Office desk at the other end of the room sliced into her thoughts. The secretary, a young woman with an air of breezy efficiency, answered.

'Colonel Meldrum will see you now, Mrs Keenan,' she said, replacing the receiver after a moment. Her eyes directed Katja towards the nearby door.

'Thank you,' said Katja as she rose, still clutching the bag to her chest. Finally, she felt she was making progress. It had not been easy to get this far. At Dover, she had spoken to an officer in charge of the evacuees from Calais, and he had been quite dismissive at first. No doubt he regarded her as some hysterical woman, whose ramblings were the result of shock and exhaustion. But when she'd mentioned Colonel Meldrum's name, his attitude had changed.

'Colonel Meldrum, you say?' he'd repeated with a raised brow, and from then on, the situation had moved forward at pace. Telephones calls were made, alongside arrangements, and after being checked over by a doctor and given clean clothes, albeit ill-fitting ones, Katja was put on a train to London, and now found herself at the War Office in Whitehall.

The colonel, a neat man with a receding hairline that had been hidden by a beret in France, leaped to his feet as soon as she walked into his office. He looked much older than she'd remembered him in the cellar in Calais, but then stress always aged people. Memories of their last encounter flashed before her eyes; the dark, the dust and the unrelenting roar of the firing above. And knowing that despite the chaos and the horror, Daniel was waiting for her outside.

'Mrs Keenan,' he greeted her. It felt odd to be addressed that way. She wasn't even used to her married name before she'd been widowed. 'They told me about your husband. I'm so sorry for your loss,' Meldrum said earnestly, holding out his hand. News of her misfortune seemed to have softened the edges of his brusque manner in Calais.

Katja bit her lip. She would not break down. Her personal circumstances must not hamper her mission. She took his hand, then sat before him at his desk.

'But you still have the transcript of the medical notes you told me about?' he asked, nodding at the canvas bag.

Katja shook her head. 'The transcript was lost at sea at Calais.'

'Oh.' His face fell. 'But they told me . . .' The familiar sharpness returned to his voice.

No one had known. Not even Daniel, but before she left Paris, she'd wrapped Dr Viktor's original notebook in oilskin and hidden it in a compartment of her camera case. Right from the start, the notebook had been a dangerous weapon and she'd needed to protect Daniel from it. He'd assumed it had been left in the safe in Paris with Sylvia. But Katja knew that, in the event of the city's invasion by the Nazis, possession of the notebook would also mean Sylvia's certain execution. In Calais, it had been the back-up in the event the transcript had been lost or fallen into enemy hands. But when her original plan of handing over the folder to Colonel Meldrum and escaping back to Paris had gone up in smoke, she'd had to think of another. It had come to her while they were sheltering from German mortar fire in the ware-house. Securing it with one of the bandages she'd saved from her hospital stay in Paris, she'd secretly taken Dr Viktor's notebook from the camera case and secured it flat against her stomach. No one, not even Daniel, knew where it was. And there it had remained until she was safely on dry land in Dover.

'In here is the original,' said Katja, delving into her bag and bringing out the leather-bound book. Laying it on the desk, she brushed it with her hand to feel the patina of the leather under her fingertips, as if it was an heirloom. 'Dr Ernst Viktor was Adolf Hitler's psychiatrist back in the Great War. In here are his notes and a detailed psychological profile of the Führer,' she explained. She slid it across the desk.

'Ah, the original notebook,' muttered Meldrum.

Katja braced herself, awaiting his reaction. This was the moment she and Daniel had dreamed of, the moment she hoped to ensure Dr Viktor's legacy would live on. But when it came it was an anticlimax. There was the familiar crump as the notebook fell open and the rustle of the pages, thankfully still dry as autumn leaves, but Colonel Meldrum's examination was only cursory.

'Hard to read in English, let alone German,' he commented unhelpfully, squinting at the last few pages.

His words couldn't have hurt more had he punched Katja in the stomach. What's more, his off-hand tone was troubling. She could see her chance slipping away from her, just as Daniel had slipped under the waves. She had to act. This time there was something she could do. She jumped in. 'I can translate it. I'm sure it'll be of interest,' she said.

The colonel pursed his lips and looked slightly offended. 'Allow us to be the judge of that, Mrs Keenan.'

Internally, Katja squirmed as she felt herself sliding towards tears. Sharply she pulled herself back. 'I can transcribe it again,' she reiterated, adding, 'sir,' just to keep him on side.

Meldrum nodded, before tenting his fingers and skewering her with a curious look. 'Yes. Yes, I'm sure you could,' he replied, as if he were thinking out loud. Taking a deep breath, he rose suddenly. Katja thought he was going to dismiss her, but he strode over to the window and looked out. After what seemed like an interminable moment, he returned to his desk and asked: 'What are your plans now, Mrs Keenan?'

The question caught Katja off-guard. *Plans?* she thought. Plans were for people who had futures. Without Daniel she did not. 'I don't have any,' she replied honestly.

'Hmmm.' The colonel leaned forward. 'Then may I make a suggestion?'

Katja shifted in her chair and stiffened. 'Please do.'

Meldrum picked up a pencil and pointed it at her. 'We need people like you. Fluent German speakers with an axe to grind with Hitler.' His brow arched. 'Would you be willing to put yourself forward to work in a most secret capacity?'

Katja's heart suddenly started to pound. 'But what about the medical notes?' There was a plea in her voice as she eyed the notebook, still on the desk.

'All in good time, Mrs Keenan,' he replied brusquely. He picked up the notebook and put it in the top drawer of his desk, as if the matter was now closed.

With this cruel gesture, Colonel Meldrum may as well have locked Katja in a darkened room and hidden the key. The notebook was her only physical connection to Dr Viktor, and to Daniel, and now even that was lost to her. She cast around the room, playing for time. In reality, she had nothing else to lose and nothing to live for unless she could be useful in the fight against the Third Reich. Colonel Meldrum had just launched into a speech – something about signing the Official Secrets Act and working for British intelligence. But she wasn't listening. Her mind was already made up. With Daniel gone, she would risk everything once more to be of service to the Allies. Without hesitation, she replied: 'Of course, sir.'

Chapter 59

Paris

April, 1946

From Colonel Meldrum's office Katja had been sent to the third floor of the same Whitehall building to be grilled by another officer, who asked her to sign the Official Secrets Act. From there she had travelled to a former stately home, just north of London, known as Camp 11. She'd later learned it was at Trent Park. Here she'd worked transcribing the recordings of high-ranking German prisoners of war, which had been made without their knowledge as they relaxed in each other's company. She'd also, to her great relief, been asked to transcribe Dr Viktor's notebook into English. Then, at the end of the war, the call had come.

At first Katja wasn't sure how she'd feel returning to France after so many years in England. Unlike the London she had grown used to over the last six years, Paris seemed remarkably unscathed. Instead of picking her way over rubble to visit the shops or choking on brick dust thrown up by demolition crews, she could stroll along the boulevards or down bijou streets without anything strewn in her way. While the Germans had occupied the city, they hadn't destroyed it. Everyone was thankful for that. The fate of Shakespeare and Company, and of course, Sylvia, was a different matter. She'd written to her a few times since the end of the war, but the letters had all been returned with the words '*Parti sans laisser d'adresse*' stamped across them. But if she'd 'gone away', where, exactly, had she gone?

A newspaper Katja read had reported how Ernest Hemingway himself had been among the first Allies to arrive in Paris towards the end of the war. The article said he'd personally dealt with the last remaining German snipers on the nearby rooftops on rue de l'Odéon, liberating Sylvia and everyone else on the street. The story brought a smile to Katja's face, and having previously heard tales of Papa's derring-do, she could quite believe it. But that was the last she'd heard of her dear friend.

When her commanding officer first told her she was being posted to Paris, Katja had jumped at the chance to look for Sylvia in person. Then the doubts had set in. And the mixed feelings. She'd worried she might find it too painful, revisiting the haunts she and Daniel used to know, remembering their bookstall browsing, or just marvelling at the view of Notre-Dame from across the Seine. And now she found herself on her way to rue de l'Odéon on a bright spring day that reminded her so much of the morning she and Daniel visited the *bouquinistes* for the first time together. Any minute now she thought she might see him, dressed in his tweeds and floppy hat, ambling along with his head in a book. Her heart beat faster as she neared the little street, but then she remembered he was dead. A crushing loneliness suddenly pulled her down, and a cloud of sadness passed over her once more. She was so deep in thought that she lost all sense of the present and accidentally brushed a man's shoulder as their paths crossed on the boulevard.

'Steady on!' said an English voice. She looked up to see a red-haired man in an ill-fitting suit.

'Sorry. My fault,' replied Katja, tugging at the arm of her jacket that had rucked up, before suddenly being aware the man remained looking at her curiously. 'Do I know you?'

The man's brows rose simultaneously, and Katja noticed he had a glass eye.

'Mr Sharples?' she said, thinking of the British press agency reporter she'd met in Calais.

Surprise shot across the man's face. 'I can't believe it,' he cried, stepping forward and taking her by the hand. 'Your husband saved my life,' he said, suddenly pulling her towards him and giving her a hug.

As he held her tight, the memories returned to Katja as fast as the incoming tide of that night in Calais. Yes, Daniel had saved his life. He'd seen that Sharples, wounded and vulnerable, had managed to scramble aboard the barge to safety, while all around the shells screeched, and as, one by one, German snipers picked off the terrified men waiting on the breakwater.

Feeling Katja's shoulders heave in a muted sob, Sharples stepped back. 'I'm so sorry,' he said, noticing tears were now streaming down her face. 'He was a hero.'

She nodded and managed a smile as she dabbed at her cheeks with a handkerchief. 'Yes. Yes, he was,' she agreed. 'It's good to see you, Mr Sharples. What are you doing here?'

He pursed his lips. 'Back at the old job with the agency. And you? I've often wondered what happened to you after we got to England.'

'I made it to London and joined the Auxiliary Territorial Service, as you see,' she replied, gesturing to her khaki uniform. She couldn't tell him the truth.

Sharples nodded. 'Good show,' he said, sensing she was holding back. 'I joined the army as soon as they discharged me from hospital.' He pointed to his forehead, now dissected by a large scar, and Katja recalled his head wound. 'Look.' He broke off. 'I'm awfully sorry, I have to go. I'm late for an assignment, but if you're around for a while, look me up,' he told her, handing her his business card. 'I owe you a drink.'

'Thank you,' replied Katja, taking the card. 'I'd like that.'

They parted then, Katja still stunned at their encounter. Seeing someone who'd been there on that fateful night when she'd lost Daniel unnerved her. It had taken her back and reopened a deep wound. Of course, she couldn't tell Sharples what she'd really done in England after she'd handed over Dr Viktor's notebook to British intelligence. For months after she'd transcribed Dr Viktor's work, she'd heard nothing. At first, she thought the transcript risked being drowned under a flood of other intelligence reports, and although she kept asking, no one had any answers about its fate. After everything she'd risked, after everything Dr Viktor and her beloved Daniel had sacrificed, it all seemed a terrible anticlimax. She'd doubted whether it had ever been worth it. But then, in 1941, the Americans had entered the war, and everything changed, although she'd only learned about what had happened quite recently. Shortly after VE Day, as she continued in her post at Trent Park, the camp's commanding officer said he wished to see her. Obviously, she'd been both nervous and puzzled by the order. She'd long ago given up all hope of ever hearing the fate of Dr Viktor's notebook. The officer, a lieutenant colonel, hadn't kept her on tenterhooks for long, informing her that after Katja had handed it over to Whitehall, the notebook had been sent to a team of psychologists at Trent Park for their expert analysis. Realising its importance, orders had finally come from 'on high', as the commanding officer put it, to show the translated notebook to the United States' intelligence service, and from there it had eventually landed on President Roosevelt's desk. It turned out the Americans were anxious to learn all about Hitler's state of mind. After they read Dr Viktor's account of the Führer's insane belief that he was the German messiah, they were convinced they had no choice but to join the Allies in Europe.

Katja carried on walking along the Seine until she finally

arrived at her destination. Rue de l'Odéon looked almost the same as when she'd left it. The little street still had its own eclectic feel; an air of faded chic with its *brocante* shop and the florist where Sylvia had bought Katja's bridal bouquet. The smell of freshly baked croissants wafted out of the bakery, just as reassuringly as the scent of lavender from the perfumery.

The war had prevented her from returning to their apartment to sort through Daniel's things like most grieving widows. She was still trying to keep her own head above water, frantically looking for something to hold on to, to stop herself drowning as well. His hat. One of his books. Anything she could cling on to, but she could find no emotional driftwood to give her comfort. Not even a photograph of him remained. Even now she had nightmares, reliving in her dreams the night he died; how he had clutched to the side of the barge and frozen as the bullet struck. She often woke up screaming at the sight of his body disappearing under the water. She supposed she always would.

Everything was almost the same, but not quite. Looking ahead along the street, something was missing. Shakespeare and Company's famous sign no longer alerted browsers to the treasures that awaited them in the store. Katja stopped outside the building where the shop should be, then paced along the narrow little street once more. Number 12 seemed to have disappeared. Where once there were windows, they were all boarded up. The door was anonymous, and of Shakespeare and Company there was no trace.

A terrible sense of loss crept into Katja's bones, and her heart began to sink. She would give it one last shot before she gave up, but when she stalked up the street again from the florist at number 6, she found herself outside the same door. There was no mistake. This was, or at least had been, number 12.

Taking a few paces back, she looked up to the shutters. They were closed, as she thought they would be, and the brightly coloured pots of geraniums had also disappeared from the windowsills. Nevertheless, she knew she couldn't leave without trying to make contact. She knocked on what she was certain used to be the shop's side entrance. It opened onto a narrow vestibule that led to stairs up to Sylvia's apartment, as well as to the shop. Even it had been painted a different colour. No longer the familiar green, but black. She waited a few seconds, but when no one came, she forced herself to bid her final farewell. This time, she knew, there was no *à bientôt*. It really was *au revoir*. Before tears could fall, she turned to leave. But then . . .

'*Oui, madame?*'

When she heard the voice, Katja wheeled round to see a young woman, standing in the doorway where she had just knocked. She hurried towards her.

'*Bonjour*,' she said, hurriedly. '*Je . . . Est-ce-que . . .?*' In almost seven years, she hadn't spoken a word of French and her tongue was twisted. 'I'm looking for Miss Beach. Miss Sylvia Beach,' she said. 'This used to be a bookshop. Shakespeare and Company.' There was a plea in her voice.

The young woman had a lustrous, dark fringe that shaded her eyes. It emphasised her sensual lips which turned down in a pout as she examined the stranger before her. 'Miss Beach is out. Can I 'elp you? I am 'er assistant,' she replied in a French accent as thick as her fringe.

'Out?' Katja repeated breathlessly. 'So, she's still alive? And she's here?'

'But of course,' replied the girl, as if there should never have been any doubt about Sylvia's whereabouts. 'At the train station, meeting a friend returning from England.'

'England?' Katja repeated. She wondered who it might be, but her relief at discovering Sylvia was still in Paris swept the thought quickly away. 'That's wonderful,' she cried, her face cracking into a smile. 'May I wait for her inside?'

'*Bien sûr, madame.* She should not be long.'

The door was opened wide and Katja stepped eagerly inside,

but her excitement soon turned to disappointment. Her face fell as she looked about her. The shop once crammed with books of all shapes and sizes, that teemed with novels and anthologies and encyclopedias, was completely empty. The walls had been stripped of the drawings by William Blake and portraits of Oscar Wilde, DH Lawrence, Gertrude Stein and the rest, and not even the shelves remained.

'What happened?' asked Katja, stunned by the sight of such emptiness where there used to be so much life. 'Where are all the books?'

'You do not know?' asked the girl, almost reproachfully, as if Katja's question simply showed her ignorance.

'No. I've been away.' she replied, adding awkwardly, 'The war.'

The girl's sullen look seemed to soften. 'Ah, yes, the war,' she repeated, as if Katja had just dug up something best left buried. 'Miss Beach kept the shop open until one day some Nazi officer wanted 'er special copy of *Finnegan's Wake* from the window. When she told him 'e couldn't have it, 'e shook with the rage and told 'er 'e'd take away all the books.'

'What did she do?' asked Katja, horrified.

The girl shrugged. 'She made a few calls, and everyone came to 'elp. We carried everything up to the third floor. We even took down the electric light fixtures and the shelves and painted over the name on the front.'

'What did the Nazis do?' asked Katja.

Another shrug. 'No one waited around to see. Miss Beach just hid with friends for the rest of the occupation.'

'And all the books. What happened to them?'

'We only send them by post now. There are a lot upstairs,' she tilted her head back so that her eyes completely disappeared under her fringe. 'And these have just come from the printers.' She pointed to a large cardboard box on the floor. It had been sliced open to reveal bright blue covers with bold white graphics.

Just then, the sound of the side door opening could be heard, and in breezed Sylvia looking elegant in a tailored blue suit with her hair in a familiar page-boy bob.

'We're back, Suzette,' she shouted from the little vestibule, unaware she had a visitor. 'Have the copies arrived?' she asked, excitedly, emerging into the shop. 'I can't wait to . . .' It was only then she realised Suzette was not sharing her enthusiasm but directing her attention behind her.

'There is someone to see you,' said her assistant, cocking her head towards where Katja had been left waiting.

Sylvia turned and looked curiously at the young woman in the British Army uniform.

'Hello,' she greeted. 'Can I help you?'

'Yes. I think you can,' replied Katja, unable to contain herself any longer as she whipped off her peaked cap. 'Hello, Sylvia.'

A pause then as Sylvia's hands flew up to her mouth to stifle a cry. 'Katja?' She said her name quietly at first, as if questioning her own sanity.

The front door was suddenly slammed shut, and the sound of more footsteps travelled along the little vestibule. 'That was some journey,' said a voice – a male voice with an Irish accent.

Katja froze at the sound; rooted to the spot.

'It's good to be back,' added the voice, as the sound of a suit-case thudded to the floor. Katja didn't have to wait long before the voice was followed swiftly by a man wearing tweeds and holding a floppy hat in one hand, which he whipped off as he entered the shop.

Sylvia, standing transfixed by the door, was the first person he saw. 'Is something wrong?' he asked, seeing her face turn the colour of alabaster. 'You look—' He broke off to follow Sylvia's eyes clamped on someone in an armed services uniform, a young woman with blonde hair. She was still as a stone in the corner, her features paralysed by shock. At the sight of her, the man also froze, as he, too, processed the sight before him.

'Oh my God,' he whispered, then louder: 'Oh my God!'

'Daniel. Daniel,' was all Katja could manage, her throat crowded with emotion.

For a second neither of them spoke; neither of them moved. The years rolled back like the Calais tide. They'd both come face to face with their past and neither could believe it was also their present. As the shock sank in, Katja suddenly became unsteady. Daniel was a ghost. *This couldn't be real, could it?* As she reached out to hold on to a nearby chair, Daniel rushed forward to catch her before she fell.

Now shaking uncontrollably, Katja clung on to him, unable to believe her own eyes. 'But you died. I saw you. The waves . . .' she blurted.

For the next few moments, nothing could have prised them apart. Crying into each other's shoulders, neither said another word.

'Katja! Oh, my darling Katja!' said Daniel finally.

'How? How did you . . .?' Katja sobbed, pulling back from his embrace to trace his cheekbones and his lips with her fingertips, as if to reassure herself he was real. 'How . . .?'

'Why don't you go upstairs to my apartment?' suggested Sylvia, through tears of joy. 'You can be comfortable there. You have so much to say. So many stories to tell.'

Daniel guided Katja upstairs to the apartment, and they sat beside each other on the sofa, his arm around her.

'Tell me what happened?' urged Katja. Her moist eyes played on his face, as if not quite believing what she saw.

'A shoulder wound,' he explained. 'The bullet missed my heart by two inches. The Germans dragged me out of the water, and for the next few weeks I was in a Nazi prison hospital until they realised I was an Irish citizen, and couldn't hold me.' He shook his head. 'They sent me back here, to Paris. So, I worked for the resistance as a courier. And you?' he said, holding her close. 'What happened to you? Where have you been? I searched everywhere. That's why I was in England. I kept trying the Red Cross and all my contacts, but you weren't on any casualty lists. You'd simply vanished.'

She shook her head, recalling the interminable hours she'd spent transcribing the Nazi prisoners' recordings at Trent Park. 'My work was very . . . I wasn't allowed to . . .' Another sob broke over her voice and he pulled her back to him. 'But I did it!' she spoke into his shoulder.

Gently, he pushed her away again. 'What did you do?' he asked with a frown, desperately searching her face.

'I had the notebook,' she told him.

'You what?' asked Daniel incredulously.

'I kept the original on me.'

'What do you mean?'

'I tied the notebook to my waist with a bandage.'

'So not everything was lost with the rucksack?'

'That's right. I delivered the notebook to British intelligence, and they asked me to translate it before they sent it to Washington.' A sudden smile lifted her lips.

'To Washington?' Daniel's voice was tinged with disbelief.

Katja nodded. 'It was one of the reasons the Americans decided to join the war. Dr Viktor's notes convinced them Hitler was deranged and needed to be stopped.'

Daniel's eyes widened in delight, and he scooped her up and whirled her round. 'I knew you'd never give up on the notebook, just as I never gave up on you. I wasn't able to rest until I'd found you, my darling.'

Just then the door to the room opened and a stout woman in funereal black popped her head in. It seemed the noise of raised voices had woken Madame Duprés from her sleep.

'*Qu'est-ce qui se passe*? What's all the fuss?' she asked, tetchily, rubbing her eyes. The old woman paused for a moment, then looked at the young female in a strange brown army uniform before suddenly realising who she was.

'*Mon Dieu! C'est toi*? It's really you?' Flinging wide her arms, the concierge waddled over to Katja and embraced her warmly. 'But we thought—'

'None of that matters anymore,' Daniel interrupted. He drew Katja closer. 'Right now, nothing matters except us.'

'And, perhaps this?' suggested Sylvia, walking into the room with one of the bright blue books Katja had seen in the box from the printers. She handed it to Katja.

'What is it?' she asked, after a moment's study. On the cover, written in large letters, was the title *Looking for Katja* and underneath, the author's name. 'Daniel?' she gasped.

Daniel touched the cover and nodded. 'I was so desperate to find you, I did the only thing I know I can do. I wrote a book about my search in the hope someone might come forward with information.' He took the book from Sylvia's hands. 'It's our story, Katja. It's about everything we went through, and how I lost you.'

'You wrote it all down,' said Katja, staring at the book.

'Yes,' replied Daniel. 'And Sylvia printed it for me. It's out in England next month. That's why I went to London, to do newspaper interviews to publicise it.' His eyes dropped to the cover. 'It's all in here, my love. All about you and me, and Dr Viktor, of course. And . . .' He turned to the first page and pointed to the dedication. 'See this?'

Katja wiped away her tears to read it.

For my beloved Katja, wherever you are, always.

'I never gave up hope,' said Daniel. 'I never gave up believing you were alive.' He smiled as she clutched the copy close to her. 'And you've proved me right.'

Taking the book from his hands, she lifted it up to her lips and kissed it. 'So now you can write another chapter about how we found each other again,' she told him, smiling softly. Finding his lips, she kissed him once more, sure there were many new chapters still to be written, and that from now on, they would be writing them together.

A Letter from Tessa Harris

Thank you so much for choosing to read *The Paris Notebook*. I hope you enjoyed it! If you did, and would like to be the first to know about my new releases, follow my social pages below.

It takes many hours of research and writing to craft a novel. Hopefully you found yourself lost in the world of *The Paris Notebook*. If you did, I would be so grateful if you left a review. I always love to hear what readers think, and it helps new readers discover my books too.

Thanks,

Tessa

Facebook: Tessa Harris Author
Twitter: @harris_tessa

Beneath a Starless Sky

Munich: Smoke filled the air.
Lilli Sternberg's quickening heart sounded an alarm as she
rounded the street corner. Lifting her gaze to the rooftops,
a roaring blaze of thick flames engulfed the side of the
building and joined the stars to fill the black sky. Her father's
shop was no more.

Lilli Sternberg longs to be a ballet dancer.
But outside the sanctuary of the theatre,
Munich is no longer a place for dreams.

The Nazi party are gaining power and the threats to Jewish
families increasing. Even Lilli's family shop was torched
because of their faith.

When Lilli meets **Captain Marco Zeiller** during a chance
encounter, her heart soars. He is the perfect gentleman and her
love for him feels like a bright hope under a bleak sky.

But battle lines are being drawn, and Marco has been spotted
by the Reich as an officer with potential. Lilli means more to
him than anything and he knows he must find a way out.

With their lives on the line, will Marco and Lilli survive the
growing Nazi threat, or do they risk losing everything in
the fight to be free?

The Light We Left Behind

England: 1944

When psychologist **Maddie Gresham** is sent a mysterious message telling her to report to Trent Park mansion, she wonders how she will be helping the war effort from a stately home.

She soon finds captured Nazi generals are being detained at the house. Bugged with listening devices in every room, it's up to Maddie to gain the Nazis' trust and coax them into giving up information.

When **Max Weitzler**, a Jewish refugee, also arrives at Trent Park with the same mission, Maddie finds herself trapped in a dangerous game of chess.

The two met in Germany before the war, and Maddie's heart was his from the moment they locked eyes.

But Maddie has finally gained the trust of the Nazi officers at the house, and her love for Max must remain a secret.

When the walls have ears, who can you trust?

Author's Note & Acknowledgements

One of the exciting things about being a writer of historical fiction – and there are many – is that during our research there's always the chance we'll come across some new or interesting facts or stories that aren't widely known. Sometimes, the details are just waiting to be spilled all over the pages of a novel.

When this happens to me, I put any promising nugget of fact into a file marked 'potential'. This is exactly what I did while researching my second World War 2 novel, *The Light We Left Behind*. Set in a former English stately home, the novel tells the story of the 'secret listeners'; men and women who covertly recorded and translated the conversations of top German generals being held in a luxury prison camp. My heroine is a psychologist, tasked with writing profiles of some of the high-ranking prisoners at the camp. The character of her boss was inspired by Dr Henry Dicks, a British Army psychologist, who studied the notorious Nazi Rudolph Hess, while he was in custody in Britain. At the same time Hess was being studied, the American secret services, the US Office of Strategic Services (OSS), commissioned a psychoanalytic report of Hitler, which was submitted in late 1943 or early 1944. One of those interviewed during this research was German psychiatrist Dr Karl Kroner, then in exile in Iceland. Kroner put it on record that Hitler had been treated for a psychological disorder by one of his respected colleagues – a Dr Edmund Forster. (Titled 'A Psychological Analysis of Adolph Hitler: His Life and Legend' by Walter Langer, the 165-page document was classified 'Secret' until 1968, but is now widely available.)

As soon as I could, I began researching Dr Forster and what I turned up was more extraordinary than I could possibly have imagined. Forster had the misfortune of treating Lance Corporal Adolf Hitler after a gas attack in WW1. His story is said to have formed the basis of a novel entitled *The Eyewitness*, which was written in 1938 by a Jewish émigré, then living in Paris, called Ernst Weiss. Weiss later committed suicide when the Nazis invaded Paris, and his manuscript was only published in the sixties. While the book was marketed as a work of fiction, Dr David Lewis, along with other scholars, including Rudolph Binion, believes that Forster's original notes formed its basis. There are striking similarities between passages in *The Eyewitness* and episodes in Forster's own life. The supposed 'novel' covers the period 1900 to 1936, and probes the relationship of a psychiatrist-narrator with a patient known only as AH. This patient is suffering from hysterical blindness and is cured by hypnosis with terrible consequences. When AH rises to power in Germany, he orders all his medical records be destroyed. The psychiatrist in the novel is imprisoned, then forced to flee to Paris.

In reality, Edmund Forster was not so fortunate. Witnessing the rise to power of his former patient troubled him greatly and he sought help from a group of Jewish émigrés living in Paris. He wanted to publish Hitler's medical records but knew that by doing so he risked his own life. Journeying to Paris with his written-up notes, Edmund Forster is believed to have passed them on to a group of anti-fascist German writers in 1933. One of them was Ernst Weiss. As for Forster himself, he became increasingly isolated in his profession and was repeatedly discredited. In 1933, he was relieved of his post at a hospital and, shortly after, was found with a bullet through his brain. Officially, he took his own life, although he may well have been murdered, alongside several other doctors who had treated Hitler over the years.

Paris in the 1930s was, of course, a hotbed for new and exciting artists, poets and writers. The avant-garde had arrived and was embraced by many. As well as famous painters, writers such as James Joyce, Ezra Pound, TS Elliott and Ernest Hemingway all lived and worked in the city. (Hemingway's *A Moveable Feast* is a love song to Paris in the twenties.) They also found a champion in the wealthy American writer Gertrude Stein. Although Jewish by birth, she became politically very right-wing and was an admirer of Hitler.

Serving this fascinating and vibrant community of English-speaking artists and writers was Shakespeare and Company, the famous bookshop founded by an American, Sylvia Beach. Her autobiography, *Shakespeare and Company*, is highly recommended. Although her original shop no longer exists, the current *Shakespeare and Company*, in a different location on Paris's Left Bank, is owned and run by the wonderfully dynamic Sylvia Whitman, who is as passionate about books as her namesake. (It was her father, George, who opened new premises after the war, with Sylvia Beach's blessing. A sign above the door quotes two lines from the poet WB Yeats: *'Be not inhospitable to strangers/ Lest they be angels in disguise.'*)

Finally, the remarkable rescue of British troops from Calais by HMS *Gulzar* is based on real accounts. Apparently, the British hadn't realised that the Germans controlled Calais, and the *Gulzar* was sent to evacuate any injured men. The Royal Navy seemed to think that the British still held the waterfront. Coming under repeated fire, the *Gulzar* beat a hasty retreat, but not before slowing to pick up around fifty British troops stranded on a breakwater, with German troops advancing over the rocks towards them. She was back in Dover by dawn. Brigadier Claude Nicholson was captured at Calais and died in a Nazi prison camp. For his heroism he was made a Companion of the Order of the Bath.

If you would like to learn more about Dr Edmund Forster, I recommend Dr David Lewis's fascinating book *Triumph of the Will: How Two Men Hypnotised Hitler and Changed the World*. As for Dr Forster's original medical notes on Hitler, presuming they survived, Dr Lewis says they are most likely hidden in a Swiss bank vault. If they ever do come to light, they will be of momentous historical significance. Until then writers of fiction like me can only speculate, hence the characters of Katja and Daniel Keenan are completely fictitious.

As always, my thanks go to my husband Simon, whose support and judgement is invaluable, to my brilliant editor Belinda Toor for her wise counsel, and all the team at HQ Digital.

Dear Reader,

We hope you enjoyed reading this book. If you did, we'd be so appreciative if you left a review. It really helps us and the author to bring more books like this to you.

Here at HQ Digital we are dedicated to publishing fiction that will keep you turning the pages into the early hours. Don't want to miss a thing? To find out more about our books, promotions, discover exclusive content and enter competitions you can keep in touch in the following ways:

JOIN OUR COMMUNITY:

Sign up to our new email newsletter:
http://smarturl.it/SignUpHQ

Read our new blog www.hqstories.co.uk

 https://twitter.com/HQStories

www.facebook.com/HQStories

BUDDING WRITER?

We're also looking for authors to join the HQ Digital family!
Find out more here:

https://www.hqstories.co.uk/want-to-write-for-us/

Thanks for reading, from the HQ Digital team